ALL OUR WARS

A NOVEL

Stephanie Vasquez

SPARKPRESS

Copyright © 2024 Stephanie Vasquez

All rights reserved. No part of this publication may be reproduced, distributed, or transmitted in any form or by any means, including photocopying, recording, digital scanning, or other electronic or mechanical methods, without the prior written permission of the publisher, except in the case of brief quotations embodied in critical reviews and certain other noncommercial uses permitted by copyright law. For permission requests, please address SparkPress.

Published by SparkPress, a BookSparks imprint,
A division of SparkPoint Studio, LLC
Phoenix, Arizona, USA, 85007
www.gosparkpress.com

Published 2024

Printed in the United States of America

Print ISBN: 978-1-68463-278-7
E-ISBN: 978-1-68463-279-4
Library of Congress Control Number: 2024941453

Interior design and typeset by Katherine Lloyd

All company and/or product names may be trade names, logos, trademarks, and/or registered trademarks and are the property of their respective owners.

This is a work of fiction. Names, characters, places, and incidents either are the product of the author's imagination or are used fictitiously. Any resemblance to actual persons, living or dead, is entirely coincidental.

NO AI TRAINING: Without in any way limiting the author's [and publisher's] exclusive rights under copyright, any use of this publication to "train" generative artificial intelligence (AI) technologies to generate text is expressly prohibited. The author reserves all rights to license uses of this work for generative AI training and development of machine learning language models.

Uno es el arquitecto de su propio destino.

One is the architect of their own destiny.

CHAPTER 1

The night Sofia De Luna's mother was murdered, the beige stucco of her family's Cuernavaca ranch home lit up blue and red, blue and red as the lights from the cop cars in the driveway spun and spun.

Now, twelve years later, that stucco wall glowed amber, warmed by torches, for the death of another sort.

"Dad's retiring," her youngest brother, Fernando, said in his brief phone call to Sofia in London.

Narcotraficantes don't get to retire. And Alberto, the capo of all capos in Mexico, wasn't the type to go gentle into that good night, so when Sofia got the call—midnight her time in London—that her presence in Mexico was requested—nay, required—her heart dropped into her stomach. She'd been out of the family business for years, so calling her back now meant they needed something from her.

A twelve-hour flight later, she shifted her weight from one stilettoed heel to the other, struggling to keep her jet lag at bay.

She sipped her *anejo* tequila, her eyes burning as she scanned the atrium. She recognized a few faces; she'd seen them on election billboards on her way south out of Mexico City. The presidential election was nearing, not that the event had meant much for the past few decades, as the war on drugs continued to rage, fueling a decades-long power struggle.

The drugs were winning because the drugs meant money. Lots of it.

For the banks. For the politicians. For all of them.

A taut tension ran through the guests. Uncertainty was bad for business. While the three cartels—the Baja, the Gulf, and the De Lunas in Mexico City and Morelos—had brokered an uneasy cease-fire of sorts the past few years, Sofia's father's stepping down would create a power void that could ripple across Mexico with deadly consequences.

Sofia was aware she should care, maybe be concerned, about what the future held for the family business. But this wasn't her life anymore. Her brothers and cousins seemed to run a tight ship, and she'd probably be in their way if she tried to insert herself now. She had a legitimate job. A career even. Far from here, far from the organized chaos.

So she'd sit through this dinner, she'd drink the tequila, stay a few days to say she did, and get back to London where she went by Sofia Torres. Where she got to do normal things like shop without a bodyguard nearby. Or go anywhere in general without keeping a gun tucked at the small of her back.

Sofia reached up to tug on the high neck of her black lace dress. The evening was warm, humid. A normal spring evening in Cuernavaca, but Sofia had spent the last eight years in London where winter stretched through spring.

"We were taking bets on whether you'd actually show," Fernando—Nando to his family—said as he approached her.

"Like I had much of a choice. Papi sent a plane," Sofia replied, planting a light kiss on his cheek in greeting.

She caught the amused uptick of her brother's lips as he glanced down at her under his loose brown curls. Curls that covered bright green eyes that could oscillate between steel and mirth.

Taking after their fair-haired Argentinian mother, Nando was built elegantly, his features fine and delicate like Roman statues. Nando was light where both Sofia and their middle brother, Diego, were dark.

"You look so grown-up," Sofia said, reaching to brush curls from his face.

"Tends to happen as time passes."

"Guilt-tripping already?" she asked. "Come on, be fair, I've visited."

"As few times as you could get away with."

Sofia tilted her head. "Don't be like that. I'm not going to be here long, so let's just try to get along in the meantime."

Nando frowned. "You're not planning on staying for a while? I figured with the changeover . . ."

"I can't. I have a job in London, little brother."

Nando nodded. "Yeah, of course," he said. "I just figured with Dad stepping down, you'd stick around a bit."

"I want no part of that, *hermano*. I haven't changed my mind."

"Sure, yeah, of course," Nando replied. "Anyway, glad you're here; it was important to him you came."

"So we can pretend we're a happy family?" Sofia asked. "Which side of the business pays for all this extravagance, anyway? How are profits in produce these days?"

The cushy life the De Luna family led was funded not just by the produce given up by the sweet soil of the farmland bearing their last name but by a different type of product. One not native to their lands. One flown into private airstrips. The cocoa leaf turned into neat bricks of cocaine, to be exact. And it had been this way for decades. The legitimate produce business the launderer for the illegitimate one. And the reason Sofia had left years earlier to carve a stable life for herself out of the chaos she'd grown up in.

But when her brother asked her to return, she couldn't turn him down.

Nando shrugged a shoulder. "We manage."

Wunderkind Nando ran the De Luna finances, essentially making him the CFO; if he said the money was good, then it was good.

"Glad to see you're putting your economics studies to good use," Sofia replied.

"And how's that foreign policy degree working out for you?" Nando asked.

She made low wages, worked long hours staring at a computer screen analyzing numbers. They called it paying dues.

"I'm learning a lot, little brother, earning that priceless experience."

Nando rolled his eyes.

Her family made it clear they thought her job was beneath her. She was a princess here. She had a kingdom here, if she'd just claim it.

"Papi's retirement seems sudden," Sofia said, changing the subject.

Before Nando had a chance to reply, a sharp whistle made him turn.

Sofia stood straighter as Diego approached, glass in hand, his black hair artfully slicked back and dark sunglasses hiding his eyes.

Only a year apart, Sofia and Diego were jokingly referred to as twins. And they might as well have been. They shared the same dark features, dark hair, dark almond-shaped eyes, and dusky skin from the Indigenous Aztec blood that ran through their father's veins.

Sofia caught flashes of the inked black-and-gray battle scenes adorning Diego's chest as he moved. A grayscale portrait of Julius Caesar peeked out from under his half-buttoned shirt. Diego had long identified with the general, earning the nickname El General as a child due to his love of all things war.

"Meeting without me already?" Diego said with a smile, but his tone didn't match the lilt of his words.

"We were talking about Dad's retirement," Nando said.

"I was saying it feels sudden to me," Sofia added.

Diego sucked air past his gold-capped incisors. "It's been in the works, Sof. You just haven't been around."

Sofia rolled her eyes. "Here we go . . ."

Diego held his hands up, his thick gold chains clinking together with the motion. "I'm not trying to fight."

"Me either," Sofia said, looking away, watching new guests enter the party. "Where's Yolotli? I haven't seen him."

Diego reached up to pull off his sunglasses, revealing two neat, stylized razor slices through an eyebrow and dark purple rings under his eyes. "Working," he said, downing the clear liquor in his glass.

Sofia glanced at the glass, then back at Diego, noting his blown-out pupils. "Working," she asked, "during a family event?"

Yolotli, the head of security for the De Lunas, and Diego's long-time partner, didn't work family events so he could be at Diego's side instead, having literally earned his position in this family.

"What did you do to piss him off this time?" Sofia asked.

Diego frowned. "Why does everyone always assume I did something?"

"Because that's usually the case. Like now, you're high, aren't you?" she asked, narrowing her eyes.

"Chill, *hermana*, it's a party, isn't it?"

Next to her, Nando cleared his throat. "Dinner's going to be served soon. We should probably take our seats."

"Give us a minute," Sofia said, her eyes on Diego.

"I'm not in the mood for a lecture," Diego began, once Nando headed toward the back patio.

"I'm not going to lecture you. I want you to remember we're still family, Diego, no matter where I live."

She wanted that to be true. She wanted to pretend she could reach for her brother now, pull him close, laugh about the stupid shit Nando used to do when he was little. But the distance between her and Diego now was a barbed wire fence.

"Are we?" he asked, his head tilted.

Sofia straightened. "Whatever it is you feel like you need to say to me, say it now."

"Family sticks it out, together, through the hard shit, Sofia."

"I was here," she replied, her jaw clenching. "You can try to rewrite history all you want, but it was me and you for a long time, doing what had to be done when Mami died."

"And then you walked away."

"Yeah, I did. But I did it for the three of us."

Diego shook his head. "Spare me that tired argument that you're going to save Mexico, that you're going to save us," Diego said, dramatically reaching for his chest. "It won't bring her back. Nothing will bring her back."

"It's what she wanted."

Diego schooled his features, his face smooth like a mask. "You better go take your seat, Sofia. You won't want to miss this."

The sudden change in her brother was like turning off a light. He had darkness in his eyes now and an ability to shift so deeply into himself that there was nothing left of the brother she used to run around their mother's garden with. He could hide right in front of her.

Sofia nodded, knowing better than to push. "Before I leave, we'll talk. Are you coming?" she asked, nodding toward the backyard.

He shook his head, cupping a lighter to the cigarette between his lips now. She waited for him to inhale and exhale the smoke. "I'll catch up with you later, sis."

Guilt was a gripping trap. The more she tried to pull herself out from under the weight of it, the more it cut into her. The more of her it took in return.

At eighteen, Sofia had left Mexico while she still had something to save, but her brothers hadn't seen it that way. They didn't understand that she had to become her own person in order to have something to offer the family once she returned.

What she hoped to offer was stability, peace, legitimacy. All the things they'd never known as long as they'd been alive. All the things their mother died praying for.

There were paths to legitimacy, but it would take time to convince her brothers that this was the right choice. This life of violence, drugs, and money was all they'd known, and for them, the civilian life would come with sacrifices. Ones they might not be willing to make. Ones their cousins, who had invested their own lives to this family business once their *tía* was murdered, might try to convince them not to make.

Sofia stepped into the backyard, glancing around the table glittering with crystal and silver.

When she spotted a familiar face, her heart stopped.

It couldn't be.

"Andres," she whispered, as if saying his name would make him real, prove that he wasn't a figment of her imagination, because to her, he was a ghost.

CHAPTER 2

Andres Herrera had disappeared from Sofia's life as soon as he graduated from *preparatoria*. There one day, gone the next. Losing him was the second significant loss of Sofia's young life.

He had been her confidant, her first love. More than that, he was her savior, her salvation. And once he was gone, Sofia only heard about him from whispers shared between teachers, women at the market. Her brothers. And when they talked about Andres, they called him *sicario*.

He had once been an idealist like her, raging against all the cruelty, the greed, all of it, and now, well, he stood on the other side. He had taken lives for a quick payday. He was everything they'd promised to never become.

Sofia's father waved to her from his seat at the head of the table, motioning for her to take the seat to his immediate right. The seat between her and Nando, where Diego would sit, was empty.

Sofia held her breath as she settled at the table in the seat across from Andres. He nodded in her direction but quickly turned his attention to his father, Don Martin, the De Lunas' longtime cocaine connection.

As Andres shifted in his seat, Sofia's eyes lowered, taking in the expanse of fair skin exposed by the undone buttons of his dress shirt. His heavy silver chain glittered against his chest, a pendant weighing it down.

But it was his eyes that drew her attention now, just like they did back in their school days. The dark hazel blue framed by thick, long dark lashes sparkled with amusement at whatever his father was saying. And when Andres looked up, surely feeling Sofia's gaze, those eyes darkened like a summer thunderstorm.

Her cheeks warmed, so she looked away, focusing instead on the plates of meat, peppers, onions, and limes of the *parrillada* piled in front of her on the table to avoid looking up.

Should have just stayed in London and avoided all of this, she thought as she reached up to smooth the hairs that had loosened from her bun.

One seat over, Nando raised an eyebrow in her direction.

Sofia debated leaving, just standing up and heading back toward the house instead of sitting in her awkward discomfort, but the conversations around the table started to wane, finally dying off as Sofia's father stood, raising his glass.

"I am blessed to see many friends here. Blessed to have my sons here and to have Sofia home."

Sofia smiled, tight-lipped.

"Many men dream of this day and aren't able to realize it," Alberto continued. "However, I am here this evening only because of all your support. Which is why I wanted to assure you that, even though I'm retiring, the De Lunas are still very much in business. Despite what you might have heard to the contrary, we are not going anywhere."

Sofia diligently memorized the etched pattern on the bowl of limes in front of her. It was the safest place to rest her eyes while her father drank in attention. The man could be long-winded, and her mind started to wander. Unfortunately, every thought was of Andres.

What the hell was he doing here, sitting with her family? After everything? Was it true about her mother? About what they say he did? When did he get that scar on his jaw? Had he missed Sofia, the way she had missed him?

"I am pleased to announce that the alliance between us as the Three Kings will remain," Sofia's father continued. "We need to lean on the strength of one another, especially in these uncertain election times."

Guess that answered her first question.

The original alliance created in the nineties by Juste Torres, Sofia's maternal grandfather, had not been a peaceful one to begin with. And it was currently a precarious truce between the De Lunas and the young men who ran the Baja and the Gulf, respectively. A truce that was losing steam as the world changed, as the game changed.

The De Lunas needed exclusive access to the Herreras' product. Cocaine was the De Lunas' lifeblood. While the other cartels shifted toward synthetics and heroin, the De Lunas stood on their cracked, decades-long foundation with the Herreras. If the De Lunas lost the cocaine, they lost their hold, not only on the other two cartels but on the politicians in their pockets as well.

Alberto had the politicians in the big city by the balls, as he had for decades. So he made the rules. As long as he kept the cartels safe from government intervention.

But a new president would be elected soon. And the heavily favored candidate wanted to make changes.

So she said. So they all said.

So where did that leave the De Lunas?

At the mercy of their connect, the Herreras.

No cocaine, no money, no pull.

And the De Lunas needed that pull, because as long as the Three Kings could operate with minimal state intervention, the De Luna family was safe at the head of the table.

There was no shortage of bad blood between the Herreras and the De Lunas in their long history. But long money had a way of making short memories.

Sofia looked up at Andres.

His gaze was on Alberto at the head of the table, but she caught the glance he gave her from the corner of his eye.

Alberto cleared his throat, silencing the crowd. "While it has been an honor to serve this family, it is time that I announce my retirement. This new chapter deserves leadership that understands the nuances of the time we are in as a country. Politically."

He turned to Sofia then. "By her mother's—my wife, Maria's—wishes, may she rest in heaven, my eldest, Sofia, will be taking my place as the head of this family."

Sofia froze in her seat, blood halting in her veins.

No. That can't be right.

As polite applause erupted around the table, Sofia looked at Nando.

He looked away, avoiding her gaze.

Sofia glanced around the table, heat rising up her neck. She looked for some sign her father was joking.

"Cheers, *prima*," her cousin Xavier, the eldest of the Torres cousins, said, his glass raised as their eyes met, light catching the thin gold rosary bracelet on his wrist.

When he winked, Sofia heard a ringing in her ears as everything else went silent.

The edges of Sofia's vision blurred.

She tightened her hands into fists, her nails digging into her palms.

Her father had planned his timing. He knew she wouldn't make a scene at a dinner like this. Sofia had over a quarter of a century of training from her father and knew better than to react in front of his guests.

Oblivious, or apathetic, to her confusion and growing anger, Alberto continued his speech. "My family, together with the Herreras, will once again control distribution and transportation. This agreement will make the entire operation seamless. And our business partners to the east and west will enjoy diminished risk. This is a win for all of us."

Sofia slid her wine glass closer to her, ready to drink. Her father was making promises Sofia wasn't sure he could keep. He promised the borders would stay open, that product would continue to move freely. But times were changing in Mexico. The people were tired of living in a narco-state. Despite the Jesús Malverde—Robin Hood—treatment some of the smaller towns received, it wasn't enough anymore, and it shouldn't be. They wanted better.

This complex, beautiful land of mountains and beaches and jungles and deserts had more to offer the world than drugs and violence. And the favored presidential candidate had a vision and a bulldog chief of police at her beck and call that kept her from being silenced like the others who had come before her promising peace.

If the family was unable to reach an agreement with the new president, their entire operation would come apart at the seams, and they'd find themselves suddenly unprotected.

The crowd around the table erupted in applause once more, and Sofia clapped politely.

As her world closed in on her, even Nando and Diego were strangers to her. Especially Diego. He was their father's right-hand man, privy to the conversations she and Nando were not. Diego must have known this was coming and didn't bother to clue her in.

Sofia blinked to refocus, her face burning with a mix of embarrassment and anger.

She reached for the Our Lady of Luján pendant around her neck, which had once been her mother's, and smoothed it between her thumb and index finger.

As Sofia's breathing slowed, she sat just long enough to be polite, swallowing down the things she wanted to say along with bites of peppers and tortilla, as guests chattered around the table.

Excusing herself, Sofia retreated into the house, the inner rooms of the home quiet with the guests outside.

She stepped into the library and took a deep breath. She had run from the reality of who she was as long as she could, and now it was like she'd run out of road. She figured she'd have to rejoin the family at some point, but not like this. She'd made it known for years that she wanted nothing more to do with the drug business. She had done enough dirt in her family's name.

While London had been a reprieve, the nagging feeling that it would all come crashing down was never far from the edges of her consciousness. Even all those miles removed from the nexus.

"Congratulations, cousin."

Sofia froze, stilling at the familiar accent.

Xavier clung to the shadows, the only light in the room spilling in from the hallway. The dim light glinted off his gold bracelets and rings as he crossed his arms over his chest.

"*Che, prima,* don't look so sad," Xavier said, sticking his bottom lip out. "I know this isn't what you wanted. I know you hoped to wash your hands of us."

"Then why is this happening?" she asked. "He can't be serious about this."

"It's what your mother wanted," Xavier replied, his gold teeth catching the light.

"Why?" she asked.

Xavier shrugged.

"How long have you known?"

"Awhile. She left it all to you in her *testamento*. The legitimate business has been in a trust until your father could no longer run it."

"And the other business?" Sofia asked.

Xavier scratched his temple with his thumbnail. "All the money goes through the legitimate businesses."

"I know that."

"So what do you think that means then?"

Sofia huffed. "I should have known a little sooner that this was the plan, don't you think?"

Xavier shrugged. "Would it have made a difference?"

Sofia chewed at her bottom lip.

Millions of dollars moved through the family's produce business monthly, laundered through the impeccable accounting of the family's financial team under Nando's supervision. It was too big an operation to trust to someone who had been out of the game for eight years. There'd be strings. Strings Sofia felt in her gut she wanted nothing to do with. There were rules to this world that made a deal with the devil seem sweet.

"And you?" she asked, "you and Joaquin, do you agree with this arrangement?"

Younger than her father, older than Sofia, the Torres cousins had come from Argentina to stay for a while when Sofia's mother passed away. They'd spent long nights either locked in an office with Alberto or out in the city learning their grandfather's business.

The Torreses had no problem getting blood on their hands, but they preferred to stick to the shadows. Alberto made the speeches, shook the hands, sat at lunches and dinners. Golfed with presidents.

But it was a well-known fact that the De Luna family wouldn't—couldn't—act without the blessing of the Torreses. It had been their grandfather Juste who had bankrolled Sofia's parents' produce business to begin with. Juste had built this empire, and the Torres cousins demanded their share and their say.

So they stayed.

"We respect our tía Maria's decision," Xavier began, "and we welcome you back to the family, Sofia. This is where you belong. You can dress yourself differently, speak differently, but you are still your mother's daughter. You are still a Torres."

Sofia crossed her arms under her chest. "What if I turn it down?"

Xavier's eyes darkened. "You are a soldier, Sofia. Soldiers get drafted."

"You would know," she replied.

Xavier had been the one to break Sofia, to make a *soldado* out of her. He was the one to sweep away the curtain and expose her to all the ugly things their family did. He called it showing her the light.

"I'm not a soldier anymore," Sofia added.

Xavier scrubbed a hand over his beard. "Amusing you think that. Maybe you've gotten soft, but the mind remembers. The muscles remember. And the things you did, they still happened."

Sofia's fingertips tingled.

She'd learned fight or flight from Xavier. So the chill in his tone now brought her back to being a teenager who had just lost her whole world. A broken teenager who looked to her older cousin to teach her how to cut pieces out of herself in order to survive.

"Look, if you really don't want what's rightfully yours, I'm sure we can work something out," Xavier said.

Of course. The cousins had been gunning to take things over for as long as Sofia could remember. She was sure they'd have some ideas.

"I think I need to talk to my brothers first. Weigh the options," Sofia replied.

While Sofia wasn't thrilled about the succession, she wasn't ready to hand everything over to her cousins yet either. Not while she had the upper hand.

"I heard things aren't going well lately," she said.

"Transition always brings challenges. Don't worry. Diego's more than qualified to take over. If need be."

Sofia hummed softly. "Are you sure about that? I don't know if he's in the best mental state for this at the moment."

Xavier laughed, but it was dark, sharp. "You deduced that from what? A five-minute conversation? I know what it is you think you can do for this family, but be careful with those ideas of yours, Sofia. There's no room for them here."

"Was that the same warning my mother heard?" Sofia asked, her blood warming all over again.

Maria must have upset someone, they'd said. *She must have done something to earn that bullet,* Sofia's neighbors, store clerks, people in the street whispered.

"You know what happened to your mother," Xavier replied.

"I know the story I was told. But I'm not sure I know the truth."

"Aye, Sofia," Xavier said as he shook his head, "you were always the better of the three of your siblings. But if you can't be the *serpiente* they need you to be, step aside. Business stops for no one, and I'm sure your brothers will agree. Besides, maybe this is your chance to earn redemption from your mother's mistakes."

Sofia watched as Xavier turned back down the hallway.

His words of vindication gave little comfort. She was right. Her mother had upset someone. Someone who needed her gone.

CHAPTER 3

Night had fallen, and now the De Lunas' backyard glittered with string lights. Absentmindedly swirling the remaining tequila in his glass, Andres's attention wandered as his father and Don Alberto chatted. The two older men bickered over Alberto's speech; Martin had apparently found it melodramatic.

Andres had seen his father's relationship with Don Alberto evolve through the years from business partner to nemesis, to almost friends, back to enemies. So this current peace between the two men didn't surprise Andres. He learned early that in this world, survival would always eclipse personal feelings.

Andres took a long pull from his drink, feeling Don Alberto's eyes on him.

He avoided the man's gaze, watching people pass. If he was being honest, he was looking for Sofia.

Before tonight, the last time Andres had seen her was close to a decade ago. The day Don Alberto chased him off a few days after Andres's eighteenth birthday, the day he showed up to say goodbye to Sofia.

Andres had desperately needed to see her one last time before he left, to ask her to forgive him. He couldn't explain, not all of it, but he needed her to know he wouldn't forget her, no matter where he went. No matter the distance between them. And he needed to know she'd promise the same.

But instead, Don Alberto told Andres that Sofia didn't want to see him.

Andres's heart cracked thinking about what she must have thought of him, of what she'd heard already, of what her father had told her.

He saw her watching from her bedroom window while Don Alberto stood guard in the doorway. Andres understood he was trying to protect his daughter, but from where Andres stood that day, it had always felt more like Don Alberto was protecting himself.

Andres should have demanded to see her or waited for her to come down. But he couldn't deny that part of him figured maybe it was for the best. She deserved a life filled with hope, and the road he was about to take was paved with nothing but darkness.

"How is Sofia taking the news?" Martin asked.

The mention of Sofia's name drew Andres's attention back to the conversation.

Sofia had looked surprised when she first saw him at the table, and he had a suspicion he shouldn't hold his breath for a warm welcome.

He was aware of the rumors about him. Hell, some were even true. He couldn't blame her for whatever opinion she'd formed when he'd gone. Losing her friendship was a price he agreed to pay when he left for Colombia.

That didn't mean it didn't kill him.

"That's yet to be determined," Alberto replied, "but she's had her time away. Her family needs her now."

"She'll have her own ideas about how things should be done," Martin said.

"Of course, but she'll have her brothers' and her cousins' experience to draw upon."

"She's her mother's daughter; she'll find a way to do things her way," Martin replied.

Andres watched the exchange between the men grow tense, Maria a long-standing sore point.

His father had been hopelessly in love with Sofia's mother. It was all very Romeo and Juliet, from what Andres had heard and seen. The clandestine lunch dates Andres was dragged along to when he was a kid, the late-night phone calls. He caught on pretty early. He'd hated his father for it at first, worried about his mother getting hurt, but then she got sick and passed away, and Andres was happy his father had Maria. She was a good friend to Martin and a kind woman to Andres when he had no mother of his own.

Which is why the rumor that he was involved in her murder had fractured the Herreras' relationship with the De Lunas, pitting one family against the other. For a while. And while his own father never believed it, the truth would have killed the person who meant the most to Andres at the time—Sofia.

So he kept his secrets and left for Colombia. He let them drag his name through the mud until the world moved on.

Until now.

Until his father needed him home.

So Andres promised himself he'd leave the war he carried within him in Colombia. He returned to Mexico to leverage his father's political relationships. Andres wanted to be a legitimate businessman.

And he needed Sofia to do it.

"You're sure you'll be able to get Sofia to that sit-down with the party's candidate?" Don Alberto asked, his gaze on Andres again.

Andres swallowed the rest of his tequila quickly. "That's what I'm here for, right?"

Don Alberto's jaw twitched at the sarcastic bite in Andres's words, but he nodded. "Make it happen sooner than later."

"*Claro que sí*," Andres replied with a half-hearted salute.

Alberto squeezed Andres's shoulder. "Let's take a walk. Just you and I. That's okay, right, Martin, if I borrow your son?"

Martin looked at Andres, who nodded.

"Bring him back in one piece, old friend."

Alberto laid a hand over his heart, then nodded for Andres to follow.

Andres fell into an easy rhythm following a step behind as they crossed the grounds to the small stone chapel anchoring one of the farthest corners of the property. An illuminated cross hung above the heavy wooden door, like a beacon in the night.

Andres followed Alberto into the small chapel, crossing himself as he approached the altar. The Virgen de Guadalupe and the Virgin Mary held dominion over the small space. This chapel was a testament to a mother's love, designed for Maria.

"Happy to be home?" Alberto asked as he took a seat at the front pew.

Andres remained standing. "Sure."

Alberto nodded. "All right, let's cut the bullshit. I don't love this arrangement either. But I trust when it comes to my daughter you'll remember your place."

"My place?" Andres smiled. "That's what you wanted to talk to me about?"

"Yes, your place." Alberto stood, adding, "I know your father, and he probably has an angle; otherwise he wouldn't have agreed to this deal. So just a friendly warning: don't think that turning Sofia against her family will get you what you or your father want."

Andres crossed his arms over his chest. "My father wants to retire with an easy transition, just like you. That's it."

Alberto chuckled. "Martin is anything but a simple man, and I know you'll say anything to protect him, you'll do anything to protect him. So I just want you to understand that telling Sofia the truth about her mother and the part you played in her death won't make her love you again, or even trust you. You'll just have made a new enemy."

Andres raised an eyebrow.

He wasn't sure he'd even get a chance to offer Sofia his connections to the new presidential candidate, let alone dig up old, buried secrets with her. He was still caught up on the whole getting-Sofia-to-even-speak-to-him-again part of this plan between Martin and Alberto. Getting her to listen to him—trust him—wasn't going to be easy.

"You're feeling guilty, is that it? Seeing me again," Andres asked. "You think everyone is out to get you. You and your secrets. Don't forget you're the one who turned her against me in the first place. And right now it sounds like you need me, so either you trust me to get this done, for all of us, or you see how well she fares with her cousins trying to start a war."

Alberto ran a hand down the front of his suit jacket, collecting himself. "You're wrong about one thing, son. She needs you. Not me. She needs the president on her side, or it's her head. And I know you won't let anyone hurt her, so I have full faith you'll do what needs to be done."

"I'm not your son. And Sofia . . . that was over a long time ago."

"Good, but like it or not, this is our secret, and unearthing the truth now will just cause more damage."

"You're right," Andres replied, "back then I would never have hurt her."

"I know. And that's why you'll keep your mouth shut now, because it's you, son, feeling that weight of guilt."

"Is that all?" Andres asked.

Alberto smiled and reached out to slap Andres on the back a touch too hard. "Go on, enjoy the party."

Andres headed back toward the patio, where guests were still convened. Dinner was over, but the drinking had just started. It would be a long night.

He still didn't see Sofia.

"Hey, *sicario*."

Andres paused to glance over his shoulder.

Diego nodded toward him when their eyes met. "Long time, brother."

Andres turned to face the man who had once been a friend, more than that, almost like a brother.

"Yeah, it has."

Diego sipped his drink, his eyes on Andres, and from where he stood, he could feel the hatred rolling off Diego like waves.

Andres steeled himself. Whatever came, he deserved it.

"Relax," Diego said with a smile that didn't reach his eyes, fairy lights and flames from the torches glinting off his gold incisors. "I just want to talk."

Andres nodded. "Sure, *'mano*. Let's talk."

Diego wiped at his nose, sniffed, then fixed his gaze on Andres once more. "Tell me, sicario, do you still solve your problems with a bullet between the eyes?" he asked, mimicking pushing a gun to his own brow.

Andres held Diego's gaze. "Not anymore."

"Hmm," Diego mused, the smile reaching his eyes this time. "I have a feeling you still would."

"If necessary."

Diego laughed then, short and dry.

"Are you worried, El General, that I might put a bullet between your eyes someday?" Andres asked. "If need be."

Diego placed his hand on his own chest. "It would be an honor, a bullet from St. Julian, patron saint of murderers."

Andres caught the mocking tone under the playfulness Diego was trying to sell. A sell that said Andres, and the things that were said about him, didn't scare Diego. Not in the least.

"I'm not St. Julian anymore. If that's what you're asking," Andres said. "Satisfied?"

"Far from it."

"I didn't ask for this either, Diego, and I know how it must feel . . ."

Diego held an index finger up, stopping him. "No, you have no idea how it feels to lose a mother the way I did."

"My mother is gone too, Diego."

"A lot of mothers are gone, Andres. And how many of them did you take?" Diego asked, stepping closer, pushing his finger into Andres's chest.

Andres inhaled deeply, exhaled slowly. "I don't kill women."

Diego shook his head. "That's not quite true, though, is it?"

"I'm only here because your family needs me," Andres began, an attempt to reroute this conversation that wouldn't end well otherwise. Diego had a hairpin trigger. "That's the only reason I'm here tonight, and we both know it."

"Need you?" Diego asked, his voice pitching. "Even if that were true, it doesn't change a damn thing, sicario."

"I didn't say it did. But you need me right now. Let me do this for you. This helps you too, and we can settle the other shit after. How does that sound?"

Diego sucked air past his teeth. "We don't need you."

"You do, and you know it better than anyone. The new presidential candidate won't take your cousins' calls, or your father's, will she?"

"But she'll take yours?"

"She will."

Diego narrowed his eyes. "Why?"

"Does that matter?"

"You're a snake, sicario," Diego said, pointing at Andres. "Why would I ever trust you? Why would we trust you to do this?"

Andres held his hands up. "Like I said, this alliance, this truce, helps my family too. We all need this president to play by the rules, our rules. Honestly, Diego, that's it."

Diego shook his head. "You're a liar."

Andres sighed. "What do you want from me, Diego? You want me to prove my loyalty to your family? After everything? I'm here, I'm right here."

"I want you to say it. I want you to admit what you did."

Andres shrank. He had entertained the idea while he was

away that he would get to come home, back to Mexico, and put the past behind him. That things would have changed, evolved as time passed. But as the night wore on, that dream felt further from reality.

Because for the De Luna siblings, time had stopped when their mother was murdered. And they would want their revenge, no matter how many years had passed. No matter what the truth was. They'd punish him like they had for years.

He knew that; he'd always known that.

"There's nothing I can say, *'mano,* that changes what happened," Andres replied, his eyes on Diego's, his voice level.

The gold flash caught his attention first before the muzzle aimed at his forehead.

"You're going to have to do better than that," Diego said, his thumb pulling back the gun's hammer.

CHAPTER 4

The stable on the De Luna property used to house two beautiful golden palomino mares. Sofia learned to ride when she was very young. Her mother would lift her into the saddle and trot her slowly around the corral with one hand on Sofia's leg, always right there. She showed Sofia how to brush the horses, how to be gentle with them. Sofia would sneak the freshest apples out to the stable, and eventually she earned the old mare's trust.

Now the stable was empty and unused, and Sofia was thankful for the quiet as she leaned against an empty stall gate, clutching her phone and scrolling through her emails.

The notifications popping up on the glowing screen gave her hope that she had a normal life still, away from this ranch home, away from her family. That it hadn't just all gone up in smoke because her father made some announcement.

She opened her text message thread, her thumb hovering over Leo's name. Sweet Leo back at home. Waiting for her.

She squeezed her eyes shut.

She wouldn't stay here. She couldn't.

Why would her mother do this to her? They had talked at night when Sofia was a young teen and couldn't sleep. When she'd sneak down to the kitchen to sit next to her mother at the island. They'd share manzanilla tea, and her mother would wax poetic about living a life away from this work. So leaving it all to Sofia made no sense.

"There's a lot of people looking for you."

Sofia gasped and scrambled to hold on to her phone as she jumped. "You scared the shit out of me."

Yolotli raised an eyebrow. "I wasn't trying to sneak up on you. You got soft."

"You're the second person to accuse me of that tonight," she said, crossing her arms. "Those days are long over."

"In light of things, I don't think that's true. Come on, we should head back to the house."

She grimaced. "Please, just give me a minute."

Yolotli reached up and pulled the earpiece from his ear. "Can't hide forever, Sof."

She glanced up, taking in the man who was just a boy when she left.

Yolotli was born from moist soil and the velvet blackness of night and the ancient light of the stars. In a past life, he was a jaguar from the jungle. He had the high cheekbones and strong jawline of the carved gods that had come before him.

Yolotli was nothing short of a Mayan god with an Aztec name. A god whose mother moved her only son north to Mexico City to escape the violence creeping up from Central America, only to run straight into the jaws of the beast. And that beast taught young Yolotli well.

He came to be known as Cizin to their enemies, a living Mayan god of death, head of De Luna security. Head of some of the most skilled assassins in the country. But to Sofia, he was just another younger brother. An orphaned boy adopted by their father. A third brother who grew up alongside the De Luna siblings.

Tonight Yolotli's linen shirt was partially undone, the humidity making the terra-cotta skin of his neck and chest shine. A gold chain with a medallion that matched Diego's lay against his chest, rising and falling with his breaths. Two pieces of one heart.

"Heard that before," she said, looking away.

"Because it's true. So who are you trying to avoid?" Yolotli asked, his eyes glinting.

Sofia smiled, hearing the teasing in his tone.

"Your brothers?" he asked. "Andres . . . ?"

Sofia didn't want to talk about Andres. She couldn't bear to make him real yet.

"Did you know? About any of this?" she asked.

Yolotli straightened. "Andres has been back a few weeks. As for the rest of it, news to me too."

"Diego knew. He had to. He didn't mention it?"

Yolotli reached up to run a hand through his black curls. "He hasn't been around lately."

"What does that mean?" Sofia asked.

Yolotli shrugged. "Same old, same old."

Yolotli was quiet for a beat, blinking slowly while choosing his words.

Sofia waited, watching the emotions shift over Yolotli's face.

"Your brother and I are having a difference of opinion," Yolotli replied finally, in a metered tone.

The two men held a few differences of opinion. Like the altar to Santa Muerte that Diego knelt before, competing with the altar for the Virgen de Guadalupe that Yolotli had erected. A difference of ideals that told the story of the two men. One prayed for peace in death. One prayed for peace in life.

"How bad this time?" Sofia asked softly.

Diego's demons got the better of him at times. When they did, the family would step in, smooth things over until Diego could get right again. But it was Yolotli who bore the brunt of Diego's inner war.

"It is what it is," Yolotli replied.

"Got it," Sofia said, looking away, sensing Yolotli wasn't in the mood to talk about Diego right now. "Listen, I think we both know I am not the right person for this position."

Yolotli narrowed his catlike eyes. "She chose you. She had to have a reason."

Sofia shook her head. "It was probably a screw you to Papi, let's be honest."

Yolotli crossed his arms over his chest. "And yet you still don't believe she was going to leave him for Don Martin."

Sofia shrugged. "I know it's what everyone says, but I don't know what to believe."

"Andres is here now, you know. You should ask him . . ." Yolotli paused, holding her gaze. "About what happened. It's probably time."

Sofia shook her head. "So he can lie?"

"You don't know that."

"You're not taking his side, are you?" Sofia asked, her brow knitting.

Yolotli sighed. "Of course not. It's just going to be pretty damn hard to work together if you don't trust him, that's all I'm saying."

"Work with him? I'm not staying—"

"What are you going to do then?" Yolotli interrupted. "Because they're serious. I'm taking you and your father to meet with the lawyer tomorrow to start the changeover."

Sofia shook her head. "I'm not ready . . . I'm not the right person."

"You were never going to be ready, but you were always going to end up back here one way or another. You were never going to be able to just forget about your brothers. And you owe it to them to try."

"Why me?" she asked, glaring at Yolotli now. "The cousins want it; they've been after Papi's seat for years. Hell, Diego wants it, doesn't he? I know he's pissed about this, that's why he wasn't at dinner."

"He has his feelings about it."

"And maybe he's right."

Yolotli shook his head. "I don't know about that. He's not well right now. The last thing we need is a war, because we won't win."

Sofia pushed away from the gate, dust settling across the toes of her black heels. "I can't do this. If it's true the family is struggling, I'm not the one to save it. Not like this."

Yolotli's nostrils flared. "Do you know how many times I stuck up for you? How many times I tried to convince Diego that you weren't selfish? That you didn't abandon them?"

"I didn't ask you to—"

"I did it because I believed in you and what you were trying to do. And if that's still true, that you want to change things, here's your chance."

She clenched her jaw and looked at the dust on her shoes.

There was a café in London where she'd go with Leo every Saturday morning. They'd huddle in the last booth, the one that got the most sunshine on the days the sun was out. They'd laugh; they'd discuss the state of the world. Politics. Always politics. And Leo, with his big heart and kindness, didn't understand Mexico. Didn't understand what was happening, *what was allowed to happen,* as he phrased it.

And Sofia Torres just shrugged, told him it was the way of things, and swiped the last piece of his toast to change the subject.

Leo didn't know who she really was, and if he did, he'd be devastated. She'd be one of *them,* according to him. The nameless, faceless cartels who raped, pillaged, and burned everything to the ground because someone had to be the bad guy. And what was less exciting, what didn't make the news were the men in suits in America, in Portugal, in Spain, in Germany who let it all happen. They opened the gates.

But Leo was right, she was one of them.

And maybe it was true that she was hiding from who she was, that her excuses had become her reality. But she knew better. Hell would have to freeze over before they let Sofia run the family business the way she wanted. The way her mother had wanted.

"They'll never let me lead. This is all for show, to say they're honoring the *testamento*."

Before Yolotli could reply, shouting from the garden caught their attention. When Sofia recognized Diego's voice, she hurried out of the stable and into the garden, pushing past party guests.

She paused as the crowd cleared and she reached her brother.

Diego stood as still as a statue, his gold-plated nine millimeter pointed at Andres's forehead.

Andres stood ramrod straight, his jaw twitching, his eyes dark, fixed on Diego.

Yolotli caught up to Sofia, pausing behind her.

After assessing the situation, Yolotli whispered behind her, "This is your problem now, *fresa*."

He turned then, herding the crowd back toward the house.

"*Carajo*," she swore under her breath.

She gave Diego a wide berth, stepping up in front of Andres, facing her brother.

"What the hell are you doing?" she asked Diego, snapping her fingers to get his attention.

Diego kept his eyes on Andres, whom Sofia felt at her back. She pushed down the thought of how different he smelled now. How much else had changed? How much had she missed after all this time?

"Diego, look at me," she said. "All those men might be afraid of you, but I'm not. Look at me," she repeated.

Diego glanced down at her, his pupils blown, sweat beading at his hairline. "He killed her."

Sofia sighed. "We don't know that."

"He does," Diego said, his eyes on Andres again.

"Do you think Papi would have him here if it were true?" she asked, her voice low.

"I know why Pops has him here. It doesn't change what happened."

Sofia reached up to gently push her brother's outstretched hand away from Andres, toward the bushes near them. "Maybe not, hermano, but also maybe this isn't the time and place to have that conversation."

Diego finally dropped his arm. "It's long overdue. You disappeared, sicario, before giving us what belongs to us."

Andres stepped up next to Sofia. "I'm here now, and I'm not going anywhere, Diego."

Diego glanced down at Sofia.

"Please," she said, "you'll get your closure, just not like this."

Her brother's jaw twitched.

He looked up at Andres. "Another night, sicario."

"I'll be around," Andres replied, his voice raspier, deeper than she remembered.

Diego dropped his gaze to look at Sofia. "*Ten mucha cuidado*," he warned before raising the muzzle of the gun to his own forehead to wave in salute before heading back toward the house.

Sofia exhaled. "Guess he's not happy to see you."

"What gave it away?" Andres asked.

She turned, looking at the flowers behind him, at the night sky, anywhere but his eyes. "I'd give him some space tonight."

"I can handle your brother," he replied. "You could have gotten hurt," he added, softer.

She glanced up, meeting his eyes full force for the first time in years.

The memories hit her like a tsunami.

His smile on a sunny day, his arm around her on a chilly fall afternoon. The *te amo* he whispered against her temple.

She looked away, her face warming with anger for what they'd lost, for what he stole.

"Yeah, well, maybe I should have let him shoot you."

"You wouldn't let anything ruin your father's party. He trained you better than that."

Sofia bristled at the bitterness in Andres's tone. But she knew how to cut too. She headed toward the house, but not before calling over her shoulder, "Like I said, probably best to keep your distance, sicario. We haven't forgotten."

CHAPTER 5

When Maria was still allowed to dream, and her father still tucked her in at night in that cramped apartment in Tepito, Maria Torres would close her eyes and picture herself grown. Elegant like her mother. Her long blonde hair cascading over an emerald dress. In this fantasy, the occasion would change—an important dinner with her husband's boss, an important dinner with *her* boss, a birthday celebration—the occasion didn't matter much. The figure she cut did. Her mother had commanded rooms. She had presence. Maria wanted to do the same.

"Your mother was a painter, *niña*," Juste whispered against her temple. "I wonder what you'll be. What do you want to be?" he asked, humming as he brushed her hair behind her shoulders. His face partially lit a pinkish red from the streetlight filtering in through the sheet hung as a curtain. Poppy synth music tinkled from the room next to hers.

"A cowgirl," Maria said, her smile toothless in the front.

Her father smiled. "I suppose you'll need some horses then."

They fled their apartment in Buenos Aires late at night. Maria remembered the way her father shushed her. How he wouldn't tell her where her brother, Santiago, was, why he wasn't coming with them.

Then she remembered sleeping. Waking up every few hours in a new town, country, city.

The home they were shepherded to, once the bus dropped them off in Mexico City, was small and cramped. But the people who owned the home were kind. They fed Maria and her father. The man of the house helped Maria's father find work.

Late at night when Maria couldn't sleep in the strange bed with foreign sounds outside, she'd sneak through the darkness of the living room to spy on her father and the couple as they drank coffee and talked around the kitchen table.

The words, Montoneros—a left-wing militant Argentine guerrilla group—and the hushed, urgent tones were familiar to Maria.

And it would be years later before Maria realized that socialism and guns and violence didn't necessarily go together, although in her experience they seemed to more often than not.

Her father had been a teacher, her teacher, at the school at the corner of their neighborhood, lush with greenery, kids, bikes on the sidewalks.

Then at night, the men would meet in the backyard. They spoke in stressed, hushed tones. Shooing her away.

"What are they doing out there?" she'd asked Santiago.

So young with such a serious demeanor. He would take his little sister by the arm back upstairs. To their books, to their mother's record player.

"Don't bother them."

In that cramped apartment in Tepito, she cried every night for them. For her mother, for her brother whom she missed so bad it felt like half of her was gone.

She cried at night and smiled for her father in the morning. She couldn't make things harder for him. That's what her mother would have told her. *Be good*, she'd say.

Eventually, Maria would ask, "The war is over now. Why can't we go home?"

"This is your home, Maria. Our home," Juste replied.

He would be tired when he came home from work, and he

smelled of dirt and sweat, but he'd still read to her, lie down next to her until she fell asleep.

He'd kiss her goodbye in the morning.

She was happy then. As happy as she could be.

Then came the job with the men who scared her.

Maria trailed behind her father as they made their way through the maze of wooden bones that would soon be their new home. It was an intimidating thing. Sprawling. So very different from their cozy apartment back in Argentina.

When Maria and her father first arrived in Mexico, they lived in a small house with sheets for curtains, shared with another family. Now, at sixteen, she shielded her eyes against the early morning sun as her father pointed out where all the rooms would eventually be in the sprawling ranch home they had broken ground on.

Her father was going on and on about room sizes, something about the good morning sunlight, the position of windows. Maria did not hear any of it. She had homework. A lot of it. She also knew she'd need to help with dinner once they returned home, before her father headed out for the night. Leaving her alone with their housekeepers in their luxury apartment in the middle of the city. Again.

Not that Maria minded the company. The three maids were sweet to her, gentle with her. They fussed over her long blonde hair. Hair that she had been proud of back home because it was like her mother's. Hair that made her stand out here, reminded her she wasn't from here.

But the women braided it tight to her scalp so she could help them with the cooking without having to fuss with it. And when they did that, she was one of them.

But they made jokes too. About her skin, about how pale she was, how pink she'd turn if she was in the sun too long.

So she'd sit in front of her vanity before bed now. Brushing that hair, watching the strokes with the same green eyes her mother had, and trying to make sense of all of it.

No longer her mother's daughter, no longer Argentinian. A soldier, that's what her father had told her she'd need to be. During the long bus ride, the short plane trip, and multiple car rides to get here, to Mexico, he whispered to her over and over about being a soldier. Tough, strong. Brave.

She didn't know what any of these things meant.

She hated her father's new work.

Before, he'd be in the kitchen, having beaten Maria and Santiago home from school. He'd have *alfajores* waiting for them. He'd ask about their days. They'd share inside jokes to keep from Mama once she was home from the gallery.

Now he was gone from sunup to sundown most days. When he was home, he slept in fits. He was always on the phone. Always had somewhere to be. Someone to meet. She had lost more than her mother in Argentina. She'd lost her brother, who stayed behind. And she'd lost her father.

"Hurry, *mija*," her father said, holding his hand out to her. "I want you to see where the garden is going to be. And your stable and the corral!"

Her father gestured to a half-built fence. "They told me we have the best in the business working on our corral and stable."

At that fence, a boy caught her eye, tall and lanky. His jaw and nose strong, sharp. Dirt dusted his bare, wide shoulders, coppered from working in the sun. Curly brown hair pushed back off his forehead, a bandanna tied around his neck. His—presumably—once-white undershirt, gray now, was damp with sweat and soil.

He was laughing, his smile wide, as he chatted with a few older men who shared a canteen among themselves. Water dripped from the boy's lips, and Maria watched, transfixed.

The boy must have felt her gaze, as he looked up and met her eyes. His smile faltered at first; then he nodded toward her.

Maria's father caught her trail of sight and cleared his throat. "Maybe we should get you home, Maria. It's getting time to help the women with dinner."

Maria's cheeks heated. She turned away before seeing the look the boy shared with her father. Neither one backing down until her father turned to follow after his daughter.

CHAPTER 6

Sofia dug her nails into the leather chair situated adjacent to her father's desk in his office. She'd been ushered up here by Lily, her father's newest girlfriend. Sofia's head ached, a dull thud at the front of her forehead, and she wished she could burrow her way into the leather and disappear. But Lily had other plans.

In a cloud of Gucci and diamonds, she hissed as she motioned for Sofia to sit. "People want to talk to you."

While the music from the party thudded more softly here, a steady stream of people ventured into the office to meet with Sofia. In true *Godfather* fashion, she shook hands. She smiled, repeated names in conversation to help herself remember and also to convince them that they liked her. A psychological trick she learned years back. She mirrored posture; she mirrored tone.

She could act, for a while. She had done this as a little girl. Going from room to room greeting Papi's friends. They'd smile, tell her how lovely she looked. It made them happy. It made her father happy. So she brought out the act for the night to get through it. All these smiling faces would ask her for favors soon enough.

She excused herself during a lull in visitors, hurrying downstairs to the front of the house for fresh air. Giving her father a wide berth so as not to trip his temper. Her heart thundered in her chest, and she was a little girl again. Desperate for space, desperate for something that made her real, not her parents' puppet.

She pressed herself against the rough stucco wall, still sunwarmed from the day. This house never let people go. Eight years had passed since Sofia left for London, and twelve years had come and gone since her mother's murder, and here Sofia was retreating to her old hiding spots. Pressing herself against the wall just like she had when the policemen spoke with her father that night. Her hands pressed against her ears because if she didn't hear the words, then it wasn't real. She had squeezed her eyes shut and told herself to wake up, wake up.

But when she opened her eyes and her father motioned for her, she'd crossed a threshold that night, one she never had a chance to walk back. That night, her arm around her father, she learned that everything you love will be taken from you.

Now she stilled when Andres stepped out onto the driveway. His long silhouette, backlit from the home's entryway, giving him away.

His lighter clicked, and soon his cigarette's cherry winked in the darkness.

She held her breath, but it didn't matter.

He glanced at her. "People are asking for you."

Out here, just the two of them, his voice sounded deeper, lusher. Intimate. Before she would have let herself fall into it, let his voice lull her, soothe her.

Tonight she nodded to herself in agreement that this wasn't like before. He wasn't like before. Ghosts can't hurt you. That's what her mother told her.

Without the judging gaze of her brothers, Sofia pushed away from the wall, stepping into the light provided by the torches.

"I know," she replied, looking out over the driveway full of foreign cars.

"I'm sorry about earlier," he said.

She let herself take a good look at him while he looked down, ashing his cigarette.

He held his body still, tight. She knew that posture, catlike, ready to act, react. Run.

He was wary of her.

Was it guilt?

"I flew twelve hours to be here tonight, and for what?" she asked, not expecting the thickness she heard in her own voice.

She sighed, began again. She didn't have the luxury of vulnerability anymore when it came to Andres, but old habits die hard.

She crossed her arms. "My father's girlfriend took ten minutes to let me know it's a shame I'm too old to marry off now. That I could have had a comfortable life as some rich *banquero's* trophy."

Andres brought his cigarette to his lips again. She was close enough now to hear the soft crackle as the tobacco burned.

She turned away. "Also, apparently, I've let myself go in London."

She meant it as a joke, to lighten the mood, but she regretted it the second the words passed her lips. These were old habits she shared with the boy she'd grown up with, the boy who lived right up the street.

And while they had ignored each other as kids, during the fall when she turned fourteen and he fifteen, their eyes opened, and they had seen one another as something more than just their parents' friend's kid.

From the corner of her eye she caught when Andres's gaze dipped, scanning her frame.

Her cheeks burned; she felt self-conscious under his obvious inspection.

Of course, her frame had filled out since she was seventeen, the last time he'd seen her. She had more curve to her hips, her thighs. Her backside. She didn't mind it, but she was also painfully aware that the girl with the always too-baggy school uniform and dirty shoes Andres had seen last was now a woman.

And she shouldn't care about his opinion. Not at all.

"You look perfect to me."

His voice, like a cold stream over rocks, raised goose bumps along Sofia's skin.

She looked up to meet his gaze as her stomach tightened at his words, at the way his thick, dark eyelashes lowered.

"Not that you asked," he added.

The hints of red and blue in Andres's dark hazel eyes sparkled with the flames from the torches. Sofia swore those beautiful and inquisitive eyes of his could see straight through her.

"I didn't."

He sighed then, flicking the cigarette to the cobblestones. "I didn't forget you, Sofia. I know you think I did."

She closed her eyes for a beat. She was here for her father, for her brothers. She didn't have the capacity to have this conversation with Andres, not tonight. Andres was a deep cut to Sofia, a slash that had never healed, and seeing him again was like picking at those stitches, like snipping them open. She had just had her world upended.

"Let's not . . . I can't do this right now," she said, crossing her arms.

"I understand you're pissed at me, but at some point, you and I are going to need to talk because it was your father who invited me here."

"He seems to be making a lot of unpopular decisions right now."

"Like I told your brother, you don't have to like it, but we—you, your brothers, me—are in this together now."

Sofia frowned. "Not me. I'm not staying. So best of luck with Diego and Nando."

Andres raised an eyebrow. "Do they know that?"

She recognized his patronizing tone she used to loathe.

She cocked her head. "Why are you back, anyway? I'm sure you're catching on that no one really wants you here."

His eyes flashed. "You don't want me here?"

She shrugged. "I'd accepted the fact that I'd probably never see you again a long time ago."

His expression shifted with the discipline she remembered from him. "I came back because my father requested it. Just like yours. So, I don't necessarily want to be here either."

"You'll understand if my brothers and I are a little upset about you being here. After the way you left . . ."

"I know, I know. And I can explain, but like you said, not tonight."

Sofia smirked. "I'm not playing this game with you, sicario," she said, turning toward the house.

Andres took a step to block her path. "My father is sick. You're the only one that knows, so don't repeat it. Please."

Sofia stilled. "I'm sorry to hear that," she said, looking up to meet his eyes. "Truly."

While her feelings for and toward Andres were complicated, he had lost his mother young, so his father was all he had left in Mexico. Angry or not, she wouldn't wish that loss on anyone.

Andres sighed. "Look, with our fathers stepping back, it creates an opportunity for us. And now is a really welcome time for change for your family. Because right now they look weak, disjointed. The president your family had in their pocket is about to be gone, and your family is losing its grip."

"And you're here to save us? You won't blame me if I don't buy this atonement act."

"It's not an act. It's not atonement. You and I used to want the same thing, didn't we, Sofia? A safer country, less violence. Legitimacy. Is that still what you want?" he asked, his eyes searching hers.

She looked away. "If it were possible, how?" she asked.

"I can get you a sit-down with Ximena Cruz; she is going to win. If you build a relationship with her, and she wins, you'll have a real chance to help change things."

She looked away from him, the expression in his eyes nostalgic, brimming with untouchable things. The specters of the conversations they used to have swimming there.

It irritated her that after all this time, after walking away from her, Andres thought he still had access to her hopes, her dreams.

"What do you get out of this?" she asked.

"The same thing. At the end of this, I get to be a legitimate businessman, maybe sleep a little sounder."

Sofia chewed on her bottom lip, her gaze on Andres.

"You don't trust me," Andres said. "I get that, but I think we both know what's going to happen if you don't step up here. They need you to sit down with the politicians, and they'll parade you out when they need you. But then they'll let you take the fall, too, if it ever comes to that. You're no more than their pawn, Sofia, and that's all you'll be if you don't make your voice heard."

"Maybe that's true," she replied, "but this isn't my life anymore, and I don't need to explain myself or my choices to you."

His eyes searched hers, looking for something, maybe a memory killed by time and distance.

He licked his lips before speaking. "I didn't mean any offense, *muñeca*."

She stilled at the use of the old nickname.

"They are going to try to convince you to give up your seat at the table," he continued. "You should think about why that is. There's a war on the horizon if your cousins continue unchecked."

Andres moved closer then, close enough that his leather-and-tobacco cologne warmed the air. Amplified by the heat of his skin underneath, the scent was strong enough to make her pleasantly dizzy.

He looked down at her. "You're going to need someone on your side here, Sofia. You've been gone a long time. Meet with me, and we can continue this discussion if you'd like. I genuinely think you and I can help one another."

Being this close to him after all that time, she expected to be angry, stay angry, but her heart beat faster every time she found his eyes on her.

She wanted to reach for him, pull him close to her, hold him so close that he couldn't run this time. She wanted to demand to know why he'd left her. Why she'd never heard from him. But the memories of who he was, a soft, kind boy who listened to her ideas, had been shattered years ago. Broken by the rumors of what he was and what he'd done.

Broken by what they said he did to her mother.

Sofia straightened. "I'm not sure we can trust each other."

His eyes flickered between hers. "Either way, I'd rather take my chances with you than your cousins," Andres replied.

She took a step back, needing some space, some fresh air, because those dark blue eyes of his made her feel like she was lost at sea.

He reached for his back pocket, pulling out his wallet. "I understand you've got a lot to think about." He slipped a business card from its folds and held it out to her between his middle and first finger. "In case you want to talk."

When she hesitated, he pulled the card back. "This is a limited time offer. This is my father's connection to Ximena that he's offering you, to honor your mother's wishes. If you turn down this succession, I can't promise he will extend the privilege to your cousins. Or your brothers. They'll be on their own."

Sofia reached for the card, snatching it from his fingers.

CHAPTER 7

According to the Mayans, humans were created and destroyed multiple times as the gods tried to create a race of beings who could worship them.

The first humans were sculpted from mud that couldn't hold their shape, so the gods washed them away and started anew with wood. When the new humans carved to worship the gods couldn't do so because they had no emotions, the gods destroyed them with a tumultuous hurricane. And monsters, just to be sure.

Eventually, the gods were successful with maize, but the new humans wandered the earth in darkness. It wasn't until the hero twins climbed up from the depths of hell and became the sun and the moon that all the water and silence and darkness was illuminated.

That was Yolotli to Diego.

Illumination.

And what was Diego for Yolotli?

Lately, Diego felt like he was nothing but the darkness.

Sitting on the hood of his Alfa Romeo Spider, Diego scrubbed a hand over the back of his head, avoiding Yolotli's eyes.

"I don't know how much more I can take," Yolotli said. "You're making my job harder. Do you understand that? Pulling stupid shit like this, tonight of all nights. This is an important night, like it or not."

Diego frowned. "Come on, I was just fucking with Andres. Honestly, he deserves worse."

Yolotli shrugged his shoulders to his ears. "What will that accomplish? A bullet in his head? What will that do for you, for us?"

Diego looked up. "He deserves worse."

Yolotli sighed. "I know you feel that way, *mi amor*, but now is not the time. You can't solve everything with that *pinche* gun and mouth of yours. One of these days you're going to pull this shit with the wrong person, and I won't be there—"

"I don't need you to protect me," Diego interrupted.

"I'm not saying you do . . ."

"Yes, you are!" Diego exclaimed, pushing off the car. "You all treat me like I can't take care of myself."

"Can you?" Yolotli asked, his eyes black as midnight. "You're slipping. I see it; we all see it. That's what we're worried about, *cariño*."

Diego shook his finger. "That's not it, is it?"

"It's not?" Yolotli replied. "Then tell me what it is because I'm tired, so tired of trying to figure it out."

Somewhere, under the fog, the pain in Yolotli's voice registered to Diego and caught like a hook, but he shook it away. "You're still pissed at me because you think I couldn't convince them to hand the business over to me instead of Sofia."

Yolotli closed his eyes for a beat. "We've been over this."

"That was your shot, wasn't it?" Diego asked, his cold cruel streak snaking into his words, hand in hand with the darkness and the urge to destroy. The darkness made the hooks not sting as much. "And you blame me for screwing it up for you."

"All right. I'm done with this for tonight," Yolotli replied, his eyes cold. "I have to get back to work. I'll see you tomorrow. Or not, depending on whether you decide to come home."

Diego settled back against the car as he watched Yolotli walk away.

It was better to let him go before they both dug in. Before they both drew knives, before they drew blood and no amount of honeyed words could walk it back.

Diego didn't want to have these arguments, the same ones over and over, but he constantly felt under attack these days. From his father, from Yolotli, and from the cousins. It was never enough; he was never good enough. No matter how much he gave to this family, it wasn't enough.

They all needed him to be El General, but no one listened to what he needed. And often it felt like he didn't have the luxury to ask for anything. Someone had to be the steadfast soldier, and it was him. Since he was thirteen years old, it had been him.

So during the long, late nights he spent patrolling the streets, he found his pick-me-up, his distraction. The *yayo* kept him awake, and it kept the voices away so he could focus. And when it was time to sleep, he'd drink to make all the shit disappear just long enough to drift off.

He closed his eyes now trying to find his breath, his center. The horizon was blurry for him lately. He was losing his equilibrium.

Yolotli had taught him about breathwork, as he called it. He was into all that mental wellness shit, always reading books about it. Diego joked that Yolotli was trying to reach enlightenment. But Yolotli hadn't smiled. Instead, he followed Diego onto their porch that night, asked him what he knew about trauma and the way brains can wire themselves, trip themselves up, but that if you worked at it you could rewire your brain. Rewire the pain and shit.

That night, as uncomfortable as it was, Diego felt seen. Understood. He couldn't bring himself to call the therapist whose card Yolotli taped to the fridge. But the breathing he could do.

He wanted the breathing to work because he wanted to be better. For Yolotli.

But sometimes the breathing couldn't tame the demons Diego kept.

"Yolotli looks pissed."

Diego opened one eye to look at his little brother. "What else is new."

Nando held out a plate of shredded meat and tortillas. "You missed dinner."

Diego reached for it and mumbled a thank-you. "What are you doing out here?"

Nando sighed. "Getting tired of being asked when I'm going to bring my *novia* around."

Diego glanced at Nando. "That's why you're moping around?"

"It'd be nice to have Maribel around for these things, you know."

Diego nodded while pushing around the meat on the plate with his tortilla. "I'm sure. But you had to have known it would be like this when you decided to date a journalist. We have to be . . ."

"Cautious. I know."

What Nando didn't know was that while Yolotli and Diego had both sworn secrecy when it came to Nando's love life, they'd taken the precaution of tapping Maribel's phones. Diego had joked that if she ever cheated, they'd be able to alert Nando. The tap ended up serving a double purpose; they'd also know ahead of time if the paper was planning on running anything about their family.

"Our choices have consequences," Diego replied under his breath.

"Yeah, all right, Dad."

Diego snorted.

"You're not going to ask?"

Diego glanced up. "About?"

"How it went? At dinner, with Sofia?"

"I assume not well."

Nando leaned against Diego's car. "We could have let her know . . ."

Diego shook his head. "It wouldn't have mattered." Diego chewed and swallowed. "Besides, she won't stay, and if she does, it'll be for that *pinche* Colombian *perro*."

Nando raised an eyebrow. "Is that any way to talk about our business partner?"

Diego sucked air past his teeth.

"Maybe it's not true," Nando said. "You know, about Andres. What they say."

"He knows something. He wouldn't have left otherwise."

"Is this going to be a problem? Working with Andres? Because we need them."

"Do we?" Diego asked. "Aren't you tired of this arrangement with them? It's been long enough; I think it's time to revisit things."

"It's been a long time because it works."

Diego placed the plate behind him on the hood of the car. "Think about it. We need them for their product; they don't need us, so why are they here? They can take their product and distribute it to Los Novillos at any time. Shut us out. They're after something here. They smell blood in the water, and they won't be the only ones."

"Sounding a little paranoid there, brother."

"It's my job to be. Listen, don't you want to be self-sufficient? Not have to rely on the Herreras or the bulls?"

Nando shrugged. "I've been thinking about that, about diversifying."

Diego snapped his fingers. "Exactly. Diversifying."

The cousins had a way. They had plans; they understood the need to watch the market, the trends.

Cocaine was steadily slipping year by year as the biggest drug export from Mexico. Opioids, synthetics, and heroin were beating out the party drug. But Pops never wanted to hear it. He didn't want to peddle trash, that's what he told Diego.

Trash was the golden ticket, and if the De Lunas couldn't find a way to get over their moral dilemma, they would be left behind. The money would dry up.

Diego hadn't floated the idea by Nando yet, wasn't sure he'd take it well either. So it was between him and the cousins for now. While they built their network, sussed out suppliers, thought through transportation.

They could do it. They could join the bulls in the future. The Gulf, the Baja, and the Morelos, they'd own the country. The government couldn't touch them. They wouldn't be able to afford to.

As long as Sofia didn't get in the way.

A rush of excitement, light in the darkness, raced up Diego's spine.

His little light.

Diego pushed at Nando with his elbow. "What are you thinking about diversifying?"

"My CV," Nando replied, his face serious.

Diego laughed. "What do you need a CV for? You have the most flexible position you can get—you're the boss."

Nando scoffed. "Flexible? I take calls at all hours of the night and day."

"Because you refuse to hire someone to help."

"It's too risky. The more people who know the numbers, the bigger the liability," Nando said, straightening. "Look, I'm third in line. I'll never sit at the head of the table, and I'm okay with that, but it means I need to have a safety net."

Diego shook his head. "Can't be half in and half out."

"I'm not."

"You let Sofia put ideas in your head," Diego said.

"No. But it's okay to want more than this, Diego."

Diego rubbed his thumb over his bottom lip.

This was all there was for Diego. He would do what he had to in order to protect it.

CHAPTER 8

Sofia dropped her heels and sent them clattering against the cold tile under her bare feet. Here alone in the sanctuary of the upstairs quiet, she paused to take in the room that used to be hers. The room where she used to sit up late at night reading or listening to music under the muted light of her bedside lamp. Back when she used to think about Andres and when they'd next sneak out to the field between their homes.

But her favorite memory of this room was of the times her mother would slip in late at night, and they'd talk about anything except the ranch and men. Her mother would ask about school, about what Sofia was reading, about her favorite songs, her hopes and dreams. In these moments, the world was wide open to Sofia. Her mother made her feel like she could be anyone, do anything.

Now the space was as sterile as a hotel room. All traces of Sofia had been packed away into a box that sat at the bottom of the closet.

Sofia frowned at the clothes that hung there now. New. Expensive.

She reached for the sleeve of a sharply tailored blouse.

"Lily thought you might want some . . . choices while you're here," Sofia's father said from the open doorway.

Her fingertips stilled on the silk shirt. "That was thoughtful," she replied.

"I hear you're talking about not staying," Alberto said.

Sofia gave her father a smile, trying to be disarming. "I think we both know my brothers—and the cousins—don't want this."

Alberto took a step into the room, and Sofia tensed against the instinct to make herself small around her father. She'd fought too hard to learn how to take up room to concede to anyone. Even him.

"It doesn't matter what they want. This is what your mother wanted," Alberto replied.

"Why?"

"Because her father had nothing when he came here from Argentina. Your grandfather built this. For her. And, for reasons entirely her own, she wanted you to have it."

"But *I* don't want this . . ."

Alberto cocked his head. In the movement, she saw the man she remembered as a young girl: strong, sturdy. Intimidating.

"It doesn't matter what we want in life, Sofia. What matters is responsibility, and this is yours. This family that you are still a part of is your responsibility now."

"Why not Diego?" Sofia asked. "The cousins have groomed him for this long enough."

"Because it's not, Sofia," Alberto replied curtly. "Each of you has your purpose. Diego has his, and this is yours."

"So if it's mine, then I can choose to give it away?"

"Why would you want to disrespect your mother's wishes in that way?" Alberto asked, his eyebrows knitting, looking very much like Diego in that moment.

"Me disrespecting Mami?" Sofia asked, her eyebrows raising. "What about you? Inviting Andres here like this, after everything they say he did?"

Her father's eyes darkened. "I thought you'd be happy to see him."

"No one is happy to see him, and I can't understand why you would invite him into this home, much less work with him."

Alberto sighed, his eyes briefly closing, a look Sofia was familiar with. She was testing his patience with her questions.

"Don Martin is stepping down. Which means we have no choice but to work with his successor if we are going to maintain our access to their product, *mija*. It's simple."

"It's always the money . . ." Sofia began.

Alberto stepped closer. "You were too young to fully grasp the situation of your mother's death. We didn't know what happened to your mother. The police didn't know. After a few years, when the rumors started about Andres, that he was a sicario, that she had been his hit, the Gulf, the Baja, saw an opportunity and pinned her death on him.

"They wanted to create a rift between us and the Herreras. They wanted us to take one another out because if we did, it made room for them. But the Herreras have been loyal to us. After all this time."

Sofia narrowed her eyes. "So you don't think he killed her?"

"It doesn't matter what I think because we will never know the truth. There are no witnesses left. And what is that truth worth now? She's gone, regardless, and you're old enough now to understand that your mother was involved in things that I couldn't save her from. We make our choices and live with the consequences."

Sofia chewed on her bottom lip, her gaze on the tile.

"But regardless of what I think, Andres is—was—a sicario, that is a fact. He didn't become the man you hoped he'd be."

"That's why you wouldn't let him see me before I left for London?" Sofia asked. "You robbed me of the chance to ask him myself."

Alberto closed the distance between them quickly, fire in his eyes. "Would it have mattered? At that time, to you he hung the stars and moon in the sky. I did what I had to to protect you from the path he was going down. You don't have children, so I can't expect you to understand."

"He was my friend . . ."

"Friend? Sofia, you've run out of time for childish things. At this age, your mother was married, had you already. And what do you have?"

Sofia felt her face grow hot. Her father couldn't miss a chance to highlight her shortcomings.

"You want to have choices; well here's your choice," her father continued. "You accept your mother's wishes, lead this family the way your mother believed you could. Or you decline. You turn your back on this family, but then you are out. We have no use for dead weight. *Entiendes?*"

Sofia clenched her jaw. "*Claro.*"

"And I trust whatever the issue is between you and Diego, you'll get it sorted out, and soon. You're going to need him. And your cousins."

"Of course," Sofia replied in the cool tone she had perfected over the years. The even tone that kept the violence at bay.

Alberto pushed a loose strand of her hair behind her ear. "Your brothers need you."

Sofia's jaw clenched, but she bit back her words. She never asked to be their replacement mother. She never asked for any of this.

"It's better this way, *mija*. We can keep you safe here. With us."

Alberto dropped his hand and turned toward the door. "Yolotli will take us to the city tomorrow to meet with the lawyer to go over your mother's *testamento*."

Sofia clenched her fingers around the medallion hanging from her chain.

Her father paused at the door, his shoulders slumping. "If you want them to respect you, you'll have to earn it first, Sofia. And you need them to respect you."

When she was finally tucked into bed after her long day, sleep evaded Sofia. The party had dwindled to a few stragglers; even her brothers had gone home. But it wasn't the voices in the garden keeping her awake.

She reached for her phone.

She'd heard the whispers all night. About the ambush on the CDMX, the Ciudad de Mexico police truck downtown.

Nasty work, they said.

She had heard very little about it back in London, but here at home, this incident made waves. There had been a sort of peace among them for years, so this attack set people on edge. While there were still skirmishes here and there, this attack was more violent, more public. It was a statement, maybe of what was to come.

Sofia scrolled through the news reports until a small thumbnail of a video caught her eye.

She knew better but clicked anyway.

The video was shaky, taken by a bystander who'd zoomed their iPhone in as close as possible.

In the frame, the police SUV rocked with the impact of bullets; even on mute she could hear them echoing one after another in her mind. Once the truck stopped rocking, smoke started to billow out from underneath the vehicle. The men, all in black, balaclavas covering their faces, retreated to a truck haphazardly parked on the sidewalk.

They held their guns out, still firing as they climbed into the truck. A golden flash made Sofia pause. She rewound the video five seconds, replayed, paused again.

A gold rosary bracelet hung from the wrist of one of the gunmen.

CHAPTER 9

The grounds of the ranch were quiet as she headed toward the stable. It was late afternoon, so Maria assumed the men had gone home for the day.

She craned her neck, letting the heavy sunlight of early evening that filtered through the planks of the roof warm her face.

"Do you like it?" a voice from behind her asked.

She jumped, then turned.

Glancing up, she met the eyes of the boy from the corral. This close, his warm brown eyes sparkled. Loose curls fell into his face, obscuring the straight, strong line of his nose, until he reached a hand up to push his hair back.

"It's nice," she replied, looking away, her cheeks warming under his gaze.

"Nice," he repeated with a hum. "I guess I'll take that."

She looked up at him again, and he smiled.

"They said this stable was for you."

She nodded, her gaze wandering around the open empty space.

"Not very talkative, are you?" he asked.

She glanced behind her, worried her father would appear again and interrupt this moment.

The boy held his hand out. "I'm Martin, by the way."

"Maria," she replied, taking his hand. His skin was rough, but the sensation wasn't unpleasant.

Martin looked her up and down, not slowly enough to be uncomfortable, but long enough that she caught what he was doing.

She pulled her school uniform cardigan tighter around herself.

"Welcome to the city of eternal spring, Maria," Martin said with a soft smile.

"Right," she replied, thinking of how things were backward here, summer colder, winter warm. Summer in July. Cold Decembers.

"So," Martin continued, "the men say your father is from Argentina."

Maria's eyebrows knit. "You ask a lot of questions."

He held his hands up. "No harm intended. I'm just a curious guy."

"Yes, we're from Argentina."

"There it is," he said, smiling. "The accent."

She couldn't help but smile back. So far she'd been teased for her accent at school. But Martin, his smile was warm, like she was in on the joke this time.

"I've been in Mexico awhile. I didn't think anyone could tell the difference now."

"We won't ever fully lose our accents," he replied.

"Our?" she asked.

He nodded. "Takes one to know one, as they say."

She schooled her face, remembering her father's warnings about boys, about their charms. About the way snakes hide in the grass.

But Martin didn't seem like one of those snakes. He was different from the slick men in fancy suits and gold chains who visited her father. Martin had dirt under his nails, rough hands, sun-kissed skin.

"So what about you?" she asked, giving him a quick once-over. "You're not from here then?"

"*Más o menos*," he replied. "I was born in Colombia, but my parents brought me here when I was young."

Maria nodded. Maybe this boy from a different country, like her, could understand her. Because maybe he also understood longing for a different place and a different time. Maybe she'd finally found a friend.

"So you know horses, I take it?" she asked. "Since you built this."

"I wouldn't say I built this; I had a lot of help," he said as he looked around, taking in his work. "But yes, my father was a horse trainer in Colombia. He taught me. I grew up around horses."

Maria pictured an older version of Martin. His father was probably handsome too, strong from years of working outside with horses. Competent. Maria, used to the way her father handled things, made things happen, found competency in a man—in a boy—not only attractive but necessary.

Thinking of her father, she knew he wouldn't want her talking to this boy alone. Snake or not.

"I should probably get back before my father finds us," she said, tugging down the sleeves of her cardigan.

Martin tilted his head. "What happens if he does?"

Maria shrugged, embarrassed. "He's old-fashioned. I don't think he wants me talking to you alone."

Martin frowned. "That so? Gonna make it hard to help you break your filly when she arrives then."

"My filly?" Maria asked.

"Yeah, your father bought a mare and her filly a couple days ago. Hired me to help you break her. So I guess that means we'll be seeing a lot of each other."

Maria clasped her hands in front of her, avoiding Martin's gaze. "I've never broken a horse before."

"Don't worry," Martin said, "we'll do it together. I'll teach you."

She hazarded a glance, and he smiled, soft, sincere.

"How bad does it hurt?" she asked.

He raised an eyebrow. "Does what hurt?"

"Falling."

His smile faltered. "It can be bad. But the point is not to."

She nodded. "I don't want to fall, Martin."

He held her gaze, his eyes questioning.

After a beat, his smile returned, affable and charming once more. "It's nothing to be scared of. Happens to the best of us."

"I should get back. Nice to meet you, Martin."

She passed him on her way out, heading back toward the house.

"Don't worry," he called after her. "I'll be there if you fall."

It didn't take long before Martin and Maria were inseparable. They talked while brushing the mare and her filly. Martin liked to tease Maria, and when she asked him why, he said he liked how her cheeks turned red. So she learned to fight back, her dry retorts surprising him, making him laugh. Which was something he did easily. At first, Maria thought it was because he was easygoing, a young man with no cares in the world. She learned quickly through watching him, listening to him, observing his behavior when others were around, that the easygoing act was just that—an act.

Maria learned many things about Martin that summer. He was enrolled in architecture school in Mexico City. He saw beauty in structure. He had a brain that never shut off. He had plans, he had dreams, he had ideas, and he wanted to know all about Maria's.

"I think I want to help people," she said as the brush slid easily over the young palomino's coat, which shone in the afternoon sun with sweat from their lunging session.

Martin was quiet. He was listening, waiting. Maria had been shy with him at first, not wanting to share too much. Her father had taught her not to talk too much. Not to share too many details about their life, their family. Maria also worried about what Martin would think of her. He was two years older, smart, charming, and confident. They had different childhoods, cultures, lives. But the more she shared, and the more he encouraged her, the easier it became.

"When we had to leave Argentina, people helped us," Maria

said. "When they kidnapped my mother, everything changed. A lot for the bad, but even in the bad, there were people who were kind enough to share what they could. What they had. We wouldn't be here now if it weren't for people helping us."

Martin nodded as he worked on a set of reins that showed signs of wear. "So maybe a teacher?"

Maria shrugged. "Not sure yet. Maybe a politician, but I want to be close to the people."

Martin whistled. "Dangerous choice of occupation there."

"Someone has to be the one to stand up."

He looked at her and held her gaze for a beat. "Our Maria."

He worked quietly the rest of the afternoon.

When the afternoons were too hot to do much other than brush the horses and feed them, Maria and Martin found solace under a large Montezuma cypress. They'd share a mango or papaya. Their conversation interspersed with the sounds of Cuernavaca's summer, the buzz of warmer afternoons.

"I had a different name before," she said as she picked at the dirt under her nails. "They called me Victoria."

Martin smiled softly. "Victoria. That's lovely. It suits you."

"I miss Victoria sometimes. Her life was easy," Maria said. "I've tried to figure out who Maria is, what Maria wants."

Martin leaned the back of his head against the tree trunk. "What does Maria want?"

Maria pulled her knees to her chest, wrapping her arms around them. "Some days I know. Some days I think I'll find a way to give back to this country that welcomed us. But other days, most days, I think I don't belong here," Maria said.

"I think maybe you were meant to be here," Martin said, letting his head roll to the side to smile at her.

His eyes were soft, his expression dreamy. Maria wondered if it was the lazy heat of the summer afternoon or something else that caused him to look at her like that.

She reached up to run her fingers through his curls, pushing them away from his forehead. "Do you ever feel like you don't belong here either?"

He stilled under her touch.

He was disciplined. She liked that. Liked that they could sit like this and talk, but their gazes held meaning. Something heavy that grew like the summer storm clouds every afternoon they spent together when her father was out. Martin was her friend first, and that was so different from the boys in her school who made obscene comments and dirty jokes. Martin was a gentleman.

He shrugged and leaned into her touch, his eyelids fluttering closed. "Sometimes, but I like it here because you're here."

She smiled shyly; when he said things like that, she felt important. Special. Even if she thought maybe she didn't deserve to.

He reached up, slipping a piece of her long blonde hair around his finger. "You don't have to choose. Victoria or Maria. You can be both. And you don't have to figure it all out today."

How she wished that were true, but there was a ghost breathing down her neck, making her stomach twist. She sensed something big was on the horizon, looming. And if she could, she needed to plant roots before she got washed away like last time. Before she got flushed out of her own home again.

"She's playing with you," Martin called from where he leaned against the corral fence.

Maria huffed as the mare pushed at her with its shoulder. Frustration made them both prickly this afternoon. Edges sharp. Maria hated to fail, even more so while Martin watched. She wanted to show him that she was tough too. That she could be that soldier that her father asked for, and that maybe one day she'd be that politician who wasn't afraid to make a difference. She wanted him to see that she was enough, but he was in university, and she knew the girls there were women, and she still felt like a little girl most days, even as her eighteenth birthday approached.

"She's testing you," Martin called, standing up straighter. "You have to push back."

"They listen to you," she called to Martin when she heard him hop the fence and enter the ring, and even she heard the pout in her tone.

"I've been doing this a long time, *mi reina,*" he said as he gently slipped the reins out of her hands.

"I have ridden horses before," she huffed, reaching to take the reins back from him.

He held them out of her reach. "Riding is different from breaking, and you know that. You have to be patient."

Maria set her jaw, crossed her arms, and looked away.

"Hey," he said, ducking into her line of sight. "Look at me—you can do this."

Maria interlaced her hands behind her head, her eyes starting to sting. "She'll never let me ride her. It's been months."

"Maria, I know you're smart, and most things come to you easily, but horses are prey animals. She doesn't care how smart you are. She cares about how safe she feels around you, or not. Do you understand?" he asked with a bite she'd never heard from him before.

He shoved the reins toward Maria, caressed the filly's muzzle, then stalked back to his spot against the fence.

The morning that filly-newly-turned-mare did throw Maria, Martin was at her side in a flash. Maria didn't see him hoist himself over the fence or sprint across the corral; she just felt his hands on her arm. Warm, solid, comforting.

She had landed squarely on her hip with a grunt, her hands sunk into the moist dirt.

"You're all right," Martin said, but his eyes were wide, his breath rushed, as his hands skimmed her arms, her thighs, her shins.

"You're all right," he said, softer this time, his breathing slowing, his eyes meeting hers.

He cupped her jaw with a gloved hand. "You okay?"

She nodded. "Yeah I'm fine."

He smiled. "You're a real cowgirl now," he said, amusement warming his eyes now where the concern had been.

She held a finger up. "Don't you dare laugh."

He ducked his head, tilting his cowboy hat to hide his face.

"You're laughing!"

"I'm not, I'm not, but I told you you had to be patient."

"You told me I needed to be the boss."

He shook his head. "I told you you needed to be a leader."

The mare snorted from across the corral.

"Now she's laughing at me too."

Martin smiled and stood, holding his hand out. "Come on, cowgirl, I think that's enough for today."

"No," Maria said, scrambling to stand on her own, wincing as she put weight on her aching leg. "I have to get it right."

She moved to step, but her knee buckled to protect her hip from the pain.

Martin reached for her waist, catching her, steadying her.

"Gotta know when to call it, cowgirl," he said, reaching for her jaw again, cupping it gently. "You're no good to her, or yourself, like this. You need ice. And rest."

"What the hell is going on out here?" Maria's father asked, and from the way his eyes blazed, she figured he already had an idea.

But when Martin didn't rush to let Maria go, his palm sliding the length of her arm to hold her hand, Maria felt the shift. Martin was a man, just like her father. A man who knew how to stand up for himself and what he wanted. He didn't shrink.

"Inside, Maria," her father said.

Only then did Maria sheepishly move away from Martin, dropping his hand. She hadn't done anything wrong, but the air had grown thick, crackled. She never disobeyed her father. She didn't fear him, at least not until that day. She respected him, respected that he knew what was best.

But alone in her room later, she wondered if maybe, this time, he didn't.

Her father was quiet for a few days, and Maria couldn't determine whether he was angry with her or Martin.

Then, finally, as she sat with her father at dinner one evening, he laid his utensils down, his face blank, his tone serious.

"There's someone you need to meet, Maria."

CHAPTER 10

The morning newspaper lay discarded on the back seat of the SUV next to Andres as he watched the sunny, hilly countryside bleed away and the metropolis of Mexico City spring up from the fields.

Andres had grown up between both, and familiarity washed over him as the scenery changed like a comforting childhood blanket pulled over his chest.

He glanced at the newspaper: *La Princesa del Narcotráfico ha Regresado.*

Sofia.

He'd known she was coming home, that she was about to be crowned queen. He knew all these things because his father had called him in Colombia three weeks earlier with the news and a request that his only son return to Mexico City.

"Things are changing," his father had said.

Don Martin explained the uneasy truce, but a truce nonetheless. It was a once-in-a-lifetime opportunity Andres's father promised. And he needed his son home to take his place. And with the right friends, in the right places, legitimacy could be theirs. No more money laundering through his father's architecture firm. They'd have a shot at owning a piece of Mexico City, free and clear. A contract with the city to ensure Herrera Architecture had first dibs on all new construction. The government had to launder their money too, and the Herreras wouldn't ask questions.

And if things went right, with Sofia, with the election, Andres could leave the cocaine behind. Hand it off to the Gulf and the

Baja. He was getting too old to sleep restlessly, listening for footsteps. Because someone would come for him eventually; it was the way the world balanced itself. He just wanted to enjoy a few years of peace before then.

So now Andres had been home for a few weeks. News of his return wasn't plastered across the newspapers but instead whispered in hushed phone calls. Sideways glances in the bank while he set up his new accounts, the way the other architects at his father's firm tensed when he entered the room.

St. Julian had returned, and his bloody past would always precede him.

Andres had left a feared man. An assassin, young and dangerous. He was praised for his steadfastness back when he handled his father's dirty work. He was lauded for his outstanding ability to point and shoot whoever he was told without hesitation. Now he was coming into this deal with his father as a partner. His sicario past just history now. At least he hoped.

Don Martin trusted that his son's time away had tamed him, and it had. Andres had taken the opportunity to obtain his architecture degree, following in his father's legitimate footsteps. While also following in his father's not-so-legal footsteps and using his eye for precision and keen ability to fly under the radar. Expanding the supply chain for the Herrera family. Flying in the cocaine Mexico needed to keep the US demand satisfied.

Andres sensed the beginnings of the torch being passed from father to son. He had a feeling his father was on his way out of this business, out of this life. This was the only reason to throw their support fully behind the De Lunas while the Gulf and the Baja watched. Andres hadn't known his father was ill. Not until he touched down in Mexico City.

He also didn't know, until he sat across from his father sharing coffee, that Sofia was an integral part of his father's plan, that somehow he'd convinced Don Alberto that she could possibly save them all.

As schoolchildren, Andres and Sofia had considered themselves a Cuernavaca version of Romeo and Juliet. Their parents' stern warnings and orders to stay away from one another did nothing but reinforce their attraction. The two refused to get caught up in the adults' feud, not understanding it. And maybe it had just always been teenage rebellion and nothing more, but the two had been one at one point.

He couldn't help wondering if Sofia had come back changed as well. Had she become more ruthless, more cunning like her father, or had her time away dulled the sharp edge the way it had his?

The Sofia he had known was gentle and caring. A worried older sister. A girl wise beyond her years. A girl who believed in right and wrong. A good friend, a dreamer, his first love and lover.

She still had it, the fire in her eyes that reminded them there was more to life than death, and he saw it now. A clear horizon, a way out. He'd wanted that, too, when they were younger. To be more, to be better. He saw the way she looked at him now, and it hurt. Because that fire in her eyes was still there. But now it didn't burn for him.

He sighed, rubbing his palm across his forehead. It was too late to debate these things. Don Alberto had made sure Andres never had a chance to get close enough to Sofia before he left for Colombia to persuade her to wait for him. Or to write to him, or whatever it was Andres was going to ask.

So yes, now it was too late, and Andres had a job to do.

His phone rang in his pocket, and he shifted to fish it out.

"Heard it was quite the party," the husky voice of Ximena Cruz, presidential candidate, purred as Andres held the phone to his ear.

"It's the De Lunas; what else would you expect?" Andres replied, reaching up to pinch the bridge of his nose.

"I also heard Sofia looked good, stunning even," Ximena continued. "At least that's what they're saying."

"No need to be jealous, *guapa*," Andres replied automatically.

Ximena scoffed. "Oh, I'm not jealous, just wondering how it went, seeing her again after all this time? Was it romantic? Like in the movies?"

Andres frowned at the bitterness and sarcasm in her tone. "It was fine, Ximena," he replied coolly.

Since she'd clawed her way to the top of the new National Recalibration Party to earn this spot as the party's presidential candidate, Ximena knew how to be sharp. She had learned to survive by making the first cut. It was why she and Andres got along so quickly after his father's introduction. Andres had deadened every nerve to become who he had to be, so the only thing he could feel now was slicing and stinging. Ximena was a black widow.

"Did you get a chance to talk to her?" Ximena asked, the acidity gone from her tone now.

"Some. I asked her to meet," Andres explained.

"I trust you know how to convince her," Ximena said.

Andres was growing bored with this conversation.

He watched through the window as the buildings slid by. He didn't need Ximena to coach him through this. The National Recalibration Party of Mexico and Ximena needed Sofia and her family's support. And Sofia wanted to feel needed by her countrymen. It would be simple enough.

"I have it under control," he replied.

"You'll invite her to the fundraiser," Ximena said, starting to sound distracted.

Andres could hear Emiliano in the background, her personal head of security and Mexico City's chief of police, who had unwaveringly thrown his support behind Ximena's campaign.

Andres had the fleeting thought that he should be jealous. Ximena had already invited Andres to her bed, and he had accepted. This thing between them was new, the chemistry palpable the first night they met. But this chief of police had a dogged loyalty to Ximena that, in Andres's experience, usually came from sharing intimate moments.

Andres reminded himself that this was about politics. And politics were more important than who shared a bed with whom.

The National Recalibration Party was in its inception, so it had been fearless—or stupid, depending on how you looked at it—to go up against the other parties in Mexico. Surprisingly, they were now projected to win.

The NRP ran on a marriage of the idea that a) Mexican citizens did not trust the government and b) the war on drugs was not working. The party promised to be the one to bring the cartels around by reintegrating them into the community.

This would be done by treating the *narcos* as legitimate businessmen, respecting their trade so the government could profit from their work. And if the party couldn't rein in the drug business entirely, they'd at least temper the violence.

At least that was the premise.

And they wanted Sofia. Badly.

She was the key, Ximena had repeated to Andres.

Sofia could walk the line between narco and politico. With her background and her education, Sofia would see the potential of this deal. And Ximena desperately wanted her as an ally of the party.

But Andres knew Ximena wanted Sofia because Ximena didn't want to take the bullet that would inevitably come her way from one of these cartels if they turned feral. Good politicians and civil servants who dedicated their lives to this country were shot down as soon as they announced their candidacy and platforms.

The underlying message was: You will never run Mexico. It belongs to the narcos.

But they'd be too afraid to take a shot at Sofia. It would upend the natural order of things. So long as the De Lunas remained the apex predator, Sofia would be a bulletproof vest for Ximena.

In theory.

"I'll invite her," Andres said. "If she agrees to work with you."

"Turn on that charm of yours. I'm sure she's still defenseless to that, right?"

Andres closed his eyes briefly.

For all her talk and bravado, Ximena didn't understand what it was he held with Sofia. How pure it had all been back then. How delicate and precarious it was now. You can only turn over memories so many times in your mind before they start to wear and tarnish.

And Andres didn't understand its power either. He had wanted to keep himself, his feelings, under control. Feelings he had burned to cauterize their edges when he left. But when he had seen Sofia again, and she'd turned those big doe eyes his way, it was like time had stopped, and with it, his heart, his blood. She was a wraith he would never be able to shake. The guilt kept him tied to her. He had done it all wrong.

"Andres?"

Ximena's voice brought him back to the present.

"It'll be fine, Ximena," Andres replied. "I'm pulling up to the office. I'll call you later."

He ended the call before she had a chance to protest.

He glanced at the screen, briefly scanning his text notifications. He had hoped to see a text from Sofia. She'd come to him. She wanted answers, and she figured he had them.

He just had to be patient.

Don Alberto's warning spun in Andres's mind more than he wanted. Because he was right. Telling Sofia the truth now wouldn't make him less of a villain in her eyes. And he needed to be the one she trusted, the one she could confide in.

He'd capitalize on that soft spot of Sofia's to offer her up to Ximena, and then his family would be free and clear. It would work, as long as he could stave off her dedication to finding out exactly what had happened to her mother.

CHAPTER 11

Sofia smoothed her palms down the thighs of her slacks as she sat in the back seat of Yolotli's SUV, her father next to her, heading toward downtown Mexico City. Sofia hadn't packed anything appropriate for seeing a lawyer, so she begrudgingly slipped on the Chanel slacks and blouse Lily had hung in her closet. And just like that, she was Sofia Torres De Luna once again. Neat, prim, proper. Controlled.

Sofia flipped her phone over in her hands. Andres's name, bold in a simple minimalist print, stared back at her from where she had slipped the business card between her phone and its clear case for safekeeping the night before.

Her father glanced at her phone, and she quickly slipped it into her slacks pocket.

"La senda de la virtud es muy estrecha, y el camino del vicio, ancho y espacioso."

He waited to see if she received his message. If she understood.

She nodded, and he patted her knee.

Andres, to her father, was a distraction to Sofia, a life that had been concluded. A life her father never approved of.

"I know, having him so close won't be easy . . ." her father began.

Sofia shook her head, interrupting him. "It's fine."

He nodded once, and she hoped that was the end of this particular conversation.

"I know what you think of Xavier and Joaquin," her father began, changing the subject.

She couldn't help thinking that, for a man she had hardly seen the past few years, he seemed very sure that he knew her and what she thought.

"Pretty sure whatever it is I think, they think the same about me."

"You think you're strangers now, but that's not true. You're still family; you've always been family."

"They don't trust that I'm the right person for the job. That's easy enough to see, and honestly, I agree with them."

Alberto reached up to rub at his forehead.

The thin gold band he used to wear, even after his wife's murder, was gone now.

"Xavier cares for you, Sofia. I'm sure he wants you to succeed, because then we all succeed. That idea can't be too foreign to you."

Sofia turned to look out the window, to watch Mexico City whiz by. London had been so different, but at the heart, so much was the same. The hole-in-the-wall restaurants with the best food, the museums, the parks.

While she enjoyed not being known, she did miss the feeling of being understood, and here, back home, people understood her.

Until they know who I am, she reminded herself.

"You, Diego, Joaquin, and Xavier were a good team once. Set aside your differences so you'll be able to move forward and do what's best for this family."

Sofia let her forehead rest against the window glass.

The towering golden El Ángel de la Independencia glittered ahead.

Freedom. The word sat in the back of Sofia's mouth.

Yolotli finally pulled the SUV into a darkened parking garage under a towering glass-and-metal building.

Sofia and Yolotli sat outside the lawyer's office in the expansive lobby. Mugs of coffee cooled on the low table in front of them.

Her father had gone in to see his lawyer alone, saying something about needing to finish up his paperwork now that he was retired.

Sofia watched the receptionist and the way her large brown eyes slid to Yolotli whenever she thought he wasn't looking. Sofia waited for the phone to ring, for the woman to be distracted.

Once she picked up the receiver on the first ring for an incoming call, Sofia turned to Yolotli. "I need you to be honest with me, since no one else is," she began. "Is it as bad as they say?"

Yolotli shrugged. "We won't last much longer if something doesn't change. That I do know. Diego talks about it all the time. Progression. He says we're dinosaurs, that we've stopped expanding. He says we're flatlining."

"Why is war even an option on the table? How did it get to this point?"

"Your cousins think we could—that we should—run the country. They're not so interested in sharing anymore. They just see a need to expand."

"But sharing is what's kept the peace."

"They've been pushing our boundaries, talking to people in other circles. The Gulf and the Baja have gotten wind of it. Made some examples of people. Left some bodies on our doorstep, so to speak. And this is just the beginning."

"The cousins forced Papi to retire, didn't they?" Sofia asked.

"'Standing in the way of the future,' I think was the exact wording they used."

Knowing Xavier and Joaquin, they had given her father two options: retire or be retired.

"What do they mean by progression, exactly?" Sofia asked.

"You'd have to ask Diego that," Yolotli replied. "Still thinking about leaving?" he asked, glancing at her.

She'd stayed up all night asking herself the same question.

This war, this election, this progression—it was all news to her. Stepping in now felt like stepping in front of a freight train.

Things were already in motion, and it would go against the law of physics to stop it now.

"I don't know," she said.

Yolotli shifted in his seat then, clearing his throat before speaking again.

"I'm going to say this once, just so I can say I did," Yolotli said, his tone serious. "If you stay, I think you should heed your father's warning about Andres."

Sofia glanced again at the card tucked into her phone case.

She wasn't proud of the way she'd reacted to seeing Andres again. She wanted him to mean nothing, like the way he had made her feel when he disappeared.

It had been so long; she should have been more disciplined. Instead, her heart raced in her chest when he met her eyes.

"That," she said, "was a bigger surprise than the bullshit Papi pulled."

"Well, Andres is here now, and I know that look . . ."

"If he knows the truth about my mother—" Sofia started to argue.

"If," Yolotli interrupted.

"Well, everyone says he knows something, right? 'Ask St. Julian,' that's what they say," Sofia replied, her voice rising.

The locals called Andres "St. Julian" now. The man named after the patron saint of assassins was a sicario. She'd heard the murmurings before he left about St. Julian and "the end of days." An elaborate fairy tale meant to keep the street kids scared straight. St. Julian was a ghost by all accounts. Untouchable. One day at your door, the next gone.

Yolotli sighed. "Does it matter? There's nothing he can say now that will make any of it right. If he had something to do with it, or even if he didn't."

Sofia's jaw clenched. She never wanted it to be true, what they say he did.

Maybe Yolotli was right. Ghosts are still just ghosts, even when they come back to haunt you.

But this ghost might know the answers, and if there was a chance he knew more about her mother's death, Sofia had to try.

The heavy oak door opened, and Alberto waved his daughter in. "It's time."

The notary was a stuffy balding man who had better places to be if the way he shoved papers toward Sofia and the lawyer was any indication.

The *radicación* of her mother's will was a rather dull proceeding. Maria's whole life had been boiled down to properties and shares, and in turn, she'd passed it all on to Sofia. There was nothing left in Argentina. Sofia had dreamed once of maybe retiring in her mother's homeland or, at the least, visiting where she'd been born.

But Sofia had heard the stories of the Dirty War. She knew how her grandmother had disappeared. She'd heard the pain in her mother's voice when she talked about Buenos Aires, so Sofia didn't blame her for wiping away those years.

"Do you accept?" the notary asked, his cheeks starting to bloom red.

"I'm sorry?" Sofia said; she'd missed what it was he had asked her. She was too busy thinking about how she'd never share a true *alfajor* with her mother.

The notary sighed. "Do you accept the inheritance of the estate?"

The estate.

A struggling produce business laundering money for a multi-million-dollar drug trafficking empire.

Sofia looked at the lawyer.

He nodded. "You have to accept so the estate isn't turned over to the state."

Sofia glanced up at the notary. "Yeah. Yes. I accept."

"Sign here," he said, his pudgy finger pressing down next to a blank line.

Sofia ran her index finger over her mother's signature. She paused at the date, the same day she died. She looked at the lawyer.

He nodded toward the page, and Sofia picked up the sleek, heavy pen and signed her name. She slid the paper back slowly, relishing holding on to this last piece of her mother, even if only for a moment.

The notary huffed and quickly scrawled his name across the single sheet of paper that made all this official. "Your lawyer will guide you through the rest. Good day, Señora De Luna."

Sofia raised an eyebrow. She'd made it to señora. No wonder Lily was so concerned. Sofia was almost thirty and unmarried, and now she was a señora.

Alberto rose to walk with the notary, the two talking in hushed tones about some piece of business he obviously didn't want Sofia overhearing.

"Your cousins and your brothers will have the chance to stake a claim on the estate," the lawyer said, once it was just the two of them. "I don't think they will, but you should be ready in case."

"I'm not worried about them. It's a family matter. We will handle it."

She could still back out; she could hand it all over to Diego or Nando. They didn't need lawyers for that. They'd take care of it. They always took care of things. She could leave this stack of worthless paper on her father's desk, sign off on it with a simple *buena suerte*.

"This is yours then," the lawyer said as he pushed a hefty folder toward Sofia.

She reached for the folder, her fingers already picking at the worn elastic tie keeping the papers from spilling out.

"She brought this will to you the day she died?" Sofia asked the lawyer.

"The morning of," he replied, his eyes on his phone.

Sofia didn't believe in coincidence. Her mother never did either.

"How was she," Sofia asked, "that morning?"

The lawyer ran his hand down his chest, smoothing his tie. "You mother was preoccupied that morning. Harried. I hadn't known her long then, but I knew that morning something was bothering her."

"Did she say anything?" Sofia asked.

The lawyer glanced at the door before reaching into his briefcase and pulling out a blue envelope. "I've waited a long time to be rid of this secret, Señora De Luna."

He reached out to hand Sofia the envelope.

"An agent who showed up the night your mom was murdered found this, addressed to you, in your mother's purse. He brought it to me to keep it safe."

"Safe from whom?"

"I didn't ask."

Sofia turned the envelope over in her hands. Her name in her mother's neat writing was instantly recognizable.

Sofia slipped her nail under the flap to open it, but the lawyer grabbed her arm, stopping her.

"I don't want to know."

Sofia nodded, shoving the card into the folder.

"Thank you," she said as she stood, "for everything."

Sofia hurried toward the door; Yolotli and her father were waiting for her in the lobby.

"Señora," the lawyer called after her, "you might want to make sure your own will is in order now. You never know."

CHAPTER 12

Sofia's high-heeled steps echoed in the quiet parking garage, the card from the lawyer burning a hole where it sat tucked into the stack of papers she cradled under her arm.

"Stop," Yolotli said suddenly, his brow furrowed and his arm out, preventing her from taking another step, his voice freezing her father in his tracks.

Yolotli turned his head as he listened.

Tires squealed on the level above them, normal parking garage sounds to Sofia.

As Yolotli punched the buttons on his key fob, the lights of their SUV blinked to life.

"Get in. Hurry," he instructed, pulling open the door for her, then her father.

Sofia slipped inside the dark cabin, turning to peer out the back window.

"What is it?" she asked when Yolotli was settled behind the driver's side, anxiety prickling at the back of her neck from the look in Yolotli's eyes and the sudden quiet from her father.

Yolotli glanced at her in the rearview mirror, but his focus quickly turned back to watching the garage.

A boxy, blacked-out SUV slowed as it passed theirs. Yolotli's eyes were steady on the rearview mirror, his hand already on the gun he kept concealed at his hip.

Sofia instinctively sank lower in the seat, even though she knew whoever was in the SUV wouldn't be able to see into their vehicle through the dark limo tint on the windows.

She held her breath until the SUV was gone, finally turning to take the exit to the street.

"Know that car?" she asked Yolotli as she pulled her mother's documents closer to her, clinging to what was left like she could somehow make her real again.

He shook his head once before firing up the engine. "Are you sure about visiting the church today?"

"If I don't, they'll take it as a slight," Alberto replied.

He had sat up straighter, smoothed down his dress shirt. His regality had returned, and Sofia let out the breath she found herself holding.

Yolotli slipped his dark glasses on, but Sofia caught the look on his face, the one he gave Diego when he didn't agree with his answer.

As Yolotli navigated traffic, and with her father's attention diverted to a phone call, Sofia's curiosity got the better of her.

She reached into the folder, pulling the blue card from the other stark white pages.

The card was heavy in her hands as she turned it over. Angling ever so slightly so the card was out of view of her father, Sofia slipped her nail under the flap once more. This time she ripped through the paper and freed the card.

Foil balloons shimmered on the front and Sofia cracked the card open, her eyes skimming quickly past the generic preprinted birthday message to where her mother's handwriting tattooed the bottom of the card.

Sofia – When the time is right, you'll know what has to be done.

Sofia frowned. What the hell did that mean?

She closed the card, quickly flipping it over, looking for more. More writing, more information.

"We've got company," Yolotli said, his eyes on the rearview mirror again.

Sofia whipped her head around. The SUV from the garage pulled up beside them now.

Sofia narrowed her eyes, trying to peer in, but their windows were just as dark, acting as a mirror for Yolotli's SUV.

Yolotli cursed the lunch traffic as he tried to maneuver the SUV through the gridlock, but there was nowhere to go. The cars ahead were at a standstill.

The driver's window rolled down, and Sofia made out the long-sleeved, deep-navy-blue button-down, and even though the man's lower face was covered with a gaiter, she knew who he worked for.

Secretaria de Seguridad Ciudadana de la Ciudad de Mexico.

Better known as the SSC CDMX.

A knotted web of electricity shot up from Sofia's stomach, burning her throat.

Something Sofia had learned quickly in this life was that every deed, every death, every blown-up police car in downtown Mexico had a twin reaction.

Yolotli lowered the passenger side window just enough to shoot a glance at the driver.

"I see you," Yolotli said quietly, under his breath.

"Yoli," Sofia hissed, leaning forward in her seat just enough to see the police officer laugh, the lines by his eyes crinkling, before the passenger behind him rolled down his window.

Sofia saw the flash, even in the bright morning, before she heard the sound.

Mas sabe el diablo por viejo que por diablo.

The devil knows more
by being old than by being the devil.

CHAPTER 13

Nine days had passed since Sofia's father had been shot in the head, his blood soaking that nice new blouse Lily bought her.

And for nine days, Sofia's life had been at a standstill, the rest of the world spinning around her. Just like when her mother died, and she was sent back to school, empty and gutted, while the other kids laughed with their friends.

Xavier and Joaquin had orbited her, kneeling with her in prayer some days, other days nowhere to be found. Lily had taken care of most of the arrangements, and Sofia had been glad of it, as her brothers were no help. *Too busy with work,* they'd mumble.

Andres had sent a ridiculous arrangement, so large it towered in the foyer. He'd been at the services too. She had felt his eyes on her, but he kept his distance with her brothers nearby.

And those smiling businessmen and women who'd gotten fat off her father's life's work were nowhere to be found. The difference in attendance between her father's dinner and her father's funeral was not lost on her. And those who did show up gave her sidelong glances. They wondered if she could be the leader she was expected to be now; she saw it in their eyes. And Sofia wondered it too.

Now the sprawling ranch home they'd grown up in was empty, save for herself and the security detail Yolotli posted there. Lily had gone back to Puebla, to be far away from the ugly parts of this life. And her brothers lived in the city, a convenient reason to not stick around.

The sun was setting again, the light filtering down through the thin late afternoon clouds.

She stood in the foyer in front of the flower arrangement Andres had sent, the fragrance of the roses still strong.

Sofia had counted the days diligently. The ritual of the *novenario* gave her something to focus on. There had been a thought, a fleeting one, that this could be her chance to repair what had been lost between her and her father.

Now it was too late, and she hadn't even tried.

Guilt sat heavy like lead in her stomach.

"Come, prima," Xavier said, his voice like an unexpected breeze, raising hairs on the back of her neck.

She turned to face him. "I thought you'd gone home."

"I thought maybe we should talk," he replied. He held an arm out. "Come, let's sit outside. Some fresh air might be good for you."

Sofia watched as birds flitted between the trees and the bushes out in the garden, twilight falling softly. She remembered this dreamlike state. Nothing had felt real for weeks after her mother was killed. Eventually, it would come back, like snapping your fingers and suddenly you can hear everything again. Car horns, airplanes. But for now, she felt like she was underwater.

"I don't want to fight you, Sofia," Xavier began as he settled into the wrought iron chair next to her, "but I think there's some things you need to understand."

"You shot up their police car," she said calmly, her gaze still on the stretch of grass. "What did you expect they'd do?"

Xavier sighed, shifting so his ankle was propped on his knee. "What did I tell you when you were younger? There's a natural order of things. And sometimes the only way to shake it up is to rip it apart."

"You sacrificed him."

Xavier snorted. "You're giving me way too much credit. The SSC is responsible. Solely. They made the first move; that's what

I've been trying to tell you. They put together this army, this national army, and who do you think that army is going to go after? Me. And you."

"And shooting up the chief of police proved what point exactly?"

"That we can. That we can reach out and take what's most important to them. They have an army; we have to strike when and where we can to keep the playing field even."

"What is it you want, cousin?" Sofia asked, meeting his eyes.

"I want what's ours," he replied.

"You can't just take from people, Xavier. That's how you lose a hand."

"I'm taking what has always belonged to us. What we never should have given up. There is so much more money to be made, but your father and your mother lacked the vision to see what could be. They played it safe. This family has been nothing but glorified middlemen for decades now. That's not what our grandfather wanted."

"And what is it that our grandfather wanted?" Sofia asked.

"Security," Xavier replied quickly. "Something that couldn't be taken from us. Our position right now in this country is not a stable one. When that army starts knocking on our doors, those men on the coasts won't protect us. We will be on our own."

"If you start this war with the government, they aren't going to protect us anyway."

"We don't need them to. All we need is a presence at the border. Then we can move whatever it is we want straight up into America."

"The borders are spoken for. There's an agreement in place, Xavier, one that has kept peace for years."

"That deal isn't good enough anymore. The Baja and the Gulf, they get a deal on cocaine because we have a relationship with the Herreras. But we're still just the middlemen making a commission. We need to move our own products."

"Being the middleman has kept us insulated."

"It's kept us at the bottom of the fucking hierarchy, Sofia, come on. The second the Herreras decide they don't want to use a distributor anymore and start selling straight to the Gulf and the Baja, where does that leave us?"

"I don't think it's any secret that I think we should bow out, Xavier."

He sucked air through his teeth, planted his feet on the ground, and rested his elbows on his knees. "And what is it you think you're going to do instead?"

"We have plenty of money; we can do whatever it is we want."

Xavier shook his head. "Not once they seize our assets."

"Maybe you should have thought about that before acting. Now they're pissed. You provoked them, Xavier. You did that."

"Better to run into the inevitable storm than wait it out."

Sofia sighed. "A war only ever hurts innocent people."

"Your mother really poisoned that head of yours, didn't she?" Xavier asked, his eyes lingering on hers. "She told you fairy tales, prima. Things to help you sleep easier at night. No one is going to save us. No one is going to save you. We have to look out for ourselves."

Sofia chewed at her bottom lip. She had to admit he was right about that.

"Give me some time."

"To do what?" he asked, his exasperation evident.

"I need to see the priest," she said, unsure how to ask for quiet, for time to think.

"The Gulf is holding us between their teeth . . ."

"And whose fault is that?" Sofia asked.

Xavier smiled. "I get that you need someone to blame for your mother's death, for your father's death, and I'll be that person for you, prima. But someday, hopefully before they're at these doors, you'll see that I'm not the enemy. You'll see that I was trying to help you. And I sincerely hope that you understand who you need to be for this family before you join your mother and your father."

Sofia stilled, watching as he stood.

"I know you don't care for me, Sofia, and I understand. But you need to think about your brothers. You need to think about what's best for them."

He glanced out over the property. "Back in Buenos Aires, when I was young, I had trouble sleeping. I'd sit in the window, watching for vans at night. Even when my father told me it was over. I didn't understand what he meant; I was too young. I just knew those vans were bad and that he promised me they were gone. So I finally started to sleep better. And what did those dogs do? They shot my father in broad daylight instead."

Sofia held her breath.

"Beautiful what our grandfather built for your mother, isn't it?" Xavier continued. "I hope you can take care of it. And yourself. Have a good evening, Sofia. I'll show myself out."

Sofia watched over her shoulder as Xavier entered the house. She waited a beat before sighing and wrapping her arms around herself.

Sofia's brothers were right: there was work to do.

CHAPTER 14

Sofia shielded her eyes to glance up at the looming Cathedral of the Assumption of the Most Blessed Virgin Mary into Heaven, located on the north side of Mexico City's Zócalo, and felt nothing. As a child she had been terrified of the four-hundred-plus-year-old building, enormous on the inside, always surrounded by tourists outside.

But as a child, she took the building's history for granted. The cathedral had been erected on the tomb of the Aztec capital city of Tenochtitlán. Built from the rocks of Templo Mayor, which had been built to honor the gods of the rain and the sun, Huitzilopochtli and Quetzalcoatl. Ordered destroyed by Hernán Cortés, who believed the Aztecs' savagery should be punished.

Cortés himself laid the first stone of the cathedral, a building whose purpose was to show off the greatness of Spain while diminishing the accomplishments of the people this land belonged to. So, whenever it was mentioned that the city was sinking, Sofia thought of the Aztecs. Maybe somehow they'd cursed this land when the Spaniards invaded. There was blood in the soil that could never be washed away, no matter what shiny monument was built in its place.

Sofia hurried past the tourists lingering outside, past the tour guides out to make a quick buck and into the expansive airy and bright vestibule.

She held her arms tight against her body, tense at being in such a large crowd. The church was off-limits, she reminded herself, and Yoli, when she asked him to hang back.

It would be better to meet with the priest alone.

The gilded Altar of Forgiveness shimmered in the afternoon light in front of her, golden from the tiled floor to the rounded ceiling. She approached the retablo as if drawn to it. This had been her mother's favorite part of the cathedral. *Forgiveness,* she'd repeat to Sofia, *forgiveness is our freedom.*

"Something you'd like to get off your chest?" a young priest asked as he stood next to Sofia, a twinkle of mischief in his dark eyes. "This altar has that effect on people. And I just so happen to be good at listening."

"Just admiring the architecture," she replied, glancing up at the tall priest cloaked in black.

He had a dark beard, dark slicked-back hair, dark eyes. A scar on his bottom lip caught her eye.

The priest hummed, his eyes on the altar. "Yes, the estipite—"

"Thinner at the top and bottom, largest at the middle," Sofia interrupted, pointing at a golden column. "First use of the estipite column in Mexico. Designed by Jerónimo de Balbás in the Churrigueresco style brought with him from Spain."

The priest nodded. "Yes, that's correct. An art history buff?"

Sofia shook her head. "No. I had a friend who was very into architecture and design. He used to say this place was simultaneously a dream and a monstrosity."

Andres used to rant and rave about how the cathedral, because of how long it had taken to build, was a mishmash of different eras. While the result was something of a timeline of architecture and design, Andres argued that it left the building without a singular identity. Instead, it had many. Too many.

Like them, she had said.

He had smiled. *Like us.*

The priest chucked. "He's not too far off. Almost like heaven and hell in one place."

Sofia thought of the remaining Aztec steps outside, encased in glass. The dark sculpture of the poisoned lord pinned to the cross, and this altar the last chance to ask for forgiveness before execution during the Spanish Inquisition.

Sofia stiffened before turning to face the priest. "I'm here to meet Father Morales."

"I know. I'm here to collect you." He glanced down at Sofia. "Follow me," he said, and she trailed behind him.

"I'm Father Raya," he said over his shoulder, "a seminarian. Father Morales is feeling under the weather today."

Father Raya held an office door open for Sofia, the din of the tourists in the nave muted here. "I wanted to extend my condolences," he continued. "I am sorry about your father."

At his words, Sofia felt the ghost sensation of warm blood on her arm, drops dripping down her cheek. She inhaled deeply and nodded stiffly. "Thank you."

He motioned toward a seat across the desk from his. "Sit, please."

Sofia perched at the edge of her seat. "My father and I were on the way to meet with Father Morales that day."

"I know," Father Raya replied.

Sofia huffed before she could stop herself. "I'm feeling a little in over my head here, Father, so can you just let me know why? Why am I here?" Sofia asked.

Father Raya pressed his fingertips together. "That's for you to decide. I am nothing more but a simple shepherd, but for you, I can be a spiritual counselor, a confidant."

"Confide in you?" she asked, her eyebrows raising. "No offense, but I'm not sure we'd have much to discuss."

Father Raya smiled. "I haven't always been a priest."

Sofia's eyes fell to the scar on his lip again. All the priests she knew had soft hands, no scars. "Fair enough."

Father Raya shifted in his seat. "Your father and I were not as close as he and Father Morales were. Your father was not a trusting man."

"And yet Father Morales sent you to me."

"Because he knows you're going to need a man like me."

"How so?"

Father Raya held her gaze. "Like I said, I can be many things."

"Why didn't my father like you?"

"Because I'm not from here. I studied in America."

"An American," Sofia said, her eyebrow raised. "Were you born there?" she asked, curiosity getting the better of her.

"Yes, in South San Diego. But I came here to find myself. Much like you when you went to England."

"You think you know who I am because my father, or Father Morales, shared some things with you?"

"No. I think I know who you are because it takes a certain type of person to know you need to leave in order to come back better. That is what you wanted, right, Sofia? To be better? For them? For your community?"

"Is that what you're doing? You're going to go back to San Diego better?"

"That's what I used to think. But I was called here. My work is here. Just like yours. Your father, however distrusting as he may have been, thought maybe you and I shared similar goals."

"Such as?"

Father Raya leaned closer, over his desk, his voice lowered. "This election is a turning point for all of us. It's an opportunity to maintain the status quo between the three arms of the Mexican government: the president, the church, and the cartels."

Sofia's eyebrows knit.

"It's a joke."

"It's not funny," Sofia replied.

"Of course it's not. But there is a bit of truth in every joke. The people need Ximena to win. Your family needs Ximena to win to keep the Gulf and the Baja in line. Because they're the only ones who can with that nice new army. Then we keep the peace between all of us."

Sofia had seen the photos hanging on the walls on the way to the office. The photos of murdered priests. Murders the church blamed the cartels for.

Sofia's family had had a relationship with the church as long as she could remember. Her mother dressed them in itchy, stiff clothes every Sunday, and the family made the drive from Cuernavaca to attend Sunday morning mass at the great cathedral. They wouldn't murder priests.

"I thought Mexico City and Morelos were off-limits," Sofia said.

"They are. For now. But what makes you think that violence won't crash these walls? And what makes priests in Morelos better than priests living anywhere else in this country?"

He was asking for protection from Sofia, from her family. He wanted her to convince the others as well.

"What exactly is it that you offer us in return, Padre?"

"Salvation," Father Raya replied.

"Don't bullshit me."

He raised an eyebrow at her language but let it pass. "We all are part of this machine now. There's no separating you, the president, us the church. Accountants are paid off to do tricks with numbers; your delivery drivers are paid off to pretend not to know what you transport in your trucks. We, in turn, comfort those people. Offer the idea of salvation so that they can live with what it is they do. You and the other cartels feed off us to keep operations running. What we ask for in return is a chance at safety. A life free from violence. We had that once."

"And you think I can convince the others?"

"I think you have to consider the fact that you might be the only one who can," Father Raya replied. "Your father understood the balance of things. He paid for our blessings. He paid for us to keep the people on his side."

Money. It always came down to money. To grease the wheels. To ease the sting. Whatever you wanted to call it.

"Padre, I think I'll have to add your concerns to the list that's been growing since my name came out of my father's mouth at his dinner. I think we're done here."

Father Raya looked up at Sofia. "Do what you want," he said, his black eyes flashing, "but it is more dangerous to let your cousins start a war you will not win."

She held his gaze. "There will be no war."

"You can't stop it once they start it. No one will be safe. Including you."

"And who are you to care about who gets hurt? It doesn't bother you? All the people your church has killed?" she asked, thinking of the bones beneath her feet.

"I could ask you the same," he replied, his eyes dark as night.

"Who saves the saviors?" she asked, a thought more to herself than to the priest.

She turned toward the door. "Maybe you should pray to us, Padre."

"Maybe," he said, standing as she pulled open the door. "Sofia, listen. I didn't mean to offend you. If you or your brothers need to talk, we're here. I'm here."

"We don't need family counseling, Padre."

"Maybe you don't. Maybe they do."

"We're fine," she replied. "We'll be fine."

"I hope that's true, Sofia," Sofia heard Father Raya call to her as she hurried out of his office.

CHAPTER 15

The morning was warm and growing warmer by the moment as Diego leaned against his all-black Giulia and waited. He hadn't slept well waiting for Yolotli to come home, and when he did, he just kicked his boots off and slipped into bed next to Diego without a word. They fell asleep like that, Yolotli curled up against Diego's back, Diego timing his breathing to match Yolotli's until he, too, drifted off.

It seemed they were back on good terms, for now. Pop's death had acted as a healing salve. A reminder of how quickly flames in this life are extinguished. A reminder to try to appreciate the moment.

Yolotli had tried asking, "Are you okay?" He gave Diego that look, the one that knit his eyebrows, his dark eyes watching for signals Diego didn't know he was emitting.

Was he okay? No. He hadn't been for a long time. But he wasn't afraid of death. Niña Blanca called to him most nights, and he dreamed of her skeletal fingers caressing his cheek, holding his head to her bony chest. There was nothing to fear in death. She promised him this.

What he was was angry.

The footage he'd found online of the attack on his father had been blurry, started too late, cut off too soon, but the dark sleeve of the shooter had been unmistakable. He pressed Sofia, was it the SSC?

She'd just shaken her head, said it happened too fast.

She was protecting someone, or something.

And Yolotli was no better.

He swore up and down he hadn't seen a patch; yes, he'd seen the familiar dark blue sleeve, but that didn't mean anything. It wasn't proof. Someone like Yolotli needed proof, but Diego didn't. He trusted the voices at his ear, the pull in his gut when something was off, and this felt off.

He drained the dregs of his coffee and leaned down into the open car to drop the empty cup into one of the cupholders in his vehicle. As he stood back up, he heard a car coming up the road.

Diego pushed the car door closed and waited for Xavier to pull in next to him.

"You're early," Xavier called as he jumped out of a truck that sat on high aftermarket tires.

"You're late," Diego replied.

Xavier grinned, his gold teeth flashing in the sunlight. "What's a couple minutes? You look like shit, cousin."

Diego reached up to run his fingers through his hair, pushing greasy strands off his forehead. "Had trouble sleeping."

Xavier squinted in the sun. "If you're serious about getting off that shit, it's going to get worse before it gets better. Wait till the nightmares start."

Diego nodded once and sniffed. It'd only been a half day, a solid twelve hours, but it was a start.

"You'll be fine," Xavier said, closing the distance between them and slinging an arm over Diego's shoulders. "Smoke some *mota* for the anxiousness, drink to fall asleep, and in a couple weeks, you'll be good as new." Xavier slapped Diego's chest. "You'll see, you just have to be stronger than it. And when you're not feeling like you are, call me."

"Thanks, cousin."

Diego wouldn't admit it if asked, but it felt good to talk to someone about this. Sofia and Yolotli didn't understand and were quick to brush it off as recklessness. They didn't know that the powder helped him keep control of himself, prevented him from being worse. There was a small piece of himself left that he wanted to stay untouched by their world. A part of himself that was just his, and the powder gave him that barrier to protect what was left of who he had once been.

Xavier squeezed the back of Diego's neck. "Of course. That's what family's for."

"What are we doing here?" Diego asked, gesturing around to the dilapidated parking lot filled with overgrown weeds and the warehouse that stood in front of them.

"A test run."

"A test, for what?" Diego asked, following Xavier, who was headed toward the warehouse.

"Come on," Xavier said, glancing over his shoulder. "I'll show you."

Diego followed Xavier into the dark warehouse. Sunlight illuminated blocks of the concrete floor where the roof had given in. The warehouse was empty except for a row of four shipping containers lined up neatly.

"How many bodies do you think you could cram in those?" Xavier asked. "Of course you have to account for the staging, right? So produce and bodies, what do you think?"

Diego glanced at Xavier. "I have no idea."

Xavier pointed at Diego. "A kilo of *coca* can get you thirteen thousand dollars. A girl, a young girl, can get you up to fifty thousand easy."

Diego wasn't sure he liked where this conversation seemed to be headed.

"We can leave some of the coke off the shipments. Make room for the girls. The driver will pick them up on the way up to Matamoros. So, Diego, I brought you here because Joaquin and I disagree on a process. I wanted your opinion."

Xavier crossed his arms again then, and gone was his light, playful tone. His eyes were cold as steel on Diego now.

Diego glanced at the container. Xavier was right. Per square inch, the return for coke was much better, but people could do things that drugs couldn't. Drugs could be sold once. People . . . well, he didn't want to think about that too much.

"It's worth it if we can sell them to *los gringos* to parade out to their rich clientele," Diego said, meeting Xavier's gaze. "They have the buyers."

Xavier smiled slowly. "You get it."

He darted over to the second container from the door. "You know there's crazy money in this, right? Like so much money. This is what I mean about progression. Diversifying. Because we can't count on the Herreras' loyalty forever. Especially with your father gone."

"Whose idea was it to use our trucks?" Diego asked, closing an eye against the sun.

"Mine," Xavier replied. "Do you like it? This is what we've been talking about! Progression, not getting left in the dust. This," Xavier said, gesturing toward the container, "is what Americans want. People. Cheap people. People they don't see as people to do the shit they don't want to do."

Diego glanced at the container. "We'll need more trucks, or to make more runs, if we're cutting the amount of coke on each truck to make space. And Nando needs to know. There's a process . . ." Diego began.

Xavier sucked air through his teeth. "Of course."

"And what about Daniel?" Diego asked. "He's not called the Bull of the Gulf for no reason. He'd not going to just let our trucks through to El Norte. He won't want to lose out on his cut by letting us move our product ourselves."

Xavier rolled his eyes. "Daniel and I have not reached an agreement yet. But don't worry about that. Come, let me show you something else."

As Diego made his way over to the container, a sickly-sweet smell, like garbage left out on the hot sidewalk, assaulted his nose.

He grimaced and brought the black bandanna around his neck up to cover his mouth and nose.

"Sick thing is, she's still worth something, even like this," Xavier said, pulling the container door enough for Diego to see what was inside and causing the smell.

A woman's body lay on the floor, unmoving. Diego didn't recognize her, but he knew his cousin well enough to know that this show was some sort of lesson.

"This is Melinda. She told Joaquin she'd rather die than get in the container," Xavier said with a look at Diego, "so he honored her wishes."

Diego clenched his jaw, looking back at the body.

"You know who she reminds me of?" Xavier said as he leaned against the container door. "Your sister."

"How's that?" Diego asked, looking at his cousin now.

"Melinda didn't see the bigger picture. I'm not sure your sister can either. The women in your family are reluctant to change, so sometimes we've had to remind them what's at stake."

"Sofia doesn't even know what she's taking on . . ." Diego began.

"And that's good. She doesn't need to. At least not until after the election," Xavier said, pushing off the container. "Come on, let's walk."

Diego fell in step with Xavier as they headed back outside. Diego was grateful for the fresh air.

"She'll try to stop this, just like your mother tried to stop your father before. For some reason, they draw the line here," Xavier said, huffing. "I don't understand it! They're fine poisoning people, having people murdered, but this is too much for them."

Diego scratched the back of his neck, the sun warming his skin.

"Don't you think it should have been yours? The business?" Xavier asked, meeting Diego's gaze, his black eyes flashing.

Xavier rapped his knuckles against Diego's chest. "Years ago when it became apparent who was invested in our future, the family's future, we wanted your mother to change her will. We wanted her to make you her heir if anything happened to her. However, she insisted it go to Sofia. You know what it is they're both after? Sofia and your mother?"

"My mother wanted out."

"So does your sister. And neither seem to care how that would affect anyone else."

Diego raised an eyebrow but let Xavier talk; instead of replying, he glanced out over the parking lot.

"Don't get me wrong, of course, we want things to work out with her, but if it doesn't happen, well . . ."

"I'll talk to her," Diego said.

"Look, we didn't get this far without having backup plans. That's all this is, cousin," Xavier said with a quick squeeze of Diego's shoulders. A squeeze meant to be reassuring but feeling more like a warning.

Diego watched Xavier get into his truck and back the vehicle up until the two were face-to-face.

"When they murdered my father, leaving him in the streets in Argentina like some dog, I felt it," Xavier said. "Like something snapped up here," he added, pointing to his temple. "He was a communist, they said. Maybe he was, maybe he wasn't. But he was mine, and they took that from me. We do everything we do to keep that shit from happening again, Diego."

Diego and his siblings had never met Xavier's father, their uncle Santiago. But their mother had an aging Polaroid of her brother on her bedroom vanity. Diego had heard stories about Tío Santiago. How smart he was. How gifted. Diego wondered if Santiago would be horrified by how his sons turned out. By how they all turned out.

Xavier sniffed. "Anyway, I mean it, Diego. Call me if you need to, about the shit or whatever."

Diego nodded. "Yeah, thank you, of course."

With that, Xavier peeled out of the gravel parking lot, rocks spraying from the tires.

Diego leaned against his car, Xavier's words ringing in his ears.

What if the business was his?

What if Sofia went away?

Things could stay the same. Maybe they'd even be better.

CHAPTER 16

Maria Torres De Luna's gravesite was ornate, the gravestone topped with white marble that glowed like fire under the orange of the setting sun. The dedication inscribed to the woman said little about who she was and more about who she was for everyone else—daughter, mother, wife.

Now with her husband newly buried beside her, her daughter Sofia wanted to make sure that Maria, the woman, wasn't forgotten.

Sofia's fingertips traced the numbers of the year of her mother's birth. Back in school, once Andres could drive, he would bring Sofia to visit the cemetery. He would hang back at the car, giving Sofia privacy.

It never made sense to her, what they said he did. He was almost like another son to Maria since Maria was so close to Don Martin. Too close. Sofia remembered the way her mother would run her fingers through Andres's hair at church, straighten his shirt with a gentle touch. Sofia remembered the look on her father's face too.

"He just lost his mother," Maria would whisper to Sofia's father.

Sofia pressed a palm against her ribs. She'd tucked the card from the lawyer under her shirt, close to her body. Her mother had left her a kingdom and its secrets.

Secrets that probably got her killed.

Sofia knelt next to the grave, not caring about soiling the expensive clothes she wore. She was playing dress-up anyway.

"Mami," she said, looking up at the headstone, placing a hand against the card, pressing it against her ribs, "what the hell am I supposed to do with this?"

She'd hoped for more guidance than this. Between the stack of documents from the lawyer and this card, Sofia thought there'd be more instruction.

The lawyer said her mother had been harried, preoccupied. Maybe she hadn't had time.

Maybe she'd known someone was coming for her.

Had she thought it was Andres? Hunting her in the shadows?

Sofia reached up and covered her face.

These thoughts did no good. She'd conditioned herself to stop them when they arose, years ago.

Diego's anger about their mother's murder was justifiable. Sofia felt it too, simmering in her veins. Their mother hadn't deserved her fate.

Tears stung Sofia's eyes, the heaviness of it all surprising her.

She'd never asked for this, the family's future set in her hands. Now her father—whether she trusted him or not, whether they got along or not—was supposed to be her sounding board, her teacher, but he was gone too, taking with him any guidance she might have had through this life she'd packed up and put away years ago.

"I can't save them," she whispered to the cold headstone.

That was what her mother wanted, for Sofia to be the savior she never had the chance to be.

But Sofia felt her brothers were in too deep now. They had made it obvious there was no other way of life for them. And it was their parents who taught them how to live like this. How to make money, how to sleep at night with what it was they did.

Business. It was all just business.

And her brothers would die before giving up their slice of the pie.

She'd had time in London to practice her argument. To perfect the words she'd say to them: *It doesn't have to be this way.*

But for them, maybe it did.

She still had her dreams.

She'd make things better, not worse. She'd get a job. Maybe she'd live off ramen, have to take the bus, forgo the expensive cars her brothers drove, but it would be her own life.

She'd hand her mother's gift back, this time to Diego.

It should have been yours, she'd say.

Then she'd be free.

She couldn't watch another member of her family die.

"I'm sorry," Sofia whispered to her mother before standing.

She started back up the path toward the entrance where she'd meet Yolotli, but a figure dressed in black made her pause.

"Father Raya," she called, nearing him, noting his missing clerical collar.

"You know, Andres has visited your mother's grave a few times since he's been back. Figured you'd show up here eventually too."

Sofia pointed to her neck, indicating the missing collar. "The priest is not his own," she said.

He smiled. "Still here to reconcile sinners," he replied.

A familiar tightness spread across her chest. Yolotli had parked near the entrance, wanting to watch the road, so she was alone with the scarred American priest.

"We need to talk, princesa."

He opened his jacket for just a second, but Sofia caught the gold flash of the DEA badge on his hip.

"*Mierda,*" she cursed, her shoulders sagged, "you've got to be kidding me."

He held his hands up. "I just want to talk."

Sofia scoffed, "Come on, you know better."

He met her gaze. "You might not trust us, but your mother did. She came to us for help."

"You think I'm going to believe that?" Sofia asked.

"Your mother notarized her will the day she died, didn't she?"

When Sofia didn't reply, he pushed away from his car. "I know that because I inherited your mother's case with the agency. I want to see it through."

"Why the hell do you care about my mother? Or what she did over a decade ago?"

"Because she was working with us right before she was killed. She saw the path your family was going down, and she tried to stop it. And they killed her for it."

Sofia shook her head.

Her mother wasn't a traitor or a snitch. She knew better. She had seen what happened to snitches. Maria's mother, Sofia's grandmother, was plucked off a Buenos Aires street because they thought she knew too much. Maria knew it would put her children in danger to work with the law. She never would have done that.

"You're a liar," Sofia said, taking a step back. "You don't know my mother."

"Neither do you, Sofia. What did the card say?"

Sofia wrapped her arms around herself.

"You read it, didn't you? You'll know what has to be done." He said each word slowly, like reading out loud. "She was talking about your cousins. Your father. This moment."

Sofia narrowed her eyes. How long had he been here, watching their family?

"How do I know she wasn't talking about you Americans? If it's true she was working with you? How would I even know that? Maybe you were forcing her, maybe you rolled up on her and flashed your badge like you did to me."

"She came to the agency for help. To save you and your brothers. I can offer you a chance to finish what she started."

"What's your name?" Sofia asked as she looked him up and down. "Your real name."

"Eduardo," he replied.

"Are you even a priest, Eduardo?"

"You can call me Lalo. And yes. I have a degree in Catholic theology."

"And yet here you are, living a double life. You must not have been paying attention in class."

"I learned about morality, Sofia," he said, stepping into her space once more. "Something you grapple with yourself, don't you? You know it too. Something has to change."

"What's stopping me from telling my family who you are?"

Lalo smiled, a chuckle bubbling up from his throat. "What? You'll tell Diego? Yolotli? I'm not scared of them. I don't care what happens to me. I've already seen worse. Besides, if I disappear, they'll come for your family. You and your brothers."

"What do you want?" Sofia asked, bored of being told what she should do, how she should feel. "Get to the point."

"I want Ximena Cruz."

"What do you want with her?"

"My bosses say she's a cartel sympathizer. I just need to know if that's true."

"You're going to have to do better than that, Lalo. My family could use a cartel sympathizer in office. I'm sure you understand. And I thought your agency wasn't welcome here anymore."

They'd gone too far, outstayed their welcome. The last straw had been the implication of a high-ranking military official in Mexico. Seems the working relationship between the DEA and the Mexican government was supposed to be ornamental. Not functional.

Lalo shoved his hands into his pockets. "I have unfinished business here."

"I see; they don't know you're here, do they?"

"Oh, they know."

"You're alone," Sofia said softly as the realization hit.

"Just like you," Lalo replied.

"What's in it for me to help you?"

"Other than keeping you out of jail? We help you get rid of your Torres problem."

"Who says I want that?"

"It will be the only option you'll have left, *doña*. Your cousins are upsetting the natural order of things. Ambushes downtown on police in the middle of the day make the wrong kind of noise. The other cartels will come for you when that happens. *Sangre por sangre*. You or them."

Sofia chewed on her bottom lip, her gaze on the tombstones around her. "They don't know who made that hit."

"I'd say it's pretty obvious," Lalo snorted, looking around. "You are running out of graves to put people in, Sofia."

She'd seen Xavier's gold rosary herself. She knew Lalo was right.

"Say I believe you and your story. What is it you expect me to do, exactly?"

"I know Andres has an in with Ximena, and I know he's offering you the same. All you have to do is take it."

"And then?"

"Just keep your ears and eyes open."

"For what, Padre?" Sofia asked, gesturing for more.

"You'll know when you hear it. You're a smart girl."

"What makes you think she'll talk around me?"

"She needs you on her side. She'll try to find a way to convince the others as well, and then all you have, all you've built, will be hers too. Under the guise of helping you, she'll reel you in close."

Sofia looked away. The sun had set now, the cemetery darkening. Headstones cast elongating shadows across one another.

"Your mother was brave. She wanted better for you and died for it," Lalo said. "She never saw justice, so maybe together we can clear Andres's name too, find closure for your mother, for your families."

"Pain makes revenge look like justice," Sofia said. "I don't care about Andres or his name."

"I don't think that's true," Lalo replied. "Your friend who was into architecture. Your friend who wants nothing more than to have a future. Just like you. You can give him that."

"He's on his own path now."

"And somehow it still involves you, doesn't it?"

Sofia's eyes started to sting with frustration.

She'd sworn off this life. She had sat cross-legged in the field between the Herreras' property and hers and made a pinky promise with Andres that she would never follow in her family's footsteps—and now here she was. She didn't build this business; she was born into it. She left so she wouldn't have anything to do with it. And now she was being dragged back to hell, her mother's cold hand wrapped around her ankle.

"Think of the blood you'll keep off your hands," Lalo continued. "Like you asked me in the church, whether I'm bothered by all the people the church has killed in their mission. What about you? They keep you up at night, don't they?"

Sofia looked up, meeting Lalo's gaze. "We can't save them all."

"We can try."

Forgiveness is our freedom. Our choices have consequences.

Her mother had been setting her up for this.

"I want a peaceful life, Padre. A legitimate one. You're asking me to give that up."

"I'm asking you to do this the right way."

Sofia glanced back at her mother's grave.

The right way seemed arbitrary.

"She has to get elected," Sofia said.

If she was going to do this, then she had to set her family up to be protected.

"If you support her, she will."

"After she's elected, I don't care what happens to her," Sofia said, meeting Lalo's eyes. "But this never touches my brothers; they never see the inside of a prison," she added, her chin held high, "no matter what."

Lalo nodded.

"You'll help me find out what happened to my mother?"

"Yes."

"You better go before my ride gets curious."

"I need an answer, princesa."

It was a deal with a devil masquerading as a priest. But she was tired of running. She felt her mother's blood under her feet just as she had felt the Aztec royalty under the earth at the cathedral the other day.

Maybe she didn't believe Lalo and his stories, but she believed that badge and that gun and the fact that her mother wanted better for them.

"How do I reach you?" she asked.

CHAPTER 17

Sofia read somewhere once about snakes eating their tails. How infinity can't be outrun. How life and death are cyclical. Then she thought of Andres as Yolotli drove in silence toward Herrera Architecture and Mexico City's buildings whizzed by, the nighttime city glittering around them.

Sofia couldn't remember a time before Andres. When they were small, they'd chase each other after church while their parents shook hands and kissed cheeks with other churchgoers. Back when Andres was just the boy up the street with the eyes like the forest and the ocean all at once and a nose a touch too big but in a way that suited him.

Andres came over for the holidays and vice versa. Growing up, Sofia was convinced her father and Don Martin were good friends. But the truth was muddy. And once Sofia's mother was gone, Sofia saw less and less of Don Martin. During lunch at school, Andres would still sit with her and lay his head in her lap as she read aloud to him. He would share his apple with her, trading for her mango slices. He'd take the ones that weren't sweet enough for her.

But her father had all but forbidden her to see Andres anywhere else. So their walks home became clandestine. It was Diego who covered for her more than once when she showed up at home late from school, having spent more time than she should in the field under the tree with Andres. When the afternoons felt endless, slowed, untouched by time.

Sofia never worked out if it was love or adoration. To Sofia,

Andres was older, brilliant. His mind was beautiful, intricate. He was soft-spoken but fearless. He was her protector. He stood up to her brothers for her when need be. Until one day, he was just gone.

She had blamed her father at first, but when no letters, no calls, no word came from Andres, she realized it had been Andres's choice all along. He could have written. And had he asked, she might have waited. She would have done anything for him then.

Now, standing in Andres's office on the top floor, dedicated to Herrera Architecture, tucked away in a minimalist steel-and-glass building south of the university, she took in his space.

His office had bright paintings on the walls, sculptures on the shelves, and dog-eared books on the coffee table. Her eyes lingered on the worn copy of Borges's *El Aleph*. *All points in space and time,* she thought, *seen in one singular point.*

"My apologies," Andres said as he appeared in the office doorway. "I was on a call. I didn't know you were coming. I was about to send everyone home for the evening."

She'd caught him off guard. Despite the smart black dress shirt tailored specifically to his frame, despite how authoritative he looked all in black, his hair slicked back neatly, his careful disposition of the other night faltered.

But his presence in the office helped the space make sense. He was all these things simultaneously, *El Aleph,* orange streetlamps glowing in acrylic, art, history, cinnamon and clove burning. The universe in one point.

"I won't keep you long," she began.

"You've made a decision then," he said, his eyes bright.

"Not quite," she replied. She pointed to *El Aleph*. "You still have this?"

"Why wouldn't I?" he asked, taking a step closer. "Brought it with me to Colombia."

Alone in this office with Andres, her skin warmed and tightened the way it did whenever he was too close. Like her skin couldn't contain her anymore. Like she was shimmering. Like she'd die if she didn't get closer to him, losing herself in the ocean of his eyes.

Andres's gaze flickered over her, and she caught the spark of their shared nostalgia in his eyes. In the way the streaks of red in his irises gave way to yellow, to aquatic green. To dark blue.

But she wasn't here for that.

She turned away, watching Mexico City twinkle beneath her.

"I meant to speak with you, at the services, but I didn't want to intrude . . ." he began. "I wanted to express my condolences . . ."

"It's okay," Sofia said, shaking her head slightly, breaking the spell. "Thank you for the flowers. That was . . . kind of you."

He nodded. "Of course, it was the least I could do."

"We were on the way to the church that morning."

Andres was still, quiet.

"He was wearing an SSC uniform, Andres," Sofia said, looking up at him. "Did she have anything to do with my father's death?"

Andres shook his head once, sharply. "No. Sofia, I know how it looks, but the SSC don't act on their own. Not like that. That's the reason they were created, why the other branches were disbanded . . ."

"You'll forgive me if I don't totally believe you, Andres."

"Why would Ximena have your father killed?" Andres asked, his eyes sharp, bright. "Think about it. How would that help her when she's trying to extend an olive branch to you?"

Sofia chewed at her bottom lip. She winced slightly as her tooth found the thin split in the skin.

"Whoever did that to you, to your father, wanted you to think it was the SSC."

These men, she thought, these men and the way they talked in circles.

If she wanted the truth behind her father's shooting, she'd have to sit across from Ximena and ask her face-to-face.

"All that's left of my mother is a stack of papers," Sofia said.

She felt the shift when he tensed.

"She deserves more," Sofia continued, "and you said something about being able to help me."

"Legitimacy," Andres said.

"That's what this woman has promised you?" Sofia asked, turning to face Andres again.

"Us," Andres corrected, moving closer, his eyes flashing. "She can advance your career in politics. Appoint you to a seat where you get to have a say in things."

"I asked what it was she promised you," Sofia said, holding his gaze.

Andres took a step back; he wasn't used to this version of Sofia, the one who pressed back. Sofia couldn't deny the spark of a thrill it gave her.

"This isn't about me."

"Then what did you promise her?" Sofia asked, looking up at Andres, taking in the scar on his jaw, the way his smile lines had deepened, the mark on his cheek where his dimple never truly smoothed out.

"You," he replied, "your support. She needs someone who can placate the Baja and the Gulf. Someone who can keep the peace. At least long enough for her to get elected."

"And what if I can't?"

He smiled then, soft, the smile lines around his eyes crinkling. "You can."

"What do I need to convince them of? That she won't screw them over? Because you know what will happen if she does. They'll come for me, not her."

"They won't," Andres said, lifting his hands as if he were going to settle them on Sofia's shoulders but thought better of it. "They won't because she won't."

Sofia cursed under her breath, thinking of Lalo.

"I can't trust this woman I don't know. I can't even trust you; it's been too long."

"Sit, please," Andres said, gesturing toward the set of couches.

Sofia debated standing, refusing the invitation, but realized she was being petulant just because. And wasn't this what she wanted? This conversation after so long.

She settled into the seat on the mid-century-inspired couch across the coffee table from Andres, crossing her leg over her knee. Spots of dust still clung to the knees of her pants from the cemetery. And she thought she should tell Andres, show him. *This is all that's left of my mother too. Paper and dust.*

Andres leaned forward to rest his elbows on his knees, his eyes on Sofia's. "I'm going to answer the question that you're too proud to ask," he said, "because I need to say it. I need you to know because we can't dance around it forever. And we have to move past it."

She noticed the way his eyes, murky blue green and red, softened now.

"I didn't want to leave you, but it had nothing to do with you. I had to go."

She stilled at his words, digging her nails into her palm to temper her reaction, an old trick she'd learned as a kid when her father berated her for a low mark or a dirty school uniform or whatever illusion of perfection she had shattered that day.

He held her gaze. "Yes, I missed you. Yes, I thought about you. Every day at first. But I hoped you had moved on, so I had to let you go."

Sofia swallowed thickly. She had waited years to hear this admission, but now it was worthless. It meant nothing.

It was too late.

They had once made out under a Fresno tree after school his last year. His hand had snaked under her skirt but stopped at her hip. She remembered how small she felt under his large hands. She remembered how safe she felt in his arms, the rough bark of the tree scratching her back as he pressed her against it. She remembered how she didn't want it to end. How that afternoon, her heart beat only for him. She wanted the moment to last forever, just the two of them, in their own world. And then he was gone.

She bit her bottom lip at the memory, feeling the skin of her chest warm. She glanced away from Andres, afraid he could read her mind.

"Why are you telling me this now?"

"Because I know you think I have the answers you're looking for. The only answer I have for you is yes, I missed you; I didn't want to leave you, but it was for the best."

"Is it true then? What they say you did," she asked. She couldn't even say the words.

He shook his head. "I don't hurt women."

"Then why do people think it was you?" she asked, frustration bleeding into her tone.

"Because I left," he said with a shrug. "Because the case had gone cold after all those years. Because your father wanted to move on. Because blaming the patron saint of death makes things make a little more sense when a mother is gunned down in the middle of the night. I don't know what it is you want me to say, Sofia."

Sofia clenched her jaw, bristling against the heat in his tone, his charming facade dissipating like vapor.

"You know who did it, don't you?" Sofia asked, her eyes on him as a thought crossed her mind. "You're protecting someone. It's the only reason you haven't fought harder to clear your name."

He looked away from her, rubbing his palms together now. "There are men who want to keep my name muddied."

"What men?" she asked.

He held her gaze, and when she didn't back down, he leaned back in his seat.

"I'm sorry, but I can't help you bury that ghost, Sofia."

Despite his cracking charming mask, Sofia could still read

Andres. Despite the way he'd grown into an elegant, intimidating man, she knew the boy too well to forget. She recognized when she hit a nerve.

"She's not a ghost to me," Sofia replied through teeth held tight.

Andres rapped his knuckles gently on the glass coffee table, his eyes on the carpet.

"Do you remember why I call you *muñeca?*" he asked.

A memory flashed as she looked at him.

"That's what you called me when I fell from that tree . . ." Sofia said.

"I think you mean when you fell *out* of that tree," he said, his eyes twinkling, "like a coconut."

"There's a reason I suppressed this memory," she replied.

"But you remember . . ." he began.

"Yes, you said I looked like a broken doll. I sprained my wrist pretty bad and cut up my elbow," she said, frowning at the memory, something long forgotten. Faded like the scar on her elbow.

"That's what you got for being so determined. Diego told you not to climb that tree."

Andres had knelt down in the mud next to her, dirtying the dark blue slacks of his school uniform. His big, beautiful eyes filled with concern.

"And you, you were sweet to me while I tried not to cry," she said, glancing at him.

His smile started to fade, the stern facade reclaiming its place, settling like a well-worn mask.

"I knew you were trying to be brave, and the last thing you wanted was for someone, anyone, to see you cry."

The tie between them that she thought had been broken by time and distance snapped taut, like a hook in her chest.

The last time she saw Andres, Sofia watched from her bedroom window as her father addressed him on the doorstep. He held a bouquet of roses in his hand, roses he handed over to Sofia's father before walking away. Roses she never saw again. Just like him.

"Andres, what did my father say to you that day you came by the house, before you left?"

Andres rubbed his index finger over his bottom lip, looking at Sofia.

"Your father didn't want you to see me. He told me to leave."

She leaned forward, her eyes on his. "Why didn't you fight for me?"

"Your father wanted better for you than a sicario, and because I cared about you, I realized he was right. I wanted to spare you."

Sofia saw the truth there in his eyes, and it took the fire out of her fight. Pain shimmered in his eyes, and for the first time, she realized that maybe leaving the way he did had hurt him too.

He looked away. "Besides, I knew you'd be fine. You didn't need me. You didn't need anyone."

His eyes trailed down from hers, down her neck and chest before settling on her bare elbow propped on the couch, her blouse sleeves rolled up over the course of the day.

He reached across the coffee table that separated them to swipe a thumb across Sofia's elbow, across the scar from her fall. The warmth of the pad of his thumb contrasted with the cool air-conditioning gave Sofia goose bumps.

He met her eyes, and her breath hitched in her throat.

She held still so as not to tremble under his touch, not to telegraph how much her fingers ached to comb through his closely cropped hair like they used to.

"I'm here now," he said softly, watching his thumb move against her skin. "Those dreams we had as kids . . . This is the way, Sofia."

Sofia wasn't naive, not anymore. Andres honeyed his words, made her remember a time when she would have done anything for him purposefully. But without her father around to run interference between her and her cousins and brothers, she'd need someone on her side who owed her a favor.

Even if this ally was her mother's suspected murderer. Right now he was offering her the only lifeline she was likely to get.

If it turned out that Lalo was right, it wouldn't matter. Sofia would have the Gulf and the Baja on her family's side once more, and Sofia, she'd take that government appointment and hold on for dear life. No matter what happened after the election.

Sofia pulled her arm away from Andres's touch and stood. "If she's who you say she is, then maybe you're on to something, sicario."

Sofia glanced at the computer monitor on Andres's desk. The stark lines of a design in progress filled the screen.

"You can't swallow a scorpion and expect not to get stung," she said, turning back to look at Andres as he stood. "She owns you now. I want to see if the price was worth it."

Sofia headed toward the door, pausing before pulling it open.

He'd never answered her question.

"Set up a meeting, but Andres, I will find out what happened to my mother. And *Díos te ayude* if I find out you had anything to do with it."

CHAPTER 18

Diego punched in the alarm code as quietly as possible before slipping in past his heavy front door.

The apartment was silent. It was well after midnight by now.

He dutifully hung his keys in their spot; Yolotli hated when he just tossed them on the counter. Then Diego double-checked the door was locked and finally eased off his boots.

Yolotli had let him know Sofia was staying over, so Diego figured he'd seize the opportunity to talk to her with no one else around. It was time to have the talk he'd been putting off.

The living room was half lit by the patio lights that illuminated his sister, where she sat curled up in one of the lounge chairs.

Diego grabbed a bottle of tequila from the bar, and on his way out to the patio, he paused to collect something of Sofia's he'd been keeping safe from its drawer in the living room before padding out to the patio.

"It's late, hermano," Sofia said.

Diego settled into his seat, the chair that he had angled best to watch the sunrise and sunset. Not that he was home much for either these days.

He pulled the cork out from the tequila bottle with a pop before extending it to his sister. "I just got off work, sis."

She shook her head, pushing the bottle back.

Diego pressed the cool glass bottle to his lips. Relieved his sister didn't feel the need tonight to lecture him about vices. Maybe because she'd been there once. Coming home at dawn. Maybe she remembered what it was like to just want to wash it all away.

"Yolotli told me you saw the priest," Diego said as he busied his hands with a rolling paper, sprinkling sticky *mota* into the small valley the paper created between his fingers.

"I did," she replied, thinking of Father Raya, Lalo. "He said if you need to talk, he's available."

Diego sucked air through his teeth. "Cha. There's no need."

If he was going to talk, it wouldn't be with the priest with the scar.

Diego slipped the freshly rolled joint behind his ear for safe-keeping while he fished for a lighter in his pocket. He glanced at Sofia before flicking the lighter. "You blame Xavier and Joaquin."

"You don't?" Sofia asked.

Diego inhaled and let the smoke warm his lungs for a beat before exhaling. "They only want what's best for this family, Sofia."

"What's best for them. They want what's best for them."

Diego shrugged. "Don't we all?"

Sofia looked away, her gaze on the night skyline.

He was losing her; he could see it in the way she drew into herself. Conversations with her had been infuriating lately. She was stuck in an old fantasy, one of an easy, carefree life. A life they never had the chance to have. So when he tried to talk to her about real life, real choices and consequences, she shut off.

Diego had learned loyalty in the way he was taught to have his sister's back. In how they'd do the runs at night, together. Only seventeen and sixteen then. They didn't know any better. All they knew was what they were told. And that consequences for them meant death. A mistake, a fuckup, meant death.

So when she ran away at the first chance she got, Diego felt that absence, that chill at his back where she used to be. He learned how to rely on himself. Only himself. And now she was pissed about it. Pissed because he'd adapted.

He looked away from her. "Yoli told me you went to see Andres too."

"Diego, it's not what you think."

"Oh, I know exactly what it is," he replied, his words tinged with the specific heat she was able to pull out of him.

Andres had already done enough to tear their family apart, and Diego worried about his sister. About her feelings for the man to whom all signs pointed as their mother's murderer. Who at the very least was a paid assassin. Sofia could do better; she should want better.

Diego feared for his sister because Sofia had found in Andres what Diego had found in Yolotli, and Diego knew that type of connection was all-consuming. Like a hurricane, it washed everything else away like discarded mud people.

"What did he promise you this time?" Diego asked, "because if I remember correctly, last time he made you promises, he broke them. And I was the one there to pick up the pieces. To make you whole again. That was me, Sofia."

She wrapped her arms tighter around herself.

"We need the Herreras right now."

Diego tossed his lighter onto the table. "Just like that, he's back in. Let me guess, he said some pretty words, told you what you wanted to hear, and you believed him. Like before. Like always."

"What would be enough for you, Diego?" she asked, her eyes finally coming to life. "That bullet you promised him? Will that fix it? Fix that canyon where your heart used to be? I know you blame him for what happened, but it's made you blind. As long as you have him to blame, you don't have to look at yourself. That's it, isn't it?"

"Why are you protecting him? After all this time."

Sofia chewed her bottom lip before replying, tasting copper. "He didn't kill her. But he knows who did."

Diego scoffed, "That's what he told you?"

She shrugged. "It's a feeling."

"He wants you to support this cease-fire, doesn't he? So that chick can get elected."

Sofia frowned. "That's one way to put it."

"He's screwing her, you know that, right?"

Sofia glanced at Diego, her eyes wide.

Shit.

"You didn't know?" Diego sighed. "Look, he'll say whatever it is he needs to to get whatever it is he wants from you."

Sofia looked away again. "I know."

Diego reached up to scrub a hand over the back of his head. "So what's the plan then, big sis?" he asked.

"I'm trying here, Diego. But I won't be able to make everyone happy. I'm not going to make my country pay with blood anymore. If there's a way to keep the peace, we need to consider it."

Diego had to laugh. He couldn't help it. It bubbled up from the back of his throat and spilled out past his lips before he could stop it.

"You care about this country, our country, so much that you abandoned it. For eight years, Sofia. Eight years."

"And what did you do in that time?" she asked, her eyes burning. "You became their *pinche* lapdog. You know what? That's your problem—you're scared to think for yourself."

"Oh, that's what my problem is? Do you want to know what yours is, Sofia? You hide behind the way you think things should be. These ideals of yours, of Mom's. Ideals that got her killed, do you understand that? She was going to leave Pops. She was going to leave him for Don Martin, for a new life, and that disloyalty, those ideas of what could be is what got her killed, and now you sit in that cemetery because you think she'll talk to you—"

"She *does* talk to me," Sofia interrupted. "She'd talk to you, too, if you visited her."

Diego shook his head. Fantasy, it was all fantasy.

"You're just like her, you know that? You've always been ashamed of this family, of what we do, what we had to do, to survive. Just like her. So you let me and Pops and Nando and Yolotli take care of all the dirty shit so you can go pretend to be someone else thousands of miles away. But that's over now, sister."

"That's not true," Sofia replied.

"It is. You always tried to distance yourself from us. You always had dreams of being someone else, something else. Anyone other than a De Luna. You and Andres. You'd sit out there in that field and make your plans, right? About doing what? Him an architect, you a mayor or governor? Or maybe president one day?"

"I was always here for this family when I had to be."

"When you didn't have a choice. I'd respect you more if you just said you couldn't handle this life."

"How can I not be ashamed!" she exclaimed. "We are killers, Diego. You're not ashamed of that? Of what we've done?"

"No," he replied. He wasn't.

They fought for what they had. Their father and their grandfather had fought to have something to call their own, and this was it. Diego left the moral arguments to others for whom it was all theoretical. This life put food on their tables. That was real.

Sofia shook her head. "Someone has to finish what our mother started," she replied, "because otherwise what was the point?"

Diego wanted to reach out and shake her.

"You're still delusional, still living in that fantasy world where we plant some trees downtown and walk away heroes to make up for all the shit we've done. You think you're Malverde."

"And you think revenge is the only way to honor her . . ." Sofia said.

"I don't want to honor her. I just want justice."

"When does it end?" Sofia asked, leaning closer. "Blood for blood over and over and over. When will it be enough? How many more shot-up cops will be enough?"

"Your politicians created an army to fight us, Sofia. An army that you saw with your own eyes. How did they expect us to react?"

"I have to do something, Diego."

"Since when?" he asked, his veins stinging now. "You think we need you, is that it? You think you're here to save us? What about that life in London, the one you were so proud of? The too-expensive, too-small flat? The shit job? It's not enough for you after all, is it? It was never going to be enough. You have a monster inside you. We all do. You point it out in me so that you can pretend you don't feel the same claws in your belly."

Her jaw clenched and released. "You're wrong, Diego. I buried that beast."

"I don't believe you. I don't think you believe that either."

"I'm meeting with Ximena," she said, and Diego felt her eyes on him.

In that moment, he felt torn in two.

The cousins had warned him, had told him things would be better without her in the way. And Diego had his suspicions about where her loyalty truly lay.

Andres. It was with Andres.

"What does that mean for us?" Diego asked, stubbing out the joint. "You and Andres figure all that out?"

"This isn't about him," she replied tersely. "Nothing changes. At least for now. But I need to understand what it is you and the cousins have in mind for expansion. Is it *hielo? La hache?*"

Diego crossed his arms over his chest. "Pops made sure those routes were closed to us years ago."

"Guns then?" she asked.

"I think this is a conversation for another day," Diego said.

The cousins' plan was news to him, even as Xavier laid it all out. Moving people. Trafficking people, while undeniably profitable, was a line that, once crossed, there was no coming back from.

Diego saw the death in Xavier's eyes. The blackness of someone who had given up having something to lose years earlier. But to bring Sofia and his little brother into this world, Diego wasn't ready. He knew they weren't either.

"I was hoping to have you on my side, brother."

He met Sofia's eyes, holding her gaze. "We'll see which side you land on, sis."

The metal had warmed since he slipped the gun into the waistband of his pants before stepping outside.

He reached under his shirt now to pull out the silver nine-millimeter Beretta, the twin to his all-gold version, and placed it on the table between them.

"One way or the other, you're going to need this."

CHAPTER 19

The heavy smell of the asado grilling outside stung Maria's nose as she entered the foyer.

They were having guests. Her father only called in the chefs and ordered enough meat for an army when he had someone over he particularly wanted to impress.

One of the housekeepers ushered her upstairs, telling her to clean up and change, and quickly.

A dress had been laid out for her. Navy with a high collar and long sleeves. She rolled her eyes but slipped it on hurriedly.

Maria took her seat at her father's right at the large table on the patio. She eyed the guests, two men, ranchers.

"Maria," her father began, "this is Alberto, and his father."

Alberto had a strong jaw, thick eyebrows, big brown eyes, a cleft chin, an aquiline nose. Broad features, all a touch too big for his face. Indigenous blood made his skin glow like sunned terra-cotta. His shoulders were rounded and thick with muscle. His forearms the same, sinewy muscles that moved like rope under his skin.

He was also older than Maria; that was obvious at first glance.

As the meal came to an end, Maria's father nodded toward her. "Maria, why don't you and Alberto take a walk," her father said in a tone that wasn't a suggestion.

The summer sun had finally begun to set, washing the property in a lush orange gold.

They passed the stable while Alberto talked, mostly about himself, some about his father. A lot about farming and produce.

Maria's blood cooled when she made out a figure by the stable.

Martin was still here. The older mare had a sore leg, and Martin had stayed late the last few days to look after her. Maria figured he would have gone by now, as he had told her he had coursework to catch up on.

Maria tried to redirect Alberto away from the stable and toward the garden, but it was too late.

Alerted by the sound of their voices or footsteps or both, Martin looked up as Alberto and Maria made their way down the path that passed the stable.

Pausing where he had been closing the stable door, he met Maria's eyes.

He glanced at Alberto, then back to Maria. And this time she saw fire there, a darkness she'd never seen in him before.

Distantly she heard Alberto remark that he knew Martin, that the Torreses had the best horseman in Mexico City working for them.

It was that moment, Maria would remember, that the truth of what she felt for Martin became clear. All the butterflies and shyness and awkwardness and the moments she counted down until their afternoons together finally made sense. She had thought it a crush, a silly crush, but it was more. From the day he introduced himself it had been more.

Maria was called to her father's office a few days later once she returned home from school.

He sat stoically behind the big desk. His desk in Buenos Aires had been small and cluttered with papers piled haphazardly. This desk had rigid order. Just like the man who had once taught literature with his head in books, dressed in all-black suits and seldom smiling.

"Sit down," her father ordered.

Maria smoothed her skirt behind her legs before lowering herself into the seat opposite her father.

"You're graduating soon . . ." he began.

"Yes," she replied, perking up. "Actually, I wanted to talk to you about that."

Her father's mouth became a rigid line. "I'm giving you this house, Maria. I'm giving you money, a lot of it. You will use it to buy a produce farm up the road from here. The accountants will work it out with you."

Maria tilted her head. "I don't understand."

"You are marrying Alberto. The money I give you for this produce business is your wedding gift. Maria, it's imperative that the produce business is successful and runs smoothly."

She still didn't understand, blindsided by the suddenness of her father's plan.

"What if I don't want to marry Alberto? I don't know him."

Her father sighed. "You should know by now that what we want doesn't matter."

Maria sank back into the chair, her eyes starting to sting, all her thoughts of Martin. Only Martin. She couldn't bear the thought of being without Martin.

She bit her bottom lip hard to stop the tears. She knew better than to cry in front of her father.

"Why produce?" she asked after clearing her throat.

"It's complicated, *niña*."

"Tell me the truth. If I'm old enough to be married off, then I'm old enough to know the truth."

"The truth is you need that legitimate business to shelter Alberto's business, do you understand that?"

"Your business. Your job that made you all this money."

Her father shook his head. "It's soon yours."

"Then I need to know. I need to know all of it."

Her father nodded and added, "In time."

"Why Alberto?"

"He's a rancher; he knows produce, and he knows my business. He will give you a comfortable life."

"I don't want a comfortable life. I want a safe life; I want to be safe. Martin could keep me safe—he's going to be an architect."

Her father scoffed, a wry smile crossing his face. "Martin is not the type of man you need, Maria."

He was the type of man her mother would want for her. Maria knew it. She needed her; she needed her mother. But they had taken her from Maria. She was left with this man, this once-creative man who now had room only for practicality.

"Let me tell you something about Martin," Maria's father began. "His family in Colombia—they do what I do times a hundred. They are rich, they are connected, they are dangerous, and they are powerful. I know you think Martin is some sort of knight in shining armor, your knight. But he's no better than me. Than Alberto. What's dangerous is that he thinks he is."

Maria looked away, swallowed her father's words down, down deep. She needed them to be lies. She needed Martin to be good.

"You need someone to take care of you," her father continued, his voice softer now. "My time will run out. I cannot stay here with you forever. That war we ran from, it never ended, not fully, not for people like us. I have to go back for your brother, for his family. Before it's too late."

"Why do I have to stay?" she asked.

"I've told you, Maria, this is our home now. This is your home. Once you marry Alberto, you will have a family here; you will have a business here. This is us surviving when they thought they would stamp us out. *Entiendes?*"

She didn't understand.

The horses neighed as Maria approached them. Her hand held out, she cooed softly. The young mare nudged her nose against Maria's shoulder.

Maria stroked the horse's muzzle as she settled against the fence to watch Martin approach the corral.

It was afternoon feeding time. Maria knew this. She knew that meant Martin would be around.

Martin carried a bale of hay, the veins in his arms protruding from the effort, his skin glistening with sweat.

She looked away.

Martin stepped up to the fence next to her. Close enough to make the palomino snort. He tutted before tossing the hay over the fence, stray pieces of the straw landing in his hair.

Maria reached for them, her fingers trembling at their closeness.

"Careful. They're grouchy today," he said, his voice soft. Raspy.

He avoided her eyes.

"Think it's the rain coming," she replied, glancing at the gathering storm clouds on the horizon. "Haven't seen you around lately," she said as her hand fell away.

"I had exams," he replied as he hoisted himself over the fence and into the corral.

The offended palomino swished its tail but made its way over to the hay Martin had dropped off all the same.

Maria stepped back. This reception from Martin was cold. It was unlike him. She decided to leave him to it, moving to turn back toward the house.

"I won't be working on the ranch much longer," he said, his voice stopping her.

She looked at him, noting how much he'd changed since they first met. How he was a man now.

"I figured that would happen at some point."

He looked down at his hands where he worked to pull his gloves on tighter, then looser, then tighter again, his forearms flexing with the nervous gesture.

"Maria, do you know who your father is?" Martin asked, looking up to meet her eyes. "What he does?"

Maria squinted against the sun. "I have an idea."

Martin reached up to wipe at the sweat beading on his forehead. "It's not safe, you know. I just . . ." He sighed. "I'm not good at this shit, Maria; I just need to know you understand. Because I don't. You told me your father left Argentina because of the violence, and now he's part of it. Here."

Maria tilted her chin up. "That might be true. But he's also a man with a daughter to provide for. He had to do something . . ."

"So you do know," Martin said, "what it is he does?"

"He's gone all night, gets calls at all hours of the day. I've seen the gun on his hip. I'm not stupid."

"I didn't say you were."

Maria looked down. "He was a teacher back home. He was a good man."

Martin pulled his gloves off, shoved them into his back pockets. "A man can be many things at once, Maria. Good and bad."

She met Martin's eyes. "You don't like him. That doesn't make him a bad man."

"It's more complicated than that," Martin replied. "He doesn't respect me. He thinks this is all I'm capable of. I'm going to be an architect, Maria, with my own firm."

"I know."

Martin's gaze softened, his sharp features less so. "Alberto will hurt you. He will get you hurt. He's in the life, just like his father, just like your father."

Maria closed her eyes. "I don't want to talk about Alberto."

"I know. But that doesn't make what's going to happen any less real."

Maria crossed her arms, clasping her hands over her elbows. Shielding herself.

"You could be in university," Martin said. "You're too smart to just be a wife."

She frowned. "What's wrong with being a wife?"

He took a step closer, his gaze holding hers. "Nothing, if it's what you want."

She looked away. "My father will never let me attend college. My future's already been decided."

Martin sucked air through his teeth. "But what do you want? What did Victoria want?"

She froze at the mention of her name, her real name. Victoria who belonged to Argentina.

She looked at the moist ground underneath her boot to avoid his eyes. "I have to do this for my family. They have to have something to come to. Somewhere safe."

Martin shook his head. "That's what your father is telling you. That's what *he* wants. I asked what *you* want."

She sighed. "There's no room for that, Martin. There's no room for wants."

"There is. There can be. If you make it." His eyes were soft, pleading.

Her face was burning with the challenge, with frustration, with all the things she wasn't allowed to say. And here was Martin, the only person who asked her to say those things, pushing her over the line she'd been toeing.

"I want you, that's what I want," she said, before clasping a hand over her mouth.

She shook her head and turned away.

Martin hopped over the fence again, reaching for Maria. "That's what I want too, Maria. I can provide for you. I can take care of us. You don't need Alberto; you don't need this place. You don't need their money or their problems."

"I owe them," she said softly, avoiding Martin's gaze.

Martin shook his head. "No, no you don't, Maria . . ."

"I do," she replied, pushing his hands away. "My brother stayed behind; we left him. I've never met my nephews. I owe this to them. They deserve a life too."

"Why does it have to be you?" he asked.

"Because this will be their home, our home. Their chance at a new life, the way I was given a chance."

"And your father?"

Maria shrugged. "I don't know. He's talking like he's never coming back."

Martin nodded and swiped at the sweat at his brow. "I never told you this, but I talked to your father. About us. About how I wanted to do things right. I wanted a chance."

"How did you know I wanted that?" she asked.

"Old-fashioned, remember?" he said with a smile that didn't reach his eyes.

"What did he say?" Maria asked, her eyebrows knit.

Martin sighed. "I think you know."

Maria looked away as the lump in her throat returned. *There's nothing I can say to make this right,* she thought.

"I'll be here for a few more hours. I'm going to get everything ready for my replacement. He's good too. You'll be in good hands."

Maria shook her head. "I don't want . . ." She bit her lip, closed her eyes, and swallowed. Swallowed it all down. There was no point in making it harder. For either of them.

She opened her eyes. "When you graduate, will you come back?" she asked. "Will you design that chapel for me?"

He looked away from her, at the ground, at the corral, at the horizon and the darkening clouds there. Anywhere other than Maria.

"Yeah," he said with a nod, "it'll be your wedding present."

The rain fell thick and heavy that night.

Maria looked out of her bedroom window toward the stable, where a light glowed.

She crept downstairs, hurried under the cover of night and rain to the stable.

Martin was closing the mare's stable door. He frowned when he saw Maria, drenched from the rain, goose bumps raised on her skin.

"What are you doing down here?" he asked. "You're going to get sick . . ."

"Don't talk," she said, reaching for him, grabbing his arm, his shirt, pulling him close to her.

She slipped her fingers through his hair, tugged his head down to press her forehead to his. "I don't want to talk."

He looked down at her, his eyes searching hers.

"Please," she said. "Martin, please."

He reached up, slid her rain-soaked hair off her forehead, pressed his lips to the skin there.

And maybe she didn't know what she was asking him for, but he knew.

His hands caged her face, the touch comforting, grounding, and for the first time, Maria felt her roots take hold. This moment was real; this moment might be all she had. And she had to know, she had to feel him, she had to be close to him. Even if it was the last and only time.

"Are you sure?" he asked.

She nodded, her eyes on his.

"He'll kill us," Martin said, the tip of his nose skimming the sensitive shell of her ear.

"No talking."

He slid a hand down to wrap around her throat, not tight, just grounding. His thumb pressed into the beat he found under her jaw.

She watched his eyelashes flutter closed, and she let hers do the same.

Then his lips finally brushed hers, light as a feather at first. His lips dry, soft, warm against hers dripping rain. She needed more.

She raised on her tiptoes to press into him, her shirt soaking the front of his now, and his arms wrapped around her, pulling her closer into him.

"I've got you, I've got you," he murmured against her ear, her temple, her lips over and over like a prayer.

And when the tears she didn't want him to see fell, he wiped at them with his thumb, kissing her gently.

"I'm here," he said, his hands slipping to her waist. "I'm yours."

Even if this is it, was left unsaid.

She needed him to lead and he did, pulling her toward the farthest corner of the stable where the light was dim.

"I'd be lying if I said I never had this exact same fantasy," he said, smiling as he pulled her close again, his nose buried in her neck, in her hair.

"Show me," she said, her hands coming to rest at his waist.

His eyes darkened, and he reached to pull the nearest saddle blanket off the rail, laying it down.

He helped pull off her soaked T-shirt, but she hesitated when his fingers reached for the drawstring of her pajama pants.

He stopped, meeting her eyes. "Come here," he said, holding her hand as he guided her to sit on the blanket.

He stood above her now, unbuttoning his denim shirt, and she watched his fingers move. Suddenly shy, she didn't know what to do with her hands.

He lowered himself to his knees in front of her. He looked like an angel and a devil all in one. A god and a sinner.

She sat up, laying her hands on his jean-clad thighs.

I want this forever; I want only you, forever. The words pricked at her tongue because they were true, but an empty promise, so they sliced and she bit them back.

"Touch me," he said, his voice bringing her back to the moment, reaching for her hands, bringing one of her palms to his warm lips and kissing her skin.

He pressed her hands to his chest, his eyes on hers, watching. "Can you feel that?" he asked.

She glanced to where her hand, small under his, pressed against his chest. His heart beat quickly under her palm.

The shyness started to bleed away as a feeling of power replaced it.

CHAPTER 20

Daybreak bathed the townhome Diego and Yolotli purchased on the city's west side. The unit was within walking distance of the natural history museum and the city zoo, and when Diego saw the way Yolotli's eyes lit up during the tour, Diego had to have the place.

Diego loved the cool gray exposed brick of the high walls and the sleek stone and wood accents. He liked the privacy of the set-back patio and tall trees. The town house had an air of minimalistic zen.

Usually.

Diego took a seat at the kitchen bar, his shoulders tense as he listened to the shower water run. He had just gotten in, his night not yet over despite the rising sun, but he wanted to catch Yolotli while he could.

Diego scrubbed a hand over the back of his head. The hair there was longer than usual. He'd need a haircut soon.

This thing between him and Yolotli had been brewing for a while. Neither really wanted to fight. Their fights were ugly things, both biting their tongues to avoid saying words they'd never be able to take back.

Their souls were twined together so tightly they could suffocate one another. Use just the right words to wound. It scared Diego how much he loved Yolotli, and he couldn't bear the idea of losing him. And when Diego was scared, it was easier to push everything away. Dance on the edge of nothingness because, really, what was the point? Of plans, of the future? He could catch a bullet tomorrow, and that would be it.

Their mother had plans and ended up face down in a ditch.

What a waste of time.

"You okay?" Yolotli asked, emerging from their bathroom, a towel wrapped low on his waist.

Diego's gaze flitted over the scene of the Mayan creation of the world, taken from the *Popol Vuh*, sketched in ink covering Yolotli's torso. Stone temples served as the background for the totems depicted in black-and-gray ink in Yolotli's deep copper-brown skin.

Yolotli had this. A history, a past to hold on to. An anchor. Diego was half this, half that. Half Mexican, half Argentinian. Half general, half soldier. Once good, now bad.

"Just some shit going on at the warehouse," Diego replied, turning in his seat to face Yolotli fully now. "Sofia being here, it's complicating things."

Yolotli shrugged, the muscles in his shoulders flexing and releasing. "She got dropped in the deep end, cariño. Give her a chance."

"She had a chance, years ago, and she decided to leave."

"And now she's here for you and Nando," Yolotli reminded him sternly.

Diego regarded Yolotli for a long moment, both men tense. "Sometimes I think you're on her side."

"Sometimes I am," Yolotli replied, "when you and Nando can't see the whole picture."

"You didn't need to tell her," Diego said, motioning between them, "about us."

"She figured it out on her own," Yolotli replied.

Diego was distracted by a water droplet that fell from Yolotli's wet curls to run down his collarbone. He took a few steps forward, wanting to reach for Yolotli. But that wouldn't solve this problem. It never did.

"We've been over this," Diego said, his tone calm.

"And yet here we are going over it again," Yolotli replied, "because you're still using that shit."

"I have it under control. I promised you that, and I meant it."

Yolotli shook his head. "You don't, though. You're supposed to be the general, but you're reactive instead of proactive. That's the shit that will get you killed, Diego. And your sister is going to need you. *I* need you."

Diego sucked air through his teeth.

"No, I'm serious," Yolotli continued, his brows furrowing. "Maybe you should listen to your sister's plan."

"What plan?" Diego exclaimed. "She doesn't have a plan. She has a fantasy."

"Then help her, asshole!" Yolotli replied, his voice rising. "I don't want to live like this forever."

"What do you want?" Diego asked, moving closer to Yolotli. "To get married? You know how that works in our world. I set you up in a house in the country. You raise our adopted kids with the nannies. If you're lucky, I visit you on the weekends. Is that what you want?"

Yolotli's shoulders tensed as he pushed them back. "Don't be cruel."

Diego shook his head. "I'm not, mi amor, I'm not. What's wrong with this life?" he asked.

"It's not a life! Look at you! How much longer can you go on like this? Not sleeping, not eating."

Diego looked around their townhome. "This isn't a life? This is a nice life, Yoli."

Yolotli shook his head and turned to pad barefoot down the hall.

Diego stood to follow him.

"You don't get it," Yolotli said quietly as he thumbed through his shirts. "It's like you've already made up your mind to die. Let what comes come, right?" Yolotli said, echoing one of Diego's sayings.

"Yoli," Diego said softly, his heart aching at Yolotli's words, "that's not true."

Yolotli said nothing. The only sound in the bedroom was their breathing and the soft rustle of clothes as Yolotli dressed.

"Why do you have to go out to the house tonight? You should stay, have someone else take Sofia home," Diego said, leaning stretched out across the bed, knowing his tank top and sweatpants left little to the imagination.

Yolotli turned to take in the sight, then shook his head. "In case you've forgotten, I get paid good money to go where I'm requested," he replied as he buckled his belt.

"I'll pay you more to stay."

Yolotli's head snapped up, his eyes on Diego.

Diego watched the dark expression falling over Yolotli's face, and he sat up quickly. "I'm sorry," he said. "That was supposed to be a joke."

Yolotli shook his head and turned his attention back to dressing. "Don't do that."

Money and titles were a sore spot for Yolotli. And Diego and his mouth sometimes failed to avoid that particular minefield. While the De Lunas had made sure Yolotli felt like one of them from day one, technically, he wasn't. Yolotli was good at what he did, and Alberto—now Diego guessed it would be Sofia—paid him accordingly. However, he was still technically a De Luna employee, while Diego was a born prince.

Diego dropped his head. "I'm sorry. I just wanted to spend some time with you. Aren't you always saying I'm gone too much?" he asked, looking up to see Yolotli's turned back. "I'll blow off some shit so I can stay home, if you stay."

Yolotli shook his head, his jaw clenching and unclenching.

"Mi amor, I am sorry," Diego pleaded from the bed where he now sat ramrod straight.

"It's fine," Yolotli said as he rummaged through his shelves of shoes.

Diego stood then, moving to crowd Yolotli in the expansive walk-in closet. He stood behind him, his hands on Yolotli's hips, his fingers digging into the skin just above the waistband of his jeans.

"I'm sorry, I'm sorry," Diego murmured into the skin behind Yolotli's ear, still damp from the shower, scented like eucalyptus.

Yolotli leaned back into the touch, letting Diego press his chest flush against his back. "I know," he said quietly as Diego peppered his neck and shoulders with light kisses.

Diego had known Yolotli for what felt like his whole life. Once, admittedly under the hazy spell of puppy love, Diego had murmured something to him along the lines of "My life didn't start until you showed up." Probably something he had heard in a movie playing in the background late at night while he dozed off, his head in his mother's lap. A lifetime ago.

Earlier in the night of this grand young teenage declaration of love, he and Yolotli had climbed the giant Montezuma cypress at the far corner of Diego's father's property. Well past midnight, the moon shone full, large, close enough that Yolotli reached out to try to touch it.

The night had been a cool one. The summer monsoons had emptied themselves early enough for the late afternoon dip in temperature to last into the evening. A breeze, cool enough to raise goose bumps, skimmed over them from time to time. Diego had reached for Yolotli then, not even sure of his own intent, but as he slid his hand up the other boy's neck, his palm resting at the back of his head, their eyes met, and he knew.

It had been Diego who closed the distance between them. He pressed his lips to Yolotli's, too hard at first, afraid if he didn't go for it in that second, he'd never get another chance.

Yolotli had smiled against Diego's lips, wiser than Diego then, still wiser than Diego now. He had eased the kiss, made it gentle, smiled at him when he pulled away. It was then that Diego knew this was all he wanted for the rest of his life, forever.

Barely a teen when Yolotli came into his life, Diego had been nothing more than a bored rich boy angry at the world for taking his mother. He had spent the summer lounging around their family's massive pool, his golden skin deepening as each hour passed.

Yolotli had shown up behind Diego's father one evening. He was skinny, his jean shorts torn, Adidas Sambas dirty and worn. His T-shirt stretched at the neck just so. His dark, curly hair falling into his eyes the way Nando's did.

"Who is this?" Diego had asked Sofia from his seat at the dinner table. They had been awaiting their father's return from the city to start dinner.

"A new companion," their father had answered as he made his grand entrance to dinner.

Whispers around the De Luna property were that Yolotli was an orphan, made so by Don Alberto. Diego brushed off the gossip. It was Diego who had been lost and Yolotli who had been found and raised like one of their father's own. As a young teen, Diego had wrestled with growing feelings that he didn't understand. Yolotli had been called his brother, treated as such by all the adults around them. But he wasn't. And Diego's feelings for him couldn't be ignored, no matter how hard he fought them.

Thankfully, he worked through that muddied water and came out the other side, positive that Yolotli had been sent just for him. Maybe by their mother, maybe by Dios, maybe just by accident, but Diego knew without a doubt that Yolotli—a word of Aztec origin that meant "heart"—was *his* heart.

"Come here," Diego said, taking Yolotli's hand. He pulled him until they reached the bed, and Diego lowered himself to sit on the mattress again.

"I can't stay," Yolotli said, looking down at Diego. He ran his hand down the length of Diego's back before gently pressing Diego's head into the soft skin of his sternum and stomach, embracing him as he stood above him. Yolotli sighed softly as he ran his blunt fingernails lightly over the nape of Diego's neck. "I should get going . . ."

"Of course," Diego murmured against Yolotli's chest before pulling back to look up at him. "Mi amor, being so close to Sofia, the things you hear, you'll pass them on to us, right? I mean, she talks to you more than us sometimes."

"Because I let her talk; I try not to judge or jump to conclusions," Yolotli explained. "Sometimes it seems as though you, Nando, and your father take losing your mother out on Sofia because she's still here."

Diego shook his head. "There's expectations when it comes to being a part of this family, and with Sofia, she picks and chooses when being one of us works for her."

"I think you should try to understand where she's coming from. Just try, mi amor," Yolotli said as he gently took Diego's face between his palms. "She cares about you, about us."

"I think she cares about you. I think she'd sacrifice the rest of us to a pack of jaguars, given the chance."

Yolotli smiled and brushed the pads of his thumbs over Diego's eyebrows. "She still wants to trust you, Diego, and you don't want to lose that." He moved away then. "I have to go. She's waiting downstairs."

Diego closed the distance between him and Yolotli quickly. He reached for his face to cup Yolotli's chin in his hand. "This life we have together, it's good, right?" he asked softly, his eyes searching Yolotli's.

Yolotli sighed and nodded. "It's good, Diego. It's good. I just worry about you."

Diego kissed Yolotli's forehead. "No need."

Yolotli gave Diego a light kiss, and Diego watched him grab his wallet, keys, and phone and head out the door. Once it clicked shut, Diego sighed, dropping back on the bed, his head in his hands.

He wanted to give Yoli anything he wanted, anything and everything. But this life required certain sacrifices, sacrifices Diego had made peace with the night the police showed up at their front door, their uniforms soaked with the late-night rainfall.

They had found a body in a ditch down the way. It was their mother.

Shot.

That was the only word Diego remembered from that night.

The universe takes because the universe also gives. Like Yolotli was given to him, Diego's mother was taken away, and that's how life works.

He explained this to a crying Nando, the last time he ever saw his little brother cry. That night red-and-blue lights flashed across his younger brother's face, illuminating the tears as they fell from his eyes, green eyes like their mother's that looked so much like hers then.

While Sofia stayed by their father's side, Nando and Diego were on the steps, becoming men. Learning how ugly the world could be.

Diego wouldn't let the universe take Yolotli from him. He'd die before that happened, and he knew that's what Yolotli was worried about. The De Lunas had enemies, and this war his cousins were suggesting would earn them more, but he'd be damned if he'd let Sofia and her lust for legitimacy take this life from him.

He hoped she'd fall in line, but if not, he wasn't sure what he would do to protect his peace, and he didn't want to have to find out.

CHAPTER 21

The administration buildings of the federal district in the Zócalo were nearly as old and weathered as the cathedral across the way but lacked the adornments. An air of austerity wafted through the hallways here. History had been made and unmade between these walls for hundreds of years.

Now Sofia's heels clicked against the smooth tile, Yolotli a step behind her.

"Why do I feel like we're poking a hornet's nest just by being here?" he muttered under his breath. Not the first of his expressions of displeasure of the day.

They were stopped at the mayor's door by the man Sofia recognized as Mexico's City's chief of police. He was a handsome, tall, broad man with a body like a boxer. His hair was slicked back and neat, his temples starting to gray, but his complexion was bright, free of any signs of aging. A fresh white bandage was wrapped around his wrist, white mesh woven between his thumb and forefinger.

Sofia glanced up to meet his eyes. They had the clarity of someone who was good at his job and knew it.

The mayor's lapdog seemed more like a pit bull.

"Don't make me search for it," Emiliano said, leaning closer to Sofia.

Yolotli stepped between the chief of police and Sofia.

Sofia saw the flash of familiarity cross the chief's face.

"Let me do my job, *chapín*," Emiliano said to Yolotli.

The two were acquainted.

Sofia brusquely untied the navy fitted wrap dress, another gift left by Lily, just enough to slip her hand under the material and reach for her side. She didn't feel like getting caught up in this particular pissing match.

So she pulled Lucia, the shining silver Beretta, from its holster.

"I expect this will be in good hands," she said as she gently handed the gun to Emiliano.

"Of course."

Sofia retied her dress as Emiliano stepped out of the way.

Ximena rose when Sofia entered the room.

Ximena Cruz was a slim, toned woman. Sofia's first impression was that she was hard, harsh almost. Ximena had razor-sharp cheekbones, accentuated by a severe bob that would have aged someone else but gave Ximena a trendy, youthful edge. Sofia sensed that Ximena was a woman trained to be tough in a world full of men. Maybe not so unlike herself.

Andres stood from the chair he'd been occupying.

He wore gray today, monochrome, a gray button-down with a silver sheen paired with gray houndstooth slacks. The light color made his eyes shimmer.

He nodded toward Sofia before addressing Ximena: "Mayor Cruz, Señorita Sofia De Luna."

"Doña Sofia De Luna," Yolotli corrected, his eyes on Andres.

"Doña De Luna, you're even more beautiful than your photographs," Ximena said, offering her hand to Sofia.

Sofia smiled politely. "Likewise," she said as she shook the woman's hand.

Her fingers were freezing, her grip strong.

"Welcome home," Ximena added as she gestured for Sofia to sit. "Mexico has missed you, I'm sure."

Sofia settled into her seat as Ximena continued, "My condolences on your loss. Your father was a beloved pillar of this community."

"Is that why you had him shot?" Sofia asked.

Andres stiffened in his seat, but Ximena smiled. "I anticipated that question. Contrary to what your family might think, we had nothing to do with the attack on your father. Which, I have to add, I can't say the same for you and your cousins' ambush on my chief of police."

"The shooter was wearing an SSC patch," Sofia argued.

"Easy to forge, unfortunately," Ximena said as she laid one hand over the other on her desk. "You might want to think about who in your circle would want to go through all the trouble to make it look like it was us."

When Sofia saw the steadiness in Ximena's eyes, the way she spoke evenly, her lack of defensiveness, she knew the woman was speaking the truth.

Sofia sat back in her seat.

"Well, now that that unpleasantness is out of the way, I've been looking forward to talking to you about your future," Ximena said. She paused. "Oh, I almost forgot. How is Padre Raya?" Ximena asked. "I've been meaning to catch up with him, and I hear you've already met with him in your short time back."

Sofia smiled tightly. "He wanted to offer his condolences."

"I'm sure, but I'm also sure there was probably more to it."

"Well, I know you're familiar with the seal of the confessional . . ." Sofia began.

Out of the corner of her eye, Sofia caught Andres's raised eyebrow.

"He's concerned about the violence," Sofia explained.

"As we all are."

"Of course," Sofia replied. "Andres mentioned you might have some . . . ideas."

Sofia caught the sideways glance Ximena gave Andres before speaking. "When I was selected by the party to run for president, there was one name that kept coming up. One name I needed to have on my side. De Luna. This is your city. Has been for decades."

"I'm familiar with my family history," Sofia said.

Ximena smiled tightly. "Of course. The point I'm getting to is you—unlike your brothers, unlike your father and your cousins—have a vision much more aligned with the party's goals for the future."

"Is that what he told you?" Sofia asked, inclining her head toward Andres.

"Andres speaks very highly of you, yes."

"And what about you? With all due respect, Madam Mayor, what makes you different? Because the people, they don't trust anyone in this room or anyone in this building. That hasn't changed in the time I've been gone. So I'm not sure what it is you think I can do for you.

"Because I know this isn't a battle to be won. Not anymore," Sofia continued. "We've already lost. So I'd rather make things work for everyone. Hemorrhaging money for a never-ending war on drugs isn't good business for any of us.

"The polls show the people are buying your message about being different. But you're not sounding that different right now to me if your only plan is to give in."

"So what's your version, then?" Ximena asked. "I've read about your work too. In London, the social service programs you helped get off the ground. All great feel-good stuff, but what did it really change? Because offering scholarships and minimum-wage jobs to kids while their friends drive the latest cars isn't going to change much in this country. You want people to value the same things you do, but they don't. They value security and the here and now because it's all they're promised."

"That's what you're promising? Security? Is that what that new army of yours is supposed to be?" Sofia said.

"Like it or not, the men who came before us have built everything based on Mexico running as a narco-state. There's too much to lose in trying to dismantle it. Doing so has never worked, and it won't work now. The Gulf, the Baja, your family will never lay down arms willingly. Not as long as one of them still stands."

"Neither will you and your army you built to try."

"You can't blame us for that," Ximena replied.

"Can't blame us either."

Diego's words of warning—about how the politicians were the real cartel in Mexico City—came back to Sofia like a neon light blinking, *I told you so.*

Sofia felt Andres's eyes on her. He was waiting for her response, waiting to see if she'd do what he asked.

"Maybe we can talk, woman to woman," Sofia said quietly, her gaze never leaving Ximena.

Ximena's jaw twitched, but she nodded, motioning for the men to leave.

"Look at us. They said this world wasn't for us, but they need us, don't they?" Ximena said in the echo of the closing door. She leaned back in her seat. "And here we are now, doing what women have always done. Picking up the pieces. And now you, swooping in to carry out your mother's wishes."

"While I appreciate the shared history you and I have, we both come from a long line of leftists, don't we? I know you like to keep it quiet, but it's there. Your disdain for the church for one. But you don't know the first thing about my mother."

"I know enough about her, and you, to know you're the key. That's why they needed you back."

"And now you want me, you want my family. For what?"

"While it's true your family's grip is slipping, it's not gone yet. And the way the De Lunas go, so go the Baja and the Gulf. I need their buy-in to win this election."

"The peace," Sofia replied.

"The longer the peace is kept between you three, the better the polls."

"The only way to keep the peace is to buy it."

"Tourism," Ximena said, her features coming to life. "If we keep the peace long enough, people will come back to the cities and the beaches . . ."

"Going to have to spread that wealth around, to the mountains, to the deserts."

"Of course."

"How?" Sofia asked.

"A commission on tourism tax. Legal rights to properties if they want them."

"Other countries will never let you . . ."

"It's already being done. It's been done for years. How else do you think the Herreras got all those prime contracts when the district started to grow?"

"That's the deal you offered Andres, then."

"More or less. And you, I have plans for you."

"Such as?" Sofia asked.

"Secretary of foreign affairs."

"I'd have to be voted in."

"I'd make sure it happened. Then you and your brothers would have nothing to worry about. You'll be legitimate businessmen and women. Most importantly, doña, no more violence."

"I can agree to that, but my cousins have other ideas."

"I know. They're hoping you'll just play at this new position of yours. Not take it seriously. And I'm hoping you will. I think it's time you separated from your cousins, don't you?" Ximena asked.

"It's not so simple. This is a family business."

"You can't buy them out? Everyone's for sale."

"My father tried once. It didn't end well. Besides, they're our access to Europe, through Uruguay. We are symbiotic at this point."

"They are a cancer," Ximena hissed, her polished mask cracking. "They'll try to swallow up this whole country until there's nothing left."

"My cousins are my family, Madam Mayor," Sofia replied.

Even if she hated it, it was true.

Ximena leaned over her desk, her eyes flashing. "They shot at Emiliano in broad daylight," she said, pointing toward the hallway. "Do you understand the significance of the line they crossed? Do you comprehend it?"

Sofia's jaw clenched. "I understand you are upset, so I will take that insult as misdirected anger."

"Your cousins have to be put down, Sofia. One way or another. That's what you do with rabid animals. I am offering you the civilized way out, for now."

"Is that what this is? How about I go back to my family, let my cousins start this war instead, because if you think they'll just lie down for you, you're mistaken."

"You don't have the manpower for both a war with the country and one with the other cartels. You'll implode."

"Like you said, maybe we take down the whole country on the way out."

Ximena tapped a perfectly shaped acrylic nail against her desk, her eyes on Sofia. "Let's try again. Your family isn't who you think they are, *fresa*. Everyone knows your mother was going to give up information on your family. That's why she was killed."

Sofia shook her head.

"You may not know it, but it's what they say behind your back. These cousins that you're protecting, they will stop at nothing. I'd hate to see you share the same fate as your mother."

Sofia stood. "They're my responsibility. Whether what you say they've done is true or not, I will handle it. Not your army."

"We will freeze your assets," Ximena said as she rose to her feet, "if you don't agree to this. Whether I lose or win, what money your family has left will belong to the state. I need you to understand this, Sofia."

"Understood," Sofia replied, "but my family doesn't respond well to threats. I'm sure you understand."

"Don't be shortsighted," Ximena hissed. "Don't let your loyalty to them get you buried like your mother. You can have that legitimacy you dreamed of. You just have to say yes."

"I learned very early that if a deal sounds too good to be true, it usually is."

"This offer won't stand forever, fresa."

"Give me a day to think it over," Sofia replied. "Offer me that respect."

Ximena nodded, and Sofia pulled open the office door, brushed past Emiliano and Andres, who flanked Ximena's office door, and started down the hall, Yolotli at her heels.

Sofia didn't speak until Yolotli had pulled the car onto the road.

She had to ask; she had to be sure.

"Did Xavier and Joaquin have anything to do with Emiliano's ambush? I need you to tell me the truth."

Yolotli glanced at Sofia before deftly maneuvering the SUV into traffic. "That's the word, but they haven't officially taken credit for it yet."

"You don't know?"

Yolotli shrugged. "Ask Diego."

Sofia sighed. "If it was them, then why? What was to be gained from something like that?"

"This war, for them, is a way of hitting reset. A cleansing, that's what they call it."

A reset. And Lord help anyone who stood in their way.

If it was a bloodletting Xavier and Joaquin wanted, how long before they started to sacrifice the De Lunas for their cause?

CHAPTER 22

Sofia wrapped her arms around herself more tightly as the afternoon warmth faded. The Zócalo grew quieter as the sky darkened and people headed home for the evening, grocery bags gripped tightly at their sides.

Lalo, all in black, stalked out of the darkness, tall and light on his feet. He was stopped more than once, silver-haired women catching him with a hand on his forearm.

He smiled down at them, offering blessings, Sofia assumed.

She glanced at the SUV parked across the square.

Yolotli would have questions. Even if he never asked. She'd need a cover. Soon.

"You know you're good at that," Sofia said, motioning toward the women disappearing into the evening. "Almost believable."

Lalo clapped his hands together. "Told you I went to school for this. Maybe you'll even let me hear your confession someday."

Sofia tilted her head. "Doubtful, Padre."

He stopped next to her, close enough that she had to crane her neck to look up at him as he gazed down at her.

"What's the problem, princesa? I'm sure you know all about the veil of secrecy."

"I do. But I also know that you, Father Raya, like to blur the lines a little too much for my taste."

Lalo smiled then, the scar stretching thin across his bottom lip. "You like your neat little boxes, is that it?"

Sofia swallowed, fighting the urge to look away. She wouldn't let him win this; she'd caught on to his little games. The way he used his height, his dark good looks to disarm, to unnerve. He thought using his looks would keep her on her toes, maybe even endear him to her. He wanted her to like him, at least enough that she'd keep talking.

"Key word—neat," Sofia replied. "I don't think you quite fit in anywhere."

"Well, that's too bad, isn't it?"

"It's probably a good thing, especially for you, Padre," she replied with the kind of half-empty words and promises reserved for flirting or dealmaking. But she wasn't here for this type of conversation.

"I'll do it," Sofia spit out without preamble. She had to say it before she changed her mind.

Ximena was everything Sofia thought she would be. A pleasing face with a pleasing message, but underneath, she was just as poisoned as the rest of them.

She was offering a Trojan horse disguised as an olive branch. A way for her to infiltrate the three cartels while promising financial security through legitimacy.

That tactic had worked well historically; it was the reason half the newer buildings in CDMX had *Herrera Architecture* etched into the stone and glass. But Sofia got the sense that Ximena hadn't sat down with Daniel of the Gulf or the Prince of the Baja. She was afraid to. She wanted Sofia to do it. And Sofia, while not afraid, wasn't sure they'd buy what Ximena was selling. So she'd have to find a way to spin it.

Sofia didn't trust Ximena, she didn't trust Lalo or Andres, and she sure as hell did not trust her cousins, so her fallback was to agree to each deal, stack them up against one another, and hope everything held.

Lalo's face shifted. "Just like that?" he asked, extinguishing the mischievous sparkle in his eyes.

She nodded. "Yeah, just like that."

"Your meeting with Cruz went that badly?" he asked.

"Look, I don't know what it is you think I can get from her, but I need whatever you can find out about my mother's death, Padre. As soon as possible . . . for a little motivation," she added with a wink.

He huffed and scratched his thumb across his bottom lip. "Sounding a little confident there, aren't you?"

"All I know for sure is you need someone close to her, closer than you can get, and right now, I guess that's me."

He nodded, turning his attention to an older couple passing them. "I guess it is."

Sofia sighed. "She mentioned something about a plan to keep the peace between us all. A way for cartels to still make and launder their money, so that the government doesn't look like it's getting in their way. That's all I know at the moment."

"And you'll get your legitimacy if you convince the others."

"*Más o menos*."

"Okay," he said, looking somewhat pleased.

"Padre?" Sofia asked.

"You can call me Lalo . . ."

"What do you think happened to my father?" Sofia asked, holding Lalo's gaze. "I know what I saw—I saw that SSC badge, but Ximena says it wasn't her."

"I think you know, Sofia," Lalo replied, his voice gentle, as if he were breaking bad news. "I'll see what I can dig up from your mom's case file," he continued. "In the meantime, my advice? The call is coming from inside the house."

Sofia frowned.

"Not a horror movie fan?"

When Sofia shrugged, Lalo continued, "There's a pattern with your family. When the status quo is threatened, people close to them start getting hurt."

"So I've heard. But that's also a good way to throw off anyone who's looking too deeply into what actually happened."

"Maybe, but I think you're starting to believe it. What I'm saying is, using Andres, a kid sicario, as a cover was pretty convenient. There was no push for an investigation. Your father wanted the case closed. Quickly. And it was easy to believe that your father just didn't want to persecute his oldest friend's son."

Sofia frowned and glanced away. "It's too easy now for people to say things. Without my father around, people feel comfortable saying things to me that they might not have before."

"There's a reason for that. And your job is to determine the why, Sofia. Why are people telling you things? What do they get out of it?"

She sighed. "They're going to try and take advantage of me. And I think it's going to be too easy to let them."

"Who?" he asked.

She looked up at him once more. "You for one."

"I just want to do my job, princesa."

"Me too," she replied, realizing for the first time that she'd finally admitted it. This was her mess now. "It's become clear to me that there's a real chance it's me or them."

"I think you're right on that one, *hermosa*."

Sofia tilted her head at the endearment. "It's going to be me, Padre, so don't get me killed in the meantime."

Lalo dragged an index finger across his chest in the shape of an *X*.

The house was quiet. So quiet. Sofia wondered how her father had stood it. So many empty rooms these days. The home had a darkness to it that clung in the corners. The voices that used to carry up and down the stairs and the halls were long gone.

Sofia had curled up into the corner of the sofa in the library, the only light a dim amber glow from the sconce on the other side of the room.

Sleep took her easily.

"Your mother liked to do the same thing," her father said, and the sound of his voice, residual in this home, made Sofia look up.

"When she needed to think. She'd come down here too. Sit in the dark. Do you remember that?" he asked as he took the few steps from the hall down into the library.

Sofia sat up. It was rare for her father to mention her mother. So she sat quietly. Waited for more.

"You have that same look," he said as he settled onto the other end of the couch. "Lost in thought."

"It's been a long day," Sofia offered, hoping her father wouldn't press.

Lalo's words sat heavy at the base of her skull. *The call is coming from inside the house.*

"Your mother used to think she could solve every problem if she had a bit of quiet time to think. She was pretty good at it. Most of the time.

"That crown . . ." he said, reaching to tuck a loose piece of Sofia's hair behind her ear. "It's heavy, isn't it?"

She wouldn't admit it, not to her father, not out loud, that right and wrong weren't as easy to discern as she always believed they were. It should be clear. What's good, what's bad. What they did, trafficking drugs, it was bad. Sure. Hurting people was bad. Stepping away from it all, leaving their future in the hands of a politician under the guise of turning "good"—was that really good? We can convince ourselves of anything. That much was true.

"You don't have to talk to me, and I understand if you don't. But you'll need a confidant. Because you'll lose sight. It will happen fast. The weeds will grow tall. You'll need someone who can listen. Who you can trust. Who can tell you when you're wrong because you won't be able to see it when you're on the brink of going too far."

"Who was that for you?" Sofia asked, her eyes on her father. Still strong and handsome as she remembered him when she was a little girl.

"Your mother," he replied, withdrawing his hand from Sofia's hair. "She was a straight shooter."

Alberto tilted his head, regarded his daughter. "It's a shame we decided not to set you up with someone. Your mother was against it, but for a woman like you, it could have been a good idea. You need someone who can understand."

The De Luna siblings had heard the talk around town: that their mother was only married to Alberto through an arrangement by their grandfather Juste. Maria always denied it to her children. Sofia understood she was trying to protect them from the uglier mechanics of life. Maria didn't want to diminish what magic was left for her children, so she let them believe that she loved their father. That their marriage had been her choice.

"Who do you have?" Alberto asked, his voice low and dark. "You're alone, aren't you?"

Sofia's jaw twitched, her eyes never leaving her father's. The air in the room buzzing.

"Whose fault is that?" she asked.

Before her father could reply, Sofia felt a sharp jerk like she was falling, and the room slipped away.

"*Perdón, doña,*" a voice said.

Sofia's eyes fought to focus as the dream slipped away.

Her cup of tea had cooled on the coffee table.

She was in the library still, but her father was gone.

It had been a dream; she must have nodded off on the couch.

She hadn't slept well recently. Her room felt like it was closing in on her whenever she entered, so she usually sat in the library and dozed fitfully until the sun rose. Tonight was no different.

She sat up straight, smoothing her hair and looking up at the guard who had woken her.

The guards on the property were quiet, so quiet, they blended into the grounds until they stepped into the light.

"*Con permiso*," he began again, "Andres Herrera is at the gate, asking to see you."

Sofia sighed deeply before following the guard to the front door where she found Andres standing in the driveway, a cigarette between his fingers, his gray button-down sleeves rolled to the elbow, its top buttons undone.

"You really should stop smoking," she called to him before stepping out onto the smooth rocks in her socks. She'd changed for the evening into sweatpants, an old T-shirt, and holey socks, she now realized, as an exposed circle of skin on the bottom of her foot pressed against a cold rock. She hadn't been expecting visitors.

He glanced up, and a look flitted across his face. Before she could place it, it was gone.

Despite her attire, she managed to look indignant. "What are you doing here?" she demanded.

"I was on my way home, thought I'd stop by to see how the meeting went. You left so fast I didn't get a chance to ask."

"Home?" she asked.

He nodded up the road, toward the Herrera property.

He was staying with his father. Just up the road, just like before.

After giving her a quick once-over, he glanced at the house. She knew the windows were dark, all signs of life gone.

"You know, maybe it's not good for you to be in this big place. All alone. After everything," he said. "I'm just up the street, my dad and I. You could stay—"

"I'm fine," Sofia interrupted.

He held a hand out, palm up. "I didn't say you weren't . . ."

She caught the annoyance in his tone. It had been years, but she still knew how to get under his skin.

Sofia crossed her arms over her chest. "Why didn't you just ask your *novia* about our girl talk?"

Andres stilled.

"Diego told me," Sofia added, "about you two."

Andres shrugged. "She didn't tell me much about your conversation," he replied, his lack of correction regarding his relationship with Ximena telling Sofia all she needed to know.

Sofia glanced over her shoulder, back at the house and the gaping front door.

She didn't want to go back inside, not alone, not yet, so if Andres was her distraction for the time being, so be it.

"I'm going to grab my shoes. Let's take a walk."

Her father's passing words about virtue being a narrow road and vice being a wide one were not lost on Sofia as she strode around the property with Andres.

Out here at night, the sky was beautiful, dark velvet dotted with glittering diamonds. The trees moist, lush, heavy with life. Out here that magic her mother clung to was still real. And vices could still be packaged as everything you ever dreamed of.

Andres cleared his throat. "So, Father Raya," he probed.

Her skin prickled. Did Andres know who Father Raya really was?

"Are you going to chastise my need for spiritual counseling?" Sofia asked, keeping her tone even.

Andres snorted. "Is that what it is between you two?"

Maybe it was just jealousy.

Sofia glanced up at Andres. His eyes twinkled in the moonlight, but the waters there were choppy.

"Father Raya is an important man to our community," Sofia replied, knowing, on the surface, that was the truth. Always stick as close to the truth as possible—Xavier had taught her that.

"He's a little . . . unconventional," Andres replied.

"Aren't we all?" Sofia asked.

Andres sighed, looking skyward for a beat. "I don't want to do this dance with you anymore."

Sofia glanced at him, and in the moonlight, she noted the darkened skin under his eyes, how tired he looked. How tired he sounded.

"I don't want to feel like I have to have my guard up around you," he went on. "I want you to trust me again, Sofia."

Sofia frowned, irritation flaring. "What makes you think I care about your wants?"

Andres stopped, taking her arm gently as he did. "You don't want this either."

"I don't want anything from you," she replied, because every time she looked into his eyes she was reminded of what might have been, and it hurt. Every time.

He dropped her arm, and her skin cooled instantly.

Her words landed more sharply than she'd intended. This close, it was hard to hide the betrayal she still felt. And why should she? Why should she shelter him from the harm he had caused?

He looked away from her. "Maybe you're right about me. I haven't been completely honest with you, that's true. There are times when I think about leaving all of this behind. Being someone else. Somewhere else. For good. You asked if this was just about the money, and it's not."

"What else is there left for you at this point, Andres? You have everything you want . . ."

"Not everything," he said, meeting her eyes. "She'll pull my deal too, Sofia. And no deal means she'll freeze my assets too. I'll have nothing."

Sofia rolled her eyes. "That's why you're here, to make sure I do what she wants so you get to keep your government contracts and shiny new career. You need me to bury your ghosts but won't help me with mine."

She turned to head back toward the house but jerked when Andres grabbed her again, stopping her in her tracks. This time his fingers were clenched tightly around her forearm, digging into the skin.

She glared at him, pulling her arm, but his grip was unrelenting, his eyes flashing. "You can curse me and roll your eyes at me all you want, but I have your way out."

"You told me that's what Ximena's deal is supposed to be," Sofia hissed, anger simmering in her veins at the way he was able to hold her there, force her to listen when she wanted nothing more than to let him remain a ghost from her past.

"I have something, no strings attached," he said, his voice softer, but Sofia felt his urgency. "I know you won't pull the rug out from under your brothers, and I have something you can give them in return for your freedom. If you want it."

Sofia looked pointedly at where his hand clung to her arm. "Nothing in this life has no strings attached."

He finally released her arm, and she pulled it close to her body.

"Please, Sofia," he began, softer this time, "hear me out. The cocaine. It's yours. Once I'm out, out for good, it's yours. Keep the connection or give it to your brothers, your cousins, I don't care. But I'll be done."

She glared up at him. "Your family won't let you out either. Not without something in return as well."

Andres continued, "If you agree to take on the distribution, then they won't give a shit what I do."

Sofia rubbed her arm and chewed on her bottom lip, the sting of the bite grounding her.

"You'll be working with the president, and you will have the entire Herrera cocaine distribution in your hands. You will be the most powerful woman in Mexico."

He wasn't lying about that. The Herrera cocaine empire was a classic monopoly. A few years before she left, the Gulf had attempted to contact another supplier directly, therefore cutting out the De Lunas, costing them their fee. And cutting out the Herreras, attempting to undercut their business.

For that indiscretion, the Herreras, those of Andres's family in

Colombia, burned the fields belonging to the other dealer, the one foolish enough to think they'd be able to take any of the Herreras' business for their own.

"Why?" Sofia asked. "Why me?"

Andres could easily have brought the same deal to Daniel or to the Prince of the Baja if he was serious about getting out. It didn't have to be her. It didn't have to be her family.

Andres reached for her again, this time laying his hands on her shoulders, his thumbs pushing into the muscle, not enough to hurt, just enough to keep her attention.

She met his eyes, which were dark out here under the moon, but the light flashes of yellow green were unmistakable.

"You don't need to do everything all alone," he said, his eyes on hers, pinning her there, holding her to him. "Let me help you make yourself indispensable before anything happens to you."

"Why?" she repeated. "Because you want me to forgive you? That's what this is, isn't it?"

He shook his head. "No. Forgiveness is a gift to yourself, Sofia. I can't ask that of you."

"Then what is it, Andres?"

"I owe you."

Sofia frowned. "I thought we discussed this. The past . . . it doesn't matter anymore—"

"Sofia," Andres said, interrupting her, "it's my fault she died."

CHAPTER 23

Andres passed the equestrian center at the base of the hill the Herreras' home was nestled into. The center, studded with reclaimed wood, natural stone, sharp angles, and buildings set into relief, was meant to be a part of the landscape; more important, it was meant for the horses. This was his father's favorite project, and most likely his last.

The electric engine of Andres's car purred whisper quiet as he pulled into the driveway of his father's home. The home he'd grown up in.

Andres killed the headlights, sitting in the silence and darkness for a moment.

He didn't know what to do with horses. Sure, he'd grown up around them, but he had picked up his father's love of books, of sleek lines and appealing geometry instead of his interest in the outdoors. Andres was no cowboy. So the horses, he'd have to figure out what to do with them. And that list of things to deal with once Martin was gone was growing.

Andres missed so many years. The good years where the two men would visit on Sundays, sit and talk about life. All the impatience of Andres's youth tempered by the experience of Martin's age. And Andres needed that because he felt like he was on the verge of losing the last grounding thing he had.

It was selfish, unbelievably so, to care only about what he was going to lose. But the old man wouldn't talk about it anyway. About the disease ravaging his body, like it had done to Andres's mother's body before. Martin was still young, and he was still strong, and he never complained a day in his life and wasn't about to start now.

The old man would never meet his *nietos*, if Andres ever got around to having any, like his father was prone to dig. The only hope Andres had was that his father would live long enough to see his son's reputation repaired. Martin had come to this country for opportunities, and Andres was his father's legacy of that sacrifice. He had to make it right.

The light was on in the main sitting room when Andres quietly entered the home.

He smiled and leaned against the wall. "What are you doing up, old man? You should be resting."

Martin looked up from the designs spread across the coffee table in front of him. His father was old-school and still liked to sketch by hand when he could. "Wanted to hear how the meeting went," Martin replied, reaching up to remove his glasses.

Andres shrugged.

"That good, huh?"

"She'll do it," Andres replied.

"You don't sound thrilled."

Andres dropped onto the leather couch across from the one his father occupied and suddenly felt suffocated by his tie, his suit jacket. "It is what it is."

Martin shook his head. "That indifference is a poison."

At fifteen, Andres had been taught how to trail a mark, how to take the perfect shot, how to avoid standing downwind of blood splatter, how to leave no trace. That indifference was how he survived.

"What do you want me to say?" Andres asked, trying to tamp down the prickle of frustration.

"You're upset that she's upset."

Andres rubbed his thumb across his temple. "I am. But I deserve it."

Martin sighed. "You don't. You could tell her the truth. Maybe it's time."

"I've kept this secret for so long now, I don't know what would happen if I let it go. It would be a bomb, and the shrapnel . . . I don't want to be responsible for that."

"This isn't your secret to keep anymore, *mijo*."

Andres leaned forward, his elbows on his knees. "She won't believe me anyway. And that's my fault. Because of the way I left."

Martin shook his head. "You were a kid. She was a kid. She should understand."

"I think she does, but I broke the trust we had. Regardless."

"That's not true. She's trusting you now, isn't she?"

"I'm the last person in the world she wants to trust," Andres said. "It's written all over her face. She just has no other options."

"You have time, mijo. To show her, if that's what you want. But right now, all you need from her is to keep the peace. You can't be everything for everyone. I know you've tried. I know a lot was asked of you. But Sofia, she's grown now; she has to figure these things out on her own now too."

"That didn't stop you, with Maria. Even if you knew better."

Martin leaned back into his seat. "You're right. But we were wrong. She was married, and not to me."

"But it didn't stop you," Andres pushed.

"What do you want from Sofia, son? Are you just upset that she's not looking at you like she used to? With those big eyes, like you were the whole world? Because if that's all you want from her, leave that girl alone. Your ego will survive."

Andres frowned. "It's not . . . that."

"Then what is it?"

"I hurt her. I want to make it right."

"This deal you offered her. It's more than generous. I'd say you've made up for it."

Andres quieted. It was hard sometimes to know which thoughts were his and which ones were imposed upon him. What he should do, who he should be. Ximena, his father—they both had ideas for how he should live his life.

"If it's your friend that you miss and not the girl who adored you, then give her time."

"We don't have time," Andres spit out, the intensity of his words surprising him.

"Give her a chance," Martin said, sitting up. "There might not be a war. This peace might hold, and if it does, you two have all the time in the world. You'll have what Maria and I never had."

Andres met his father's eyes. "Which one is the truth? About Maria. Were you two planning on running off together? Or was she working with the DEA?"

Martin sighed. "What Maria and I had was complicated, but I'd never ask her to leave her children. And she'd never do that."

Andres looked at his hands, rubbed them together. "Why didn't you two just leave, before she was married?"

"You know the answer to that, son. She was asked to be someone specific for her family. We can't say no, can we?"

Martin sighed then. "I'm going to head up. Try and get some sleep yourself. You're looking a little worse for wear."

Andres nodded, his father patting him on the shoulder as he passed.

What am I supposed to do with the horses? Andres almost asked. His father would want them looked after. Not just sold off. Maybe he could open the center to the community. His father would like that.

Andres's phone buzzed in his pocket before he could give it much more thought. He inhaled deeply once and let the air pass slowly through his nostrils before he answered. "Ximena."

"You know you can stay with me, in the city. You don't have to make that commute every day."

"I know."

"How is he?" she asked, softer.

"Hardheaded."

"Did you see Sofia?"

"I did. She's going to agree to keep the peace. She's talking to her brothers tomorrow."

"That's good. The peace is good. But Andres . . ."

"I know."

"We need more than her good relationship with the Gulf and the Baja. We need the routes before her cousins get them because once they do, they won't give them up easily."

"I know."

"If she can't do it or won't do it, you know what needs to be done."

"Claro," he replied before ending the call.

The Torres cousins' murders would have to be green-lit, eliminating them from the game. It had been a long time coming. And Andres, the former sicario who desperately wanted to bury that piece of himself, would have to see it was done. This was his deal with the devil. And if two bullets stood between him and the life he'd worked so hard for, so be it. He'd pulled the trigger before, and he could do it again. Hopefully, this time for the last time.

There was nothing left to lose. He'd lost Sofia a long time ago. And while he saw the struggle in her eyes—wanting to believe that he hadn't killed her mother but having to side with her family, her brothers—she'd never choose Andres over them. And he couldn't ask her to.

But he could do this. He could take out the poison before it spread any further.

CHAPTER 24

Sofia leaned against the SUV, dark sunglasses shielding her eyes. The sun was bright this morning, and the sky cloudless.

Yolotli stood next to her, his arms crossed over his chest.

They waited.

Sofia's mind turned over Andres's admission the night before, that he should have been there the night her mother died. That had he been, he would have been on that road earlier, likely at the same time Maria was headed to Don Martin's house because that's where she had been going that night. That part was true.

But, according to Andres, because he had a job that night, he was late coming home.

But was that the truth?

Sofia had no clue and no way of knowing for certain either way. And that was the sticking point for Diego; Andres had been there that night. Whether before or after her mother was shot was still unclear. Diego had said it himself, and Sofia couldn't argue: Andres would say anything to get what he wanted.

However, the peace needed to be kept for Sofia's house of cards to stand, so she agreed to do this for Andres. She also didn't really have another option. He was right; if she didn't make herself indispensable to her brothers and her cousins soon, she had no doubt they'd find a way to move on with or without her.

So she placated Andres, told him for this, for the legitimacy, for the cocaine, for her, for right now, it didn't matter what she believed about the night her mother died.

A war would obliterate what was left of her family; Ximena was right about that. Her cousins were just in too deep to see it. So Sofia's sole objective right now was to bring the family back from the brink.

She'd deal with Ximena and Lalo and all the rest of it later.

"Any words of encouragement?" Sofia asked, her stomach churning, tight with anxiety.

Facing her brothers was one thing. Nando tended to be generally agreeable, so long as his processes weren't disturbed. Diego was a wild card, but it was the thought of facing the cousins that had kept her up last night.

"Don't put your corn in baskets full of holes," Yolotli offered.

Sofia tilted her head. She thought about that for a moment, and decided it was sound advice.

"I need to ask you something," she said, "and I understand it might be a conflict of interest, but I have no one else."

Yolotli turned to look at her.

"It's been brought to my attention that I need someone to confide in."

"Isn't that what those visits with Father Raya are for?"

Sofia bristled. "That's business. I need someone closer to me."

"You're asking me?"

Sofia shrugged. "You're the only one I trust."

Yolotli shifted, toeing a few of the pebbles that made up this parking lot. "You know, Diego has me reporting back."

"Have you?"

"There's not been much to report."

Sofia nodded. "We can keep it that way."

"He's El General. I can't keep things from him forever."

"You won't. I just . . ." Sofia sighed and turned to face Yolotli. "I need to know what it is you want too. Not what you want for Diego. What you want for you, because you're my family too, and I want to do what's right. For all of us."

"What I want is not an option," he replied, his dark eyes on the road.

"What do you want?"

"I don't want to be this anymore," he said, gesturing around. "We've been lucky so far. But everyone pays in the end, and I'd like to get out before someone comes to collect."

"Do you believe I have a plan for just that?"

Yolotli shrugged. "I want to believe you, Sofia, but one wrong move topples everything over the edge."

"I know. I know."

"If you're asking my advice, you need to talk to the kid," Yolotli said, nodding toward where Nando stood at the back door of the warehouse, his phone pressed tight to his ear.

"Diego could be persuaded to go as Nando goes. At least he used to be," Yolotli explained. "Maybe put a bug in the kid's ear. See if it takes."

The sleek shape of Diego's Alfa Romeo and the big-body frame of Xavier's truck came into sight as they headed up the road, putting her conversation with Yolotli on hold.

Sofia patted Yolotli's arm.

It was now or never.

Xavier huffed as he paced the back room of the De Lunas' warehouse. "Peace?" he asked, glancing at Diego. "Am I hearing this right?"

Diego sat slumped low in his chair, his arms crossed over his chest. His sharp eyes flitted between Sofia and Xavier.

"It will pay off in the end," Sofia argued.

Nando ran a hand through his curls, pushing them off his face. "Are you sure?" he asked. "Because if Cruz decides to collect information on us—and she will because that's what working together means—she'll have a case built ready to go, against us, the Gulf, and the Baja—and we will have handed it to her. And that war you're trying to avoid will be inevitable."

"It's not going to get that far," Sofia said.

"You can't know that!" Xavier exclaimed, his voice rising. "These people want you to think you're doing the right thing, the honest thing, the virtuous thing," he said, venom dripping off his words. "They're using your weaknesses to blind you so they can bury us. And they are far from honest how they go about it."

"Who are you to talk about virtue?" Sofia asked, pushing off from the folding table she leaned against. "Taking potshots at police chiefs—"

"Like he doesn't deserve it?" Xavier interrupted. "They will happily use those tanks against us, use those shiny new assault rifles. How is this *perra* going to sit across from you and say she wants peace? They could have left us alone. They could have let us be businessmen. But true peace was never an option, was it? Because it's not lucrative. They want to be partners so they can shove their hands in the cookie jar. They want to smile at the Americans and say, *Look at what we're doing to fight your war,* while they steal from our pockets. You have to see that, Sofia."

"What is it you're really after, Xavier?" Sofia asked, her brothers and Joaquin quiet in the room around them. "What is it you think this war with the Gulf and the Baja is going to get you?"

"I want what is ours," Xavier replied, his gold canines flashing. "I want Mexico. All of it. It was ours once, before we knelt and let them take ribs from us. A rib to the west, a rib to the east. What's left of us now? A shell."

"What is it that you think is ours?" Sofia asked.

Xavier sucked air past his teeth, his canines glittering. "Everything."

"And who is it you think will fight this war for us? That move you made against the police chief scared people. And we need the people on our side; that has always been our bargaining chip, but you're too bloodthirsty to see that. We don't have an army anymore, and forget recruiting for one."

"*You* don't have an army," Xavier said, his tone dark enough that Sofia's brothers shifted in their seats.

"No war," Sofia said through clenched teeth.

Xavier smiled. "Look at you getting brave, prima."

"Give me at least until after the election," she added. "We can revisit—"

"Revisit?" Xavier interrupted again, amusement sparkling in his tone. "This is not a boardroom, prima. This isn't jolly old England."

"What about the other candidate?" Nando asked, the irritation evident in his voice at the derailment of the conversation.

"They won't deal, refused every sit-down," Diego replied.

"Seems like we need Cruz to win then," Nando said. "At least she's willing to play ball."

Xavier shook his head. "It doesn't matter who sits in that seat when we can remind them how easy it is to take it away from them."

"The cocaine will be ours soon, all ours, only ours," Sofia said, crossing her fingers. Andres was right about pulling this card, about being indispensable.

Xavier narrowed his eyes. "That's what that sicario promised you?"

"It's his to do with as he wishes."

"And why would he give it to you?" Xavier tilted his head. "What is it you're giving him?" he asked, a smirk on his lips. "I was wrong, prima. Maybe you are just like your mom, on your knees for a Herrera while you turn your back on your family."

Sofia's hand prickled with heat from the impact before the sound hit her ears. The echo of her palm against Xavier's cheek bounced around in the silent room.

When Xavier wiped his lower lip, his thumb came away scarlet red.

Sofia trembled with anger, with fear. This was the same man who had held a knife to her throat when she was sixteen just so she "could see how it feels."

She wasn't a kid anymore, and she was in charge. But that did little to convince her the bogeyman wouldn't finally swallow her whole.

"Don't you ever speak to me like that again," she said, her voice low, attempting to hide her fear from Xavier, but she knew he could smell it on her.

He grabbed her before she had time to react, his hand on her throat.

His smile stretched as his fingers squeezed the column of her neck. "Glad to see you haven't lost your fight."

Sofia knew her brothers, and Nando, while concerned—she sensed his movement behind her—wouldn't take on Xavier, not head-to-head. But Diego, whether he agreed with his sister's decisions or not, wouldn't let their cousin choke the life out of her in front of him.

Not yet at least.

So as the darkness started to set in around the corners of her vision, Sofia waited. She wouldn't give Xavier the satisfaction of struggling.

"That's enough, primo," Diego said finally, rising to stand.

Xavier pulled Sofia closer, his eyes black. "You think running cocaine distribution is the answer?" he asked, his eyes narrowing. "I forget, all the time, that life has been nothing but abundance for you, for your mother, while my father was shot in the back, left to bleed out in the street. While we fought for what life we had in Argentina, you and your brothers rode horses, played in gardens." He shook his head. "The cocaine is not enough."

Sofia's lungs burned, and her eyes watered.

Xavier released her suddenly, and Sofia gasped in air with as much dignity as she could manage.

"Cocaine is antiquated," Xavier added.

"It's commission on all sales . . ." Sofia interrupted, her voice thin.

"Okay, and . . . ? What about the guns, H, meth? They beat us to it, to all of it!"

They, the Gulf.

The man they called Novillo, "Young Bull," had turned the Gulf and the ports there into a veritable swap meet of America's favorite vices. The Gulf was also the De Lunas' juicy vein into the artery of America. A vein they had been barred from through the years of her grandfather's and her father's dealmaking.

That's what Xavier was after. The border. Because without the border, it didn't matter how many and what the De Lunas tried to move.

"And what, you're going to take it all back from them?" Sofia asked. "In case you forgot, we're a little landlocked here. Pretty far from the border too," she said, her voice thin, scratchy. "Also running low on people to move those types of things."

"You think they don't know that too?" Xavier asked. "We are obsolete; they are just waiting to strike. Which is why we need to make the first move."

"And the Baja?" Sofia asked, glancing at Diego. "We're going to take their ports too? Their border?"

Diego shifted in his seat. "I can talk to them. Like you said, we need an army. At least some allies."

Sofia shook her head. "No. No war. Diego, you'll go to the Baja, you'll tell them it's Ximena Cruz, it's peace."

Xavier sucked air past his teeth. "You're making a mistake, prima."

"Yeah, well, it's my call. Like it or not."

"Well, *jefa*." Xavier spit out the word, and it dripped with disdain. "What is it you'd like Joaquin and me to do while you play patty-cake with the Baja and the Gulf?"

"You'll do your job; you'll run the loads like always. Nothing changes." Sofia looked around the room, meeting Diego's eyes. "Do you hear me?"

Diego nodded.

Nando hitched a thumb over his shoulder toward the warehouse floor. "Are we done? I need to get back."

Sofia caught the worry lines between her youngest brother's eyebrows.

She'd probably underestimated her brother's dedication to their family business, his cold, calculating demeanor masking the stress he'd taken on over the years.

Sofia nodded, and the men in the room started to file out, Joaquin first.

Xavier lingered by the door as Diego and Nando passed him, leaving him alone with Sofia.

"You got that shot, prima. Try it again, and I'll make sure I catch you when you're on your own."

It wasn't a warning. It was a promise.

Sofia waited for Xavier to clear out before heading to Nando's office.

Nando glanced up at her before looking back at the large monitors on his desk. "Not smart," he said before leaning down to type at the keyboard.

"What's that, hermano?" Sofia asked.

"Egging on Xavier like that. You know how he is."

"He doesn't listen otherwise," Sofia replied. "What's going on? You look stressed."

Nando paused and leaned his hands on the desk. "You realize the difference between a promise made and a promise kept?"

Sofia tilted her head. "Of course."

Nando straightened, reaching up to push his curls back once more. "Well then, I hope you have a plan that doesn't count on promises made."

"I'm working on it, but I was wondering what you think. About all of this? Haven't seen you much since Papi's funeral."

Nando raised a delicate eyebrow, his attention back on one of the monitors.

"Nando?"

He shrugged his bony shoulder to his ears. "What do you want me to say?"

"These businesses that you've run so smoothly, what is it you want out of them? What's the point? For you."

He sighed and dropped into his desk chair. "Infinite growth is not possible. That's what I told them."

"So what is possible?"

"What we had," he replied, his green eyes still focused on the monitors.

"What is the point of this for you, Nando?" Sofia said each word slowly, hoping it would filter into her little brother's consciousness, make its way past all the numbers he held there.

"I wanted this, do you remember?" he asked, finally meeting her gaze, and she saw the way the light, delicate skin under his eyes was purpled and hollow. "I used to beg Dad to bring me with him to work. I liked how the men would greet him. I liked the power he had. I wanted that."

Sofia leaned against the doorframe, listening.

"Now I have that. I have it all: his desk, his office, the *power*." He said the word like it tasted rancid on his tongue. "And truth be told, I'm starting to resent it because that power—it comes at a price, and that price is everything," he said, his tone lilting with the fuzzy tendrils of humor that mania creates.

"So if you don't want this, what do you want?" she asked, stepping closer and lowering her voice. "You can talk to me."

She missed the boy she used to see on their video chats, the one who carried on about economics and numbers and ideas Sofia didn't quite grasp, but from him they sounded magical, like incantations. Because he believed in that work, because he loved it. This he didn't love. Not anymore. Not with the way his gaze avoided hers.

He shrugged again. "I have no idea what else is out there, Sofia. Do you? Yes, you left, but you were bankrolled; you were safe while you tried on being another person. We won't have that protection anymore."

"We don't need money to be protected, Nando. We have all this money now, and I don't know about you, but I don't sleep well at night."

His green eyes, sharp on her now, flashed. "None of us do. None of us ever did."

"Is that life?" she asked. "Is that really all there is for us?"

He picked up a pen from his desk, tapping it against the metal. "Maybe," he replied finally. "We made promises to people. This family keeps its promises."

He glanced out onto the warehouse floor where men and women sorted and boxed the produce fresh from the family's farmland into crates with efficiency and precision.

"What can I do for you?" Sofia asked. "How can I help?"

Nando looked up at her. "Right now? We need more trucks."

Sofia frowned. "More? I thought business was slowing down."

"Not for Daniel, it seems. Diego ordered two trucks for Daniel's weekend shipment this time. So we're down a truck for the Baja."

"Did Daniel ask for more?"

"Not that I'm aware of. I was just told this morning to get two trucks loaded, so I did, but now I need to free up another."

"Maybe that's good news," Sofia replied. "A show of good faith from Daniel."

Nando glanced up at Sofia. "Knowing Daniel? Doubtful." He leveled his gaze at her. "Speaking of which, you should sit down with him. And soon."

"I'll ask Diego about it."

"The sooner the better."

"Noted."

Nando turned back to his screens, and Sofia excused herself, but not before pausing on her way out the door.

"Think about what the point is, Nando, for you," she said.

"What's it for you?" he asked, glancing over his shoulder at her.

"You," she replied with no hesitation. "You and Diego. That's all that matters."

CHAPTER 25

Maria shifted her weight from foot to foot, crossed and uncrossed her arms, her eyes on the door.

"They'll be here; you're wearing a tread in the tile," Juste quipped before making his way outside.

Her father's sour mood wouldn't ruin hers today. She hadn't seen her brother, Santiago, since they'd left him with their grandparents, and now he was finally able to visit.

The large front doors swung open as her brother lightheartedly quibbled with her father's waitstaff about carrying his own bags.

"Santi!" Maria exclaimed, hurrying toward her older brother, her arms outstretched.

He smiled widely, pulling her into a tight embrace.

"I thought I'd never see you again," she said.

"Can't get rid of your big brother that easily," he replied. "So good to see you."

Her nephews, whom she had never met, clung to their father's legs.

"They are so big already!"

"Time flies. Xavier is eight and Joaquin six now."

Santi leaned down to address his sons. "Go give your tía Maria a hug; she's waited so long to meet you."

They held their arms open, letting Maria pull them in close and tight for a moment before squirming.

She smiled and let them go.

Once free, they ran straight through the home to the backyard.

"Hey!" she called after them with a laugh.

Santiago smiled. "I told them there were horses."

Maria sighed. "Well, I can't compete with horses."

"You look so grown-up," he said with a sigh. "We've missed so much."

"Come, let's catch up," she said, giving her brother's shoulder a squeeze.

"Excited about the wedding?" Santiago asked.

Maria huffed. "I wouldn't say that."

"Listen, I know you didn't really have a choice, but I'm glad, you know, about all of this. This way we can be together again. It's good, Maria. Good for the family."

"Hopefully," she replied.

They meandered over to the corral where the boys were watching the groom brush the aging mare.

The new horseman was old. Grouchy. The mares liked him well enough, but Maria ached for Martin's kind, encouraging words, his faith in her. Faith that transcended the corral, the stable. This ranch home.

She missed him so bad she couldn't breathe when she thought about him, so she tried not to.

"You won't be alone anymore," Santiago continued, "once me and Ella and the boys can move out here."

It could be nice, she thought, having family around.

Alberto was not a warm man. The two went on chaperoned dates, a last-minute attempt to get to know one another before the wedding in the spring. It wasn't going well. Alberto had no motivation for anything other than money. He didn't care for horses or art or books or music or even her, probably.

She missed the way Martin would look at her, smile at her

jokes. Push her, make her prove—not to him, but to herself—what she was capable of.

Alberto dismissed her more often than not.

"I'd like that," she finally replied to Santiago.

Winter passed, and spring came quickly.

The wedding was large and ostentatious. Many serious men, with guns on their hips and their eyes hidden by dark glasses, attended. Men Maria didn't know but men her father dutifully introduced Alberto to.

Her new husband thrived under the attention.

Maria kept herself busy dancing with her nephews, politely receiving well-wishes from guests.

All the while she hoped the floor would open up and swallow her whole. She knew what would be expected of her tonight. Once everyone left. Once she was alone with Alberto.

She found herself in the kitchen, the one place no one would look for her. The kitchen was her sanctuary, for the women who helped raise her did so around the large island while she helped cut peppers and onions. She'd sit there with her math homework when she was younger and listen to their gossip. She found their laughter and jokes comforting.

She sought out that comfort now.

They fussed over her, offering her food. She hadn't eaten during the reception, they remarked. She blamed nerves. They knew she was unhappy. But they spoke words of faith, devotion, hope. Steadfastness. All the things women were tasked to be.

"Señora." The voice came from the back doorway, the one that led out to the patio.

The women's chatter waned, the three suddenly very interested in helping the catering staff set up platters of canapés.

Maria looked to the doorway, but she already knew who the voice belonged to.

"Do you have a moment?" Martin asked, a hint of a smile tugging at his lips.

For you, she thought, *anything, always.*

She clenched her jaw, the pain radiating but grounding.

He held his hand out as she approached him. She took it tentatively, and when she glanced over her shoulder to see who might be watching, she could swear she saw one of the women smile.

Maria directed Martin to a small, rarely used office off the side of the kitchen, in the opposite direction from the party roaring outside.

Martin closed the door, locked it, and turned to face her.

"They'll be looking for me soon," she said, inspecting the spines of the books on the shelf nearest her to avoid his eyes.

"You look so beautiful," he said, his voice soft.

She sighed, looking up to meet his eyes. "I didn't think you'd come."

She needed him to not be there. As much as she ached to see him again, it felt like her heart was cracking when she envisioned him standing next to his father in the church as she walked down the aisle. If she could have choked on her own feelings, it would have been then and there. She was drowning.

During the ceremony, she couldn't meet his eyes when she passed him; she felt lightheaded as it was. He was so handsome in his black tux, a blush rose pinned to the lapel jacket. His curls were slicked back, and she thought it was a shame, as she preferred the way they fell loose across his forehead.

But now, alone in this room together, there was nowhere to go, and her throat hurt with the longing she had tried to suppress.

"I didn't want to, but I wasn't sure when I'd see you again, so . . ." he trailed off with a shrug.

"You brought a date. She's pretty."

Martin nodded. "Yeah, she's a good girl."

Maria smiled, but it didn't reach her eyes. "You stole me away, locked me in here, to tell me that?"

He turned toward the door. "You're free to go . . ." He held her gaze.

"What are you doing, Martin?" she asked.

"I wanted to say goodbye," he said, closing the distance between them.

He wrapped his fingers around her neck so gently she thought if she moved she'd break the spell.

His thumb brushed over her jaw. "I'm not the best with words, you know that."

She leaned into his touch. "Show me."

He leaned in and kissed her before she could protest. Soft this time. Their first kiss in the stable had been a wild thing, unbridled. This kiss was slow, meticulous. Purposeful. He was trying to create one last moment to remember her by.

She kissed him back with all the pain in her chest, and she hoped he felt it too; she hoped he knew. She hoped he could feel the crack in her heart because words weren't enough.

He pulled away, dragging his thumb softly over her bottom lip.

"I don't want this to be goodbye," she said, smoothing her hands down the front of his crisp white shirt, feeling his heart beating under her palm the same way she had in the stable that rainy night.

"Nor do I," he said, hooking his index finger under her chin, tilting her head up. "I'll be around. You'll know where to find me."

A few days later, she was tasked with opening the mountain of gifts. A cylindrical shape caught her curiosity.

Plans for a chapel.

The months passed, then a full year, then two and three, and Maria fell into a rhythm with Alberto. It wasn't love, but he let her run the produce business, the legitimate business, while he took care of the drug business. It gave her something to do. She found she liked being lost in the numbers. She was good at finding inefficiencies. Mostly she enjoyed her time getting to know the De Lunas' workers. Good people she would provide large holiday bonuses for. Expensive gifts when their wives gave birth. Money for college.

Alberto never said a word about the way she spent their money. It was the one thing he could give her. He was gone more than he was home, but Maria didn't mind. When they spoke, it was about business. Maria didn't mind. He had other women. Maria didn't mind that either. She had Sofia coming.

Maria lived for the days her brother and her nephews visited, not yet able to move to Mexico full-time, and Maria could hear it in her brother's voice. Ella didn't want to leave their home. Maria understood.

Some days Maria thought, *If this is as good as it gets, I can survive it*. Survive, that's all her father had wanted.

CHAPTER 26

Sofia reached up to smooth her intricate French braid. Her emerald-green cocktail dress shifted with the movement.

"No security tonight?" Andres asked as she approached where he stood on the sidewalk outside one of the newest restaurants in CDMX's Condesa neighborhood.

Nightlife teemed around them. The evening had fallen, and it was beautiful weather. Cafés and art galleries propped their doors open. Couples passed on the sidewalk, their eyes only for one another.

"Not tonight," Sofia replied.

Andres placed his fingertips on the small of her back, her skin warming where the heat of his fingertips pressed against her skin through the cool silk of the dress.

He hesitated, his eyes searching hers, but Sofia tilted her head, leaning in just so for him to place a kiss on her cheek in greeting.

If her cheek tingled where his lips, dry and warm, had met her skin, she wouldn't show it.

"Thank you for coming," he said.

"Of course," she replied.

The memories she shared with Andres, the way her heart ached when he looked at her, clamored against the stitching she had sewn it all away with. And everything she said about what mattered and didn't matter she only half believed. He still mattered to her. Her body would always tell the truth.

When they were thousands of miles apart, years apart, it was easier to deny. But here, now, back home, he woke something in her, something warm, soft, organic. And she saw the same in his eyes.

Andres cleared his throat. "There she is," he said as he smoothed down his blazer.

"Señorita," Andres teased as he approached Ximena.

She smiled broadly at Andres, showing those perfectly white teeth, her eyes squinting closed. Andres took her outstretched hand in his and pressed his lips to the back of her hand.

For a fleeting moment, Sofia felt a twinge of jealousy. While she thought of Andres as her Andres—that's what her brothers called him—he was, in fact, not hers. Maybe never had been.

Sofia reminded herself not to let the sharp heat make its way up her spine. She had no reason to be jealous. Even if she did, she wasn't about to show it. So Sofia stood straighter, pushed her shoulders back, and put on her most congenial smile.

"Glad you could make it, doña," Ximena said.

Andres smiled at the two women. "I'll leave you two to it."

"Thank you, Andres," Ximena said, returning his smile.

Sofia waited for Andres to walk away before speaking. "I didn't get the chance to thank you for the opportunity."

Ximena took a sip of her white wine and waved off Sofia's words.

She swallowed, set her glass down on the table behind her, and reached for Sofia's arm. "There was no one else, doña. I knew you could do it," she said, her dark eyes flashing. "Men are not so complicated. I knew you'd find a way to convince your brothers. Your cousins."

"They're not exactly sold."

"But you are," Ximena replied, a sharp eyebrow raised.

"Not exactly either."

Ximena let go of Sofia's arm. "Let's walk."

Lalo needed intel on Ximena, and Sofia needed something to give to Lalo before he started wondering if she was going to keep up her end of the bargain. Though she hadn't gotten much information about her mother from him yet either. But she wasn't here for that tonight. One move at a time.

"I'm just curious," Sofia began as the two women made their way down the cobbled pathway that led around the restaurant and toward the back patio. "If it's just about the money, our money, staying in the country, then what benefits will the people see?"

"Well, that'll be up to you, won't it? Once you're in office, you'll have a say."

"The people you've promised our money to, they won't have an issue with that?"

Ximena's jaw tightened. "You let me worry about that."

Sofia huffed, "Come on, you realize you're asking me to be the shield against the cartels for your campaign, catching any stray bullets that come your way, right? Then I think I deserve to know some of the ins and outs of this deal I agreed to. Because it will be me the Gulf and the Baja want answers from."

"You'll keep your money, you can promise them that."

"So what?" Sofia asked between tight smiles in greeting to Ximena's guests as they passed. "They make money off our money? The banks?"

"Something like that," Ximena said. "Your money makes them money. Who does that hurt?" Ximena asked, her thin shoulders scrunched to her ears. "You promise to stop the violence; I promise to keep your money flowing. It's a win-win."

Sofia nodded, her heavy chandelier earrings twinkling in her ear.

It was the banks behind this whole setup.

"And the DEA?" Sofia asked.

Ximena smiled. "Useless."

"But they're still here, *y los Estados Unidos* . . ."

"Are still poking around our business, yes, and why do you think that is?" Ximena asked. "Ask yourself what reason would they have to care about violence in Mexico? They don't even care about the violence in their own country."

She had a point.

So what was it Lalo was trying to do? The banks were too big to jail, and the government of Mexico would never let the DEA get close enough to indict their own again.

"So, doña?" Ximena asked.

Sofia bit at her bottom lip, waxy with lipstick.

"I care about the people, Ximena," Sofia said, "and I will hold you to that promise."

Ximena smiled, patting Sofia on her shoulder. "Whatever helps you sleep at night, doña. If you'll excuse me."

Sofia found herself suddenly standing alone. She was there to rub elbows, to make Ximena look good, but Sofia couldn't be bothered now.

She started to head toward the front of the restaurant, ready to leave.

"Sof," Andres called after her, wrapping a hand around her elbow.

She whipped around, pulling her elbow from Andres's grip. "Save it," Sofia said.

Andres released her elbow. "Let me walk you out," he said, the blue of his eyes dark. "You shouldn't be walking alone at night."

"I don't need you to worry about me. Stay. Enjoy your girlfriend's party."

It was childish, but Sofia enjoyed the discomfort that shifted across his handsome features.

He opened his mouth, then closed it, then began again. "It's—"

"No," Sofia interrupted him, holding a hand up. "I don't need an explanation," she said, turning back to push through the restaurant and out the front door, Andres at her heels.

"I did what needed to be done, Sofia," Andres called out to her once they were alone on the sidewalk. "We need a party in the government that will protect our interests as well. It's the only path to legitimacy. Idealists will lock us up the first chance they get. To prove a point."

Sofia stopped and turned to glare at him. "That's all that matters to you? Protecting your interests. What about stopping the violence? Or that was never actually part of the plan since it's easy for you. You sit up in that steel-and-glass castle and look down on everyone else."

"You think you're the only one who's lost something?" he asked, his eyes darkening. "That because your mother was taken away, the world, this world, owes you?"

"Doesn't it?" Sofia asked. "There are many like me in this country, and this world owes them too."

"What is it exactly you think you're going to do on your own, Sofia?" Andres scoffed.

Sofia glared at him, his dismissive tone too familiar.

She curled her fingers into fists, her nails biting into her palms. "You know what the worst part is, Andres? That you didn't come to me as a friend, the friend you want me to be, with the truth. Instead, you used our old friendship to pay your debt to Ximena under the guise of helping me."

Andres frowned, his eyes softening. "Why do you think that, Sofia?"

"Because I'm not naive, Andres."

He shook his head. "Sofia, I made this deal for us. I knew the second you got back here, the men in your family would cut you out as much as possible, and they have, haven't they?"

"There is no *us*, Andres. You're just like my brothers, my cousins. Just like my father. And I hope it was worth it. Whatever it is she's done for you, because you're in her pocket now."

Andres's eyes flashed as they searched hers.

"You need her, Sofia," he said finally, retreating into his armor.

"No, you do. You believe her when she says she'll wash away all your family's sins. That you'll be born anew. She's a politician, *querido*. You can't trust her."

Andres's jaw twitched.

"You know this cease-fire won't last," Sofia went on. "Being the king of Tijuana, Matamoros, wherever, is not enough. It's never enough. For anyone. They will start fighting again because they all want more. What we need to do is ensure they trust in this alliance. Xavier is right; they smell the blood in the water, and they're probably planning to strike at any time."

"And then what?" Andres asked, shrugging. "Same old same old. Sofia, alliance or not, they'll still want more—you said it yourself."

"And we can promise it. Once we set the rules with the president. Us. Not them."

Andres sucked air through his teeth, shook his head. "No. It's not good enough. I don't want to rely on the cartels to decide my fate anymore, Sofia. I want a new life. We both do."

"Don't do that," she said.

"Don't destroy your future because you're angry about our past, Sofia," he replied, his eyes dark and his tone cool.

She smiled, reaching up to pat his chest. "No, sicario, I'm not angry. Not anymore. I have a business to run and a family to protect; those are my only concerns now. Good night, Andres."

She turned away and quickly tapped out a text on her phone.

She needed to talk to the priest.

Parque Mexico was lively this evening; Sofia had expected no less, and the crowds spilling over from the nearby restaurants made it easy to blend in.

Lalo walked next to her, his clerical collar sitting flush against his neck. She watched it when he swallowed, his Adam's apple bobbing against it.

"If you wanted to spend a Saturday evening together, all you had to do was ask."

Sofia raised an eyebrow. "I did."

"True," Lalo replied. "Was the fundraiser as boring as I imagined it would be?"

Sofia nodded. The glimmering lights of the city reminded her of London and her late-night walks.

"She's promised our money to the banks. She's answering to them," Sofia said, "but I think you already knew that."

Lalo shrugged. "Assumptions don't hold up in court."

"None of this does," Sofia replied, pausing to watch the water of Lago de los Patos. "I need some answers, Padre."

Lalo stopped next to her, his hands clasped behind his back. "Have you asked your cousins about your mother?"

Sofia shook her head.

Lalo stepped closer, raising his hand to brush her hair off her shoulder. The light touch gave her chills, goose bumps breaking out along her skin.

"Because I think you know what the truth is," Lalo said, his dark eyes on hers. "And you know who you need to ask, and you're too afraid of what he'll say to make him tell you."

Sofia crossed her arms over her chest, her eyes back on the water. "What's the point? Everyone lies. Andres will lie; he's been lying."

Lalo's eyes searched her face. "You're still in love with him, aren't you?"

The question hit Sofia in the chest like a concrete block. She hadn't said it out loud, but now that someone had been braver than her, speaking the truth she'd erected walls around in her heart, those walls started to tremble.

Lalo cursed under his breath, his gaze on the lake now. "He knows it too, Sofia. Don't let him make you look like a fool again."

Sofia tightened her arms around herself, trying to stave off another chill.

"Don't lose sight of what it is you're trying to save here, princesa," Lalo said before walking her back to her waiting car.

CHAPTER 27

The flight from Mexico City to Tijuana had been an uneasy one as Xavier's parting words bounced around Diego's brain.

He was paranoid, he wouldn't argue that. Whether from his drug use or the life he led, probably both, but that paranoia let him know when something felt off.

Xavier had licked at the fresh cut on his bottom lip when he told Diego to have a safe trip to Tijuana, and Diego flinched when Xavier clapped a hand on his shoulder. "We'll take care of things here."

Xavier's words were as dark as his eyes in that moment. He wouldn't let a slight like Sofia's show of dominance slide. There was no way. And the fact that Diego wasn't included in Xavier and Joaquin's next steps for their plan to traffic women, girls, through the Gulf made Diego's stomach twist. He'd attempted to be the voice of reason when Xavier and Joaquin pushed too far, but Xavier had shown him his canines, backing Diego off like a dog in the street.

So now Diego navigated the SUV into the dark parking lot of the weather-beaten pastry shop. He glanced at the clock on the dash. It was nearly eleven at night, but fluorescent lights burned brightly in the lobby.

Diego killed the engine and hopped out of the SUV.

He scrubbed his hands over his face, trying to shake the anxiety nipping at his fingertips.

He rapped his knuckles on the glass door.

A young girl in a hoodie unlocked the door and pushed it open a crack.

"Is he in?" Diego asked.

"Yo!" came the call from a deep, raspy voice, somewhere in the lobby.

The girl pulled the door open, her eyes never leaving Diego.

"Well, I'll be damned," the tall, lean man dressed in all black said in comfortable English as he crossed his arms over his chest. "A De Luna. In the flesh."

The girl who let Diego in raised an eyebrow before taking up her post at the door once more.

"Dragon, long time no see," Diego said as he crossed the small lobby, his English rusty in his mouth.

"Tell me about it," the man known as the Dragon, aka the Prince of the Baja, replied, suspicion glittered in his large doe-like eyes.

The Dragon was a specter. He didn't attend meetings; he didn't travel. He hid out in this run-down bakery, camouflaging himself in the Pacific Ocean–washed streets of Tijuana instead of holing up in some mansion farther down the coast. He didn't drive an expensive car, and he wasn't dripping in gold, though if you gave him the chance, he'd share all he knew about the Aztecs and their appreciation of the metal.

Diego frowned. The heady smell of the sugar and oil of the bakery was already going to his head. "How do you work like this?"

"You get used to it. So what the hell brings you out here, General?" the Dragon asked, those doe eyes on Diego.

Diego pinched the bridge of his nose, then let go. "Your boss isn't picking up his phone."

The Dragon shrugged. "He's not my boss."

"You know what I mean. When we call, he needs to answer," Diego replied. "Come on, it's just common courtesy."

"Not my problem," the Dragon said, then waved a finger in Diego's direction. "Should have thought about that before giving him the family blessing, right?"

Diego's smile faded. "Where is he?"

The Dragon rubbed a hand over his closely cropped hair. "I don't know, man. He's busy now. Shaking hands, kissing babies. All that shit."

Diego sucked air in through his teeth. "We bought him that election. And that border. Which, in turn, buys us face time with him."

The Dragon leaned his head back, the tattoo across his throat stretching with the movement. "I know that, D. I'll pass that on when I see him."

Diego nodded. "I appreciate it."

"Anytime," the Dragon replied as he shifted to clasp his hands in front of him. "Anything else? You didn't come all the way out here just for that now did you?"

Diego let his eyes wander over the Dragon's long, lean frame, held his gaze just to look into those big, pretty brown eyes of his, framed by long, thick dark lashes.

There had been a time when Diego would have flirted with him; he had in the past, just to tease. He liked the way the other man reacted—annoyed, unamused. But Diego had always caught the way the Dragon's eyes slid to him when he thought Diego wasn't looking.

But Diego was trying to be a better man now. And he knew the Dragon was just an admirer of beautiful things.

Diego stuck out his bottom lip and shook his head. "*Pero no*, just wanted to chat."

The Dragon smiled slowly. "Let me guess. This has something to do with the shit storm in Mexico City. A shoot-out in the street? Ballsy. But not the best idea. You De Lunas are getting messy."

Diego leaned a hip against the glass case, surveying the few remaining pastries below. "Sofia is serious about keeping this peace between the three of us."

"Because that's what's going to get Cruz into office," the Dragon replied.

"Maybe, but who cares who's sitting in that seat as long as we can keep the business rolling right?"

"How's that going, by the way," the Dragon asked, "having your sister back?"

Diego shrugged.

It was adversarial, that's what it was. He had missed his sister deeply when she was gone, and now that she was back, the betrayal stung like alcohol over a paper cut. So he couldn't help feeling like he owed her nothing. But at the same time, he couldn't just let her drown. All they had was each other.

He had chosen the worst time to try to get clean. The powder, the alcohol numbed all these feelings, all these complicated thoughts. Made it so things were simple. Lately, nothing felt simple anymore. His one job was to keep the family business running and keep them safe, and he was failing at both.

The Dragon cleared his throat. "Thought you all had the politicos in your pocket. That was the deal, right?"

"Things change."

"Your money is running out," the Dragon said.

Diversify. The word circled Diego's brain.

It was true that the De Lunas were keepers of the cocaine, thanks to their codependent relationship with the Herreras. But the family had no routes of their own, no access to America. Xavier and Sofia were right about that.

In the Gulf, Daniel kept a stranglehold on his routes. The Dragon might be more agreeable, which is why Diego was in Tijuana standing on cinnamon-sugar-covered linoleum.

"This peace," the Dragon began, "what's it going to cost me?"

"*Nada*."

"Come on," the Dragon replied with a slow smile, "nothing's that easy."

From what Diego knew about the Dragon, he wouldn't like

working with the government either unless certain guarantees were in place; *firewalls*, that's what Nando called the separators. While this was Sofia's deal, and Diego didn't exactly love it, he wasn't sure blowing it up was the right move either.

"Cruz wants to work with us."

"Your sister, is she as smart as your little brother? About numbers and shit?"

Diego huffed. No one was as smart as Nando when it came to numbers.

"Look, I like peace. I like quiet," the Dragon said, "so I'm naturally inclined to keep the peace between the three of us. But I'm going to need some numbers because it sounds to me that this candidate of yours might be thinking about promising our cash flow to someone else. That would be the only reason to let us keep doing what we do. The only reason to try and get in our good graces—access to the money."

The banks.

The cartels had made them millions over the years in return for laundering their money right under everyone's nose. If anyone wanted to make sure the cartels didn't go out of business, it would be the banks.

Diego reached up and scrubbed a hand over the back of his head. "You'll get your numbers. Sofia wouldn't screw you. She knows better."

Diego would see to it. They needed El Príncipe at this point with the way the cousins were going at Daniel.

"And the Gulf?"

"Hopefully we can get them on board."

"Seems your cousins have a vendetta going with Daniel. I'm just saying I don't want to wake up to a Torres at the foot of my bed some night."

Diego thought the bad blood between his cousins and Daniel was shortsighted, but Xavier would convince him otherwise. Talk about how Daniel started it when he tried to cut a side deal with the Herreras a few years ago.

"Cousins think Daniel's after more than his fair share."

The Dragon leveled his gaze at Diego. "What do you think?"

"I think there's enough to go around, for all of us. Cousins want to diversify. Might be interested in your routes."

The Dragon tilted his head. "This coming from Sofia or your cousins?"

"Me."

The Dragon rubbed his fingertips against his chin. "You want my routes? They're pricey."

"Figured that."

"So what happened, huh?" the Dragon asked. "Now that the old man is gone, your family finally sees the light? Because, as I remember it, he didn't want me to run things out here before. Didn't want to diversify either."

"Obviously it's not his call now."

The Dragon regarded Diego. "I'll think about it. But if this soon-to-be-president puts whatever deal it is she's making with your sister on the table, and Daniel doesn't like it, this country will be even more of a war zone. You'll be trying to move product through a *Mad Max* hellscape."

"It won't come to that."

"You better hope not."

Diego nodded and glanced around. He reached up to squeeze his nostrils between his index finger and thumb, sniffing hard.

"You okay, man?" the Dragon asked, his dark eyes concerned. "I know that look."

Diego reached up to run his hand through his hair. "I'm good, man. I'm good."

The Dragon shook his head. "You can't fuck around with the Herreras' product. You should know it's a point of pride of theirs that they barely step on it before it gets here."

Diego nodded. "Yeah, thanks. I know. I just need the kick sometimes."

The Dragon nodded. "I hear that."

Diego glanced out the window. "Want to get dinner?" he asked, looking back at the Dragon. "I'm not really in a rush to get back."

The Dragon nodded, his expression softening. "Yeah, sure. We can do that."

Diego's Pops used to talk shit about the Dragon because he was of two worlds—born in America, raised on the streets of Tijuana. Pops would say something about how the Dragon was a chameleon, a shape-shifter, that they couldn't trust him.

But Diego saw a lot of himself in the Dragon.

Both had been left to be the protectors of their families; both had lost more than they'd ever be able to replace.

"The food is so good here sometimes I think about staying," Diego said as he ran a hand over his stomach. Remnants of his last taco lined the paper of the red plastic basket in front of him.

The Dragon chuckled and wiped his fingers on his napkin. "Better than that pretentious CDMX shit."

"Hey, it's not all bad."

The Dragon raised an eyebrow. "So, you can try and bullshit me again if you want, but is everything good?"

Diego sighed. "Family shit, man." He noticed his own leg shaking, rattling the aluminum table. He cleared his throat and leaned forward on his elbows.

"How long have you been on that shit anyway?" the Dragon asked.

Diego reached up to scrub a hand over his face. "I don't know, man. A while."

The Dragon rolled his shoulders back. "Gonna take a while to come off then. Meditation," he said, pointing at Diego. "Discipline the mind."

Diego ran a hand over his jaw. "Yolotli says the same shit."

"It works, if you let it."

Diego's leg started to shake again, and he looked out over the empty parking lot of the taqueria.

"My sister has real shit taste in men."

The Dragon smiled. "I mean, we can't all be as lucky as you, D."

The corner of Diego's mouth ticked up before sobering again. "Got some real bad shit I might have to do if things don't go according to plan."

The Dragon swallowed, and Diego watched the tattoo on his throat flutter.

"Comes with the territory," the Dragon said, his dark eyes assessing Diego.

Diego chuckled. "That's what we tell ourselves, at least."

The Dragon hummed before crossing his arms over his chest. "I assume it's for the greater good."

"Whose?" Diego asked, his pitch rising.

The Dragon nodded like he understood. Maybe he did.

There was a darkness that followed Diego. Sometimes it lifted enough to let him take a breath, to feel the sun. Usually it weighed him down, saturated the corners of his mind. As a kid he'd run from it, found out early enough how to stay ahead of it, but now? These days? There was no outrunning it. Some days it suffocated him. Some days he didn't know what was real.

Diego took a long swig of his beer, waiting for the buzz to dull the edges.

The Dragon nodded toward the bottle. "That shit will keep you sick. Keep you on a cycle of ups and downs. Coke one minute, alcohol the next. Doesn't usually work out too well."

Diego wanted to make a joke about the Dragon not being his

father, that he was a big boy, all that. And maybe it was a trick of the quiet night, but the Dragon actually sounded concerned, so Diego bit his tongue.

"They'll replace us, you know, as soon as our bodies hit the pavement," Diego said. "Blood still warm. They'll replace us."

The Dragon shook his head. "Can't think too long and hard about the end, D."

"Why not?" Diego asked. "What else is there?"

"This real bad shit you might have to do, I suggest you get it over with. Move past it. Keep moving forward. It's all we can do."

"Until the next real bad shit." Diego sighed. "It might be a good deal what we offer your *príncipe,* but if I'm being honest, it'd probably be best to wait this shit out. I'm not sure who's going to come out the winner anymore."

The Dragon stilled, his face a mask.

After a beat, he nodded. "Be a shark, D. Keep moving."

Keep moving.

Diego was a shark, a shark sinking to the bottom of the seafloor.

CHAPTER 28

Sofia had been dreaming of London. Of an easy Sunday morning stroll, her mother, older, at her side. Her golden hair, streaked with silver, shiny in the rare English sun. They smiled, they laughed. Sofia didn't remember what they were saying, but the details didn't matter—it was the feeling of having her mother at her side that lingered.

She woke with a start as her phone rattled violently against her nightstand in the quiet late-night hours in the De Luna ranch home.

She grasped for it to silence it, the number flashing across the bright screen in the dark room familiar.

"Nando," she said into the phone, her eyebrows knitting, "what's wrong?"

"Turn on the TV," he said.

She scrambled out of bed, and her brain, struggling to wake up, snapped to attention now. She pulled open her bedroom door. The monotonous tone of a reporter wafted up the stairs from the *sala*.

She padded down the stairs, the phone still pressed to her ear.

The glow from the mounted flat-screen TV threw her shadow into the hallway. Sofia leaned against the doorframe watching a semitrailer engulfed in thick orange flames burn against the black night sky on the screen.

Desperately she scanned the ticker at the bottom for more information. *As the coming election heats up, cartel violence spikes.*

"Where is this?" Sofia asked into the phone, remembering her brother on the other end.

The *De Luna* painted along the side of the semi's container was clearly visible, even as the flames licked higher.

"Matamoros."

The Gulf.

"What happened?" she asked.

"I don't know," Nando stammered, repeating it over and over. "The truck with their shipment left yesterday, just like normal."

Over Nando's rushed words, Sofia keyed into the news anchor explaining that it seemed the truck had been ambushed, the driver locked inside.

"They did this . . ." she said, Nando not hearing her.

Xavier and Joaquin wanted their war for the routes so bad they'd push until the Gulf had no choice but to react. And that time had come.

"Diego?" Sofia asked.

His brother's name made Nando focus. "Still in Tijuana."

Sofia looked away from the TV. "Fernando, stay inside, stay home. I have to go."

She ended the call, and her shaking fingers clicked off the TV.

"This is what you wanted?" she asked, her throat tight with adrenaline.

The ghosts, they were there with her. Her mother. Her father.

She already knew the answer, because that was her name on that truck too. This was the crown her mother had placed on her head, thorns and all.

Her father's shadow disappeared into the home's dark corners.

The phone vibrated in her hand, making her jump.

Unknown number.

She answered the call as fast as she could.

"This is how you do business?" the voice, tight with controlled rage, asked. She couldn't place it, but she had a guess.

"Daniel . . ."

"Sofia," he replied in a voice smooth as silk dragged across embers.

She felt herself about to trip over her words, stumble the way she used to when her father would give her a hard time about her grades, or ask why she was home from school so late and was she with that *pinche* Herrera boy again.

But this time, she swallowed down that insecurity and stood taller.

It was her name on that truck, too, after all.

"I got your message," she said.

"Good," he replied. "Shame I had to go through all that trouble to get you on the phone. I think we're overdue for a chat, *reina*."

"All you had to do was ask," Sofia quipped, needing him not to hear any uncertainty, any fear, in her tone.

"Do you know what the meaning of my name is, Sofia?" Daniel asked after a beat so long Sofia thought the line had disconnected.

"God is my judge," she replied, the dark hallway she stood in closing in on her like a confession booth.

He hummed, apparently pleased. "Look at you, living up to your name."

Her mother had a song for her, rhyming "Sofia" with increasingly more absurd words until Sofia ended up in a fit of giggles. But her mother had explained once why she named her daughter Sofia, meaning "wisdom."

It's the knowing *inside of you*, she had said.

"You'll come here," Daniel continued. "No brothers, no cousins. I want to talk to you only. And Sofia, I am not a man who is afraid of what has to be done. I hope you understand that."

The line did go dead this time, but a text message quickly followed, a pin to a location in Matamoros, followed by a date and time to meet. Tomorrow.

Her hands never stopped shaking as she threw items into the duffel bag Lily had unpacked for her upon her arrival.

Sofia picked up her phone once more and shot off a text to Nando. She needed a plane and the pilot ready to go ASAP. But she said nothing about Matamoros because he'd want to come, and she was well aware she could be walking into a trap.

Her phone buzzed again with a call, and she hurriedly answered, pressing the phone to her ear as she slipped out of her bedroom and started down the steps.

"Where are you going?" Yolotli asked.

"To meet Daniel."

"I'm coming with you—"

"No," Sofia interrupted. "I need you to talk to Diego, get the truth from him about what Xavier and Joaquin are doing. Nando said something about sending this extra truck to the Gulf. They've been planning this."

She paused at the front door. "Yoli, I need to know if Diego knew about this. I need to know whose side he's on."

"He'll say the same for you."

She had expected this battle with the cousins, but she hoped it wouldn't come to war with her own brother. If this was the path he was choosing, Sofia wasn't sure she could save him from the vultures that circled.

The sun was starting to warm the horizon as Sofia watched the pilot prepare the jet.

A car pulled up to the hangar, setting Sofia's teeth on edge. She hadn't slept since being awoken; hell, she couldn't remember the last time she really slept, her nerves were so rattled.

When Andres stepped out of the sleek sedan, all long lines and quiet authority, she sighed.

"Doña," Andres said as he approached. His voice was thick and raspy from disuse this early in the morning.

"What are you doing here?" she asked, focusing on handing her bag to the pilot's son.

"Nando called me."

Sofia turned to face Andres, meeting his eyes, surprised by the worry she saw there.

"Why?" she asked, her eyes on the plane again. The sooner she left, the better.

"He sounded concerned. Said you asked for a plane. Pretty easy to put two and two together."

"So you saw the news," Sofia said.

"Hard to miss."

"You're here to protect your investment," Sofia said, meeting his eyes once more.

"Look, I can talk to Daniel. Maybe reason with him . . ."

Sofia huffed and turned toward the plane. "This is my family, Andres; I can take care of it."

"Stop, stop," Andres said, reaching for Sofia's arms, his eyes searching hers. "I'm not letting you go by yourself. And right now it looks like I'm the only person you have."

"Señora," the pilot's son called from the top of the stairs, "*lista?*"

Even if Andres was only trying to protect Sofia, his key to his deal with Ximena, Sofia had to admit she lacked the numbers for a meet like this. The extra body would help. Andres Herrera was still the Gulf's cocaine connection. Daniel might tread more carefully with Andres in the room.

Her phone buzzed, and she glanced at the number.

"All right," she told Andres, "get your bag."

She took a few steps away from the plane, the phone pressed to one ear, a hand to the other.

"Not a good time, Padre."

"Just calling to wish you safe travels."

Sofia glanced over her shoulder, where Andres stood at the top of the jet's staircase, his eyes on Sofia.

"I'll let you know how it goes," she hissed before ending the call.

Andres held his hand out to her as she approached.

She took his hand, accepting his support as she started up the stairs. Her hand fit in his the same as it always had. The thought came before she could stop it.

Up here in the quiet, the drone of the engine lulled away the sharp edges of adrenaline. The crash was coming; she felt it in the way her limbs were loose, soft.

"What the hell are your cousins trying to do?" Andres asked.

"Diversify," she replied, her eyes on the mountains below them. "They want to save us by culling anyone they think is in their way. They're so afraid of being left behind," Sofia continued, more to the window, more to herself than to Andres. "They think it's better to strike first. Maybe it is."

"They'll lose, Sofia. They'll get you killed too. How far are you willing to let this go?"

Sofia turned to him. "Maybe you don't get it yet, sicario, but I'll get killed either way."

Andres looked away. "Is that what you and the priest talk about?"

Sofia watched the natural water lines of a mountain as it passed beneath them.

"The priest is trying to save my soul."

CHAPTER 29

Alberto stood in their walk-in closet, his dress shirt hanging open unbuttoned.

"We're having guests tonight," he said, glancing over his shoulder at Maria.

"Oh," Maria replied, "does the kitchen staff know?"

"You'll let them know," he replied.

"Of course," she said.

"Get dressed," he said before brushing past her.

Men, some Maria knew, some she didn't, trickled in that evening as she played the part of hostess, guiding the men to the back patio where dinner was set up.

She was about to head to the kitchen to see if the staff needed any help when she heard the front door open once more.

She stilled, recognizing the wide set of shoulders, the curly hair.

Martin made his way over to greet her.

He was dressed sharply, in all black. The way his frame had filled out, the low-trimmed beard now reminded her how long it had been since she'd seen him.

"Señora," he said, his voice low, as he leaned in to press his lips against her cheek in greeting.

She closed her eyes, giving herself this moment to feel close to him again after so long. His lips on her cheek made her blood burn.

The scratch from his beard made her skin buzz. Instead of sun and dirt, he smelled like ocean water: salty, crisp, clean.

She laid her hand on his arm, the leather of his jacket warming under her touch.

"Martin," she replied once he pulled away, "I didn't know you were coming."

He nodded, reaching up to run a finger over his bottom lip, his eyes dark.

For anyone else, the gesture might have been a subconscious one. But Maria knew Martin, knew he was savoring the feel of her skin on his lips.

"It's good to see you," she began, not sure what to say after all this time but needing to fill the silence between them. She was flustered, felt the heat rising up her neck. "The men are out back; I can show you."

"I remember my way."

She huffed, "Right, of course."

Then it hit her.

She narrowed her eyes. "Why are you here?"

Martin's jaw twitched. "Your husband invited me."

Maria glanced behind her, toward the chatter of the men outside.

"Oh," she replied, glancing back up at Martin. "I didn't realize you and my husband had business in common."

Martin's eyes held hers. "Things change."

He glanced at her hands folded over where her dress skimmed the slight bump of her stomach. She was just starting to show.

He met her eyes. "*Felicidades*."

She bit back, *It should have been you, it should have been yours,* on the back of her tongue. Instead, she glanced down, the dull silver of the nine millimeter at his hip catching her eye.

"*Gracias*," she replied, pulling her shawl tighter around herself. "And you, congratulations, for all of it."

Martin worked at a large architecture firm in downtown Mexico City. And he had a wife now, and she was pretty, pretty like you'd expect a rose to be. And he had a baby boy named Andres.

Maria knew these things because the house staff, the women who used to braid her hair, would come in from the city, having done their shopping, and they'd fill Maria in on all the *chisme*. They knew she wouldn't ask but would always wonder about Martin.

Martin had a gun at his hip now, silver and shiny. He had a large house now, too, just up the road from hers. And now Martin, who had always wanted to just be an architect, seemed to be working with her husband.

He nodded, smiling faintly. "Yes, thank you. You'll have to meet the little guy one day."

"I'd like that."

"I better get back there," Martin said.

Maria nodded, stepping aside as he walked past.

"You know," he said, stopping, his dazzling smile finally appearing, "it would be nice to see the girls again."

Maria smiled. "The horses. Of course. You're welcome to visit them."

"Later," he said, holding her gaze, "maybe you can join me, if you can get free."

She nodded once sharply, then turned away.

"They've missed you," Maria said as Martin entered the stable, the mares rousing, standing near their gates to see who was coming.

"And I've missed them," Martin replied, reaching over the stable gate to pat the younger mare. "Ramon told me you didn't listen to his directions very well."

Maria scoffed and reached up to rub the older mare's muzzle. "You taught me everything I needed to know. I didn't need Ramon."

Martin smiled. He was gorgeous like this, lit by the soft amber lights of the stable, right at home where she'd first met him.

"How are you feeling?" he asked, his gaze dropping to her stomach.

She laid a hand there instinctually. "I've felt better."

"It's a delicate time."

Those little reminders of his wife, his life. Maria couldn't deny they stung.

"How was dinner with Alberto?" she asked, needing to think about anything other than Martin's wife.

Martin smiled slowly. "Fine."

"I thought you'd be longer."

"Are you worried he'll catch us," Martin asked, stepping closer to her, "like you used to worry about your father catching us?"

Maria shrugged. "We aren't doing anything, right? Besides, he's drunk, and he's got an audience. He won't miss me."

Martin's eyes were dark, watching hers. "So we have some time."

She wondered if he was thinking about it too, the last time they were together alone in this stable. When they had made love on one of the scratchy saddle blankets while the rain drowned out everything.

He had kissed her like it would be the last time, and she'd clung to him like it was. She had replayed that night over and over so many times she sometimes wondered if she had dreamed it instead because it had been perfect.

But here now with him, she remembered how the muscles in his shoulders flexed under her palms, the way his gold chain dangled in her face as he braced his weight above her. His eyes—she remembered his eyes the best because they never left hers. She saw the concern there, softness, fondness. Love.

"So," she began, clearing her throat, "how have you been?"

Martin shook his head. "Let's not do that."

"Do what?"

"The small talk."

"Okay," Maria said, raising an eyebrow, "why are you here?"

"I told you, Alberto invited me."

"Don't do *that,*" she said. "I'm a grown woman, Martin; I know what goes on in this house. You can be honest with me."

"If you know what happens in your house, then you should know why Alberto called me here."

"You have something he wants; that's the only reason he pays attention to anyone."

"Your father promised him my family's coca. Alberto wants what he was promised when he agreed to marry you, I suppose. He wants his own source of cocaine. He wants to be the biggest supplier to the Americans."

Maria frowned. "And you, what happened to taking me away from all of this? I thought you wanted nothing to do with this."

"Alberto and you and your family need my family's product."

"Say that's true, what do you get out of it?"

"I have a chance to make real money here. Life-changing money. Money I can use to start my own architectural firm."

Maria shook her head. "There's other ways . . ."

"You've never been poor, not like I have. Those six months your father worked in the fields is nothing compared to a lifetime of wondering when your next meal will come. So I can't expect you to understand."

Maria tilted her chin up, set her jaw. "Don't be cruel."

"I'm not being cruel. I'm being honest," Martin replied. "I have a wife now, Maria . . ."

Maria bristled at his words. They still broke her heart.

Maria hadn't chosen Alberto, but Martin had chosen his wife. It wasn't fair to ask Martin to wait, but that didn't stop Maria from hoping he would.

"I have to provide for her and for our son."

Martin was watching Maria's face; she could feel it.

Maria crossed her arms over her chest. "Welcome to the business then, Martin. Alberto might make you rich, but he will take just as much. Excuse me," she said as she moved to walk past him, back toward the house, but his voice stopped her.

"He needs you, Maria," Martin said. "He won't last long in this world. He's too arrogant. Too cocky. He rubs people the wrong way. Your father had a way with people. You have that same grace. If Alberto is going to succeed, he's going to need your charm. Your way of talking to people."

"I doubt he'll want my help, but I'll keep it in mind."

"Do you still want to give back? Do you still want to make a difference?" Martin asked, challenging her. "Sit down with these men, at these meetings, make them hear you."

She shook her head. "Not like that, Martin. This business of my father's, of Alberto's, it's a poison."

"And how else will you learn how to fight it?" he asked.

She huffed, "Wouldn't that ruin your plans? I thought you had money to make."

"I have a number, and when I hit it, I'm out."

"They won't let you walk away."

"I have a plan."

Maria shook her head. "They don't care about plans."

Martin shrugged. "What else can they do to me? What else can they take?"

"Your wife, your son . . ."

"They took you from me, Maria. Took something from both of us. I can protect my wife now, and my son. I know how, but back then . . ."

"It's done," she snapped, moving to continue through the stable.

"Please," Martin began, "talk to me."

She sighed. "I don't know what there is to say . . ."

"What else was I supposed to do, Maria? You had married Alberto—"

She held her hand up to stop him. "Yes, I know how this story goes, Martin."

"Do you?" he asked, his eyes wild now, glittering in the low light. "Do you know how badly I missed you? Do you know how much I thought about you? How much I still think about you?"

"I know," she hissed. "I know because I did the same. But what good is it, Martin? What good is it to talk about it?"

"I just need to know, Maria."

"That I felt the same? You knew, you knew that night."

He shook his head. "No. After," he began, holding her gaze. "Was it true?"

Her blood flushed, rushing to her core.

"Was what true, Martin?" she asked carefully.

She had a secret, one she locked away so deep down the pressure of everything else crushed it, distilled it to one sharp blade. A secret she kept lodged in the soft tissue, to protect him, hoping he would never know. Because she hated herself for it.

"That not too long after we were together, the women who looked after you got you a pill from the pharmacy in Tepito—"

"Martin . . ." Maria interrupted.

"The truth, Maria," Martin said, "please."

At the time she had been angry, so angry that the universe would do that to her, bring her so close to Martin, bless their union or curse it. She had thought she was being punished for going after what she really wanted, but now that she was older, she realized that actions have consequences.

The reasonableness of that statement never made it hurt any less.

Maria's eyes started to burn and sting. "I had to . . ."

"You could have told me," he said softly.

Maria shook her head. "There was no point. My father would

never have let me keep it. He never would have let me be with you. Who do you think sent those women to Tepito?"

Martin's eyes flashed, and his jaw twitched. "I should have known."

"I'm sorry, I am. I never wanted you to know. I never wanted to hurt you."

Martin smoothed her hair, let his hand rest at the base of her neck. "I'm not angry with you, Maria. I wish I could have been there for you; I should have been there for you. You shouldn't have gone through that alone."

"It wasn't what I wanted, Martin, you have to know that. It's not what I would have chosen. And for a few days I let myself dream about you and me. Our baby . . ."

Martin's jaw clenched, and she remembered his discipline. The way he controlled his emotions. The way he let himself be only whatever it was she needed. He thought she needed him to be strong, to not be angry. He was right. She'd hurt him enough. She felt guilty enough.

"You should probably get back. Before he sends someone to look for you," Maria said.

"Yeah," Martin replied with a nod. "Yeah." He reached up to push his curls off his forehead.

"Manzanilla tea," he said, shaking a finger in her direction. "It will help you sleep."

He headed toward the stable entrance but stopped after a few steps before turning back to face her.

"Just so it's said, just so you know, I would have married you. If you had wanted that too," he said. "When I told you I've got you, I meant it. I still mean it. I will always mean it."

"Did you have a good talk with Martin?" Alberto asked later that night when he slipped into bed next to Maria.

Maria turned to click off her night table lamp. In the cover of darkness, she replied, "He wanted to visit the horses."

"I'm not a blind man, or a stupid one, Maria. I know he covets you. But he will never have you, do you understand?"

Maria closed her eyes. "Good night, Alberto."

CHAPTER 30

It had been a long drive to reach the Meyer-lemon-colored home set deep off the main road outside of Matamoros proper. The furniture here was sparse, a mix of cheap particle board and junkyard pickups.

And the smell—it was barely there, but it settled on the back of Sofia's tongue just enough so she could taste it. Acrid: a mix of sweat, fear. Blood.

She and Andres were led to the back of the house to a sprawling, nearly empty room.

Men lingered, leaning against the paint-chipped walls, guns at their hips, their eyes on Sofia and Andres behind her.

Muted sunlight filtered in through the sliding glass door. The grass in the backyard was thick and overgrown.

Daniel turned to face them when they entered the room.

Daniel of the Gulf had skin that glowed like the sun from within, bronze like Sofia's father's. Daniel's hair, his eyes, black like hers. Assessing, blank. Maybe they had been family once, before Cortés.

He smiled, a tight and precise thing. White teeth straight like a bare skull. "St. Julian, what a nice surprise."

Andres stiffened next to Sofia. "Daniel," Andres said in greeting.

Daniel turned his attention to Sofia. "Well, here she is. Took you long enough to meet with me, reina."

"My apologies that it had to be under these circumstances," Sofia replied.

Daniel eyed her. "So different from your cousins. They would have waltzed in here demanding a new truck."

"Our driver?" Sofia asked, omitting any hope from her tone.

Daniel shook his head once, sharply.

"Then you owe me more than a truck, after all," Sofia replied.

Andres glanced at her, but she stood her ground, her spine straight and her chin up.

She wasn't scared of men like Daniel. They were predictable in their unpredictability. He wanted her to push back. He wanted the challenge.

Daniel smiled. "I knew there was a Torres in there somewhere."

He stepped up next to Andres and reached out to pat his shoulder. "I'm going to borrow Sofia for a moment."

He turned then to Sofia and held out his arm. "The backyard is not in the best of shape. I'd hate for you to twist an ankle."

She slipped her arm through his, and he pressed her arm close to his body, his black eyes on her. He smelled of *mota* and heady, expensive cologne.

"Let's walk, reina."

"Maybe we start from the beginning," Daniel said as they stepped out into that muted afternoon sunlight. "Maybe they've left some of the pieces out of the story so far for you, since you've come back."

"You tried to steal from us," Sofia said, wishing she had her sunglasses. The lack of sleep was catching up to her. Running dull razors across her brain, behind her eyes.

He smiled, and this time it was soft, amused. "That's what they told you?"

"They've told me many things," she replied.

Everyone lies.

"It has been a complicated relationship with your family, I

won't deny that. But I wouldn't call what I did stealing, exactly."

"You tried to undercut my family. You tried to break the alliance. What would you call that?"

"Sometimes you have to break things to put them back together better," he replied. "Someone like you should understand an idea like that."

"I do."

Daniel was leading them out to the far end of the property where an empty in-ground pool sat.

His guards were out of earshot now. It was just the two of them.

He paused, still holding her steady, still.

"You've had your nose here and there, sniffing out other sources. Hard not to feel slighted by that," Sofia added.

Daniel shrugged. "Price comparison." He looked at her. "Let's cut the bullshit. I know your cousins want my routes, my access to the north. But this isn't the way to go about getting them."

"We're stagnating. They thought we had to do something."

Daniel considered her words, his dark eyes on the clouds briefly before turning back to her. "Your family, your father and mother, had a chance to have a piece of what I do, and they turned their nose up at it. And I was fine with that. Happy to take the work off their hands. But when I tried to build something for myself, your family wouldn't allow it. Now I'm asking you, reina, why should I limit myself because your family has some false sense of morality?"

"I don't care what you do. I'm here to ask if we can find a way to do it together."

Daniel laughed then, a short huff that seemed to surprise him. "What did your family tell me when I asked for a bigger cut of the cocaine since they made it very clear to me I couldn't shop elsewhere? When I tried to ask your family if we could do this together?"

Sofia laid her hand on his arm. "I wasn't here for that. Wasn't my call."

"This is true. This is also why you're standing here. Your cousins, however—this pool, it's for them. Pieces of them," Daniel said, leaning closer to Sofia, his eyes black as night. "They think they can cut into my business now, after what your family did to me. I won't allow it. I can't stand for it, Sofia. Surely you understand."

"What is it exactly they want in on?" Sofia asked. "Maybe we can find a way to work something out."

Daniel frowned. "You don't know?"

"It hasn't exactly been a happy family reunion."

Daniel leaned back, taking Sofia in. "Do you know what was on your truck that I blew up?"

"Your shipment," she replied.

He shook his head, then nodded. "Well, yes, but there were girls on that truck. Girls your cousins were attempting to keep from me and send up into Texas without my knowledge, my approval, or my cut. As you can imagine, I felt very disrespected by this action. So, even though I kept the girls and the drugs because I am not a wasteful man, who is stealing from who in this scenario, reina?"

"I didn't know . . ." she began, having to say something while her brain caught up to what Daniel had just shared.

Her own family attempting to get involved in trafficking? One of the few lines her grandfather never wanted crossed. She couldn't, wouldn't stand for this.

Rabid dogs, she thought, *get put down.*

"I can see that," Daniel said.

"Join us," Sofia said, swallowing, blinking to regain control of herself. "The three of us together they can't stop. No one can stop."

Daniel sighed. "The old, dysfunctional alliance again."

"It works."

"For your family."

"Look, I don't give a shit what you do here," Sofia replied. "What you send up to America, keep it. All of it. What I care about is the people here in this country. This shouldn't touch them any more than it has to."

Daniel frowned. "What if, instead, I sit back and watch that politician disembowel your family? Then I still get to do what I want. I don't need your blessing, reina."

Sofia chewed at her bottom lip, then stood straighter, leaning in. "Screw that politician. I'm not doing this for her. This is for us. The three of us. We control the president; that's the way it's supposed to be. But we can't keep that power if we're fighting each other."

"Interesting take," Daniel said, patting her hand on his arm. "But I heard you wanted out. That you want to play politician. And coming to me like this, talking about how we can help each other, blah-blah, sounds exactly like what a politician would say."

"You're right," she replied, "I do want out. I want a quiet life, Daniel."

Daniel tilted his head. "Your brother Diego, he keeps the Bony Lady, Santa Muerte, close to his heart, doesn't he? And Nando, well, he has Diego to watch over him. Now, what about you?" Daniel asked, leaning closer, so close that to anyone else they might have looked like lovers sharing secrets. "Your father, your mother—gone. Grandparents, well, they're long gone. Your only uncle killed, left for dead in the streets. And what about your father's family? Oh, they never wanted anything to do with you and the Torreses, isn't that right? There's no one to protect you, so if you don't claim that crown and hold on for dear life, they will snatch it from you."

He reached up with his free hand, pinching her chin between his thumb and forefinger.

"Reina, this is who you are. This is your legacy. It will all be for nothing if you step away, have you considered that?"

"What's it all worth now?" she asked.

"There's another way. When you drove through my city, it was quiet, wasn't it? Kids are in school. People are off the streets. You can reign however you want. It's yours now. Why not be a king? Why fight it? You have to ask yourself, where, how, can you make the most difference."

He was right. His city was clean and quiet. She knew he ruled with an iron fist, but he was also ruthlessly protective of his town, his people. And that money, he poured it back into the community. She had seen the new buildings in the modest downtown. New buildings meant new jobs.

"I'll tell you what, reina. I see this alliance, this so-called peace we used to have, is important to you. And I forgive you the sins of your family since you were not here, but you owe me for your cousins' disrespect."

"What is it worth?" she asked.

"You should ask yourself that. Your cousins know what they are doing. Maybe they lost a truck, but that truck—though easily replaceable—well, burning on the news, it looks very bad for you. Especially when you're trying to build peace and appease that skinny CDMX mayor. It makes what you're trying to do look like a joke."

He guided them back toward the lemon-colored home. "The only way it stops is when you stop them."

They paused at the sliding glass door. "I want them dead. Then I'll believe that you want peace."

This time Sofia didn't argue.

Daniel pushed the glass door open. "After you."

When she stepped back into the room, Andres uncrossed his arms and took a step toward her. Relief showed on his face, but he caught himself and regained his regal composure.

Daniel nodded toward his guards who stepped back, giving them room.

"I appreciate the visit, reina. Are you staying a while?"

Sofia glanced at Andres, then back to Daniel. "We were planning on heading back."

"Please, you'll stay the night. As my guest. It's not often you come all this way. Plus, you two look like you could use a little rest."

Andres and Sofia shared another look.

"We have an Argentinian restaurant," Daniel continued. "Sofia, you must go."

"We'll stay," Sofia replied before Andres could argue.

She needed a night away and some time to process what she'd just learned from Daniel. And where to go from here since Daniel was right.

She'd tried to talk to Xavier and Joaquin. She'd tried to give them another way, another option. But if this was the future they wanted for her family, she couldn't allow it. She couldn't allow her brother to be a part of it either.

CHAPTER 31

True to his word, Daniel set Andres and Sofia up with a reservation at the Argentinian restaurant close to the border, next to the river. Sofia had the suspicion Daniel was trying to show off, to show Sofia what his money was doing for his city. For his people. And Sofia was impressed. Daniel had pull here that Sofia envied. Mexico City was large and lumbering when it came to change, bogged down by the cogs of government.

There used to be migrant camps in this city, thick with tents filled with the displaced. But Daniel had found a place for them. Made a place for them. He had the power, the opportunity to transform, and he did it by running the worst vices this civilized world had to offer right into the arms of America. But they asked for it, didn't they? They were never asked to be saviors—her, Daniel. Andres—just suppliers.

Across from her, Andres picked at his chicken Milanesa.

Sofia, in a forgiving mood this evening, this far from home, where she could feel herself coming back to herself, cleared her throat. "My mom used to make that for us."

Her voice was softer than she'd like. Showing Andres her soft underbelly did nothing but get her hurt. But she was nostalgic, sentimental as the moon rose large on the horizon.

Andres set his fork down, his eyes still on his plate.

"What is it?" Sofia asked, lowering her own fork.

He shook his head once, sharp.

Maybe he didn't want to show her his underbelly either.

"I meant what I said the last time I saw you," Sofia began. "You should have come to me as a friend . . ."

"But we aren't," he replied, sharply, quickly. "You said it yourself. I can't sit here with you like this," he hissed over the bubbling classical music.

"It's a business dinner, isn't it? What's the problem?" she asked, unnerved by the electricity in his movements. "I thought you wanted this? You wanted us to put the past behind us."

He met her gaze, held it. The murky green, blue, and red swirled like a cyclone. "But it's not," he replied as he stood, the sudden movement causing his chair to scrape across the tile.

She watched him stalk across the restaurant, his shoulders high and tight.

She sighed, then downed the rest of the wine in her glass, letting the last swallow coat her tongue before standing to follow Andres out to the restaurant's balcony.

Out here the breeze was cool on the thin layer of perspiration covering Sofia's skin, raising goose bumps on her legs.

Andres leaned against the balcony, his eyes on the Rio Grande, taking a slow drag of his cigarette.

Sofia leaned against the balcony and watched the cars pass on the busy city street below.

"I won't apologize," she began, "for feeling the way I do toward you. You can't blame me for being confused."

He shook his head. "I don't. I understand," he replied, his voice dark and deep. Cool like a hidden stream.

Sofia looked up at Andres, impossibly handsome in the inky cover of night with the moonlight reflecting in his eyes. The silver light threw his high cheekbones into relief, but the tight skin of the scar on his jaw shone.

She reached before her brain said no. She ran her index finger over the shiny skin along the strong, straight line of his jaw. He let her touch him, his eyelids fluttering closed for a beat. When her nail grazed his bottom lip, he reached up, grabbing her hand, holding it in his.

Her heart beat against her chest, a violent thing in this delicate moment. She was forgetting her anger. She was forgetting the searing, aching pain he had left in her when he went away. When she heard the rumors. When he wouldn't answer her. When he kissed Ximena's hand.

Andres looked at her for a long beat before dropping her hand and turning to watch the cars as Sofia had.

"I've been thinking lately about how love is a strange thing," he said, the long line of his tall frame rigid.

His fingers toyed with the lighter in his pocket, turning it over and over.

Sofia swallowed air back into her lungs as her fingers found the medallion against her chest, grounding her. She wondered what made him think about love tonight.

She rubbed the metal between her fingers. Love . . . a funny thing in their world. It came only in glimpses for them. A rare funny idea. Whimsical, like a forgotten childhood toy.

Andres turned and took a long beat to look her up and down. Slowly enough for Sofia to feel her skin warming under his gaze. Slowly enough that she knew that was the point.

Sofia met his gaze. His eyes were glassy from too much liquor.

Anything he said tonight would be lubricated, slipped away from wherever he'd locked himself up.

"I think love is the thing that takes the sharpness of the world and dulls it just enough," Sofia said, searching his eyes for the source of the heat in his tone.

"Is that so?" he asked darkly.

"I like to believe that love is real for others," she replied.

There was an emptiness buried deep inside her that she spent her days trying to outrun. In London, she used to play a game. She'd pick a man, any man who caught her attention. Then she would set about laying a trap for him. They would always come to her, falling easily into her spiderweb. Once she captured them, Sofia was bored again and released her prey.

It was an ugly game, but it kept her preoccupied. Her roommate gushed about love and the way it warmed everything. Sofia knew early on that love wasn't for her. It wasn't something that would find her. She'd be left behind, and she had made peace with that fact. What she had with Leo was the picture of love, but really it was just comfortable. Easy. Not painful and vengeful and ripped from her with sharp claws like everything about Andres was.

While it sounded melodramatic now, the idea was born out of heartbreak. The truth was that when Andres left, he took her heart with him. So when she said she didn't think she was capable of the type of love Diego and Yolotli had, she meant it.

Andres shook his head. "I don't know," he said. "To be half a heart means to always be missing a part of you."

"That's the point, isn't it?" Sofia asked, not sure what they were talking about anymore, her brain warm and fuzzy from the heady wine. This conversation felt dangerous, the narrow precipice of something else.

"Diego said once, 'You pay a price in this life,'" Sofia continued. "Life gives, and life takes away. When you have something like what they have, then no matter what, you have someone for you. Just for you. Even if it's only for a short time. It's a gift."

Andres turned to face her fully, his back against the balcony now.

She tilted her head. "What are we doing, Andres?" she asked softly, gently.

"I know you, Sofia. As much as you hate it, I do too, and I know everything you're doing now is out of love for your brothers."

"You've promised me a lot of things since I've been back, Andres. And that picture you've tried to paint, I see it now. So tell me, isn't this what you wanted? Daniel has agreed, in his way, to this. To what Ximena wants."

Andres chuckled, smoke haloing him, his dimples deepening. "The idea was to get you out, to get us out, but seeing you with Daniel today—"

"This is what you asked me to do," Sofia interrupted.

Andres frowned. "I know, I know. It's just easy to get caught up and lose what it is that keeps us, us."

"You'd know," she said, her tone cool.

"Yeah. I do," he replied, moving to turn his back on her again.

"Andres," she said, stopping him, tired of the way he hid from her when she felt so raw. "If things were different, if they were your way, what would you want?" she asked, moving closer. Close enough to feel his body heat. Close enough to touch. Close enough to feel the beat of the other half of her heart if she held her breath long enough.

She reached for the medallion hanging from his neck, her thumb tracing patterns over the warm medal like she had done to hers.

"What would you want from me then?" she asked, looking up at him.

His eyes darkened like an oncoming storm. "Are you sure this is the game you want to play?" he asked, laying his hand over hers, stilling her fingers against his chest.

"It's not a game to me, Andres," she said, losing herself in his eyes, in the way that being this close to him made everything else fall away. "You were never a game to me."

"What are you doing?" he asked, tilting his head, his dark eyelashes dropping as he glanced at her lips.

Sofia figured this close he had to hear the way her heart rattled so loud in her rib cage now.

"What do you want from me?" she asked again, unsure of what she herself wanted in this moment.

He leaned closer to her, his lips near her ear, his stubble tickling her cheek, the tickle making her shiver. "Wanting is a dangerous thing, Sofia. We should be careful. Let the past be the past."

Had he forgotten so easily?

The rain—it had been raining that day. He walked her home before her brothers had a chance to protest. He stopped at the thick patch of trees right before the De Lunas' gate. There he pulled her into the thick of them, her hands in his. "Don't forget me," he had said, before pressing his lips to hers. Their last kiss.

"*El pasado es el pasado,*" she repeated.

Was he trying to convince himself or her?

She moved away, Lalo's words in her ears. "If you had it all your way, Andres, would you tell me the truth then? Because this limbo you're keeping me in—telling me nothing so I have to keep you close—will end. There's nothing to lose now."

He tilted his head back, his eyes on the sky. "Maybe for you."

"What you agreed to with Ximena is not freedom, Andres, if you're this afraid of her and what she can take from you."

He nodded, pulling one last drag from his cigarette before putting it out under his shoe.

"*Lo se.*"

When he didn't protest, when he didn't fight, she sighed.

"I'm here because of you. I'm here because what you offered me, what you promised her I'd do, keeps my brothers safe. So, for now, I'll let you keep your secrets. But when it all falls down around you, don't expect me to get cut picking up the shards."

With an ache sharper than the others, she turned her back on him once more, leaving him standing alone on the balcony. All those miles between them, all those years—maybe it was too much to reconcile after all.

CHAPTER 32

Sofia stepped out of the shower and dried her body off quickly, willing her mind to not think. Trying to blink away Andres's dimples, his long lashes, and his cloudy blue eyes from her mind.

She slipped the silk hotel robe over her shoulders and walked barefoot over to the floor-to-ceiling windows. The Rio Grande flowed beneath her, Texas glittering on the other side.

All these borders, man-made. All of them.

She pulled the curtains shut.

Nando had sent her a number of urgent texts while she was at dinner. She texted him back. Now she held her phone in her hand, the message from Diego still unanswered.

The ghosts she kept were there with her. Sofia felt them in the way she doubted herself. It was naive to think the men in her family would protect her. They protected one thing, and that was the money. The blood they all shared meant nothing if it got in the way.

The ticking on the countdown of Sofia's freedom grew louder each day.

A light rapping at the door pulled her from her ghosts.

She stood on her tiptoes to peer out the peephole.

"It's me, *muñeca*," Andres said as she caught a glimpse of him in the hallway.

Sofia leaned her forehead against the door, the wood cool against her skin, grounding her.

It was well past midnight now.

She took a deep breath to steel her resolve and opened the door. "Andres, it's getting late."

His hair was disheveled just enough to look alluring. A line of sweat had formed at his hairline, and his cheeks were flushed a soft shade of pink, his dress shirt sleeves rolled up to the elbows. But his eyes were a clear sparkling blue, and the look he gave her was hungry.

He nodded. "I know," he replied as he raised his arm to lean against the open doorframe. He pressed his forehead against his forearm, his eyelids fluttering closed.

This close he smelled sinful. The mix of his spiced cologne, alcohol, smoke, and the familiar scent of his skin underneath it all made her blood thrum, her heart beat in her ears.

Sofia crossed her arms under her chest. "What do you need?" she asked, hoping he'd take the hint she wasn't in the mood to talk. He'd made himself clear enough at the restaurant.

"*Soy un cobarde*," he said, pointing at himself, "it's true. You think it too, but I've always had my reasons, Sofia."

Sofia bit at the inside of her cheek to stop from rolling her eyes. "Andres, it doesn't matter what I think about you—"

"It does," he said, interrupting her in a voice soft and raspy from too many cigarettes. His eyes sparkled now like they were lit from within.

He frowned. "Can I come in, Sofia? I just . . ." he began, meeting her eyes again. "I just need you to understand."

She stilled, paralyzed by the question.

He lowered his head, his beautiful eyes glinting under those long eyelashes. "Please, I only need a minute."

"One minute," she said before stepping aside and pulling the door open, letting him enter.

Once Andres was in the room with her, Sofia remembered she

was wearing only a thin robe. She pulled it tighter around herself and leaned her back against the door.

Andres looked around her room, his gaze catching the dress she'd been wearing slung over the hotel room's chair. He eventually sat on the back of the too-stiff modern couch that occupied the front room.

"I know what your family tells you, that you should forget about me."

"Do you want me to?" she asked as his eyes trailed up her bare calves to her waist, chest, neck, and finally her face. Her skin warmed under his slow, deliberate gaze. "Because your being here now says otherwise."

He shook his head. "Come here," he said, holding a hand out to her, his fingers beckoning. His voice even duskier now.

When she made no signs of moving, he stood and took a few steps her way, his eyes on hers. Those eyes willing her to understand—*I'll bend for you, but you have to meet me halfway.*

She took the few steps needed to close the distance between them, her feet moving of their own accord. It had always been like this between them. The world that conspired to keep them apart fell away when it was just the two of them. Fighting that pull was futile.

He tentatively reached for her, cupping her face in his palms at first. "My muñeca."

The possessiveness in his tone made her melt into his touch despite everything—the rumors, her family, Ximena.

This moment felt crystalline. Like looking back into a magic mirror, she could almost smell the guayacan trees they used to sit under.

He rubbed the warm pads of his thumbs against her cheek softly.

Under those guayacan trees, Andres would pull her close so she was pressed fully against him. She relished those moments when she could feel the tall length of him pressed against her. No one, nothing, coming between them.

She shook her head gently in his hands. "I don't want to talk anymore tonight, Andres."

He hummed as he took in her features as though he were memorizing them. "What would you like to do then?" he asked, his hands sliding down her back to eventually rest at the dip of her waist.

Dizzy from the warmth of his closeness and his sweet, spicy tobacco scent, she huffed, "That's a loaded question."

He reached up to slip a strand of her hair behind her ear. "Tell me."

His eyes searched hers, and she knew he was waiting for a sign, a word from her. Something, anything, but in the delicateness of the moment, she didn't know what to say.

Challenging Andres by pushing at the cracks in his discipline had been a pastime of Sofia's for a while now. His gentlemanly restraint was frustrating but powerful, and when it broke, it crashed like a tidal wave. He'd drown her, and she'd welcome it.

"Why did you come here, Andres?" she asked, her eyebrows knit.

He slipped his fingers under her chin. "For you. It's all for you, Sofia."

Her heart hammered in its cage now. Under the full weight of Andres's gaze, her cheeks warmed. "Don't say things you don't mean," she said, the words a whisper.

Sofia held his gaze, afraid to touch him, afraid to make him real under her hands the way she used to spend so many nights dreaming of. Afraid he'd vanish under her palms like he did in her dreams.

"I mean it," he said, his gaze dropping to her lips before flickering back to her eyes. "I've always meant it."

Sofia shook her head. "Andres—"

"I need you," he said, interrupting her. "I need to feel like not everything in this world is ugly." His fingertips dug into her hip now as he drew her in closer to his body. "You want this too. I can feel the way your heart is beating," he said softly, lowering his lips to her ear, his fingertips kneading the flesh of her hips now.

He pressed his forehead to hers. "I'll leave if you tell me to, but it has to be now, Sofia."

She was terrified of what he was asking. Terrified that she couldn't say no to him, even after everything. She was too afraid to say yes, but too deep in her want and too in over her head to say no. One foot over the precipice, the other on solid ground.

She chose to give in. She let herself touch him. Her hands came to rest at his sides. And this time, he was warm and solid and real under her palms.

"I want you to stay," she said, turning just so to meet his eyes, now willing him to understand that she couldn't say yes to what he was asking. Not with words. Not out loud.

"Are you sure?" he asked, his eyebrows raised.

She nodded. The heat flushing her chest was rising up her neck, making her voice thick. "I am."

He tilted his head then and leaned in close. "I want to forget everything else tonight," he whispered as he lowered his mouth to dust her earlobe with light kisses, raising goose bumps on her skin. "I only want to remember us," he said, meeting her eyes again.

This was him breaking. This was the tidal wave cresting, so she closed her eyes as his lips finally met hers again after all those years. It was as if no time had passed, even though he tasted different now, like smooth rum and smoke. But his lips were still as soft, his kisses as gentle, as explorative as before.

When she nipped at his bottom lip, needing more, he pulled her closer until she was flush against him, like they used to be under those trees.

To hold her own against the force of his embrace, she slid her hands up his back, clinging to him. And even though she found the muscles there more filled out now, he still felt like home. Her home.

She pressed up onto her tiptoes then and crushed her lips against his too hard, so their front teeth clinked. But he didn't mind if the way he moaned into her mouth was any indication.

He slid a hand up her back, into her hair. Breaking their breathless kiss, he paused, reaching up to cup her face in his palms once more. "I did miss you," he said, his eyes large, soft, vulnerable in the dim hotel room. "Don't ever think I didn't."

She reached up to run her nails through his short hair, remembering how he liked the feeling of her nails scraping lightly against his scalp.

He leaned into her touch, his eyelids fluttering closed. His impossibly long lashes resting against the tops of his cheeks.

"I never stopped," she replied.

Then he kissed her so deeply it was as if he hoped he could make up for lost time in one night.

CHAPTER 33

The funeral for Martin's wife was held on a Sunday. Flowers spilled out of the old church, down the stairs, across the aisles. The small church smelled like a spring morning, despite the dreary weather outside. The flowers were fitting. Martin's wife had been beautiful, lovely as a rose.

Sofia fussed with Diego at Maria's side. Maria shushed Diego as she held the crying baby close to her chest. Despite the toddler and infant they shared, Alberto was no help. His sight was trained on Martin in the front row, who had his head bowed, speaking quietly to his son, Andres, a comforting hand around the young boy's shoulder.

Maria's heart broke for the boy. While Martin would survive, the boy needed his mother. He was young still. Only a year and some months older than her daughter.

At the thought, Maria pulled Sofia closer.

This time she didn't fuss.

Maria leaned in as Martin pressed his lips to her cheek. She felt guilty for the hand she laid on his arm, for lingering near him a beat longer than socially necessary. *The man just lost his wife,* Maria chided herself. But her time with Martin was so scarce now she had to savor it. Drink every drop.

"How are you, Martin?" Maria asked as she shifted a sleeping Diego from one shoulder to the other. "What can I—what can we help with?" Her eyes scanned Martin's, looking for the things he couldn't say.

He reached down, his arm protectively wrapped around Andres, who stood still and serious next to his father.

"We're good," Martin said with a nod. "Managing. Her family is staying with us for now. They're helping . . ."

Maria nodded when Martin's words started to trail off.

"If there's anything—" Maria began.

"I know," he interrupted with a nod.

She looked down at Andres, who was gazing up at her with his big blue-hazel eyes.

She smiled and rubbed her thumb over the boy's cheek. "I'll always be here for you too," she said softly, her words only for Andres.

"I should get going," Martin said.

"Yes, sorry," Maria said.

He nodded once then and turned away.

Maria's hand shook as she raised it to knock on Martin's door. It was midmorning. Her kids were down for their naps under the nannies' supervision at her house, and Andres would be at preschool. She could talk to Martin. Alone.

"What are you doing here?" he asked after pulling the heavy door open.

She held up the plate. "They're Andres's favorite."

Martin reached for the plate, an eyebrow raised. "You made arepas?"

Maria shrugged. "I had some help."

"Does Alberto know you're here?"

"Probably," she replied.

Martin nodded but pulled the door open, and Maria followed him into the kitchen.

"What are you doing here?" he asked again after sliding the plate onto the kitchen table.

His home was quiet. So quiet.

Hers was filled with the laughter or the screaming of Sofia and Diego most of the time. The noise comforted her. Reminded her of what was instead of what could have been.

But here in Martin's quiet home, with Andres off at school and no Katherine, the soul was missing. And Maria couldn't help it then but to think of the life she and Martin might have had. It could have been filled with laughter too.

"I just wanted to see how you were," she said, standing straighter. "It's been a few days since the funeral," she added, narrowing her eyes, "and I worry about you."

He huffed and crossed his arms over his chest. "Nothing to worry about, Maria."

"Martin," Maria began carefully. The exhaustion was written all over his face. He blamed himself for losing Katherine. "She was sick, and you watched her die. It's okay if you're struggling with things."

He shook his head. "No, I killed her," Martin said, his voice catching.

Maria reached for his hand. "That's not true, Martin."

His jaw clenched. "This life, it isn't easy."

"She knew that," Maria said. "She knew that when she chose you."

"Maybe," Martin said, his eyes on where Maria held his hand.

Maria should have pulled her hand away, should have stopped there.

Instead, she intertwined their fingers. "It wasn't your fault."

"I could have stopped. I should have stopped. That's what she wanted. She wanted to move. She wanted to leave."

"Why didn't you?" Maria asked.

He looked up then, meeting her eyes. "You know why."

Maria tilted her head. "Martin . . ."

"Be honest with yourself, Maria. If you loved him, if you had made it work the way you promised yourself you would, then you wouldn't be here right now. You wouldn't have met up with me in the city all those summers. You wouldn't have taken my calls at night . . ."

Maria let go of his hand. "Martin, stop."

"No, this is what you came here for, isn't it?" he asked. "You needed to see me, you needed to know."

She looked at him, took in the hard line of his jaw, his flashing eyes. "I wasn't trying to hurt you . . ."

"But it did hurt. It's always hurt. And it hurt you too."

"I thought you'd moved on."

"I didn't have a choice once you married him."

"I hoped you had moved on."

He shook his head. "No, you didn't. Because you couldn't either."

"Martin, I wanted you to be happy. I always wanted that."

"She made me happy."

Maria nodded. "I know."

"She gave me Andres."

"I know."

"She still wasn't you."

Maria's breath hitched in her throat.

"I was a shit husband," he said, crossing his arms over his chest.

"I doubt it," Maria replied. "You're a good father."

He nodded, his gaze somewhere out the large kitchen window. "He deserves better too."

"He's lucky to have you," Maria tried to convince him.

"It's not too late to leave," Martin said, crossing the kitchen to reach for her, his hands around her arms. "Let's take the kids, we can go to Colombia . . ."

"He'll kill me. He'll kill us. You can't walk away anymore, Martin. I warned you about the cost . . ."

"Leave him," Martin repeated, his hands cupping Maria's face. "Let him have it."

Maria shook her head. "He'll never let me take the children. I can't leave them."

Martin swept the pad of his thumbs over her cheeks, collecting the tears there. "If this is all I can have of you, Maria . . ."

She pressed up onto her toes, kissing the words from his lips.

He returned the kiss, pressing into her lips so hard she knew they'd be sore.

And the bruise on her lower back from his kitchen table would take days to heal, and she would press against it in the shower, just to feel that familiar sting. To replay the feeling of his hands on her bare skin.

If this was all they could have, she'd hang on until her nails bled.

She felt the warm sting of shame as she watched her children run around the garden. If their father knew the promises she had whispered against Martin's skin, it would destroy her. It would destroy them.

And Alberto spent his days trying to destroy everything her father had built. Her nephews all too happy to tag along and learn how to bully, how to intimidate.

So the night they all four sat around the kitchen table and Alberto raised a hand to silence Maria, she sat up straighter.

"No," she said, her eyes locked on her husband, "this is my business; my father gave it to me. I will be a part of this; I will make decisions because you need me. You need me to get into those rooms, and you need me to sit by your side and make you look good. You need me because I can get to people you can't. You need me because they like me. They listen to me. It's you who needs me. And there's a better way to do things."

Martin scoffed, "Those men in the east and the west, do you think they care about a better way of doing things?"

"You'll let the kings be. You'll oversee things from here, and you will get a percentage, but if you get greedy, you will make enemies. Two coasts against us are terrible odds, Alberto."

She excused herself before standing to brush past her husband. He grabbed her arm, holding it tight enough to burn. His dark eyes held hers.

"I have let you continue your friendship with Martin out of respect for our marriage, for our business arrangement with him. However, if you don't stop seeing him, Maria, I will see to it you never see your children again. So it's up to you. Who do you choose?"

She slipped out of the bed once he'd fallen asleep. She padded quietly down the hall to Sofia's room.

The door was open a crack, just enough for Maria to peek in. Diego had dragged his blanket and pillow into his sister's room. Maria smiled. He did this whenever the summer storms got too loud, too powerful. He'd seek refuge in his older sister's room. And Sofia, while annoyed, never turned him down.

It was in that moment that all the hatred Maria had for her husband and for her father, for forcing this life on her, hardened into a diamond. A spark.

She laid her hand on her stomach.

She had an idea then. A way to get out from under them. A way to be with Martin for good. A way to keep her children safe.

This was all hers, and she'd burn it down before she let them take anything else from her.

CHAPTER 34

The room was still aside from the white noise of the air conditioner. The chill raised goose bumps on Andres's skin as the sweat along his spine and neck started to dry.

He traced a smooth line up and down Sofia's bare back in awe of her beauty once again and the way her dark hair fanned out on the pillows. His eyes trailed over the black inky lines of the snake tattoo crawling up her thigh and over her hip, remembering the way the skin there tasted under his tongue. But mostly he was in awe of the way she looked at him, her face half hidden by where her head rested against her forearm.

In the silence that should have been warm and sated, the *What now?* was loud. She still needed the truth. He owed her that and more.

"Do we ever have to go back?" she asked, her voice muffled by her arm.

He smiled softly. He wished with everything he was that they didn't.

"Soon," he said instead.

She frowned, closed her eyes.

Obviously the wrong answer.

"You could have told me," she said, reaching up, her palm soft against his cheek. Her thumb smoothed over the lines where his dimples hid. "About why you had to leave. What they made you do. I wouldn't have thought less of you."

Andres lay back. "You would have." And it was true. After all they promised each other, he'd become the opposite.

"I know how these things go. I'm sure you weren't given a chance to choose," Sofia said, shifting to lie on her side, her head propped up by her palm.

He looked away from her, his eyes on the ceiling. "When I turned fifteen, I was told it's who I am now. I didn't think too much about it. I went on foot to where I was told the man would be. I walked up to his car, called his name like I was taught, and when he turned around, I shot him between the eyes."

He looked at her. "Is that what you wanted to know?" he asked, crueler than he intended. He couldn't help himself. What was left between them balanced on their shared pain.

"Were you scared?" she asked.

"Were you?" he asked her, looking down at her. "The first time?"

She shrugged one shoulder, her nails paused where they were drawing circles on his chest, tracing a fading outline of a compass.

"Then you understand," he said.

"You asked me not to forget you," she said.

"I know," he replied, his fingers curling gently in the ends of her hair.

"Then what happened," she asked, "between us?"

"I came back once," Andres said, "to Mexico, a year after I left. I came to visit my father. He told me you were leaving, so I went to see you the day before you left to ask for your address in order to keep in touch. Your father turned me away at the gate. Again . . ." He glanced down at Sofia then. "I did try."

Sofia looked up at him. "I didn't know that."

"It was for the best, Sofia. I hope you see that. Besides, I figured eventually you'd find someone else. I thought I wouldn't be enough now, once you saw what the world had to offer."

"*Y tú?*" she asked. "What did you find?"

His eyes turned to the ceiling again, remembering. "You. Everywhere. I tried my damnedest to forget you. After your father turned me away, I told myself that was it. But it didn't change the fact that everywhere I went, I saw you. I went thousands of miles from Mexico, only to stand on the grounds of Casa Olivi in Le Marche, Italy, to think, *Sofia would love it here*. It was so peaceful, so quiet. You were everywhere with me, Sofia."

He slid his hand under her jaw. If his words weren't enough, he needed to show her with his touch. He needed her to know.

"I'm sure you weren't lonely," she said with a teasing smirk.

She rubbed the St. Julian pendant on his chain between her thumb and index finger. "I wish you had never left," she said quietly. "I wanted that more than anything, for you to come back. I was alone. I lost my mom, then you."

"I am sorry," he said, reaching for her hand. "I'll always be sorry, but it was dangerous for me to stay."

Sofia shifted to prop her chin on his chest, meeting his eyes. "You could have been anyone, Andres. You're smart; you could have just worked at your father's business . . ."

"Sofia, it's a nice fantasy; I had the same one when we were younger. We'd own a modest but nice house just outside of Mexico City. We'd live quiet but fulfilling lives. But that was never in the cards for either of us. Your father, your mother, they didn't protect you. Just like my father didn't protect me when my family decided that I would make a good killer."

Sofia sat up on her knees, pulling the sheet with her. Andres mourned the loss of the view of all her soft skin.

"That's it?" she asked softly.

He sat up, reaching to gently brush her hair from her eyes. "It's the game, *querida*."

He wanted to make this night last because tomorrow held no promises for them. But it was too late, the spell already broken. The reality of who they were, outside this room, was seeping back in under the doorframe, through the cracks in the walls. In their words.

"Then why are you trying, Andres? What's the point of all of this with Ximena if you think your life is predetermined?"

"This is my last chance to take what I was given and make something more of it," he said, his words metered so she'd feel the importance behind them. "I'm running out of time."

They all were.

"At least tell me why my father wanted me to stay away from you so badly. Tell me, please, what happened that night."

If he had said he was a coward before, then this was his chance for redemption.

"He didn't trust me not to hurt people he cared about."

"And why would he have thought that?" Sofia asked coolly.

"I know too much," Andres replied, brushing his thumb across her eyebrow. "I've been keeping a secret of his for a long time."

"What are you talking about?" Sofia asked, pulling away, batting at his hand. "What secret?"

Andres sighed, shifting so he sat at the edge of the bed, his eyes on Texas across the river. "I know who killed your mother, Sofia. I know because he was the first man I was paid to kill."

"Who, Andres?" she asked. "What man?"

Andres looked at Sofia. "Hector. Your mother's driver. He killed your mother because your father paid him to."

Sofia swore under her breath. Andres heard her shifting away from him.

He reached for her, cupping her face in his palms, making her look at him. He couldn't lose her now. Not yet, not until she understood. "Your father paid me to kill Hector so his secret would die with him that night. I got there too late to save her. I promise that had I known . . . Sofia, your father knew what it would do to you and your brothers if you ever found out . . ."

Sofia moved away from Andres. "Then why does everyone say you did it?"

He stilled, his stomach cold as iron. "They needed you to believe that because if you believed I was the monster, then your father wouldn't be. He wouldn't be the one keeping us apart; he wouldn't be the one who took your mother from you."

Andres reached for Sofia again, but she moved to the other end of the bed. "Stop, Andres."

He stilled, his hand dropping to his lap. "You believe them."

"I don't know what to believe," she said, her pitch rising. A tear splashed on her cheek, and she wiped at it violently. "Why?" she asked, not looking at Andres. "Why would he do that?"

She was curling in on herself, an old wound reopened. A wound he bled twice.

"Your mother was talking to the DEA."

Sofia shook her head. "They knew . . . ?" she said softly.

She'd known. Somehow Sofia had already known this about her mother.

Andres reached for her, this time pulling her close to him, even as she resisted, her hands slapping at his arms.

"Why did it have to be you?" she asked, her voice rising, shrill in the once peaceful quiet of the room.

"Your father wanted to hurt mine because my father still loved your mother. But I swear to you, Sofia, I didn't know . . ."

She scrambled off the bed to stand in front of him, shaking in her makeshift dress of the hotel bed's sheet. She raised her arm and he braced himself, knowing what was coming.

The slap stung, but the heat behind it was contained, dull, more pain than anger.

"You should have told me," she hissed through clenched teeth.

He stood, reaching for her. "This is why I didn't," he said as she tried to push him away. "I didn't want to hurt you, but you need to know the truth now because it will come down to choosing sides. And you can't count on the men in your family to protect you."

"Oh, and you will?" she asked, her voice gone high as she struggled against his embrace.

She was afraid of him now. She hadn't been before, when the rumors were just that. But now, she avoided his gaze, shrank from his touch.

He let go. Maybe she was right to be afraid.

She wrapped her arms around herself.

Andres sighed. "You need to know what they're capable of before it's too late." He paused, giving her space. "I know you have no reason to believe me . . ."

"My mother visited the notary that morning," Sofia said, her eyes on the carpet. "She was changing her will. She knew. She knew something was going to happen to her."

Andres reached a hand up tentatively to run over Sofia's hair, stopping at the back of her neck when she didn't pull away. "I am sorry," he said.

"You're an asshole," Sofia said quietly, letting the tears fall now. "You knew, all this time, and didn't tell me."

"I couldn't hurt you."

"It hurt worse to not know," she replied.

"I had to try to spare you because you had already lost your mother. I didn't want the truth to take your father from you too."

"What am I supposed to do now, Andres?" she asked, searching his face. "I can't trust my cousins, my own brother. They don't trust me, and maybe they're right not to. When does this end?"

Andres's grip on the back of her neck tightened just enough so she'd feel his emotion, the words he couldn't say. "Leave with me. For Colombia. Forget all this. We can start over."

"I can't abandon my brothers. Not like that. And you, your plans . . ."

Frustration clawed at Andres. "Maybe they don't want to be saved, Sofia. Maybe they want what it is your cousins want. This dream of yours is yours," he argued.

"They'll lose everything if I don't see this through. Your girlfriend promised me that."

Her tone had gone cold. She reminded Andres so much of Diego when she withdrew like this, when she pulled into herself.

"And then what?" Andres asked. "Even if you stay, it will always be something, Sofia."

"You sound like my brothers," she said.

He shook his head. "No, I just wonder who you are, what you want underneath these grandiose ideas. Maybe none of us can save our families, have you thought about that?"

"I can't just walk away."

"You could," he countered. "Your mother had a dangerous loyalty to a country that wasn't even hers. It was guilt that drove her, Sofia. That's not your burden to bear."

"It's not?" she asked, her eyebrows raised. "How have I been any better? How have I helped?"

"Maybe you can't, Sofia."

She shook her head. "No. I said it before. Sometimes we don't have choices, but sometimes doing the right thing is the only choice."

He leaned down to meet her gaze. "You can't atone for decades of destruction, no matter how much you want to believe it. Sofia, there are gorgeous farm homes with stables on the outskirts of Medellin that I could show you. You can pick which one you want. If you still ride, we could get you a Paso Fino or two."

"Don't," she said, maneuvering out of his grasp to stand and reach for her discarded robe.

"Why not?" he asked, angry now. Angry at her for denying the truth that she'd pressed so hard for. The truth that he would still drop it all, forget it all, for her.

"Tell me from the moment we saw each other at your father's *pinche* party that you haven't thought about it too," he said.

"Of course!" she exclaimed. "I wanted this before you left. I wanted this in my dreams in London. I always wanted it to be you, Andres. But it's not. And it won't be."

"So what was this then?" he asked, motioning between them. Anger made his hands shake. Anger at himself for letting himself have this moment that he knew would end just like this.

"You tell me," she said. "I assumed just business."

He stood then, his eyes still on her. "I know you know the answer to that, Sofia."

"I get it now," Sofia began in that rare, cruel tone of hers. "That's why you like her, isn't it?" Sofia asked. "Ximena doesn't remind you of who you really are. A killer."

His hands paused for a second as he pulled his pants on. He repeated the motion with his shirt, avoiding Sofia's gaze.

She was angry with him. She wanted to say hurtful things that slashed like the knife he had just put in her chest.

He understood.

Andres nodded and buttoned his shirt. "I just hope that those men would do the same for you," he said before pulling the door open and letting it click shut behind him.

CHAPTER 35

Diego leaned against the wall of the old church, a crumbling building just outside a small town on the De Lunas' truck route to the Baja.

The headlights of the running semis outside lit up the inside of the small space, illuminating the young women and girls as they lined up along the back wall.

"So you want to know how it's done?" Xavier had asked, and Diego had agreed.

"There are a few ways to go about it," Xavier stated, his gold teeth shining in the headlights. "You can say you're a coyote, taking a trip up north. Or that you're a recruiter for work in the States. That works better for boys. If we get a request for soldiers, that's what you'll say—you're recruiting for work."

The more Xavier shared with Diego, the deeper he pulled him in. It's why Xavier had gifted Diego with El Brillo when he turned thirteen. The twin to Sofia's nine-millimeter Beretta, gold where hers was silver, El Brillo had been a reward. A reward for acting as stakeout for Xavier. A reward for learning how to point and shoot and not ask questions. A reward for keeping his mouth shut. But Xavier's rewards came with strings.

"Girls are harder," Xavier continued as they headed into the church. "Better to get females to recruit them. Makes things easier."

Diego's attention turned to the quiet shuffling he heard toward the back of the room. He scanned the line, where about fifteen girls huddled together, so quiet it was like they were holding their breath.

"Do they know where they're going?" he asked.

"Of course."

"Do they know why?" Diego asked.

Xavier turned to Diego. "Does that matter?"

The girls had turned now to follow Joaquin outside, toward the semis.

"I guess not," Diego replied, looking back at Xavier.

Xavier's eyes were on him, observing. "Y El Príncipe?" he asked.

"He won't stop the trucks. But I'm sure Daniel will. He seems pissed, if our burned-out semi is anything to go by."

"I'm not concerned with Daniel. He got his show; he got your sister to jump for him. But it won't last. Your sister can't handle someone like Daniel for long. And it doesn't matter; the Gulf will be ours soon, Diego."

"We should wait," Diego said. "Let this election play out. I think we need Cruz in office and on our side, if we want to keep making money."

"You've been listening to Sofia too much," Xavier replied with a bite to his words. "Can't trust any politician, Diego. Including that sister of yours."

"I'd say the safer bet is the politician willing to sit down in meetings with us," Diego argued. "Besides, Cruz promised less funding toward this pinche war and more funding toward social services. The people are eating it up."

"And you believe that?" Xavier asked, his eyes on the trucks outside, watching as they closed up.

"Of course not. But the people do, if the polls are anything to go by."

Xavier glanced back at Diego. "Look at you, watching the news."

His eyes had gone black, lifeless. He was daring Diego to keep pushing.

"I'm not as uncultured as you think I am," Diego replied with a snappy smile. It was meant to be a jovial quip, but his eyes stayed on Xavier's, neither backing down.

"Cultured," Xavier repeated. "You're just buying into the bullshit, the make-believe, just like your mother did."

"What about my mother?" Diego asked, sharp this time, quick.

Xavier stood straighter then, encroaching on Diego's personal space. "Your mother wasn't cut out for this, little cousin. Why else do you think she ended up the way she did?"

Diego saw it, the way Xavier took joy in the anger and rage that passed over Diego's features.

"She was your aunt," Diego said through his teeth. "How can you talk about her the way you do?"

Xavier sucked at his gold teeth. "I've been trying to tell you, primo, but you just don't want to hear it. Your mother was a rat. She wasn't a martyr, she wasn't Jesús Malverde, she wasn't Mother Teresa. She was more than willing to hand us over for her freedom so she could run off with another man. With Martin. That's not how you treat family. She's not family. She got what she deserved, I promise you that."

Diego held his cousin's stare, and those eyes that looked nothing like Diego's mother's stared back. Diego wondered then how far Xavier would go to protect what he thought was his.

"And how is it you're so sure of it all? Of what happened to her?" Diego asked, his brows creasing.

Xavier sniffed. "Nothing happens on that ranch that I don't know about, primo."

"You mean, that you don't approve?" Diego asked.

Xavier winked and patted Diego on the back. "I know hearing the truth hurts, but it's over now, right? It was handled. Why are we talking about it? Look, we're here now, because she's not, and that's all that matters. So what is it you suggest we do, Diego, about Daniel?"

Diego's blood had frozen in his veins. The easy way Xavier

talked about Diego's mother's death made him queasy. Xavier knew what happened to Diego's mother. But it was more than that. Maybe he'd had a hand in it.

Diego cleared his throat, glanced outside. "We can't send the girls through the Gulf for now. Let Daniel cool off first. Once Cruz gets elected, then we make our move."

Xavier ran the tip of his tongue over his gold teeth. "Can't stop now, primo; there's bills to pay." He smiled then, a poisonous grin. "You know what, though? I'm proud of you. And once your sister is out of the picture, I promise you, that throne will be yours."

Diego nodded, knowing he'd pushed far enough for the day. Trying to argue his sister's case right now would not go over well. He also knew that throne would never be his. Not as long as Xavier was around.

Xavier patted him on the back. "Go home. Get some rest. You look like you're dragging."

At the mention of rest, Diego felt sleepiness tugging at him. He'd been clean for a few days now, but his body was playing catch-up after surviving on adrenaline, coca, and caffeine for so long.

He nodded. "Yeah, probably a good idea."

"Hey!" Xavier called after him, once Diego started his car. "*Ten cuidado.*"

"*Siempre.*"

The townhome was dark when Diego got in. It was late, almost early morning, the sky starting to lighten to the east. He hung his keys in their spot, toed off his boots, and slipped out onto the patio where Yolotli sat.

"What are you doing up so early?" Diego asked as he dropped into the seat next to him.

Yolotli didn't move, didn't blink, his gaze on the sunrise. "Do you remember when I told you about my mother, about how she came to Mexico?"

Diego nodded, sinking lower into his seat, his eyes on Yolotli. "Of course."

"I told you about how we had to leave everything, everyone, in Guatemala to escape the war among our own people, I told you that, right? How we came to this country with nothing?"

Diego clocked the set of Yolotli's jaw. Diego remembered that and more. He remembered how Yolotli had come to them with nothing, his mother's blood on his cheek.

"When were you going to tell me," Yolotli said, his eyes reflecting the fire of the sunrise now, "about the girls?"

"Yolotli . . ." Diego began.

Sofia must have told Yolotli after Daniel probably laid it all out to her. Everything about the trucks, the girls.

"My mother trusted someone to help get her across the Mexican border," Yolotli said. "That man took the last of the money she had. Imagine, Diego, she was alone, with me only a year old, left at the border, robbed, penniless. Can you imagine?"

Diego could lie and say he could. But he couldn't, even if he wanted to. Diego had never known what it felt like not to have money. Not to have help.

"It's not about the girls . . ." he began.

"Bullshit," Yolotli replied, venom in his voice now, his eyes blazing when he met Diego's gaze. "You can try to lie to yourself all you want, but I can't justify it, Diego. There's no money, no power, nothing in the world worth selling the last bit of your soul for. You won't come back from this. That demon you talk about will consume you. Do you understand?"

Diego looked at the rings on his hand, unable to meet Yolotli's eyes. "It's for us, Yolotli . . ."

"I didn't ask for this!" Yolotli exclaimed, jumping to his feet. "This home, this life was enough for me; you were enough for me. Even if we had nothing, it would be enough because all I ever wanted was you."

"You don't believe in me," Diego said quietly. "You don't believe that I can give us more."

"I have always believed in you, but I do not believe in this, Diego. You're better than this. The man I love would never . . ." His voice trailed off, his throat thick with emotion.

"If I don't do this, do you know what will happen to me?" Diego asked, looking up at Yolotli.

Yolotli shook his head. "It's not right."

"Whose side are you on, Yolotli?" Diego asked, standing up. "Why can't you trust me?"

"Because I can't! I can't trust you to do what's right anymore."

"And you think my sister can?"

"I think Sofia is right about one thing for sure. It's time for your cousins to go, and if that's what it takes to save you, Diego, I'll do it if she can't."

The slam of the patio door left Diego alone in silence.

He couldn't have been so wrong about this, could he? Sofia, she was already planning on chopping up their piece of the cocaine distribution, removing them as the broker, the middleman who charged a fee. And now she'd laid herself at Daniel's feet, promising who knows what for a cease-fire for some politician who had her hands in all their pockets. Working with the cousins to expand was the only promise of consistent cash flow.

But there was one thing that Yolotli, the person who knew Diego best, was right about: to do this, to do what the cousins wanted, would leave an indelible mark on his soul. And while Diego didn't fear death, he feared an eternity in the afterlife without Yolotli.

Diego flipped his cell phone over in his palms once, twice, before shooting off a quick text to his sister.

CHAPTER 36

According to the K'iche' people, Xibalba was the underground court where the Mayan lords of death reigned over their servants and those unlucky enough to find themselves visiting the realm. Xibalba was a place where death flourished, and according to legend, in Xibalba a river flowed, filled with scorpions.

Sofia thought of how they must have stung one another, in confusion, in frustration. Too many too close.

Their mother's marble grave glowed supernaturally bright under the night's thin crescent moon. Sofia wrapped her arms tighter around herself while she waited in the darkness for Diego. He'd sent her a text asking to meet in the dead of night in the cemetery, told her she'd know where.

The scorpion in Sofia's life had the same flaw. Diego, hard as he was, felt too much too deeply. Too much confusion, too much frustration. All of it. He'd drink it down, distill it until he produced venom. He'd been taught to drown that empathetic boy. He learned to sting first, ask for forgiveness later.

Despite it, he'd been the one keeping the family afloat, the bridge between the old and the new ways, so who was Sofia to demand anything from him? She'd confused wanting him to be *better* with her need for him to be *safe*. Turned her own frustrated sting on him because she thought he could take it. Out of all of them, he could take it.

Diego appeared out of the shadows, as quiet and still as the night around them.

"Wasn't sure you'd show," he said as he reached up to adjust the hood of his leather jacket.

"For you? Of course I'd show," she replied, taking a step away from their mother's gravesite. "We have some things to talk about."

Diego kept his head down, stayed out of patches of light spilling onto the pathway, anxious tension radiating from him.

"We do," he agreed. "When I was in Tijuana, I had some time to think. I thought about how you are protected, how you've always been protected. No matter how alone you might look. That El Príncipe will work with you, whatever you decide, because of me, because I did my job. Before, I resented that. That the family handed this all to you, even though it was built off my sweat, my blood."

There was a waver in his voice, and Sofia wrapped her arms tighter around herself to keep from embracing him, pulling him close like she would when they were younger and he'd just woken from a nightmare. The only soft touch left in their home.

"But now, I'm proud," he said, lifting his gaze to meet hers, "because you've been safe, Nando's been safe, and that means I've done my job."

"I know we've asked too much . . ." Sofia began.

Diego held a finger up. "Everything I've ever done in my life was for this family," he said through clenched teeth. "For you, for Xavier, for Nando, Joaquin, Pops. But now I'm done."

He swallowed, and for the first time Sofia saw the light glinting off the tears that had run down the hollows of his cheeks. "We are all family, and as much as we might not like it, they're all we have left of Mom," Diego said. "Of who she was."

Sofia did reach out then, tightening a hand around her brother's forearm.

"But she wouldn't want this," he said finally, sniffing, raising his head once more. "And I won't lose anyone else. Not to them, not because of them."

"Diego . . ." Sofia began, trailing off because she knew that tone. He knew something; something had changed.

The moment Sofia had touched down back in CDMX she'd gone to Yolotli and told him the truth about what it was Diego was doing with the cousins all night. About what their plans to expand really meant. About all the girls who were already lost.

She watched the color drain from his face. Watched as he shook his head. Watched as something shattered deep in him.

He must have said something to Diego. Yolotli was the only person in the world Diego feared.

"I had to tell him," Sofia said softly.

Diego shrugged. "I know. And I'm starting to think that maybe you've been right all along about Andres. Maybe it wasn't him."

Sofia bit her tongue so as not to speak without thinking. She believed Andres, she believed what he'd told her in Matamoros, but she wasn't ready to try to convince her brothers. Not yet. So the cousins must have said something to Diego. Let something slip.

"It's too late now, though. Doesn't matter," Diego said, shaking his head as if shaking away tendrils of other words he wanted to say. "I'll give you the location of the pickups. And I'll let you make that *puta* politician look good," he continued. "But Sofia, you ripped this all apart to clean it, to gut it, so it's you who has to sew it back together. For all of us."

Sofia sighed. "Thank you, Diego . . ."

"I'm not doing this for you," he replied, handing her a slip of paper. "You better hope whatever it is you're going to do with this information works. Because I don't need to tell you what will happen if it doesn't."

The next morning, Sofia watched people passing as she waited for Lalo at Alameda Park where she sat under the monument erected for former president Benito Juárez. She thought of the scorpions again. Wondered if that's all they were. Her, her brothers, Andres, Ximena, Daniel, El Príncipe. Lalo. All scorpions, scrambling over and stinging one another.

Her time in Matamoros with Daniel had given her a clarity she'd been chasing. Even reinforced the idea that what she was doing was right. And something had spooked Diego. She'd seen it in his eyes the night before. Whatever it was had been serious enough to get him to flip on their cousins.

"Have a nice trip?" Lalo asked as he sidled up next to Sofia, his eyes shielded by dark sunglasses in the early morning sun.

"Nice" wasn't the right word for it. But she'd gotten what she wanted, what she needed. The truth about her cousins' plans and the truth about her mother.

"Andres told me," she began, looking up at Lalo, "about what happened to my mother that night."

Andres had said that it was his fault her mother died, that he should have been there that night. He had just left out the part that he was there, just too late to stop Hector from pulling the trigger.

"Do you believe him?" Lalo asked.

What did he have to gain by placing himself so close to the murder? She'd known Hector died that night too. They'd said he was probably trying to protect her mother. Now Sofia knew that wasn't true. What was probably true was that Hector turned on Maria. What is it they say about the simplest explanation?

Sofia didn't blame Hector. He probably needed the extra money. Sofia couldn't fault him for that.

As for Andres, he knew that telling her, after all this time, would do nothing but hurt her and push him away. He had no reason to keep her father's secrets now that the man was gone.

"I do," she replied.

"I know that was a hard conversation. I know how much he means to you."

"And why do you know that?" Sofia asked. "Why do you know

so much about us? Seems like you could have locked us up and thrown away the key a long time ago."

She was hurt by the lies, hurt by the truth kept from her. She needed somewhere to put that thorny pain. And Lalo was here. Here talking about what he knew about her, how he knew this and that.

"I already told you. I'm not interested in putting you De Lunas in jail, although I will, if it comes to that."

"What do you really want from Ximena?" Sofia asked. "What is it you think I can get you?"

This gray line with Lalo worried Sofia. He was too close—to her, to her brothers. To Andres, despite what she felt about him now. Sofia had been the one to bring Lalo in. She'd been too trusting. It had been too easy for him.

"Why did he say he did it?" Lalo asked, ignoring her question.

"He said my father green-lit my mother."

"Sofia, I know it's not what you want to believe, but it is true. Your mother was working with us, I told you that. She was desperate to save her children because she'd seen enough to know how it all would end otherwise."

"And what was she giving to be in the good graces of the DEA? That they'd go out of their way to help her?"

"She was willing to give up that big house, all that jewelry, the cars, to take on some shitty witness protection life to keep you and your brothers away from them. To keep you safe."

"And you?" Sofia asked, resisting the urge to push at his broad shoulders. "You sent me right back."

"And you marched right on in, didn't you?" Lalo asked, a bite to his words. "Doing things your mother's way didn't work out for her. You're doing what you have to. Try not to be so hard on yourself."

Sofia paused.

Lalo didn't mention exactly who her mother had flipped on because she never promised the DEA her nephews. She was never planning on it.

"She wasn't going to give them up, was she? Her nephews, my cousins?" Sofia asked.

Lalo's features contorted, and disgust passed quickly like a wisp of a summer cloud.

"You've been trying to convince me this whole time that she was going to flip, but she wasn't, was she?"

"She gave us everything we needed on your father, Sofia. But we always knew he was just a pawn. Your grandfather, your mother, your cousins have always been the ones running the show. Now Xavier and Joaquin are all that's left. You're doing the right thing, Sofia. Your mother was trying to play both sides. Didn't work out great for her."

"I hope you're right, Lalo. But I have a feeling you won't stop there."

"Hoping to recoup is what ruins the gambler," Lalo replied.

Sofia inhaled deeply, then let the breath out through her nose slowly before speaking. "I know where Xavier and Joaquin are operating. I gave the information to Emiliano. Once his cops roll in, Ximena will get to look like a hero."

Lalo smiled. "I wasn't sure you had it in you. Maybe you're braver than I thought, braver than your mother."

Sofia shook her head, once, sharp. "No. She was trying to do the right thing."

She thought of her father: *The weeds will grow tall,* he'd warned.

"There's no way this story ends with all of us De Lunas in one piece if Joaquin and Xavier find out what I've done."

"You knew that."

"I've always known that. But I had to do something."

"So, will you tell your brothers about what Andres told you about their father?" Lalo asked. "They deserve to know."

"Eventually," Sofia replied, reaching up to adjust Lalo's clerical collar. "Check the news tonight, see if my information was good. See how I keep my promises," she said before walking away.

Later that night, Sofia stood in the *sala* watching as breaking news flashed across the screen. She watched as girls were pulled from an old, decrepit church. She watched as Emiliano took all the credit. Watched as Ximena smiled alongside him.

Waited to see her cousins marched out in cuffs. Waited and waited. Until her phone vibrated urgently.

CHAPTER 37

When Xavier first came on his own to visit Maria, she hardly recognized the boy he used to be. The wild, toothy smile was gone, replaced by a mouthful of gold. All that metal came accompanied by a serious demeanor, one surpassing his age.

He sat with Alberto and Maria at dinner and discussed the business. Alberto was all too willing to share their family's proprietary information.

Her father and her brother, Santiago, both wanted this. Wanted Xavier and Joaquin to be a part of this business. Wanted them to have something for themselves, wanted them safe from Argentina. So Maria gave Alberto and Xavier their space. Let Alberto show off and let Xavier absorb all that his grandfather had built.

Nando, her youngest, was growing quickly, but still young enough that he liked to spend time with her. So she bided her time sitting with him in her garden, caressing his loose curls while he read through his assigned books. Eavesdropping when her husband's and nephew's voices grew too loud.

Despite honoring her father's wishes for her nephew, she found it unnerving how easily Xavier was able to influence Diego, her oldest boy quickly looking up to his older cousin.

Sofia, barely a teen now, was skittish, kept her distance as best she could. Andres took up her time most days anyway, and Maria was happy to let him. She wanted that happiness for her daughter. Wanted her to have some light before the darkness set in.

Xavier was ambitious. He was gunning for Maria's spot in the hierarchy, that was obvious. He argued against her long-standing belief that endearing themselves to the community would shelter them in the end.

Xavier had called that notion antiquated. "You've given them jobs, money, protection. What else do they need from you?" he asked her.

Maria glanced at Alberto who averted his eyes, sipped his tequila.

"You know what happens to those who stand in the way of progress, don't you, Tía Maria?" Xavier continued.

"Tell me, Xavi, what happens to them?" Maria asked.

Xavier shrugged. "The future will decide," he replied cryptically.

"I'm worried about him," Maria told Alberto later that night as they undressed for bed.

He shrugged off her concern. "He's a teenager."

"He saw his father killed," Maria countered.

"Don't coddle him," Alberto replied.

And while Alberto might not love her, Maria loved her family, her brother, and her nephew fiercely, so she was determined to figure out how to change this path she feared her *sobrino* was headed down. The darkness in his eyes was like a limitless pit. Never-ending. She had to try to bring him back to himself before it was too late.

"You can talk to me, you know," Maria said as she set a plate of *medialunas* in front of Xavier early one morning.

They were alone; Alberto wasn't up yet, and the kids were at school, so Maria seized the opportunity to speak to her nephew without anyone else around for him to try to impress. She wanted to speak to the real Xavier, the one she remembered.

"I am so sorry about your father," she said as she took the seat next to Xavier.

Xavier tore into one of the breads. "Are you?"

"Of course, Xavi. You lost your father. I lost my brother; that would be like you losing yours."

Xavier looked up at her, his eyes black. "You lost someone you've barely seen in the past ten years. I lost all I had left. No offense, Tía, but there's a difference."

"Is that why you think you need to be a man now?" she asked. "You're trying to convince Alberto that you're ready to be a man, is that it?"

"I am a man," Xavier replied, his tone dark, sharp.

"You'll have what's yours, Xavier, you and Joaquin, once he joins us, but there's time. Let yourself be young first."

Xavier chewed and swallowed, his eyes never leaving Maria's. "My mother is dead, Tía; I don't need another one."

Maria clenched her jaw.

He was young; he was hurt. She'd need to have patience, but she owed it to her brother to see to it that Xavier grew up differently than they had. He wouldn't have wanted his son to have to watch his back, like he had. Or be out in the city all night like Alberto. They didn't build all they'd built just to run from one war to another.

"This life looks nice from the outside, *sobrino*, but it's just as ugly underneath as what you left behind."

"There's a difference here; we're in charge."

"That doesn't mean you won't get shot down in the street one day if you're not careful."

"My father was careful."

"I didn't mean it like that."

"Diego and Sofia, they aren't ready for what your life will show them, are they?" Xavier asked.

"They'll learn. When it's time."

Xavier nodded, pushed his chair back as he stood. "I'd say it's time. The name of your family, De Luna, doesn't strike the fear it should. This business should have always been ours. It was built with our blood. You were a Torres once. I'll remind you of who we were. Excuse me, Tía."

She watched Xavier walk away, his words sinking her heart like it was iron.

"This isn't working," Maria said to Alberto when he finally returned home that night.

He'd taken Xavier and Diego out with him, claiming it was an easy work night, they'd be safe. But he was taking pieces of Maria's heart she wasn't ready to let go of yet every time they left.

Alberto downed the tequila in his glass, reaching up to loosen his tie. "What exactly is it you're upset about now?" he asked.

"They're too young, Alberto . . ."

"They are damn near men, Maria."

"They are teenagers. Teenagers who we, you and I, promised to give better lives."

"I never promised that," Alberto replied. "You promised them that. I promised that I would provide, and that's what I've done, that's what I'm doing. So how is it you're so unhappy? Others are happy with so little, and you, you have a kingdom and more surrounding your castle."

"All of this is not mine; it's not yours. It was my father's castle, that his money built and you took over as your own. None of this was ever ours."

Alberto scoffed. "You don't want this; you never wanted this. You like your easy life of fancy brunches, drinks with politicians who don't take you seriously. You've never had to actually work, Maria. You have all the free time in the world to meet with Martin in the city; don't you like it that way?"

Maria's nostrils flared at the mention of Martin.

They had tried to be discreet, at first. But Maria's disdain for Alberto, and his for her, had made her careless of late. She'd heard the talk. People had seen her and Martin together. But she'd shrug it off; their meetings were easy enough to explain away. He had introduced her to the politicians she'd have drinks with. He was her connection to a legitimate life. The life she yearned for, the life Alberto would not let her have. Plus, he was still in business with her husband.

"This isn't about him," Maria replied.

"Then tell me what it is you want me to do," Alberto said, stepping closer to Maria, too close.

She looked away to avoid his gaze as he glowered down at her.

"Keep it up, *mi juguete*. You think I don't know what you and Martin talk about?" he said, curling his fingers under Maria's chin to tilt her head up so she met his eyes. "You think I don't know what it is he wants from you? What you want from him? What it is he promised you? You think he'll whisk you away to Colombia, away from me, away from your children? Give you a different life, the life you thought you wanted?"

Maria ground her teeth but held Alberto's glare.

His fingers tightened on her chin, enough to hurt. "You can try. I give you my blessing. Leave with him. But I will see to it you never see our children again."

Maria pulled away from Alberto. "I will die before I let you do that. I'm not leaving. I'm not getting chased off my property."

"Good, glad to hear it," Alberto replied, moving away from her. "Your nephew has some ideas about the future of *our* business."

"I'm sure he does," Maria replied, "but there's a reason we operate the way we do. Staying under the radar—"

"Is how you get buried," Alberto interrupted. "It's been decided. We will be sole distributor. Xavier agreed it's the best path. For all of us. We're moving forward with this, Maria."

Maria shook her head. "Your ego, his ego will get us all killed."

"Perhaps, but that's why we need Diego to know how to run this business. It will be his someday."

Usually a thrill ran up Maria's spine while she waited for Martin at their usual weekday lunch spot in the city. But not today. Despite the shining sun, the singing birds, the familiar, predictable sounds of traffic, of the big city, fear was unfurling itself low in Maria's gut.

Alberto spoke like a man who'd already made his plans, made up his mind. And the more Maria listened, the less it sounded like she was a part of those plans.

So she was glad she'd made plans of her own.

The DEA had been sniffing around Mexico for a while now since the grisly murder of one of their own a few years back. Maria knew they were aware of her family. She knew they had little photos of them taped up to some corkboard somewhere. That they played mental gymnastics to connect them together like puzzle pieces. She knew this because one of them had come to her.

He'd sidled up next to her as she grocery shopped. While she was alone.

This *agente* told her it wasn't safe to be that accessible. She had asked why. He had mentioned the corkboard. But his warnings had come with a deal. One Maria wasn't sure she could turn down. Not after the way Alberto held her children over her like a noose.

She'd come close to making her choice, but she wanted—needed—Martin to hear her. To understand. She had to see if maybe his offer still stood. They were only a plane flight away from Colombia. And when he offered before to take her away from all of this, he had urged her to bring her children. She'd never leave them anyway. Alberto had it wrong.

Despite the cold heaviness of dread sitting in her stomach, her heart still skipped a beat as Martin strode up to their table, one that sat on the street because she liked to feel the sunshine on her skin.

Martin, dressed all in black with clean, sharp lines, leaned down, his hand on the back of her chair. She inhaled deeply. The familiar scent of his cologne, woodsy and warm, the same after all these years, made chills run down her spine.

He pressed a quick kiss to her cheek before settling into the seat across from her. "Heard your nephew is in town again," he said.

"He's staying this time," Maria replied.

"I know."

"Alberto mentioned something about being the head of distribution, that all the buyers will have to come to him. Is that true?" Maria asked.

Martin sighed and leaned back in his seat, stretching his long legs out beneath the table, bracketing hers. It was a subtle gesture, but Maria realized it was an intimate one. They had years of this, whatever this was, between them now. Maria had been fooling herself that no one else saw it.

"It makes sense. There's no efficiency in piecemealing deliveries all over the country. I'll fulfill the orders; your family will distribute."

"Yes, until someone decides they don't want to pay the extra tax that comes with having Alberto as a middleman. Until someone decides it's cheaper to go straight to you."

"I get my money either way, Maria."

"And what about my family?" she asked, glaring at him behind her dark sunglasses. "I'm worried, Martin. All the time. I worry for my children. Their father is gone all night, just like mine was. What kind of life is that? They deserve better."

"I'm sorry, Maria, I can't tell you what you need to do for your family. But I have to do this. My money is tied up here. I've invested here, in this city. I need this."

"I warned you about that," Maria began. "About owing Alberto, about being *owned* by Alberto."

Martin shook his head, frustration making the vein in his temple pulse like it used to when she wouldn't listen to him all those years ago in the corral.

"I'm talking to someone at the DEA," she said.

"Are you insane?" he hissed, leaning closer.

"They have taken everything from me—Alberto, my father. They've won. They broke me; this life that I have left is cursed. I won't put my children through the same thing."

"What exactly are you going to do, Maria?" Martin asked, his tone low.

"I have connections now, people who believe in what I believe in. Which is ending this."

Martin shook his head, sliding his chair closer to Maria's so he could lower his voice. "It's too big, Maria; it's bigger than us, bigger than those politicians and connections. There are cartels under Alberto. You remove him, someone else will just take his place, and along the way someone from one of those cartels will figure out it will be easier to just kill you and remove the issue all together. Especially if anyone finds out you're talking to the DEA. We aren't snitches, Maria."

"I don't care what happens to me, Martin. I don't care what they call me. And maybe you're right; you're probably right. But I have to try. For my children's sake."

He shook his head. "This is not the way."

Maria narrowed her eyes. "I thought you understood. Or is it because this affects your money now too?"

"I don't care about the money, Maria . . ."

"That's not entirely true, is it?" she asked, leaning away from him. "You and my husband seem to have more and more in common each day."

Martin's temple pulsed.

"Why can't you be honest with me?" Maria continued. "Be honest with yourself. You still need Alberto and those other cartels because, without them, you can't afford to pay the politicians who approve your work in the city."

"It's just for now; it's just until—"

"When?" Maria interrupted. "Until you find another buyer? You told me, to my face, years ago that you were only doing this to create something legitimate . . ."

"And I have."

"Not when you have to pump dirty money into it."

"That's how things work in this city . . ."

"Don't patronize me, not you, Martin."

He pressed his palms together, and his nostrils flared. "I'm not, I'm not," he said as he reached for her, cupping her face between his hands, prying eyes be damned. "I am trying to protect you. Your children need their mother."

She shook her head. "I won't live like this anymore. It's not a life. I should have left with you when I had the chance."

He passed a thumb over her cheek where a tear had fallen. She cleared her throat then. It was too late for tears.

She reached up to gently pull his hands from her face. "I'm leaving it all to Sofia. It's the last chance I can give this family at redemption. Promise me you'll look after them. Just in case."

Martin's eyes were soft now, filled with understanding. "He will never let that happen."

"You'll find a way."

She pressed her palm against his cheek, the neatly trimmed stubble of his beard soft against her skin. "I love you, Martin. I have always loved you. I never stopped. Not ever."

"I know," he replied.

"I wish it could have been different . . ."

Martin reached for her hand and squeezed it tight. "Me too."

With a nod she stood and headed back up the sidewalk, and it took every ounce of self-control she had not to look back.

"Does he still have curly hair?"

Maria paused, turned on her heel.

"The youngest one," Martin continued when she met his gaze. "I haven't seen him in a while."

She nodded, then swallowed, clearing her throat. "Yeah, he pushes it off his forehead all the time but won't let us cut it."

Martin gave her a half smile. "Don't."

CHAPTER 38

Sofia sat alone outside with a book during school lunch most days. Until one day, the skinny boy with eyes like the winter Atlantic she'd seen pictures of asked to sit with her.

Andres Herrera had always been the boy from down the street to Sofia. The son of her parents' friends. Andres was older, but not by much, so the two of them circled one another in school as the years passed.

Until one day, when the sun was riding low in the sky with the approaching fall, and Andres made the choice for both of them.

They didn't say much that first lunch, just sat together and ate in silence with their books in their laps.

But when Andres stood to leave, Sofia spoke up. "Will I see you tomorrow?"

"If you'd like," had been his response.

Something sparkled inside Sofia that day and warmed when she answered a little breathlessly, "Yes."

The first time they kissed, he had been laughing at something—she couldn't even remember what now, but she remembered his dimples, his eyelashes, the way his smile made her forget everything else. And she rose on her tiptoes to press her lips against his quick as a hummingbird. The smile he gave her afterward was soft, sweet.

The first time they made love under the tree where they had shared everything else had been rushed and awkward because they were young and had no idea what they were doing aside from just needing to be closer. Both so filled with feelings they didn't know how to put into words. Sofia held that particular memory locked away deep because that afternoon he had been hers. All hers. Only hers.

Now Andres stood behind his desk as night fell on Mexico City. He looked up at Sofia for only a second as the door closed behind her.

She watched him, noted the way he wouldn't meet her gaze. She also noted the faint wrinkles at the corners of his eyes, the deep lines where his dimples hid, and she wondered where all their time had gone.

She took a deep breath, exhaling to get his attention. "You wanted to see me," she said, crossing her arms under her chest.

He rapped his knuckles against his desk. "Yes. Well actually, Ximena wanted me to talk to you."

"About what?" Sofia asked sharply.

About Matamoros? About how we shared a bed? she wanted to ask. She wanted to claw at him, rip away this persona he had put on once again, wearing it like an ill-fitting suit.

"I gave her what she needed, a nice Election Day buzzer-beater," Sofia continued.

"Not quite," Andres replied, his eyes on Sofia now.

"What do you mean, not quite?" Sofia asked, frowning. "I saw her on TV, with that cop of hers. So proud of the work they'd done. I did notice she didn't thank me in that speech of hers, but that's okay. I won't take it personally."

"Where were your cousins, Sofia?" Andres asked, leveling her with a gaze. "I thought they'd be part of that raid."

Sofia narrowed her eyes. "What are you asking, Andres?"

"Come on, Sofia, how does it look?"

"You tell me."

Andres sighed. "Ximena is concerned that your cousins weren't brought into custody."

"She thinks I tipped them off?"

Andres shrugged.

"Why would I do that?"

Andres sucked air through his teeth. "Because they're your family. Isn't that what you kept telling me? And family protects family."

"You know how I feel about them, Andres."

"Ximena thinks you're playing multiple sides here."

"She would know all about that, wouldn't she?"

"Where are they?" Andres asked.

"I don't know, but I have a feeling I'll see them soon enough. I'm sure by now they know it was me who gave your girlfriend's attack dog the information. Information I risked my ass for. So I'm sure they'll want to have a chat about it."

"You know what?" Andres said, his eyes burning now, the red swirls overtaking the dark blue and green. "I actually don't give a shit about your cousins. They'll get what's coming to them by someone at some point. You know what I do give a shit about? I couldn't help but notice the DEA showed up to your stunt, and I was *un poquito* confused as to how they knew where to be."

Sofia stilled. Lalo must have found out where she sent Emiliano. He probably sent some of his people to show up.

Sofia shrugged. "People hear things."

"Oh, I know," Andres replied as he opened the folder sitting on the top of his desk, "especially when they're told."

Sofia's gaze flickered down to the glossy black-and-white photos that had been hidden away in the folder.

They were of her and Lalo, together at the park.

Andres looked down at the pictures, using his fingertips to spread them out. "Ximena had these taken. I'm sure you can understand with the election why she'd want to keep track of her investment. I didn't believe her at first. Until she handed me these.

She wanted me to be sure she wasn't lying. Making it up. Because at first, she was right, I didn't believe it. Not you."

Sofia felt Andres's gaze on her, hot on her face.

"You and your priest, hmm?" Andres hissed, leaning over his desk. "He's DEA."

When Sofia said nothing, Andres cursed. "How could you?"

"You and Ximena don't know shit just from some pictures," Sofia replied.

"Don't lie to me," Andres said, raising his voice, the heat in his gaze simmering in his tone now.

And Sofia, for all her fight, knew better than to argue with Andres. Because he was right. There was a strict code detailing what should be done with snitches. And it had been a part of Andres's life to handle those with big mouths.

She swallowed, her eyes still on the photos. There was no lie she could tell Andres that he would buy. He knew her too well, and he'd done this job for too long.

"What does he want?" Andres asked.

"Your girlfriend," Sofia replied quietly.

"Why?"

"I assume for the same reason we do, control of the routes, for his country."

"What did he offer you?"

"My family's freedom," Sofia replied, meeting Andres's eyes, daring him to challenge that.

Andres looked away, cursing under his breath. "How could you be so trusting?"

"Me?" Sofia asked, her tone pitching. "It's all the same, isn't it? You, me, Ximena, the priest. At least I gave up lying to myself about why I'm doing what I'm doing."

"Here we go . . ." Andres began, moving away from his desk, toward the windows.

"She's so obvious, Andres. That DEA agent didn't need me to tell him anything. I always knew what Ximena was after. I saw that look in her eye. I recognized it from the moment we met. A hungry dog with the scent of bone in its nose. And you, me, my family, your family, the prince, Daniel—we were that bone. So you, Andres, how could you be so trusting?"

He said nothing, his back to her.

Sofia scoffed. "Oh, I see, you thought you were going to be El Primer Caballero."

He turned, crossed the room, closed the distance between them so quickly Sofia's breath caught in her throat as he came to stand in front of her.

"You're wrong," he said, his finger in her face, his eyes blazing now. "That's not what this is about. You still don't get it, do you?"

"Stop lying to yourself, Andres," Sofia replied, shoving his hand out of her face, her heartbeat in her throat now.

"I've done everything I've done so that there will be a life after all this. I've told you that, Sofia, and you, you just gave it all away."

"This has nothing to do with you . . ."

"Bullshit!" he growled. "I supply the drugs, Sofia; I keep the Gulf and the Baja and your family in business. Me. I do that. Who the hell do you think they're going to come after next?"

"You're fooling yourself if you don't think they already know all that, Rey," the moniker rolling off her tongue with all the bitterness she had left for Andres fueled by all the lies between them.

His eyes searched hers, the heat of his anger bleeding the murky blue of his hazel eyes away until just the yellow green and red remained.

Sofia reached behind her back, pulled Lucia from her waistband. She looked at the gun in her hand, traced a nail over the designs raised from the pearl handle.

"My mother died for this. It was the least I could do to try to finish what she started because all that matters now is my brothers.

I won't let my cousins take them down this path." She looked up at Andres, then offered him the gun. "I know what it is you think you need to do now, sicario, and I understand. But for what it's worth, you—your freedom—was part of my deal. This was never going to touch you."

"You think that will matter to them," Andres said, his voice strained, "once they get Ximena, once they get the routes? Whatever they promised you will disappear like it never existed. It's never enough for them."

"And it's never enough for us, is it?" Sofia asked. "Maybe if we had known when to stop—me, my brothers, my cousins. My father. Even my mother. Maybe we wouldn't be here right now."

She pushed the gun toward Andres, pressing it into his palm. "You might not have killed my mother, but for what it's done to you and me, it might as well have been you."

She looked up at him, surprised to see tears shimmering in his eyes.

"Finish it then," she said.

His Adam's apple bobbed as he swallowed. He looked away, wiping his face with the back of his free hand. "No," he said, shaking his head.

He pushed the gun back toward Sofia, gently but firmly. "Not this time."

Mexico City was sinking. It had been sinking for decades. And right now to Sofia, it felt like the bottom of the city was about to fall out completely underneath her feet.

The facade that what they had together was real—the facade they had spent weeks hiding behind—was finally shattering. There's hope in a cracked thing. Hope that all the Band-Aids and tape and finger-crossing will keep it together. That hope disappears for a shattered thing.

She slipped the gun back into her waistband and moved to step past him.

He reached for her, wrapping his long fingers around her upper arms, pulling her close to him, his eyes shimmering, searching hers. "I've loved you since I was too young to even know what that meant, Sofia. Your long hair, your big dark eyes, your smile, the way you cursed just like your brothers—all of it. And I still love you now, Sofia."

Sofia's shoulders slumped. "You said it yourself, Andres, we never had a chance. That fantasy was always going to be just that."

"What if I was wrong?" he asked, his eyes hopeful. "The offer still stands," he added, his fingers at her elbows now.

He bent down slightly to meet her eyes. "Come with me to Colombia. Leave with me. Forget all this bullshit, all this living for someone else. Our children will have the life we never had, a life where they get to decide."

Sofia swallowed slowly around the lump that had formed in her throat. "Andres, you know I can't."

"Can't or won't?" he asked, his eyes darkening. "Be honest this time."

"You're right, Andres, I do have a choice, and it's them," she said, moving out of his grasp. "My brothers," she added, looking up at him, "and you chose Ximena and your future, and I understand."

His jaw clenched, but he nodded.

A beat passed between them.

"That offer of yours sounds like heaven," Sofia said, because in another life it was all she wanted. But what had her father said? It was time to put away childish things. Too much had been done that couldn't be undone now.

"It would have been," Andres replied, his eyes dark and cold.

He was locking away everything he had ever felt for her, suffocating it. Killing it. She'd seen that look before.

"People like you and me don't get to have that ending," Sofia said. "You taught me that a long time ago."

She felt his eyes on her as she headed toward the door.

Walking down the hall, she knew he was right, that there never was a happy ending for them. But if anyone had asked, at that moment, she had wanted that ranch in Colombia, those children. That man.

She wanted it so bad it ripped her open.

CHAPTER 39

Sofia avoided Yolotli's gaze as he pushed away from the wall near the elevator where he'd been waiting for her as she came up the hall.

"You all right?" he asked, his eyes on the elevator buttons as he punched the G repeatedly.

Sofia sniffed, swallowed around the lump in her throat. "He's an asshole."

The elevator doors popped open with a ding, and Yolotli reached to hold the door open for her. "I could've told you that."

The way her heart felt jagged in her rib cage, the way it hurt to swallow, she knew she still loved him, asshole or not. Even while that dream—that maybe somehow their wish could come true and they could end up together—had died back in that office, in that hotel room.

Yolotli gave her a gentle push on her lower back. "Got to keep moving, fresa."

The elevator ride was silent, Sofia taking a moment to reorient herself.

She'd called Yolotli after seeing the news. She had a target on her back now, one she'd put there herself. Xavier and Joaquin wouldn't, couldn't, let this type of betrayal slide. And they would have already figured out by now that it was her. They'd be out for blood, and she'd be able to duck them for only so long. And with no one else left, Sofia had turned to Yolotli for his protection.

She kept her head down as she hurried behind Yolotli across the now empty parking lot of Herrera Architecture.

Yolotli stopped abruptly ahead of Sofia, reaching a hand back to stop her.

"Hey, prima," Xavier said from where he leaned against Yolotli's SUV. "Thought you would have had an army by now."

"An army can't stop the inevitable," she replied, reaching behind her slowly.

"Don't even think about it," Joaquin said as he jostled Sofia, stopping her from pulling her gun from her waistband.

"Think we need to talk," Xavier said.

When Sofia didn't reply, Xavier pointed his gun at her. "Get the fuck in the car, Sofia."

The SUV bounced down a utility road outside of Mexico City. They'd been driving for a while, but the sack Joaquin had pulled over her head kept Sofia from seeing anything.

The vehicle slowed, then stopped.

"We're here, prima," Xavier said, pulling off the sack so quickly he pulled her hair with it.

She winced and then looked around. It was dark. Very dark.

Xavier held his hand out. "Let's go."

She pushed his hand aside and climbed out of the vehicle. Yolotli already stood on the roadside, Joaquin's gun in his back.

She heard voices not too far off the road. There was a building a hundred yards or so in from the road they stood on. It was illuminated by a single floodlight.

"Where are we?" Sofia asked.

"New place of operations, since you kind of ruined our last one. Walk," Xavier instructed, his hand on her neck.

She followed behind Yolotli as they headed toward the nondescript concrete building.

"I really wish things could have been different," Xavier lamented. "But no, you have too much of your mother in you."

"She cared for you," Sofia began. "When you came to live with us. She loved you like her own."

Xavier huffed, "That's not entirely true, is it, prima? We were strangers to her. She resented us for surviving."

"That's not true. She resented you for letting the violence win. You let them break you."

"Thirty thousand people were disappeared in our country's Dirty War, prima. My mom was one of them, my father, your grandmother, and eventually our grandfather. They got him too, years after he returned home. But this is about your mother. How she let the comfort of all the money our grandfather made lull her into her righteousness. She got what she deserved because she forgot where she came from. But," he said, stopping Sofia as they reached the building, "I'm going to give you the choice your mother didn't get."

Sofia now saw who the voices in the night air belonged to, young girls, just like the ones who'd been paraded out for Ximena's cameras the other night.

A semi was waiting nearby, its engine rumbling lowly. Yolotli was staring at the entrance to the building, and Sofia followed his gaze. Diego stood leaning against the building, watching them.

He would have known where Sofia and Yolotli were going to be that night. That if Andres called for her, she'd run. Maybe it was Diego playing multiple sides too, just as she always suspected.

"I need you to hear me, Sofia," Xavier said as he stood in front of her now. "I'm not the bad guy you think I am. I have done nothing but try to build a legacy for us here. You have no idea how hard we've fought for this. For what we have and what we will have. You are blinded by the search for justice like you accuse me of. But I understand why my father was killed. And you, you need to understand why your mother was killed."

He snapped his fingers in Diego's direction. "Let's make this a family meeting, shall we?"

Xavier waited for Diego to join them.

Sofia recognized the position Diego was in, the position he'd put himself in. Xavier and Joaquin weren't stupid; the options as to who would have told Sofia the location of their pickups were very limited, and not many were brave enough to tell on the Torreses.

"I'll tell you what it is you really want to know, Sofia. What you've been running around Mexico City begging for instead of just coming to us. To me."

"I already know, Xavier," Sofia replied. "I know it wasn't Andres who killed my mother."

"Your sicario told you that?" Xavier asked. "Did he tell you everything? Did he tell you that your father was too much of a pussy to make the call? Did he tell you that it was me?" Xavier asked, his teeth glinting and his eyes burning. "That we had her killed before she could ruin us?"

Sofia caught the way Diego's jaw clenched.

"She wasn't going to give you up, Xavier. Not you or Joaquin. Just Alberto . . ."

Xavier smiled. "That's not how these things work, prima. You want to believe that, you need to believe she wouldn't turn on her family, but she did. She was. I protected us."

"She just wanted out, Xavier. She would have let you have it all."

Xavier reached up to run a hand through his hair, strands falling loosely back onto his forehead. "Look, Sofia, I get it. I do. You're trying to protect your brothers. But I'm doing the same for mine. You, Diego, Nando—you all deserve better than this. We all do. All that government of yours has done, all this country has done, is take and take from us."

Xavier reached for Sofia, grabbing her arm. "Join us, Sofia. This is your family; we are your family."

Sofia shook her head. "No, Xavier. Not like this," she said, nodding toward the girls.

Sofia saw the change in Xavier, like he'd pulled a mask over his face.

"You know what, prima, since we are telling the truth, let's put it all out there. Why don't you look at your brother, tell him about your friend the priest?"

Sofia clenched her jaw.

"Go on, tell him," Xavier said, glee on his face. "Tell him you're a snitch just like your mother."

Diego looked at Xavier, who nodded. "Yes, yes. It's true. The DEA likes to play dress-up. I wonder if Sofia took confessional with him, alone, just the two of them, spilling every fucking secret this family has."

Xavier slung an arm around Diego's shoulder. "What do you think, primo? Maybe I should call Andres. Have him clean up this mess of ours, just like before, since that's all he's good for, isn't it?" Xavier asked, his eyes on Sofia.

Diego didn't respond, he didn't move, his eyes, too, on Sofia.

It was one thing for Andres to know the extent she'd gone to to escape her cousins, to try to dig her family out of this grave. But it was another thing for her brothers to know. Snitching wasn't something she'd be able to walk back or easily explain away. While maybe she'd escaped a bullet from St. Julian for now, it was doubtful her own family would let her off that easily.

"You are just like her, aren't you? Just as selfish," Xavier continued, walking back toward Sofia, kicking up dust with his boots. "She wanted one thing in this world more than anything and that was Martin Herrera, and you, Sofia, you want Andres just the same, don't you? Us for him, us for his freedom, was that the deal you made with your priest?"

Sofia shook her head. "No. You for them," she replied, nodding toward Diego.

"Finally, a clear answer," Xavier replied. "I'm done asking you, Sofia; I am done begging you to understand. You think because you played Daniel's game, kissed his ring, that he'll spare you? He's a bulldozer, and you have no idea what he's capable of. The Gulf, the Baja, they have no allegiance to you. So once your crooked politician starts taking more than her fair share, they'll come for you to recoup what they've lost."

"Let them come," Sofia replied. "They have every right, since you think stealing from them is the only way. Stealing won't make you the king you've longed to be, Xavier. Stealing keeps you in the mud with the rest of us."

"I am bored, Sofia. Bored with this conversation, bored with your never-ending self-righteousness you inherited from your mother. We could have had an agreement. We could have worked together. Instead," Xavier said as he cocked his gun, "since you won't listen, how about I make you suffer instead?"

As the gunshot echoed in the quiet night, screams rose from the semi where the girls were being loaded.

When Sofia opened her eyes, she watched Diego crumple to the ground, his hands clutching his thigh.

Sofia was frozen in place by Xavier, who pointed his gun now under her chin, close enough that she could feel the heat from the barrel.

"Nando is next, prima. And when they're both gone, you'll sit with that until it kills you from the inside. Do you understand?"

The semi started to roll, followed by Xavier's truck with Joaquin behind the wheel, Xavier in the passenger seat, but all Sofia could hear was ringing in her ears as she watched Diego's blood, too much, dark, black as night, pooling around his thigh where he lay bent over in the dirt.

"Therefore, a lion from the forest will strike them down. A wolf from arid plains will ravage them. A leopard stalks their cities. Anyone who leaves them will be torn to pieces because their rebellious acts are many, their unfaithful deeds numerous."

—*Jeremiah* 5:6

CHAPTER 40

El Paraiso had once been a resort. Now it was home to a makeshift hospital. Nestled up against the hills between Mexico City and Cuernavaca, the old resort had been a popular tourist spot before the drug wars.

Now the pool was empty, lined with leaves and branches blown in by the wind. The hotel rooms abandoned.

Except for one room just off the main lobby. In this room, machines beeped, an IV was hung. In this room, there was life. Just barely.

The doctor, an expat army trauma surgeon, adhered to one rule: it was his job to put people back together, no matter who they were. And if you looked hard enough, you'd catch the ghosts of those he'd lost swimming in his eyes.

El Paraiso had earned some notoriety among the cartels, a place where no questions were asked when you needed a bullet pulled from your shoulder or thigh at three in the morning.

Now, for Sofia, El Paraiso had become limbo.

"So do not fear, for I am with you; do not be dismayed, for I am your God. I will strengthen and help you; I will uphold you with my righteous right hand . . ."

The murmured prayer from the nurse in Diego's room continued, floating down the hall.

Sofia had never known the precipice between life and death like this before, and for that, now in this empty hotel lobby, Diego barely breathing in the room down the hall, she felt thankful. Here, then gone, was easier than this.

She was desperate with hope, sick with worry. So overwhelmed she couldn't move. Hadn't moved. Her eyes tracked the clock's hands on the wall. Vaguely she was aware sunlight had started to fill the lobby.

It was Election Day. The thought was strange, intrusive.

She had tried to pray herself, but the words failed her now. The words her mother would repeat over and over while their eyes shut for sleep. Sofia could no longer remember them.

Blood had dried on her hands, her neck, her hair. It was everywhere. Diego's blood, she was sticky with it.

The doctor had murmured praise as his steady hands quickly worked over Diego. Something about the pressure, about quick thinking, but Sofia had only done what Yolotli barked at her as they loaded Diego into the truck, as he sped as fast as he could to El Paraiso. Sofia had held on to to her brother for dear life, for *his* life.

Now they waited.

Nando shifted next to her. He'd driven out to this hotel that didn't exist as soon as he'd heard. He was pale, paler than usual.

The doctor, his eyes bright, had come out a few minutes ago, an hour ago—Sofia had no idea—to say Diego was stable, and she heard the word "lucky." But all she could think about was the blood. The way Diego slipped out of consciousness, the sweat on his brow, the blue tint to his lips.

"I wish she'd stop," Nando murmured.

Sofia lifted a hand to reach for her brother's but stopped when she saw the blood under her nails, in her rings. She let her hand fall back into her lap.

"She's just trying to help," Sofia replied.

"What happened?" Nando asked, his voice a whisper, torn from crying himself hoarse.

"I fucked up," she said. "I fucked it all up."

Nando stretched his legs out, sinking lower in the aging leather chair.

"They're punishing me," Sofia continued, "for getting in the way. Maybe they were right. This whole time. They found a way to keep us relevant. And what have I done?"

Nando reached up to rub his hands over his face. "I can't do this anymore. I can't do what it is they're going to ask of us."

"I know," Sofia replied.

They'd come for Nando next. They'd promised her that. So now she had to find a way to keep him safe. Now she had to pray and pray and pray with everything she had left that Diego would survive this. There was nothing beyond that.

But this was Nando, her little brother she'd made up stories for when nightmares and rainstorms kept him awake.

"We'll be done with this. Xavier and Joaquin can have it. Then you'll finish school," Sofia began with a firm nod. "You'll run the produce business. Marry that *pinche* journalist girlfriend of yours if you want."

Nando snorted. "That's the idea, isn't it? The thing that keeps us going. Knowing damn well it'll never end like that. It ends like this. Alone, hiding. Scared. Bleeding."

The horses, the ranch in Colombia, none of those things Sofia ever had the chance to lay her hands on. That dream was never real, while this one, the life of peace, she had come close enough to taste it. To make a difference. And she would have been good at it. She would have been good at building things instead of breaking them.

But this is what she had been called home to do. To sit in this room that smelled of antiseptic with her youngest brother and convince him that no matter how many wolves were at the door, wolves she had called, everything would be all right.

Her mother said Sofia would always protect her brothers, but they protected one another in the end. It seemed Sofia did know what needed to be done after all.

She'd let Xavier win this. Let him have his war with Daniel. Let it blossom into another with the Prince of the Baja because, at this point, there was no other option. They'd take her men, remind them what they did to dissidents. All Sofia had left in the world was in this run-down hotel with her.

"For what it's worth, I get why you left for London," Nando began. "I just missed you."

"I had to prove I was somebody too," Sofia replied.

Nando turned to Sofia. "You were always somebody to us. Diego won't admit it, but I will. I always looked up to you. You were Mom's favorite. I wanted that, what you had."

"You were the favorite. Ask Diego if you don't believe me."

"I was just the baby, that's all."

Sofia smiled, and it felt foreign at first, like she'd forgotten how. "You got away with everything, and Diego and I were always in trouble."

Nando shrugged. "She was hard on you because she knew you'd have to be tougher."

Sofia watched him for a moment. "I know what really happened, with Mami."

Nando stilled, his gaze on his lap.

"The cousins thought she betrayed the family," Sofia continued with a sigh. "She wanted to go legitimate, but our father and our cousins wouldn't allow it. So she turned to the DEA for help, for a way out."

"She was going to talk?"

Sofia felt a prickle of anxious guilt in her spine. Nando didn't know about her deal with the DEA yet, but he'd know soon enough. For what it was worth, Sofia worried that he would look at her the same way, disgust and confusion in his eyes.

Sofia sighed. "I can't imagine, as a mother, the choices she had to make. But I know she made them for us."

Nando sighed. "All these secrets are tearing us apart."

Sofia regarded her little brother, the gold that glittered at his wrist and neck, the trophies for the heaviness in his eyes, shoulders, words. Sofia noticed for the first time the fine lines that were starting to form between his eyebrows.

Sofia's younger brother was cerebral, controlling, precise, meticulous, and competent. Lethally unforgiving, he was shielded from the worst of it like Sofia in a similar way. The younger brother went to university, managed their warehouse. He didn't work in the shadow of night the way Diego did. He didn't get his hands bloodied the way Diego did.

It dawned on Sofia then that Nando was always trying to protect Diego, not the business. This whole time Nando saw the violence that had been kept at bay the past few years starting to crash at the gates of their peaceful kingdom. Sofia and her new ideas were the harbinger of deadly change. Turned out he wasn't wrong.

Nando turned to look at her, the shadows in the room putting his already sharp features into stark relief. "What now?"

Yolotli emerged from Diego's room for the first time since they'd arrived. The blood on the front of his white shirt had dried to a burgundy stain. He met Sofia's eyes for just a moment before heading for the front doors. His eyes were as vacant and wild as Sofia felt.

She didn't have an answer.

"When you asked me before what my reason was, what my 'why' was, I didn't have an answer," Nando said. "I do now."

"And what's that, little brother?" Sofia asked, her eyes on the front door still.

"I think the point was, for all of us, that we thought we'd be the ones to escape this. That somehow we'd be the chosen ones. That we'd get to retire. Maybe I thought the same as you. That we could step away."

"And now?" she asked.

"There is no stepping away. There is nothing after this."

She reached for his hand then, squeezing hard, smearing their brother's blood between their hands.

CHAPTER 41

The car purred around Andres while it idled in his father's driveway. The radio filled the silence as the election results trickled in. The sun set behind him as he listened to the early projections.

Ximena had argued with him, asked him to stay in the city with her so they could celebrate her victory. She was so sure of it. She wanted him there; she begged and whined.

But Andres had looked at Emiliano, the way his fingertips lingered at Ximena's lower back, just long enough to be on the other side of professional, and Andres decided he should be home with his father. The old man was getting sicker by the day, though neither of them mentioned it.

And he found Sofia was right, Ximena collected bones, and he was just another to add to her pile. As long as once she won, she kept her word, and he got his contracts, then all this shit would have been worth it.

He'd deal directly with El Príncipe and Daniel for now until he could hand off the distribution entirely. It was what he'd wanted from the beginning, a way out of the cocaine business, but lately Ximena made it sound like she had other plans for him. Plans that kept him at the head of distribution. "They know you," she argued.

While Andres understood that familiarity and trust were hard to come by in their business, being head of distribution was never a part of his deal.

And with the Torreses still around, it complicated things. They'd still want their share of the cocaine—and hell, everything else—so Andres knew what Ximena would ask of him soon. To eliminate the threat. But when he retired, he'd made a promise to himself, and it was the last one he had left unbroken. He had hoped someone else would have done it by now. Put a bullet between Xavier's and Joaquin's eyes so he wouldn't have to.

The rules, the laws they lived by, were a necessity. A way to keep order in an otherwise chaotic world. Sofia had broken those rules when she decided not to play the same game anymore. They'd kill her for that. Her cousins, once they knew—hell, maybe they already knew. Maybe she was already dead. Just like her mother.

He slammed his fist against the steering wheel. "*Carajo!*"

Andres had screwed things up between them, and he understood that, accepted it. But what Sofia had done, bringing that agent into their lives, was inexcusable. Even if he saw in her eyes, heard in her tone that she'd do anything to protect her brothers. They were grown men. Men she couldn't help if anything happened to her anyway. She'd sacrificed herself for them. Just like her mother had.

Andres rubbed a hand over his face. Her loyalty would be her undoing. But he couldn't help her now. Even if he wanted to, they'd made their choices.

He finally made his way inside, greeting the nurses who lingered near his father's bedroom door before entering.

"Thought you'd be with Cruz," his father said, struggling to sit up before a coughing fit took over.

"Yeah, yeah," Andres said, hurrying to his bedside. "Take it easy."

Once his father had caught his breath, Andres dropped into the recliner near the bed. "Rather be here," he replied.

Martin rolled his eyes. "I doubt that. How's it looking?"

"It's early," Andres replied with a shrug, "but projections look good."

"I'm proud of you, *mijo*."

Andres scoffed, "Still a lot of work to be done."

"Always. But you're your own man now. Keys to the city and all. It's what I wanted for you. What I hoped for."

His father had worked his entire life to lay this foundation, this pathway straight into politics and legitimacy. Andres was grateful the old man would be able to see the fruit of his labor.

He reached for his father's hand. "Thanks to you."

When Andres was sent away to Colombia to learn how to become his own man, to learn how to be who his family needed, he had resented it at first. He'd been torn from everything he knew and loved. He never had a chance to say goodbye. Not to Sofia, not to anyone.

But now it was all worth it, to see his father at peace.

"Y Sofia?" his father asked.

Andres shrugged.

"Don't blame her for her family's mistakes."

Andres shook his head. "It's not that. It's more than that. It's complicated."

"No. These things are very simple. We make them complicated."

"Not this time," Andres replied, "but she's right, we made our choices."

Martin held his son's gaze. "I've been visited by your mother in my dreams."

"Oh," Andres said, leaning back in the recliner.

"I know what that means. The time is close."

Andres looked at his hands in his lap, studied the grooves in his watch band, taking note of the years' worth of thin scratches in the metal from wear.

"There's something that I need you to know, son. Maybe it will shed some light on your complicated situation."

Andres shifted in his seat, sitting ankle to knee as he waited for his father to continue.

"Maria and I . . ." he began, and stopped. There was a faraway look in his eye. "We never got the chance we should have. That doesn't mean our love ever went away. Or that it ever ended."

Andres knew this. He'd been at the secret lunches. He'd heard the way they spoke to one another, and the way his father never remarried after his mother died.

"We had an idea once—or should I say, I had an idea? That we could leave this place. Take you children and just leave it all. I know you've had the same idea; I've seen that look in your eye."

Martin cleared his throat, took a deep breath. Continued. "She turned me down. Multiple times she turned me down. And I hated Alberto for it until I realized it was because I was supposed to be better than this. She wanted more for me than I wanted for myself, but once I had you, this was the road that opened to me. To provide for you."

He stopped then, rubbed a hand, rough from years of horse training, over his silver-and-gray beard. "Things got darker and darker with her family, with her nephews, with Alberto, until one day she came to me for help. She felt trapped, boxed in. It was no secret she wanted out of this life. And that time, I turned her down. My life was here, with you, with what I was building. It was too late."

Martin stopped again, swallowed a few times. Andres heard the thickness in his voice now. "That was the last time I saw her alive."

Andres reached for his father's hand again. "You can't blame yourself . . ."

"I absolutely can, mijo. I'm the one who told Alberto that Maria had reached out to the DEA for help. I just didn't think they'd . . . do what they did."

Andres frowned. "I'm sorry? I don't understand . . ."

"I had to save you, mijo. I had to. I didn't sacrifice everything for you to end up with nothing. You have to understand that. That's why I did what I did. I couldn't risk losing everything. She had no way of promising what the DEA would take and where they'd stop. She could have told them everything. I had no way of knowing."

"But you had to have known what Alberto would do to her. What else do we do with rats?" Andres asked, trying to wrap his head around what his father was saying. Trying to put himself in the same position. While he was pissed at Sofia for betraying them, he could never, would never, willingly stand her up in front of the firing squad, and that is exactly what his father had done to Maria.

"I didn't think Alberto would let the mother of his children be murdered. But once her nephews knew, there was no bottling it back up. I'm sorry, Andres. I know the rift between you and Sofia started because of this."

"I understand why you did it," Andres replied. "I just don't know how you could have."

Martin looked away. "For you," he replied. "For you. They could have swept in, taken everything. Sent me away, sent you back to Colombia. I couldn't have a life without you in it, mijo."

Andres reached up to run his hands over his face.

Sofia had been right: all of it, everything, was always about the money. The business.

Martin squeezed Andres's hand. "I'm telling you this to say I failed Maria. I had the chance to keep her safe from them. Don't blow your chance like I did. You'll regret it for the rest of your life."

"I can't save her," Andres replied. "Even if I could, she doesn't want me to."

"Then be there when she falls. Sofia was your friend, Andres. No matter what else has transpired between the two of you, I can promise you that if you don't try to be there for her now, whatever the outcome, it'll always weigh on you."

One of the nurses knocked at the door, an apologetic smile on her face. "It's time for his medicine."

Andres nodded, wiped at his face. "Sure, yes. Of course."

Martin stared at his son, a stare that was willing him to understand. "*Lo pensaré. Te lo prometo.*"

Outside his father's room, Andres pressed his back against the wall. His father's voice and the soft, upbeat voice of the nurse intertwined. They were joking together, a bond forged through necessity, but a special one nonetheless.

In these last days, his father had found someone who knew how to be strong; she understood what he was going through, and Andres had to swallow down the pang of guilt he felt.

He'd watched his mother get sicker and sicker until there was nothing left. Watching his father go through the same thing only made him think of his own mortality. Except when it was his turn, there would be no one waiting in the recliner, no one cracking inappropriate jokes with him. He would be alone. And it would be his fault.

He slipped his hand into his slacks, tightening his fingers around his phone.

He couldn't ask Sofia to sit in that chair for him. It wouldn't be fair, and she'd rightfully say no. But what his father said, about regretting not trying—Andres didn't know if he could live with that.

CHAPTER 42

The sun was setting on El Paraiso. Nando, curled up now on the lobby's couch, slept fitfully, his curls spread out wildly across the cushions.

The nurses had shown them where they could shower, freshen up. Brought Sofia and Yolotli dark navy scrubs to change into. Yolotli declined the change of clothes.

Sofia rinsed off under the lukewarm water in a daze, muscle memory propelling her through the motions of her shower.

The staff brought them pastries, sandwiches, and cold coffee from the underutilized kitchen. The nurses urged them to rest, and Sofia watched over Nando as he drifted off, but sleep evaded her.

The doctor had retired for a catnap, as he called it, and the nurses took turns visiting Diego's room.

It was as quiet as a dream. The late afternoon air languid, stuck in time as if jellied.

Sofia stood then, needing to stretch her legs.

Walking to Diego's room, her feet moved on their own. She hadn't been brave enough to look in, telling herself she was just giving Yolotli his space, his time, with Diego. The truth was, she was scared to face reality. She was a finger crosser, believed in superstition, believed thoughts had power so it was better for her to stay rooted in her seat as to not disturb the universe's forces at work.

But now she peered into the darkening room. And Diego met her eyes.

She gasped, hurrying to his side, her voice hushed. "I didn't know you were awake. I'll call the nurse . . ."

He laid his hand on hers and shook his head.

"We need to talk," he said, his voice hoarse as he swallowed around it.

Sofia glanced at Yolotli curled into the chair in the corner of the room, his knees to his chest, which rose and fell gently as he slept.

She turned back to Diego, laying her hand over his. His skin was so pale, too pale still.

Diego swallowed once, twice, before speaking. "Do you remember when Mom died, and you'd spend all night in that chapel of hers?"

Sofia nodded.

"What did I used to tell you then?" he asked, holding her gaze, his brown eyes soft.

"You can't pray her back to life," Sofia replied.

"Maybe I was wrong."

Sofia lowered herself into the chair by Diego's bed. "I didn't know what else to do back then. I had to do something."

"We weren't allowed to mourn, me and Nando. While you got to be sad, we were told to act like men. Then you got to go away, see the world. We didn't."

"I didn't leave to hurt you or Nando," Sofia said, careful with her words, careful that she might break him.

Diego frowned, his eyes closing briefly. "I get it now, don't worry, Sof. And I get why you told Yolotli about the cousins, the trucks. The girls."

"He wouldn't shower," Sofia said, her eyes dry, burning now. She reached up and rubbed at them harshly. "He didn't want to wash your blood away."

Diego sighed. "It's complicated between us. It always has been."

"You have to fix it," Sofia said, her throat tightening. "I'm worried about you without him."

"I don't need a babysitter."

"No. But you do need a voice of reason."

Diego sucked air through his teeth. "You know, Pops told me something once. He said, 'You'll try to do the right thing, and you'll think you're right, but you'll never be right.' I figured he was referring to himself and Mom, but now I get it. Neither of us was right, Sof. It's always been you and me. You and I did this."

Sofia was quiet, nodding in agreement. Letting her brother talk. These moments of insight into Diego's feelings were rare. He prided himself on being a rock, their rock. Unmovable and unflinching.

And he was right.

"I didn't see it then, but now I see it," Diego said. "How we shut you down too quick, didn't listen to your vision."

This was the closest she'd get to an apology from Diego.

"I'm sorry too," she said.

He nodded, his eyes on the cross hanging above the door.

"The day has come when we have to stop running and face who we are, what we've become," he said.

She shook her head. "No. We're done. We're out. I won't risk—"

"There is no out, Sofia," he interrupted. "You have to make what's left of this alliance work if we're going to survive."

"Diego, none of that matters . . ."

She thought of how her world had stopped, crumbled around her as she watched Diego collapse in the dirt.

She'd died herself as she pressed with all her weight to stop his bleeding, her hands, wrists, forearms covered in his blood. She couldn't put any of them at risk like that. Never again.

"I didn't almost bleed to death for you to give up," Diego replied, his teeth clenched, the familiar sharpness back in his eyes.

"What am I supposed to do now?" Sofia asked. "I cut us out."

"Not entirely," he replied. "If Cruz wins tonight, then she still owes you her part of the deal."

Their family was still the one with the strongest ties to the politicians who would inevitably try to strong-arm more out of the Baja and the Gulf. She could position the De Lunas as the cushion between them and the politicians.

"Cut the government in just enough that they leave Daniel and the Prince alone. You'll have your peace," Diego replied, "and we need them on our side. We need the borders because those pinche politicians want them. That access is the only thing keeping us from being shot in the street like Pops."

"I don't disagree," Sofia replied.

Diego shifted slightly, wincing as he did so. "The question is then, what are you going to do about it?"

She looked at his leg, padded thickly, covered by the blanket.

It was like an illusion. Almost like nothing had even happened. But the grayness to his usually glowing skin, the hollow look in his eyes gave it all away.

What was she going to do about it?

"I think you forget, hermana, we were born to be kamikaze pilots, right?"

Sofia sighed. "Perhaps," she said, her eyes on the cross nailed to the wall.

"You know what has to be done, don't you?" Diego asked.

Sofia's fingertips itched with the phantom feel of Lucia in her hands.

"This is why she left it to you, Sofia," Diego continued.

Sofia glanced at Diego. Handsome Diego, who cleaned up the messes.

Her brothers were yin and yang, one the engineer, one the executioner. And where did that leave Sofia? The idealist forced to be a realist.

When Sofia was fourteen, dressed in her school uniform, her long hair in a braid cascading down her back, Joaquin had marched her into a De Luna warehouse. Had her stand in front of a man she had never seen before. This man was crying as he sat restrained in a folding chair.

This man was praying. Sofia could hear his whispers. "I forgive you." That's what he said to Sofia as she raised her gun, pointed it at the man's head. *The only place we aim*, as Joaquin taught her.

"He forgave me," Sofia said to herself, to the cross on the wall, to Diego, to whoever was listening.

"They won't," Diego said as if he knew precisely which memory Sofia was replaying, and maybe he did. He'd been there that afternoon, begging the cousins to have him do it instead of Sofia.

There were others after that man, and some before, but it was that man's face Sofia saw before sleep would come some nights.

What she knew had to be done was risky, but worse than that, it was dangerous. If Lalo changed his mind, if she couldn't take care of her cousins, there was a possibility they would all end up in cuffs.

But what was worse, every second her cousins lived, Nando wasn't safe. Sofia, either, for that matter, nor Diego, once word got out he had survived.

Sofia looked at Diego and held his gaze. "You'll fix this shit with Yoli?"

"I don't know, hermana."

"You'll try?"

"Always."

Sofia leaned back in her seat. "For a moment, one fleeting moment when I was in Matamoros, I had this thought: What if I just stay? Nestle myself somewhere near the beach, only come to town for groceries. Never come back here."

"Stay with Andres, you mean," Diego said.

"Yoli said something when I asked him once how he knew you were it, and he said when he could trust you not to let him fall. That was Andres for me."

Diego was still next to Sofia, listening.

"He was a world," she began, "like a snow globe. He was a world where things could have been good."

Diego tapped her hand. "That's the thing about first loves. The possibility of what could have been will always be golden."

Sofia said nothing, closing her eyes against the sting.

Finally, after a long beat, Diego spoke. "There's no time for sentimentality, Sofia," he said. "I need your word when the time comes. You can do what I know you can do, what Mom knew you could do."

Sofia nodded. "The cousins, they're ghosts. And you were the one who said we need to let go of ghosts."

Diego nodded. "*Claro que sí.*"

They were quiet together for a beat, as the realization set in for Sofia of what she'd have to do. Of what should have been done.

"Do you know why I pray to Santa Muerte?" Diego asked.

"She came to you in a dream, I remember."

"Yes. She chose me. She chooses me now, Sofia. She chooses those who otherwise don't have a chance."

The room darkened; the sun had fallen behind the hills now.

"Let's pray," Diego said, squeezing Sofia's hand that just hours ago had been covered to her elbow in his blood.

They prayed for safe passage, and they prayed to Santa Muerte for steady hands, and they prayed to the Virgen and asked for forgiveness for what Sofia was about to do.

CHAPTER 43

Sofia's eyes darted up and down the street as she crossed. She wasn't thrilled about Lalo's suggestion to meet in the middle of the day. Now, as she felt her cousins' breath at the back of her neck like a bull, she would have preferred moving under the cover of darkness.

But daylight offered her a false sense of security. As if her cousins, or whoever they'd pay to put a bullet in her skull, would be deterred by light or witnesses. They'd already proven they didn't mind an audience.

Thankfully, she wasn't completely alone. Yolotli waited for her in an SUV at the corner. He had insisted that he come with her. That she couldn't handle the cousins alone.

For Sofia, leaving Nando and Diego back at the hotel-turned-hospital felt like leaving a piece of herself behind. She imagined it must feel the same for Yolotli. But he didn't hesitate, standing to leave when she did. "I won't let you get murdered on my watch, doña," he had said.

And Diego knew better than to try to argue with Yolotli.

The woman at the front desk of the sleazy faux-Japanese motel near the south end of the city was well manicured, her makeup heavy but impeccable.

She handed Sofia a key, told her to enjoy her stay. Sofia glanced at the sign on the wall offering rates by the day or half day.

The hotel was small, and she quickly found the room she was looking for. She knocked once sharply on the door labeled

Mermaid Room. Lalo pulled the door open, and Sofia pushed past him.

Neon lights glowed under the bed, and a blue spotlight was centered on the sleek floor-to-ceiling pole in the corner of the room.

She turned to look at Lalo. "Really?" she asked, her eyebrow raised.

He tossed his phone onto the bed. "Not sure the reputation of this hotel is the biggest of your worries right now."

"Yeah, I'd say," Sofia replied. "They know. They all know who you are: Ximena, my cousins, my brothers . . ."

"I know. Why do you think we're meeting in this shithole?"

"What are you going to do about it?" Sofia asked, crossing her arms over her chest.

"Me?" Lalo asked, pointing at his own chest.

"Yes! This was your deal, Padre. Don't you owe me some type of protection?"

Lalo narrowed his eyes. "I thought you didn't watch movies."

Sofia sighed, exasperated. "They are going to kill my brothers. They've already tried with Diego. They will probably have me watch once they get ahold of Nando. Then they are going to kill me. What does that get you and your government then, Padre?"

Lalo lowered himself to sit at the foot of the bed. "Looks like Cruz is going to win after all. Despite your missteps."

"I don't give a shit about the election right now."

"You should," Lalo warned, his eyebrow raised, "because you made a deal with her, and that deal goes both ways. You're in her pocket now. Her regime will own you."

"Not if I'm dead."

Lalo tsk-tsked. "Well then, lucky for you, I need you alive. As it stands, you're my only connection to her office. And it looks like you're about to get much more involved."

Sofia didn't like the implication in his tone. That whatever deal she and Lalo had wasn't coming to an end, even as the election wound down.

"I gave you information, and you said you'd keep my brothers out of prison. That was our deal."

"I said out of prison, not out of the dirt."

Sofia stalked over to where Lalo sat on the bed. "We have an enemy in common, Lalo. I won't be close to Ximena if I'm in the dirt with my brothers, will I?"

"Fair point." He cursed under his breath. "In light of these circumstances, I'm proposing a new deal."

"You've got to be shitting me . . ."

"I get your cousins. You get to live."

Sofia shook her head and stepped away from Lalo.

The orange neon under the bed lit him in such a way that he resembled a summoned demon, and with every ounce of fight she had left, that's what he was to her now. Another obstacle to ending this.

She dropped into the chair across from the pole, her eyes on Lalo. "You dragged me into this. You asked for information, and I gave it to you. My brothers are at risk because of you."

Lalo shook his head and leaned to sit forward, his elbows on his knees. "No. No, I don't think that's quite right. You acted on information of your own volition. You thought a small-time SSC officer would be able to take your cousins in. You doubted them because you hate them and their way of doing things. So you know what? You can only blame yourself. You dug this hole. Had you trusted me, had you worked with me, it wouldn't have come down to this."

"That's bullshit," she replied. "You've known all along that all roads lead back to the banks. You've known all along what Ximena would want from me. You just wanted a front row seat. So you tell me, Padre, what is it exactly you're doing here? Why use me? My family?"

"I don't think you really want an answer to that."

Sofia glared at him. Glared at the way he sat so calm, so sure of himself and the situation, dripping with American arrogance.

"I think I know," she began. "You thought we were weak."

"I thought *you* were weak," he corrected.

She clenched her jaw but couldn't argue. She'd been weak. She'd made mistakes. She'd been just as arrogant.

Lalo smiled and pressed his hands together. "I need your cousins alive, princesa."

"My cousins have to go. It's the only way this ends."

Lalo rubbed a hand over his beard. "I need them, princess. Alive. That's nonnegotiable if you want your get-out-of-jail-free card for you and your brothers."

"I'll be dead before you even have my cousins in handcuffs, and you know it."

Her cousins couldn't walk away from this, even in cuffs. If they did, they would hunt her down for the rest of her life. There would be no protection, no city far enough away to hide from them.

She'd already resigned herself to the idea that she would pull the trigger herself. Lalo could be as pissed as he wanted about it, but there was no way those animals could see another day.

Lalo crossed his arms over his chest. "I have to be honest; my boss might want one of you De Lunas then, to set an example. Close the loop, that sort of thing."

Sofia looked up at Lalo. The weight of his words settled on her shoulders. She cleared her throat and looked away. Absentmindedly, she pulled at the fringe on the rip in her jeans.

"If that's true . . . if that happens, it has to be me," she said finally. "My brothers didn't have any part of this deal between you and me."

"What about Andres?" Lalo asked. "Maybe you'd be more willing to trade him in instead. Since he's not blood, since he's kept an important secret from you for so long. This would be your chance for revenge. For justice."

Sofia sighed, tired in her bones, so tired her joints felt like rubber. "He's done, Padre; he's out."

She didn't know why she did it; it was automatic. To lie, to cover for Andres. To protect him. Regardless of it all, he'd never meant to hurt her. He never lied when he said that. He just had a life he had to live, just like her. And it was no one's fault that their paths had split the way they did. She couldn't blame him for that anymore.

Sofia pushed herself to her feet. "Be ready tonight. My family's ranch."

She moved to pass him, but Lalo stood, towering over her.

They shared a quiet moment, a look with the weight of her life in it. While she was handing her future over to him, she hoped he saw in her eyes that she meant it. She meant it all. That all of it had always been out of love, her love for her brothers.

"It will always be him, won't it?" Lalo asked.

"What do you mean?" she asked.

"This life, the next. It's him. It's Andres."

Sofia held Lalo's gaze. His eyes were soft, like there was a man under that badge, under the clerical collar he wore so well, under the lies. And that man was lonely, searching for someone who understood him.

Sofia shook her head. "It's no one, Lalo. You know how it is. I think maybe you and I are not so different."

He raised one hand then, and with the lightest pressure, he ran the back of his knuckles over Sofia's cheek. "Don't make me have to hurt your family, Sofia. It's the last thing I want to do to you."

She searched his dark brown eyes for the truth. "But you will," she said finally.

"If I have to."

She frowned. "Do you really believe what you're doing is helping?"

"I have to," he replied.

"So do I."

He nodded then and pulled the door open. "Maybe you're right about us not being so different."

CHAPTER 44

Sofia rubbed her arms as the night, chilly in early summer, made her shiver. The grounds were silent. Animals, she'd read, knew when danger was near. They knew to be quiet; they knew to be still. They knew to flee, and Sofia thought they were smarter than any of them.

Xavier would be here soon, Joaquin at his side.

Neither of them would miss the opportunity to hear Sofia concede, to hear her beg. To hear her admit her mistakes.

That's what she promised Xavier in a text as Yolotli drove her back to the old, empty home.

She was done fighting, she told him.

And she was. After tonight.

"I'll do it," Yolotli said as they walked out into the back of the house, toward the garden.

"It needs to be me," Sofia argued.

"I know you think that because, for some reason, you think you have something to prove, but I'm telling you you don't, Sofia."

"I can't ask you to kill for me."

"I'm volunteering, Sofia. You need to be the good one."

Sofia shook her head. "If we're talking about saving my soul, it's too late for that."

"Not necessarily," Yolotli replied. "You came back to do good things for the people you love. This isn't the way. It doesn't have to be you."

"I made a choice. I need to face the consequences of that choice. It's the right thing to do."

"You don't need to kill to prove you're right, Sofia. You have a chance to start clean, to start fresh. What they made you do when you were young, people will forgive; you were just a girl. But if you do this, there's no chance of forgiveness. Even if they deserve it."

"I don't know what life there is for me after this. It might not matter at all."

Lalo had warned her. He'd take her in, close the loop.

The sun was long gone behind the hills now, leaving a purplish-blue sky in its wake.

"An angel of death," she said under her breath, more to herself than Yolotli.

"Can I ask you a question, Yolotli? Do you believe that it all evens out in the end? Killing to save lives?" she asked, her gaze on the neon cross at the entrance to her mother's chapel.

"I think sometimes we have to believe that it does. I'd like to think it's true. But in the end, we can only do what we think is best."

"They're here," Yolotli said in a quiet voice that unnerved Sofia. The gravity of what was at stake was not lost on him. The idea that they wouldn't walk away from this conversation was a real possibility in his mind too.

Xavier stood golden and righteous on their patio. Joaquin leaned against one of the pillars.

The quieter of the two was the first to greet Sofia. "Took you long enough to come to your senses, prima."

"Well, you two have shown me the error of my ways," Sofia began, taking the few steps to meet Xavier and Joaquin on the tiled patio, Yolotli at her side.

She forgot sometimes that this man she considered a little brother, a part of their family, was a killer like Andres. A weapon in his own right. But she hoped against hope that tonight he'd be able to just be a man. Just be her brother, her family. Unlike her cousins.

"I see it now, Xavier," Sofia said. "It's true, I thought the same as my mother, that we could protect ourselves by bowing down. But you were right all along. When you kneel, all you're doing is exposing your neck."

Xavier narrowed his eyes.

Sofia read his body language easily. His arms hung at his sides; he was suspicious of her, of her words. Of this.

"What exactly was I right about?" he asked, his head tilted, his eyes on her.

She shrugged. "All of it."

Stick closely to the truth when lying. They'd taught her that.

"I underestimated you, what you were capable of, but now I see it. Now I understand. What you can do. What you could do given the opportunity."

Lalo was right; she might have underestimated them, or the lengths they'd go to to make their point. But she understood now.

The rigid line of Xavier's shoulders relaxed, not by much, but she caught it.

"That's all I ever wanted," Xavier said, "was for you to see what was possible. Instead, you came back here with your head held high like you had all the answers."

He chuckled, but it was dark, thick with anything but humor.

He stepped toward her. "While we bled. While we mourned. While we picked up the pieces that you turned around and handed it away. To the priest, to Andres. To that woman who now you'll have to answer to. *Tu jefa*. I don't want a boss, not like you. I won't answer to anyone!" he roared.

Sofia flinched.

He was so close now she could see the light smattering of freckles on his nose. The ones that got darker as summer progressed.

His dark eyes flashed. "All our wars for nothing," he said. "Our parents." He looked over Sofia's shoulder at Yolotli and pointed. "Your mother."

Xavier's chest was rising and falling faster now, his nostrils flared. "You disrespected all of them," he said to Sofia through his golden teeth.

"When they came for our grandmother, your mother was saved. When they came for my father, yours was sitting on his throne here. Safe and sound. And you disrespected those who came before you. A traitor, weak like your mother but with the mouth of a man."

The crack the back of his knuckles made when they connected with Sofia's cheekbone was deafening to her ears.

Yolotli had his gun drawn before Sofia righted herself.

"Aht, aht," Joaquin clucked, his own gun pointed back at Yolotli, "not so fast."

Xavier leaned down, his face centimeters from Sofia. "You want to behave like a man, Sofia, then I will treat you like one."

She pulled her hand away from her cheek, warm blood, her blood, coating her fingertips.

"I deserved that," she said quietly, the pain in her cheek just warm heat for now, until the adrenaline wore off.

"What was that?" Xavier asked, raising his hand, the one with rings now dotted with her blood, to his ear.

"I deserved that," she repeated, her eyes on his as she pressed Lucia's barrel, his gift to her, into his stomach, "and you deserve this."

She squeezed the trigger.

Xavier's body fell backward from the force of the shot, crumpling to the tile.

A second shot rang out and Sofia ducked, covering her head.

CHAPTER 45

Sofia looked up; the shot had come from the balcony. Andres stared down at her, his eyes hard.

Sofia glanced at Joaquin, who was sprawled face down on the tile, blood pooling around his face.

Xavier's groans of pain cut through the ringing in her ears. She stood, her legs shaking, to stand over her cousin. He held his hand to his stomach, blood flowing over his fingers, just like Diego's had done to her hands.

Sofia knelt next to Xavier, her knee resting in his blood. "You were right," she said to him, thinking she was speaking quietly, but she couldn't be sure. The gunshots had been too close, and everything was muffled now like they were underwater. "It didn't have to be this way," she continued, finally meeting his eyes.

His jaw was clenched, his body vibrating from pain, from the cold he was inevitably starting to feel from blood loss. "This won't end it, prima," he muttered.

"No," she replied, "but this will," and she reached up to hold his face still, pressing the barrel to his temple.

"Do it," he said, his eyes closing.

Sofia didn't feel the tears falling until the salt stung the cut he had given her on her cheekbone.

The third shot silenced them all.

She had squeezed her eyes shut, too afraid to watch. After a deep breath, she opened them, and in her arms she didn't see the bogeyman; she saw nothing but her older cousin, the boy who had lost everything.

She laid Xavier's body down as a fondness she'd forgotten washed over her.

Biting down hard on her lip, she tried to stop the tears, to stop the sob that bubbled at the back of her throat. Her fingers, slick with his blood, reached for the necklace she wore, the one she never took off, the one from her mother. It took a few tries, her hands shaking and bloody, but she unclasped the chain and leaned to fasten it around Xavier's neck.

In the picture of her uncle Santiago, the one on her mother's dresser, he'd had the same necklace as her mother. She remembered the agony she had seen in Xavier's eyes when he talked about his father. She knew that pain all too well when she thought of her mother. Maybe he didn't deserve it, but she'd let him have this one last thing from her.

Sofia heard them before she saw them. Men in drab brown uniforms, bulletproof vests, and boots pouring in through the open doors of the home.

"Put your guns down! Get down on the ground now!"

CHAPTER 46

A rush of noise—more yelling, boots on tile, weapons clanking—overtook Sofia.

"Get down," a man's voice said behind her in heavily accented Spanish. An American.

The man who stood behind her didn't yell. He knew the gun pressed to the back of her skull was enough.

Sofia laid Lucia on the ground before lacing her fingers behind her head. The agent behind her grabbed her hands and pulled them behind her to zip-tie her wrists together, causing her to nearly fall forward.

Her eyes were on Andres as another agent pushed him to the ground of the balcony where he had lowered himself to his knees. With one cheek pressed into the tile of the balcony, Andres looked down at her, his expression blank.

"Let's go," the agent with the American accent said as he easily lifted her by her arm to stand. He reached down to grab Lucia and tucked the gun into his waistband.

Sofia tried to look back over her shoulder for Yolotli, but the American holding her arm tsk-tsked.

"Nothing to see back there, Señorita De Luna."

She frowned at her name in this stranger's mouth. The shouting continued behind her, growing quieter as the agent marched her out of the house. The driveway was once again bathed in flashing red-and-blue lights, this time brimming with unmarked trucks.

The American pushed Sofia toward an SUV parked near the

end of the driveway. He quickly pulled the back door open with his free hand once they stopped.

"Giddy up," he said as he practically pushed her into the back seat.

She winced as she landed roughly on her side in the seat. Sofia only had a few seconds to take in her surroundings before the door opened again. This time Yolotli was thrust onto the seat across from her before the door slammed closed again.

"Are you okay?" Sofia asked in what she hoped was a whisper.

Yolotli nodded, his jaw set. In the darkness of the SUV, she saw his eyes were wide, but not with panic. They were cool with something else, like an unending pool.

Sofia was worried about him, and she was concerned about Diego and Nando; she'd had no communication with them since she'd left the hotel hospital. Xavier and Joaquin could easily have sent men there to finish the job. And she was anxious about Andres, who wasn't supposed to have been here, and what might happen to him now that he was.

It had been a gamble to trust Lalo, and now, with a Herrera in his grasp, he might not be willing to let him go. Sofia craned her neck as she tried to look out the windows to get a sense of what was going on. Lalo was nowhere to be seen.

It was all falling apart. Sofia's cousins were gone, and she was thankful for that. But they would go to prison. Diego, when he recovered, would probably join them.

She swore and banged the back of her head against the SUV seat.

Just then, the door opened abruptly, and the American who had tossed her into the back seat smiled. "Word is you two are free to go." He reached for Sofia, pulling her arms toward him so he could cut the zip tie binding her wrists.

The American agent motioned for Yolotli. "You too, gorgeous, let's go." Yolotli turned his back to the man so he could free his wrists. The officer motioned for him to step out first.

"Go home," he said to Yolotli, motioning toward his SUV.

The man reached a gloved hand out to Sofia then, taking her hand to help her down. She moved to follow Yolotli, but the agent held his arm out, stopping her. "Jefe needs to see you."

"Go check on my brothers," she said to Yolotli, nodding to him reassuringly.

Sofia followed behind the agent as he led her to another SUV, this one parked closer to the house. The man opened the back seat door with a salute to whoever was sitting inside. "She's all yours, Jefe."

Sofia stepped around the agent, peering inside the dark vehicle. She sighed, then reached for the pull bars to climb into the seat across from Lalo. "So *you're* your boss?" she asked once the car door slammed shut.

He shrugged. "Out here, yes. Are you hurt?" he asked, his eyebrows knitting together as he assessed her and all the blood that covered her.

She looked him over. He was wearing the same tactical gear as her new escort.

"DHS?" she asked. "Homeland Security. I thought you were DEA."

"I thought you would have figured it out sooner. Your government kicked out the DEA, remember?"

"I do. And I remember asking you about it. So what is Homeland Security doing in my neck of the woods, Agent . . ." Sofia trailed off, leaning forward to take a glimpse of his last name stitched into a piece of removable Velcro. "Serrano," she read out loud. "That's nice."

Lalo sighed and stretched out his legs. "As of four this afternoon, I was dead set on arresting all of you. Anyone who survived. It's my job, after all, to remove people like yourselves from the game."

"So what changed your mind?" Sofia asked.

"What you said to me in the hotel. About how maybe we aren't so different. You kept your end of the deal. You were willing to sacrifice yourself for your brothers' freedom. Self-sacrifice in our line of work is rare. It's commendable. And above all that, I believe you when you say you want to keep the peace."

Sofia shifted in her seat, rubbing at her wrist again. "So, Mr. Homeland Security, did you get what you came for?"

Lalo glanced out the window at the men and women swooping in to the De Luna estate. "Yet to be determined."

"I told you they couldn't live," Sofia said, her tone cold as steel.

Agent Serrano looked at her again. "Our new president is determined to take a stand against human trafficking. It was my job to make them look good. Sound familiar? Once you showed me what your cousins were up to, it was easy to connect the dots to Ximena. She wants the routes and the girls your cousins were trying to steal from the Gulf. She found a way to keep the banks fed, through your cousins. That's why I needed them alive. So to answer your question: I am a boss, but not my own. We all answer to somebody."

"I can help you," she bargained. "Like I told you, you need me close to Ximena. Not in the dirt. It would have done no good for anyone had they killed me. And they wouldn't have stopped trying to kill me as long as they continued to breathe."

His gaze fell to her bloodied hands. "Was it you?" he asked.

She shook her head. "It doesn't matter."

He leaned forward then, resting his elbows on his knees. "Promise me, Sofia, that you'll keep your brothers and the Herreras in line. This peace you promised me is the only reason you're not in the back of a car headed to an American prison."

"That was the plan, Agent Serrano, as long as I didn't end this night dead or locked up," she replied, meeting his dark eyes. "What will happen to Andres?" she asked, trying not to sound hopeful.

She didn't miss the way Lalo's jaw clenched for just a second. "About to be put on a plane home," he said. "For good. The deal is he goes back to Colombia and stays there."

Sofia shook her head. "He wasn't part of our deal."

"Andres has been a wanted man for a very long time," Lalo said, shifting to the edge of his seat. "What I'm offering you is the best you're going to get. It's you and your brothers free, and Andres disappears. Goes back to Colombia and never returns to Mexico, or my bosses keep him. They keep you. They keep everyone."

She chewed her bottom lip for a beat. "Can I say goodbye?" she asked.

Lalo swore under his breath and pushed the door open. He hopped out, slamming the door behind him.

It wasn't long before the door opened again, and Lalo pushed Andres toward the vehicle. "Make it fast."

Andres settled into the seat across from Sofia, and when he looked at her she saw the anger in his eyes. "What the hell is going on, Sofia?" he asked, his voice cool.

"This wasn't supposed to happen. You weren't supposed to be here," she said, shaking her head.

She swallowed rapidly to stop the tears from falling. It wasn't supposed to end like this. If this was the last time they saw each other, he'd leave thinking she set him up.

"What was supposed to happen, Sofia?" he asked, his tone measured.

She shook her head. "I was supposed to give them my cousins," she said, holding Andres's gaze. "That was the deal."

Andres glanced out the window. "You know how it looks, Sofia."

"I promise you, you were never a part of this . . ."

He looked at her then, his gaze hard. "You've never been good at lying to me."

Sofia's shoulders sagged. "I did this for them," she said.

Andres looked away from her again. The flashing red-and-blue lights illuminated the rigid set of his jaw. "They're saying I can't come back to Mexico."

"You're out," she said. "It's what you wanted."

He shook his head. "Not like this."

"Why did you come?" she asked, reaching for his hands, blood be damned.

His cold demeanor crumbled at her touch. He sighed, turning his hands over so their palms pressed together, their fingers clasped around one another. "I told you I owed you."

"I forgive you," Sofia said, holding his gaze, "and I'm sorry."

As the door was pulled open again, the lights and noise from outside flooded the back seat. "Come on, Andres, you've got a plane waiting for you," Lalo said.

Andres raised their hands to his mouth to press a kiss to the back of her hand. "We're even, muñeca," he said before climbing out of the SUV. "*Buena suerte*."

Sofia watched as an agent led Andres away. She waited for him to glance over his shoulder, but he never did.

"You too, Sofia, you need to get out of here," Lalo said, holding his hand out to her to help her step down.

He looked at her once they were standing face-to-face. "If I can give you some advice, call Tijuana. You're going to need them."

"Is that it?" she asked, willing her eyes to be cold, hard. She wouldn't let Lalo enjoy taking Andres from her.

"For now," he replied. "I'll call you soon, princesa."

EPILOGUE

Sofia slipped into the back row at the gravesite, high on a hill in Medellin, Colombia, her umbrella shielding her from the drizzle.

She searched for Andres and found him quickly. He was elegant as ever, clad in a stark black suit, a black button-down shirt, and dark sunglasses despite the rain. His hair was damp and slicked back.

He stood near the gravesite, welcoming well-wishers and accepting condolences. He smiled from time to time, bent his head, and spoke graciously.

Sofia watched him from afar until the crowd began to thin. She closed her umbrella and stood, walking over to Andres carefully, the earth soft beneath her heels.

"*Lo siento,*" she said, her eyes on the buttons of his shirt, not his eyes. "For your loss, for all of it," she said before dropping the bundle of flowers she had brought onto Don Martin's coffin.

Andres watched the flowers fall. "You came." His voice made goose bumps rise on her skin.

"It was the least I could do."

"There's nothing to be sorry for," he said. He turned back to look down at her. "I heard Diego's recovering well."

Sofia nodded, looking anywhere but up at Andres. She knew once she did, she might cry, scream, reach for him, kiss him in front of all these people. Maybe all of the above. All she knew was that her body hummed when he was near, like the pull of a magnet. She wanted to hold him and not let go this time.

He shifted next to her. "Thank you for coming," he said. "Are you in town long?"

"Going back to Mexico tomorrow," she said, swallowing around her dry throat. "There's going to be an investigation. I need to be there," she rambled.

"We should walk," he said, placing his fingertips at the small of her back as they headed away from the gravesite.

While Sofia had come to pay her respects, she also wanted the chance to clear the air.

"That agent was my way out . . ."

Andres shook his head. "I don't care about that, Sofia. It doesn't matter now."

Sofia fell silent as she walked beside him. "So, what will you do now?" she asked after a few steps.

He paused at the roadway. "I'm burned to the family, so I'm out. For good. I'm going to relocate my father's architecture business here." He shrugged. "It's what he always wanted. To come home."

Sofia glanced back at Martin's grave.

"He told me he was proud of me," Andres said.

"I'm proud of you too," Sofia said, turning back to Andres. "You became the man you wanted to be."

He cursed softly under his breath before reaching to pull off his sunglasses. "Can I see you tonight?" he asked, his blue-hazel eyes warm in the muted gray afternoon light.

She never dared to think about what it could be like with nothing in the way, nothing forcing them apart. She wanted to make up for all the lost time because in this life, nothing was promised. But it would be only one night, and leaving would hurt that much more.

He was waiting for an answer, his eyes on hers.

She cleared her throat. "Andres, I . . ."

He leaned down then and pressed a soft kiss to her cheek, his hand coming up to cup her jaw in his palm. "I understand if you have to say no," he said near her ear.

Of all the things she imagined he'd say once he saw her, this wasn't it. It felt like the entirety of Colombia shook beneath her feet. But he was solid and real, her hands resting on his arms.

"I do love you, Sofia De Luna. I always have," he added so quietly, so gently she knew the words were for her to hear and her alone.

"Yes," she breathed out with a nod. "Yes, Andres," she said, looking up at him. "Come see me tonight."

The slight flare of his nostrils was the only sign he gave, but the churn of emotions inside him, like the tidal wave he was, crashed in his eyes.

He pressed his forehead to hers. "I can't go back with you."

"I know."

"Stay."

"I can't," she told him.

He closed his eyes. "I know."

"I do too," she said.

His eyes flickered up at her from under his lashes.

"I love you too, Andres Herrera. I always have."

One night couldn't hold a candle to the lifetimes of nights and days she wanted to spend with him, but she was thankful for what she'd been given.

The next morning she'd be on a flight back to Mexico.

Without a cocaine supplier, she and her brothers had no choice but to survive on the legitimate produce business. It had always been a gamble, and the thought that Sofia might need Andres, and his family, again in the future had come up.

But maybe she'd taken the right chance, and maybe one day in the future she would come back here, back to Andres. Both of them finally free.

ACKNOWLEDGMENTS

First and foremost, there would be no novel without the never-ending support of my mother, who was my first cheerleader and editor. Without her encouragement and willingness to read, and re-read, my work, I never would have made it this far.

To my father—thank you for sharing your love of reading.

To my husband—there aren't enough words; I love you and thank you.

To my sister—thank you for your support of this project.

To my cats, Squeaky and Ivan, my ever-present writing companions—it's not dinner time yet!

For those interested in reading more about US–Mexico border issues, pick up Francisco Cantú's *The Line Becomes a River: Dispatches from the Border.*